FORBIDDEN FATE

MARY GEBHARD

Line editing by James Gallagher of Evident Ink
Proof Reading by Rumi and My Brother's Editor
Cover by Hang Le

Forbidden Fate
ISBN-13: 978-1-7338510-7-7
An Unglued Books Publication
www.MaryGebhard.com
EDT: BL

For the girls whose broken hearts never stopped beating.

ONE

STORY

Fate is a thread; you can tie it in a thousand knots but you'll always come to the same end. My mom loved to whisper that whenever things didn't go her way, which was...often. As I stood across from Westley only hours after Grayson's wedding, I pictured our thread. The thousands of knots we'd tied together. And in the end...Lottie's wedding dresses hung up behind me. Her lingerie too. I would have to help her into them.

Help *Mrs. Grayson Crowne*.

The one and only...the one who should have always been.

"Grayson's guards will be here any minute," I said to West.

He smirked, quirking his plump lips just enough to flash his bright-white teeth. "Lottie is Grayson's wife now." I clenched my teeth at the pain those words brought as West walked closer, sliding one hazelnut finger along the vanity.

"She gave me permission to be here. Something about forgetting her garter."

As Lottie's girl, *I* was supposed to bring it to her, but West picked up the lacy garment, twirling it around his finger. My eyes darted from it to him as fear crept up my spine. Westley had never been violent. Still, I was nervous. A few weeks earlier I had finally said what had been weighing on my soul: Westley du Lac raped me.

I don't know how a man like West would respond to that...how any man would. I still wasn't sure if I believed it myself. Rape, to me, was supposed to be bloody and vicious and cruel, not filled with sweet words.

"What do you want?"

"I told you I would be here," he said for the second time. West was close enough now that I could smell his rich cologne, see his dark tux straining across his thick biceps.

"I don't know what you're talking about," I lied.

Though West had promised to pick up the pieces that he said would inevitably fall after Grayson, he couldn't be serious. He was just fucking with me. The boy who had ghosted me and taken my virginity for a bet didn't actually *want me*.

Didn't actually care for me.

West took a step closer, but I stayed put, refusing to let another man push me back.

"I can give you what you want, Angel."

I scoffed through my nostrils. I should just ignore him, get back to work, stop poking at the wound, but I couldn't stop this gnawing in my gut. *Why?* After everything we'd been through, why did West think I'd want that? It must be a rich thing, right? Being so arrogant. Believing everything belongs to you, even people.

"You can't give me anything. I want nothing to do with

you." I turned from him, fidgeted with the second of Lottie's dresses.

"So you're just going to stay here?" he asked. "You know what a girl has to do for the bride."

I swallowed. "I'm doing it. I'm getting her dresses ready."

"Angel, you know that's not what I mean."

My fingers froze on the delicate lace, eyes traveling to the spiderweb lingerie just beside it.

A girl did *anything* for her mistress, whether it was dress her, clean her, listen to her woes. Rumors of old, ancient rituals crawled with a shiver up my spine. Girls forced to bring the bloody evidence back and, in some cases, help the bride after—anything to ensure a baby.

West laughed, but it was mocking. "You do know."

Months ago I'd already come to terms with what I might be asked to do, because I would do anything for my uncle, even if it meant readying the bride for the love of my life while I was still sticky with his come.

"I'll take you out of this place." West's touch found my shoulder, feather-light. "I'll give you the happily ever after you deserve."

I tried to focus on the lace, the window, anything but my heart rising into my throat.

Push him off.

Shove him away.

Do. Something.

"You know...we never kissed, Angel." His low, smooth voice was in my ear now. "It's all I can think about." He pushed my hair to one side.

I exhaled a breath that scraped on the way out.

Then I spun and shoved him off, snatching the garter

out of his hand, and exited Grayson's wing without a glance in West's direction.

My fast-beating heart was anger.

Grief.

Nothing more.

The wedding was in full swing, the big band carrying from the ballroom. Patrons in silk and sequins laughed, paying no attention to me.

"Angel—"

I looked over my shoulder, cutting off West before he could speak. "Why—*how* could you think I'd want to be your fucking mistress? Just leave me alone, West."

I didn't give up everything to throw it all away on the man who'd thrown me away—

Grayson.

I came to a full stop.

Seated above everyone else in the ballroom, he tangled a hand in his rose gold hair as he talked to paparazzi. I looked at the garter in my hand, the one I was supposed to bring to the wife on his arm so he could peel it off her leg.

My heart crumbled like old granite.

He didn't see me...and that was a good thing. I was back to being a ghost. My eyes found the bruise forming on my finger in the shape of Grayson's teeth. A vicious wedding band, the only kind someone like me could ever have with someone like him.

"Marry me," West said to my back.

I froze, and his hand clasped my shoulder, forcing me to spin. To look into his deep brown eyes.

"Marry me, Angel."

I would have laughed if I wasn't so disgusted, so broken, at the thought.

My soulmate left me in pieces, and the boy who ruined me—*raped* me—wanted to pick them up.

"You can't offer that. None of you can!" I yelled before I could control my emotions. "You give away...you give away promises you don't own the right to keep."

I swiped at my tears.

West blinked. "I'll take you down to the courthouse right fucking now."

I glared at him.

He'd been the one to call me out on my naïveté, for believing in a happily ever after with Grayson. When I'd once thought Grayson and I were speaking in truth, it turned out West was the *only* one to offer me real truth.

There is no such thing as a happily ever after.

"I don't know what your goal is here. I don't know what bet you're involved in again—"

"It's not a bet—" he all but growled.

I cut him off. "But how little you must think of me. If you honestly believe I'd fall for that."

Again, my brain supplied.

If you honestly believe I'd fall for it...again.

Not once, but twice, I'd fallen for a happily ever after. I was Cinderella in bare feet, walking across nails, pretending the only reason I couldn't see my shoes was because they were glass.

I exhaled a shaky breath.

"There's only one person keeping me here, and when he dies, I'm not staying around for another prince peddling his lies."

Except a small, *tiny* piece of my heart wanted to go back to West. Wanted to make what happened between us okay. Because then, maybe, I wouldn't have to look back on that memory with sadness.

It might wash away the stain.

"If you'll excuse me," I said. "There's a wife missing her garter."

West gripped my elbow. "Not even for revenge?" He thumbed my chin. "We can make him regret everything."

TWO

GRAY

"Can I get a photo of the couple of the century?"

A man dressed in an ill-fitted tuxedo held up a camera to take a picture of us.

The wedding of the century. At least, that's what was getting shoved up my ass from every angle, written in twenty-four karat gold on the six-foot wedding cake, spelled in diamonds across tables and walls, trending across social media because mother had paid for millions of bot accounts.

The Crowne-du Lac merge was the biggest marriage to happen in our world and my mother wasn't going to let anyone forget it—or maybe it was an attempt to draw their attention from the blurry girl I'd brought to the engagement party, leaked in photographs online. *We* were the wedding of the century, the *couple* of the century.

"You could at least pretend to smile," Lottie whispered. "It's not like we don't know how to pretend."

Every Crowne is taught a wedding is just another business deal.

I had hoped to avoid that fate, but here I was.

I grasped Lottie's hand, trying to offer her some kind of support.

She shot me her pretend smile. Sad, hollow, willowy. Fuck.

The paparazzo looked at his camera. "Perfect. Look how happy you are." He snapped another few pictures and left, disappearing into the crowd.

We were seated above everyone, and I felt like some kind of royalty at a feast.

We had an entire year of this facade, an entire year of photo ops and pretending. Of paid paparazzi and paid magazine covers that were staged to look organic. Shit, we didn't even get a fucking weekend to rest. This weekend we were headed to Asheville to celebrate Labor Day with Lottie's family.

We were going on a veritable royal tour.

The food was made by some Michelin chef, a fucking steak I had to scarf down. It shouldn't have bothered me. I did this all the time.

They think your favorite food is steak...

"Rare, like you like it, right?" Lottie asked.

I shot her another winning Grayson Crowne smile.

Our wedding planner appeared before us, and she bobbled her head in front of our long table for a good three minutes before I realized she was talking to us.

"It's our first dance," Lottie said quietly.

"Oh shit."

I stood, offering my hand to Lottie so we could make our way into the center of the ballroom. The music started, and bright-white camera flashes went off one after the other. My eyes connected across the room, and I tripped over my shoe, into Lottie.

Snitch.

A few feet behind her was West.

Fucking *West*.

It was a brief glimpse, but I would always and forever recognize her. Only hours ago I'd been inside her.

Come inside her.

"Grayson?" Lottie's concerned tone drew me back.

I started dancing again, plastered a smile on my face. Fuck, I really didn't like that he followed her.

Snitch rounded a corner out of the ballroom, and Westley followed.

It's not my place. Not my place to wonder if she still dripped me between her thighs. Not my place to care that Westley fucking du Lac was once again riding my girl's ass —not my girl anymore.

Shit.

Fuck.

"Is something wrong?" Lottie asked, then blew out a breath. "I mean, other than the very obvious."

My eyes were still on the door, but a small smile quirked my lips at Lottie's honesty.

"I just think Strauss is a really trash waltz," I said. "Couple of the century and our first dance is to the one song everyone plays for their first recital."

Lottie laughed, and for a minute I forgot about Snitch and that I had no right to think about her anymore. For a second, it was normal and almost *okay*.

I fingered the rubies in her ear. "You hate red."

She shrugged, as if it wasn't even worth mentioning *why* she was wearing something she hated.

I couldn't believe any of this was how Lottie had imagined it. Walking down the aisle to an empty altar, married to a man like me. Though her makeup had been fixed, her eyes were still red.

"Lottie, if you could do anything right now, what would it be?"

Her throat bobbed. "I don't want to play this game."

I wanted to give her something.

Anything to prove I wasn't the man I'd taught her I'd become.

"Lottie—"

Her eyes flashed to mine. "You can't give it to me."

"I'm Grayson Crowne. I can do anything."

Her eyes narrowed at the challenge. "I don't want to smile for pictures. I want to take off this dress and this tiara. I want to talk to you and get to know you again in private. And..." She looked away, as if ashamed. "I don't want to see *her*."

I stopped dancing. "Let's get out of here, Lottie."

"Really?" She blinked. "Just...leave?" She looked around us. Our song ended and couples had surrounded us on the dance floor.

"We've taken enough pictures. Let's go have your perfect wedding night."

Her mouth parted, and I clasped her hand, dragging her with me. Her laugh echoed as she gripped my shoulder.

"Are we really going to leave?" she whispered.

"Yeah—"

My mother stepped in front of us with a hiss. "Keep smiling."

Naturally our smiles wavered.

"I said, *Keep smiling.*"

She shoved a phone between our chests. It was a shaky

video, half the image obscured by something...flowers. White roses. Beyond them an obscene dance took place. A man's naked ass, a woman groping him.

It was me. Me with Snitch, just hours before. Luckily there was no sound. They would have heard the words that were seared into my mind.

I love you, Story Hale. I'll never stop loving you, Story Hale.

"It's clear it's a maid," my mother said, pulling the phone back. "They don't know which maid. But it's clear it's *a* maid. On your wedding night." Her nostrils flared.

Lottie dropped her grip from my shoulder, and our hands separated.

"How many people have seen it?" I asked, voice rough.

"Just—" My mother held up her finger. "I'm going to fix it. So far it's only on small forums. It hasn't hit any major news. I'll fix it—we'll fix it. This should go without saying, but don't do anything that would draw attention to this. Go mingle or go dance and *smile*." She shot a pointed look in Lottie's direction.

Mother walked away to presumably bribe some web hosts.

A spiny silence crept up in her wake. Lottie rubbed one arm, eyes on the floor.

A thousand words ran through my head, something to rewind the time, all of them useless.

"Lottie, believe me, I had no idea someone was filming."

"I think this is the worst day of my life," she whispered.

"Lottie—"

She picked up her dress, walking swiftly across the ballroom.

Fuck.

Fuck.

Who filmed that? How had we not seen? It wasn't exactly private back there...*fuck*. I needed *out* of this facade, even if for only a minute. I headed past the bastard table minus the bastards who couldn't be fucked to attend. I'm sure my mother would rip my ear off about that later. Past people I'd never met in my life, who I'm sure were only here so Mother or Grandfather could use this invite as a way to manipulate their interests. Past *friends* who didn't give a single shit about me.

In this world, those are friends.

Snitch was in my head, in my blood. Every step I took, she swirled like a shimmering ghost around me, her wide as walnut eyes following me. I couldn't reach the columns fast enough. I pulled a joint from my inner suit pocket, lighting it quickly and taking a long drag, trying to banish her.

Mother really wanted the world to believe we were perfect. The ballroom was covered in white roses. Morbidly fitting, white roses were the symbol of both weddings and death. The goodie bags—sponsored by designers and including boutique tech, streetwear, items you couldn't get anywhere save this wedding—were already trending.

I couldn't wait to see that shit pop up on eBay.

Everyone here was smiling, laughing, enjoying the couple of the century's *wedding of the century*.

I'm the only one you don't have fooled, Grayson.

I inhaled smooth smoke, staring out windows lining the ballroom at stars piercing the velvet sky. This party would last all goddamn night. Another inhale, and a rocky, jagged exhale.

I'd once thought Snitch was poison ivy, but getting her out of me was going to be like ripping out thousand-year-old tree roots. If I ever managed to succeed, I would die with it.

I must have stayed between the columns for at least thirty minutes, getting so stoned the gold-and-white wedding started to blur.

I watched Lottie as she made the rounds. She wore the Crowne tiara and glimmered under the chandelier light. Her dress hugged her curves...I remember something being said about hand-cut lace roses.

Whenever she thought someone wasn't looking, her smile flickered and died.

Sometimes I watch you.

I shook my head, trying to lose Snitch's raspy whisper.

Lottie was beautiful, perfect, gorgeous—and just a few hours of being my wife was slowly draining her. I kicked off the wall, determined to join her and salvage as much happiness as I could from this wedding.

"I told you to stay the fuck away." Snitch's angry whisper perked my ears.

I stopped short. For a second, I thought my ghosts were actually talking back.

I must really be going fucking insane.

Then West spoke, and ice filled my veins.

"You'd rather stay here and work for my sister?"

I looked around, trying to find them.

Why the fuck was she with West?

"What you're offering isn't much better," Snitch hissed.

West laughed.

"You *raped* me," she snapped.

I must've heard wrong.

This is a nightmare, not a dream.

"Stop fucking saying that!" West growled. "If I raped

you, then why did you want me to call you back? Why did you cry over me, Angel?"

An icy calmness came over me as I listened to West dig his own grave. I focused on where I'd heard them. It sounded like they were just on the other side of the column, probably near one of the chocolate fountains.

I'm gonna kill him.

"Pictures!" My mother's wedding planner appeared before me like a specter. "I've been looking everywhere for you. A little birdie told me you like to hide. First the bride and groom, then the family, then..."

I could barely hear her. The muscles in my hand fucking hurt from how much I flexed them.

"Grayson?"

If he could breathe after I finished breaking all the bones in his face, maybe I'd let him live.

"Are you okay?"

I always knew Westley du Lac was a fucking snake.

Pot calling the kettle black, maybe. I shook out of it, pushed past the petite woman, but she grabbed my arm.

The fuck? She might not be a servant, but she had no right to grab a Crowne. I stared at her fingers, then slowly lifted my gaze to hers.

Lottie.

I blinked, coming out of a fury-fueled daze.

Lottie had grabbed me.

"Lottie?" I looked at her hand on my arm again.

Lottie snatched my hand, tugging my fist open. I stared at my hand numbly, at the streaks of char against my golden palm and the red burn marks from squeezing it so hard. I forgot I'd had a blunt.

"What's wrong with you?" she asked.

"I...uh, zoned out."

She gave me a bereft look, eyeing my burned palm. "Do you need to go to the doctor?"

We both knew that wasn't an option.

Grayson Crowne couldn't disappear from his own reception, not after the video.

She handed me a thick cloth napkin. "Hold it until the bleeding stops." Her lips thinned, and her stare hadn't let up. "You were supposed to lie low. You're making a scene. Can't you just play pretend for a few hours?" She shot looks at the wedding planner watching us with shrewd eyes, the paparazzi a few feet behind her. "We've been doing it our entire lives..."

I gripped Lottie's shoulders and her eyes grew. "I want to do more with you than play fucking pretend, Lottie."

Her eyes grew at my words.

I looked around, trying to spot Snitch.

"You're still looking for her," Lottie said, hollow.

I owed Lottie. Now there were people in the world who knew the truth of our wedding night. Knew I'd fucked someone else.

But rape?

Fucking rape?

I found Lottie's eyes. There was nothing to make this right. I'd ruined the most special day of her life.

She exhaled, trying to shrug out of my hold. "Let's go take pictures."

I tightened my grip, holding Lottie in place.

Everything in me said to go find Snitch. To make sure she was okay.

Or to beat Lottie's brother to a pulp.

What do you do when you want to do the right thing,

but whatever right you choose will end up wronging someone? How do you choose?

"They're waiting," Lottie said softly.

It was tense. Awkward. Wrong. My mother knew I'd
fucked someone else. Her mother knew. Hell, I'd bet the
famous photographer positioning us, muttering something
under her breath about *contrived*, knew.

The only one who didn't know everyone knew yet was
Snitch herself.

Still I couldn't stop thinking about Snitch. All the times
I'd been jealous about West, had goaded her, had used it
against her.

I was fucking trash.

She hadn't opened up to me. There was still so much
she kept from me.

"Grayson, you're not smiling," Lottie whispered
miserably.

I affected *the smile*. The famous Grayson Crowne
smile, the one no one knew meant I was miserable.

No one but Snitch.

We took photos until the reception blurred into glittery
gold. Until I didn't feel the muscles at my cheeks twitch.
The bodies next to mine were interchangeable, so I didn't
pay attention to the arm landing on my shoulders until he
spoke.

"Hey, bro," West said, the smile in his voice like oil.

My blood went cold.

The music died.

I craned my neck slowly, meeting his dark brown eyes.
It seemed to happen in slow motion. He smiled and made
jokes with the photographer, joked with his dad and
my mom.

As everyone—my mom, grandfather, sister, Lottie and

her brother, parents and grandparents—posed for a family photo, I threw a right hook, crunching into West's jaw.

It was a sucker punch, but I still felt pretty fucking good when he landed flat on the marble floor.

"Brother-*in-law*," I corrected.

THREE

STORY

I swear everyone was staring at me. Whispering. Snickering. I knew the servants were going to do something, get back at me somehow, and the hair on my neck was stick straight. It didn't make sense that the elite would be watching me though.

The room crashed silent.

Then the sound of cameras went off, like a thousand bugs clicking their wings.

I lifted my head in time to see West fall into Beryl Crowne, and Beryl hit the marble. Grayson stood over Westley, shaking out his hand. I knew what that meant better than anyone

He looked like the boy I used to watch. The arrogant Playboy Gray.

But wilder. Messier.

I don't know what preceded it, and I know I should've stayed away, but I ran over.

Beryl was already on his feet, adjusting the lapels of his black tux, but West was on the ground, blood coming out of his mouth and nose. I dropped to my knees.

I knew what it meant if this kind of incident continued unchecked or spiraled. You could never blame a Crowne; you rarely blamed a guest. But *someone* had to be blamed, and it was always a servant. If someone like Beryl Crowne was affected in the incident? The blame would burn like acid.

"I think that's her," someone said.

Her?

"What the fuck?" Grayson said. "Him? You're choosing him?"

Another slamming silence, followed immediately by more clicks and bright lights, this time directed at *me*. Everyone was staring at me.

Choosing him.

Did he have any idea the consequences of his choice of words? I wouldn't look him in the eyes. And while seconds passed, it felt like an hour as I tried to navigate the thorny, sharp maze he'd just erected for me.

"It's her," someone said, more loudly.

"Definitely her."

The cameras kept clicking, and I could tell some were videoing. *Her?* What did they mean by that?

I knew Grayson and I were already a rumor.

The servants had made that clear by excommunicating me. While the Crownes had stopped the rumor at their gates, and the du Lacs had cut it off at the press, it was still out there. In blurry photos. If we weren't careful, others would get wind of me, and I wouldn't be able to live my life.

Hidden. Unseen. The way I'd always been.

I cautiously looked away from the crowd.

"I apologize, Mr. Grayson," I said quietly, tension threading my words as paparazzi snapped my photo. "I didn't mean to pick someone over a...Crowne."

I chose my words like I was picking the best, most precious jewels. It wasn't that Grayson was jealous; he was furious at me, an untrained servant. "I understand Crownes always come first."

Grayson snatched a champagne glass and downed it in one gulp, as if what I'd said just drove him to it.

"That's not what I fucking mean—"

"We always value our guests," Tansy said, cutting him off. "You've done well. Grayson is just tired from giving all of his attention to his newlywed. You know, boys will be boys!"

She finished with a dismissive laugh, but I heard the tension in her words. What she wouldn't say to a room full of paparazzi.

Silence descended once more.

"What's your name?" someone yelled, breaking it.

"How did you meet Grayson?"

"When did you fall in love?"

Fear strangled my spine.

I couldn't speak. Staring into a thousand lenses and phones. How did they know? How could they possibly know?

"Come on," West said, lifting me off the floor. "I think we should go." His tux was wrinkled, his fluffy curls in disarray, but he acted like it was nothing.

"I'm supposed to be helping *you*," I replied numbly. He shot me a smirk with his now-bloody plump lips.

Tansy immediately launched into damage control, but Beryl stared at me.

Icy.

As did Grayson.

Grayson watched me, Lottie watched me, Beryl watched me. So did a few reporters, even as Tansy played damage control.

We exited under the gold leaf banner that read *Couple of the Century*.

GRAY

I itched to throw another punch when West put his arm around her like he was an injured deer or something.

It was one fucking punch.

That guy used to win in fight nights at Rosey.

Lottie placed her hand on my elbow. "Grayson, please." Desperation weighed Lottie's words. For the first time, I looked outside my anger, at the reception.

My grandfather, whose tux was wrinkled and eyes were hard. Yeah, I'd hear about this all right. Past the press, who would be paid off not to write this story with some other steamier piece, to the crowd. A crowd filled with cameras, vicious smiles, and a desire to sate whatever bullshit following of a few thousand sycophants they had.

A crowd who could *not* be paid off.

"This wedding is a fucking disaster."

"It's all anyone is talking about now."

"We said lay low."

"And you punched him."

Multiple family members were whispering at once. My mother, Mrs. du Lac, my grandfather, her father...all saying basically the same thing: What was I thinking?

Lottie's mother and mine, her father and my grandfather, stared at me, waiting for an answer I couldn't give. How the fuck did I explain this? I'd heard West is a rapist. Was I supposed to just let that slide?

But it would devastate Lottie. And I'd already devastated her enough for a lifetime.

I rubbed the back of my neck, finding Lottie's eyes only. "Lottie..."

"If you say you're sorry—" She broke off, then shook her head on a scoff. "You couldn't even go one *hour* without making it about her. All that 'I'm your husband now' stuff was just bullshit. When she appears, you don't seeing anything but her."

Lottie went back to our table.

I dragged my hands through my hair, watching her leave. I reached into my suit pocket, retrieving a sucker, slamming it into my mouth.

Somehow I'd fucked up everything with Lottie and yet still hadn't done enough for Story.

"I have been planning this day for years." I glanced to the side, surprised to find my grandfather hadn't left with everyone else. "Since before you were born. This was the start of a new era. We'd have not just a kingdom, but a dynasty, a world in which everyone bows to the Crowne."

"Do the du Lacs know that's what you've planned?" I gritted.

"You know I still remember your father's wedding night," he responded instead. "It was also very...memorable."

He was much too calm. This was the time he should be threatening me. Reminding me he could send Story to jail. Instead he reminisced.

"He also left your mother high and dry," he continued.

"Something about a pregnancy. He was so..." Grandfather took a breath, sounding annoyed. "So unreasonable."

I narrowed my eyes. "The triplets weren't born until years later."

"I wasn't talking about the triplets, Grayson. For her sake, I hope you wore protection."

The lemon sucker seared my tongue, biting. "Excuse me?"

"Your father barely got away with it the second time."

"You might have had to threaten me into this marriage, but I'm here now. Unlike you and Father and every other goddamn male Crowne, I will honor my vows."

Grandfather laughed. "Funny way of honoring her."

He patted me on the shoulder; then, adjusting his tie one last time, he affected a smile and joined the reception. I stared after him long after his body had disappeared into the crowd, his real meaning falling over me like ice water.

My father didn't have any more children than the triplets outside his marriage.

Numb, I rejoined Lottie at our table. I said nothing, because there was nothing I could say to make it better. She pulled out her phone as the music continued.

"The marriage of the century." She held up a gold plate engraved with the words *Marriage of the Century*.

She pushed her cheek out with her tongue.

"Online they're calling us the sham of the century. Fraud of the century. Joke of the century."

"Lottie..."

She dropped the plate with a clang. "We have a wedding night to finish."

She stared out at our reception, dead eyed and determined.

FOUR

STORY

The minute we were out of the ballroom I shoved West off. He could stand—he was barely hurt.

"I'm sorry—" West started, but I turned on him.

"Stop! Stop saying you're sorry. I'm really tired of the men in my life using me to make themselves feel better. If I have to feel like shit, so do you."

He looked like he wanted to say something, but to his credit, didn't.

I could still hear the ballroom, the music playing as if nothing had happened. The way Grayson had looked at me seared into my chest like a brand. Scarring. White-hot.

"What was on their phones?" I asked quietly, afraid of the answer.

"This is you, right?" West held out his phone for me to look at.

Grayson.

Me.

Hours ago, as we'd said our goodbyes behind the altar. I lifted my eyes from the phone, colliding with West. A wedding full of people who'd seen me at most my vulnerable moment.

"How many people have seen this?" My eyes locked with West's warm chocolate ones.

"Only a couple hundred thousand. Don't get a big head. You'll be forgotten in the morning."

I spun, finding Mrs. du Lac.

A couple *hundred* thousand?

Only?

She stepped past me to her son, dabbing West's nose with a silky white cloth. Her floor-length gown flowed across the marble, seeming to repel wrinkles and shadows, the silky cornflower color bringing out the complexion of her skin. Both elegant and intimidating, like her.

"What a way to ingratiate yourself with our new family," she said lightly.

She reminded me a little of Tansy, in that she had that graceful air. She didn't rush, even as her son bled.

A couple hundred thousand. Hundred. Thousand.

They hadn't seen my face, at least.

West paused and said, "I was serious about my proposal."

Mrs. du Lac threw an unreadable look over her shoulder, before following after him.

Then I was alone, only the distant sound of music and laughter my company. The quiet grew the longer I stood, until I felt so insignificant I couldn't breathe.

A couple hundred thousand.

I shook my head, walking to the kitchen. I had a moment before Lottie's next dressing, a few minutes I could spend with Uncle. I went to the pantry, piling up boxes of my uncle's favorite biscuits. He couldn't leave his bed, and he's too prideful to ask. I piled the boxes until I couldn't see. Until the sharp cardboard edges bit into my biceps.

A couple hundred thousand.

I walked in a daze to the servants' quarters, mind spinning between Grayson and West. Serious about his proposal? Even if West wasn't fucking with me...I didn't want revenge against Grayson.

Maybe I should.

I just want an *answer* for why it all fell apart.

A couple hundred—

My foot caught, and the boxes went flying, scattering across the marble. I fell to the ground, scrambling to pick them up.

A couple hundred thousand. A couple hundred thousand. A couple hundred thousand.

"Ow, fuck." I caught myself on a sharp cardboard edge and dropped what I'd barely managed to pick back up. Exhausted, I fell to the marble, legs spread like a child.

I guess it was a good thing the hallway was empty, that everyone was busy with the wedding.

No one was here to witness me collapse.

"A hundred thousand," I whispered aloud.

A rustling to my left yanked me out of my daze. Someone had bent down to help me. Quickly re-entering servant mode, I scrambled to get on my knees.

"Oh, please don't. I can do—" I broke off, voice dying.

Two big hands joined me, veins throbbing along the golden skin.

These hands had held me, had bruised me, had been *inside me*.

Cautiously, I lifted my eyes.

One by one, Grayson Crowne piled the boxes as if they

were the most precious things in the world. His rose gold hair was wild and messy, like he'd been running his hands through it, and it veiled his face at the angle he was bent.

His eyes cut to mine like an electric shock.

I jumped off the floor, running my hands over my uniform, looking anywhere but his eyes. Grayson slowly stood, his back to his wedding, and mine to the servants' quarters.

We were stuck between worlds.

Silence buzzed between us.

His eyes locked on the locket I wore—the one *he gave me*—and I shoved it under my collar. He clenched his jaw, then held the boxes out for me, his hand bloody from punching West.

I yanked them back. I wanted to yell at him, but what would would I say? Don't help me? Only a few hours had passed since he'd told me he loved me, but it may as well have been eons.

So I just turned on my heel.

I was almost at the servants' quarters when Grayson's cold voice drifted back. "Stay away from West, Story."

I stopped short, fingers digging into the boxes until they crinkled.

"Or what?" I asked, refusing to turn around. "You've already done the worst thing you can ever do to me."

Left me. Abandoned me. Forgot me. Chose her.

His hand was suddenly on my shoulder, pulling, as if trying to turn me around.

"Story..."

I nearly caved. Nearly let him pull me back, just to see the look on his face, what would accompany such an ache in his voice. But I dug deep for my dignity and yanked my shoulder free, disappearing down to the servants' quarters.

I wound my way down the familiar tunnel to my uncle's room. Some rumors say that the first Crowne believed in magic and built the secret doors and tunnels for ritual sacrifice, others say he built it to hide his mistress.

Either way, they've long been usurped for our purpose: servitude.

I knocked lightly on my uncle's door. He was asleep, and I wasn't going to wake him, so I just sat next to the bed, watching him. He looked so much smaller, frailer.

My mind drifted to Grayson. I don't know why he punched West. I could think of a million reasons. It wasn't like they ever got along.

A million reasons...and in all of them, none of them should include me. The woman who was most definitely not his wife.

"You breathe very loudly for someone who isn't asleep."

"Uncle!" I leaned forward. "You're awake."

"It's hard to sleep through that noise." He sat up.

You breathe like Hannibal.

I exhaled the sad memory through my nostrils. As if my uncle knew.

"When I die—" he started.

"Whoa." I cut him off. "That's an awful way to start this conversation." Nausea swamped me at the thought.

"When I die," he continued, "promise me you'll leave."

I wished he'd stop telling me he was dying.

"That's not happening for a very long time, Uncle."

He didn't respond, but the way he rolled his lips told me everything. My gut sank. The one person I had left in this world was going to leave me.

He took my hands in his, eyes red.

My uncle never cried, but the tears were there, on the lids.

"I promise," I choked out, the thought of leaving closing my throat. But once he was gone, there would be nothing for me here. No reason to stay.

He slowly withdrew his hands from mine. "There are things you need to know."

"You keep talking like you're leaving me. You still have so many months left in you," I said weakly.

"I'm not leaving you with a fortune. I've saved a lot, and it will be enough to leave Crowne Point and to start over, not underneath someone's foot."

"I don't mind it here..."

"There is a coin." He took a raspy breath. "The coin is the most valuable thing I own. Now you own it. It is buried..." he broke off, taking another breath. "It's buried beneath a poem."

"Uncle you're not making any sense." I worried his mind was deteriorating with his health. "Maybe you should rest, I'll read you a poe—"

"Listen to me, Storybook!" He yelled, and I snapped my mouth shut.

My uncle never yelled.

"That coin grants wishes, but only one. Anyone in the Crowne world will understand what it means and does. If you ever need a wish granted, use it. Remember." He grasped my wrist, and I was again struck with how much weight he'd lost, his fingers skeletal. "You only get *one*."

My brows knitted.

A coin that granted wishes? Buried beneath a poem?

Hot tears bubbled up my throat.

This wasn't fucking fair. My uncle was the smartest man I knew but he was losing his mind. I didn't want to make him yell again, and I knew that trying to reason with a deteriorating mind was pointless.

"Why didn't you use it?" I croaked.

His grip loosened, and he fell back against the bed, eyes closed. "I did. My wish was to give you a wish."

I lifted my eyes, but my uncle had sunk back into his cushions, his breathing steady.

If the coin had been real, I knew my wish. But I somehow doubted even a magical coin could make him live longer.

I leaned against the closed door, head spinning with the day's events. I pulled out my phone and scrolled and scrolled past various blogs and tweets. The video was trending.

My lungs felt like they were shriveling up inside my chest. What would my uncle think if he knew? And would this *really* be forgotten in the morning?

"You're late." I quickly scrambled off the door, finding Ms. Barn glaring at me.

"Just because you've slept in Grayson Crowne's bed doesn't mean you can lie around and do nothing. You're Mrs. Grayson Crowne's girl, and she's waiting."

FIVE

STORY

I went to go attend to Ms. du Lac—*No, Mrs. Grayson Crowne*—but I stayed outside for longer than I should've. Once again, my eye fell to the bruise on my ring finger. I was supposed to help her into her lingerie. It was my job. I was nothing more than her girl.

But I'd fucked her husband—and now ruined her wedding because of it.

The Crownes wedding rituals dated back centuries, before they came to America, and that was one of the tamest. I shuddered, thinking about the ones that used to include me.

The door swung open and Lottie stopped short. She looked surprised to see me; then her smooth features faded into exasperation.

"You're here."

I lifted my head. "Mrs. Crowne."

"Mrs. *Grayson* Crowne. I'm not his mother."

I pursed my lips, nodding.

"I've been waiting an hour for you," Lottie clipped. "I barely have any time to get ready before he comes."

Before he comes.

To fuck her.

His wife.

Whatever I *thought* I'd heard in Grayson's voice was a mirage of my own desires. Over and over again he chose her.

"If we have to be stuck together, can you just...try a little?" Lottie wasn't haughty or imperial with her request, like the Crownes; she was beseeching. Of *me*. A servant.

I blinked. "I'm sorry. I...lost track of time." I quickly dashed past her, pulling the ivory lace off the window.

I wanted to apologize again, but I knew there was no point. I trailed after Lottie back into Grayson's wing.

Grayson and *her* wing.

Sometime while I'd been away, someone had come and decorated the hollow room with flowers and candles. *Who?* I wondered. They couldn't have made my uncle? But then, West had gotten in as well...A distant part of me worried for Grayson. His fortress was slowly eroding.

Lottie made a noise, and I realized I'd been standing for too long. I quickly got to my knees, placing the soft fabric at her feet.

"Your foot, miss," I said.

I had to go inside myself, numbing to the situation. At least I had practice—it was how I'd lived when my mother was alive.

"It's *Mrs.*" Lottie stepped into the hole I'd built in the fabric.

"Of course." I lifted the spidery fabric up her naked hazelnut curves. "I apologize."

I adjusted the corset material that pushed her breasts up, made sure everything fit properly, but I didn't step back right away. My fingers rested on the thin satin bows at her shoulders. I was so close to Lottie I could smell her sweet floral scent, but my eyes had wandered. Silky white roses left a bread crumb trail up to the second floor, and against everything in my body telling me not to, my eyes followed them up to the bedroom.

I'd taken Grayson's virginity. Was Lottie a virgin? Would he take hers tonight? Unless...had they already done it? I felt possession grow inside me. This must be that ugly, patriarchal disease men get when they learn women are virgins.

Now I have it.

I took Grayson's virginity, and I don't want anyone else to touch him. He's *mine*.

Lottie cleared her throat.

She was just an inch taller than me, and our eyes locked.

"Are you a virgin?" I asked.

I stepped back instantly, eyes finding the floor. Oh my god.

Oh my *god*.

A stale silence threaded its way between us.

"You're wondering if he slept with me already," she said at last. "Is it killing you?"

I swallowed but said nothing.

It wasn't killing me, because I was pretty sure all the important pieces of me had already died.

"Because I *know* he slept with you," Lottie said. "The entire fucking world knows now."

I crushed a petal beneath my foot.

"All night I've been wondering which of us felt worse...

but I think we're both in the same hell, just different wallpaper."

Lottie took a deep breath. "I hadn't planned for the world to know, but I guess I probably should've prepared for that."

Planned? Prepared?

I couldn't help it. My shock had me lifting my head, and I found her already looking at me.

"Oh no. Did you think he did that on his own?" she asked softly. "Who do you think gave him permission? He had to get you out of his system someway."

My breath rushed out of me, as knowing washed over me.

The letter.

I shouldn't have been surprised Lottie knew we'd slept together; it was exactly what I'd come to expect from the rich.

Still, I felt dirtier than before, when I'd only been a cheater. Now I was used. *Stupid,* too. I grasped my hand, rubbing my ring finger. Every good thing about that memory stained and tarnished and ruined.

I turned on my heel, ready to get out, end this night as quickly as possible.

"Where are you going?" Lottie asked to my back. "I need my girl."

"I've already dressed you. What else do you need, Miss du Lac?"

Her nostrils flared. "Mrs. *Grayson Crowne.*"

I clenched my jaw, but this time I didn't say sorry. I just stared back.

"What do you need, Mrs. Crowne?"

She glowered. "It's my wedding night. What do you think?"

My blood temperature dropped. "You can't be serious."

She blinked and looked away.

"You're supposed to be my girl." I realized tears had filled her eyes. She honestly looked terrified. "You stole my girl's spot. You stole *my* spot. You can't even do this? Do you think I want—" She broke off on a sob. "You'll come and get the sheets."

Just as the door opened behind us.

GRAY

Snitch was talking to Lottie when I came to her. It was some kind of perverted fantasy, seeing my girl before my wife.

Lottie lifted her eyes to mine. "Remember what I said."

"Of course, Mrs. Crowne," Snitch said, and bowed her head and left.

My head swiveled to follow her down the hall. I wasn't sure if she was wearing her locket. I didn't fucking like that. Didn't like when she'd tried to hide it from me.

"Sure you don't want to chase after her?" Lottie asked.

Shit.

Caught.

"Lottie—"

She put up a hand, turning away. "This is the worst wedding night in the history of wedding nights."

At least Snitch was gone. For a horrifying second, I thought it would be her taking the sheets.

"I don't want her as my girl anymore. I don't care that her uncle is dying. I don't care if her whole family is dying. I can't do this anymore. Why can't we just pay for them to live somewhere else?"

"This is their home," I said. "It's...his home. He's been like a father to me." I gripped her hands. "If it was just Sn—Story, I would do what you ask, believe me."

It burned coming out, the idea of kicking her out onto the streets.

I knew it was better for everyone. Safer for Snitch, even, with my grandfather around. But I still couldn't stomach the thought of never seeing her again.

"That old man is the only father I've ever known," I continued. "I can't abandon him when he only has a few weeks left to live. Story is his only real family."

Her jaw clenched until the muscle popped.

If my wife had been anyone else, she wouldn't have given a shit over my explanation. So what? Kick him out.

Instead she fell down, defeated.

"You know we can't suppress everything. If you google her name, do you know what pops up now? Cinderella stories. She's like a folk hero on the internet. Forums are dedicated to her. They call me the wicked wife. I'm the villain."

Lottie stared abjectly at the floor.

"When I pictured my wedding night, there were sweet kisses, and tender passion. Instead I let my husband fuck someone else, and now the whole world knows how little he wants me."

I got to my knees in front of her. "Let me make it up to you."

"The longer she stays, the worse it will get. So I guess I'm praying for someone to die now. Is that who I am?" She looked up at me, eyes wet.

I thumbed the tear about to fall off her cheek.

"Every day for the rest of our life, I'll prove to you that I'm a worthy husband."

I *won't* be my father.

I won't abandon my wife.

I won't put Snitch in danger.

I slid my thumb from Lottie's cheek, into her curls, cupping her neck, forcing her to feel my earnestness in my grip. "I'll give you a baby, I'll give you a life, I'll give you the world."

Tears shimmered in her eyes. "I can't stop seeing you two together. It was one thing to imagine it."

I gripped her tighter, pulling her closer. "You are my wife. My loyalty is to you."

"I want to believe you. But you threw a punch for her on our wedding night, Grayson," she whispered.

"Lottie, you were my first love. You will be my last love. I just need time. Can you give me that?"

Her eyes softened. "I guess."

"We won't be the couple of the century, Lottie. We'll be the family of the century. This isn't a nightmare. We'll make it a dream. I promise."

"I want to believe you..." she repeated on a whisper.

"So do. Let me make it up to you." I tugged on her hand. "I'm serious when I say you're my wife."

"But you still love her. Will you ever stop?"

I couldn't imagine that day ever coming. I'd told Snitch the same earlier. I would love her. I would *always* love her. Snitch had sewed herself into the very essence of me.

But for Lottie's sake, for our marriage's sake, I lied. "I just need time."

"They expect us to have sex," she said miserably. "They want bloody sheets. I already lost my virginity. What fucking year is it?"

I made a face. That didn't mean shit.

I stood up, giving her my hand, and led her up the stairs to my bedroom.

Our.

I undid the bandage on my knuckles, scraping blood onto the sheets. Maybe it was a twisted poetry, bleeding from skin I broke against her brother's face, because of the girl still between us.

"There. Done."

She smiled weakly.

I tilted her chin up with my thumb. "I haven't seen that all night." Her smile dropped, and I gripped her chin softly. "Charlotte."

"You don't want this, Grayson...I don't want to force you into this."

She looked away, but I drew her face into a soft kiss. "Tell me if it's too much. If you want me to stop." I peeled one thin satin strap past her shoulder, kissing the soft skin as I went. "You said you had a vision for your wedding night."

She watched me, eyes wide, plump lips parted. I could do sweet and tender for her. I had been getting other girls off my entire life without any regard to my own feelings. Why should my wedding be any different?

SIX

GRAY

"I'll make you feel so good, Lottie," I promised. "Your wedding night will be perfect. Tell me what you like. I'll give it to you. I'll give you everything." I pressed her body into the mattress, lightly grazing her ear with my teeth until she shuddered.

"I don't know what I like," she admitted. "I...I haven't had sex very much."

I trailed my hands up the inside of her thigh.

"This?"

She nodded and sighed a breathy moan.

I grazed a thumb over her pussy but didn't part the lips.

"This?"

A hot, needy moan.

I pressed my thumb, barely parting. Wet.

You're already so fucking wet.

Snitch slammed into me as Lottie's hand slid up my

thigh. The two images collided in a dark dance. Snitch was always *so fucking wet*. So fucking *needy*. Lottie reached for my cock, and Snitch vanished like smoke.

I could feel myself going soft.

Fuck.

I grabbed Lottie's wrists, holding them together with one hand and slamming her flat against the bed in one move. Her eyes popped at the new position, and I plunged a finger inside Lottie, trying to banish Snitch.

I couldn't bring her into this.

Not on our wedding night.

Lottie's mouth fell open on a silent gasp, back arching. Her soft hands grasped mine, so unlike Snitch, nails manicured down to the pad. Not the furious, heated scratching I loved.

Fuck. There Snitch was again, crawling up and sliding inside my thoughts.

Lottie reached for my cock again, and I pulled away before I could stop myself. An awkward second passed, my finger still inside her.

"Will it help if I pretend to be her?" she breathed against my lips. "Story."

My dick twitched at her name. I rubbed my thumb along Lottie's clit, hoping she didn't notice.

"It will," she gasped. "I can feel it."

"Stop." I tried to be firm, but my words came out strangled. I worked the finger inside Lottie, trying to turn back time with her moans and gasps, before corruption had sunk inky into our wedding night.

"Does she like one finger or two?" she asked.

I didn't respond, but she grasped my hard cock. This time I didn't pull away.

"How many, Gray?" She tightened her grip on me, pumping up and down.

"Lottie—"

"No!" Lottie cut me off, working me harder in a rhythm until I couldn't think past the pleasure. "How many?"

"She'll take as many as I give her," I grated.

Lottie looked me in the eye. "So give her what she deserves."

We were tumbling down this hill now, too fast to stop it.

"How many does she deserve?" She all but cried her words when I tweaked her clit. I buried my head in her shoulder as she worked me, letting myself get lost in the dark spell Lottie was casting. As Lottie pumped me, I returned the favor, her moans getting discolored, distorted, in Snitch.

"One or two?" Lottie's soft question was at my ear, urging me to fuck her, fuck my wife while I pretended she was another woman.

"Three," I growled, sliding two more inside. A sharp gasp slipped from Lottie's lips. Concern I'd hurt her shattered the moment. I lifted my head, finding her eyes.

"Lottie?"

She grasped my cheeks. "Don't call me that name."

I got Lottie off, making her scream, cry, say words I never knew could come out of her mouth. As I came into my wife's hand and on her thigh, I groaned Snitch's name into my wife's shoulder.

Our breaths were heavy. I pushed myself up on my elbows. I'd come in Lottie's hands, but she was covered on her inner thighs and pussy.

I'd promised her a family, but I was fucking terrified of that sticky substance sinking inside her... Just as quickly as the dark, dirty primal heat that had corrupted us and had made what we'd done okay came, it dissipated. All that was left in its wake was an icy hollowness.

"Lottie—"

"Don't," she cut me off, pushing me off at the same time. Lottie slid to the edge of the bed, giving me her back. I could count her breaths by the way the elegant notches in her spine moved.

Fuck.

Fuck fuck. *Fuck.* That was so not how we should have spent our wedding night. Instead of taking Snitch out of the equation, we'd brought her into our bed.

And I couldn't stop the dark, fucked-up thought in my head telling her to go clean up. She was my wife, and I'd promised to be loyal to her, so why did I hate the idea of her getting pregnant?

It was unlikely, right? She'd have to be, like, crazy fucking fertile.

I reached for her. "Lottie."

She flinched at my touch. "I just...I need a minute."

My hand was still outstretched when there came a knocking on the door. Lottie snapped her head at the sound, then at me, eyes wide. She scrambled across the bed, lunging on top of me.

My face must have betrayed my confusion.

"Can you just act like you aren't totally repulsed by me for five seconds?" she asked, looking over her shoulder at what sounded like someone coming up the stairs.

"Lottie, I'm not...do you think that?"

"We can use her," she whispered. "If it will help, we can use her in the bedroom."

Use Snitch, as if she were nothing more than a toy?

It had been done in the past, when girls were seen as nothing.

I would never fucking do it.

But I couldn't respond, because whoever had come to get the sheets had arrived. I lifted my head off the pillow to see who had come, and all the air left my body.

Story.

"I'm here for the sheets."

SEVEN

STORY

Lottie naked. Gray naked. Lottie on top of Gray, flushed from exertion. Her lips flushed. The sheets stained red.

"Story," Grayson breathed as if he'd been punched.

I swallowed. "They are requesting the sheets, Miss—Mrs. Crowne."

Slowly they got off the bed. Grayson stared holes into me. Chiseled arms. Back exerted. Muscles slick. Lips plump from kissing. Hair wild.

Bed sheets messy.

I gathered the sheets in my arms, silky and soft, and red. Red and bloody. Once again I was reminded of the beginning, when I'd come here with a mountain of my only belongings. Now I was back with a mountain of their wedding sheets.

I swallowed. "Thank you."

I turned from Charlotte, catching Grayson's eyes. Brittle, bruised. I said I would learn to hate Grayson Crowne, but I wasn't sure I knew how.

"Stay," Charlotte said, and I froze. "My girl is supposed to finish what you started."

Lottie spread her legs, and I saw sticky white drip down her thighs.

I froze.

"Lottie." There was iron in Grayson's words. Between them passed a look I couldn't read, but it made shivers run up my spine.

Lottie looked me up and down, calculating, as if I were something to use, something to buy.

"Push it up inside me," she said.

"Leave, Snitch. *Now.*"

The way Grayson spoke made me sprint out of the room without a second's hesitation.

I quickly scrambled away, running before my tears fell.

Push it up inside her.

I carried a mess of bloody sheets. Numb.

In the past, a girl is less than a ghost, she's air. Invisible. So no one thought twice about what she witnesses or does. It's not vulgar. Because the girl isn't someone who fucked the bridegroom hours before.

She isn't someone whose heart bleeds for the bridegroom.

She isn't someone whose soul is tethered irrevocably to his.

She's no one. Nothing.

So why did his words, his proclamation, still throb inside me?

I love you, Story Hale. I will always love you.

I settled against the wall, fingering around the edge of the fruity stain, being sure to avoid it. Mesmerized by it.

Mom always did say when you bleed, you're a cut away from bleeding out.

I feel like I'm going to faint.

I walked down to the servants' quarters in a daze, so numb I was barely cognizant of handing over the sheets to the one who would take them to Tansy and Mrs. du Lac.

I checked in on my uncle, wishing to talk to him, but he was already asleep. I hated that I'd taken this job—stayed in this hell—for *him*, but that very job kept robbing me of my opportunities to spend time with him.

I quietly shut the door.

When I got back to my room, I knew something was off. It felt...different. When I touched the knob, my fingers came back sooty.

"You really shouldn't have come back."

I turned around, finding all the servants who weren't working, including Ellie.

Ellie held up the letter Lottie had sent Grayson. *"Grayson. I'll give you this one night to get it out of your system..."*

It was one thing to have Lottie say it, another to have the inked words read aloud. It took everything inside me not to fall to the ground.

"What a find," Ellie said when she'd finished. "But that video more so for the press."

"You videoed it?" My heart crushed, shattered—whatever was left became bloody jam. I used to think they were my family. My *only* family.

"You know as well as anyone there are no secrets that can be hidden from the servants."

"You could all lose your jobs..." But I knew they wouldn't. The servants looked out for one another, and whatever power I might have had before was in the wind.

They laughed, because they knew it too.

"Cinderella of Crowne Hall..." she continued. "That's what they're calling you, you know."

She looked over my shoulder at my closed door, and my gut twisted at what was behind it, at what they could have done now. Steeling my spine, I turned the knob and opened it.

Ash.

Ash from the fireplaces, the stoves...in my bed.

"Cinderella should sleep in the ashes, don't you think?"

They laughed, leaving me with my dirty bed.

GRAY

"What the fuck was that?" I opened and closed my fists, struggling with my anger.

"She's my girl, Grayson, at your request—no, at your *insistence*. She is supposed to do way more than that and you know it." Lottie took an angry breath she tried to hide, and it blew out her cheeks like a chipmunk's.

Then a faraway look overtook her eyes, like fog swallowing the horizon of Crowne Beach.

"I've been dreaming of my wedding night with you ever since our first kiss..."

Just like that, my anger evaporated into sludge.

I went to her, went to my wife. Taking her soft, manicured hands in my own. She still wouldn't look at me, eyes downcast.

I tilted her chin with my knuckle, her brown eyes on mine. In this moment, I finally saw Lottie. Rage, hate, bitter betrayal. Charlotte du Lac was not someone who showed emotions, because she wasn't allowed to feel them. I could relate to her on that level. It took a thief to burrow inside my heart and steal all the emotions I hid before I could feel them myself.

"Lottie."

"Don't." She swallowed and took a step back, that familiar distance swallowing her eyes again. "I don't want to talk about what we just did. If we have to do it again, we have to do it. We just don't *ever* talk about it. If we need to use her, then we need to use her."

Worse than being surprised by her words was expecting them. It was exactly what someone in our life would say. Before Snitch, before all of it, I wouldn't have so much as blinked at them.

Now?

"No. No, Lottie. Never again."

I dragged her into a hug, but she wormed her way out of it. The waves crashed and she rubbed her bare arm, ridding it of goose bumps.

"You can't bring her to Asheville, Lottie."

I tried to drive Story out, and that obviously didn't work. Story was made of metal. She was stone. She was going to stay until Woodsy died, and I couldn't fucking drag her around. The old man was gonna die soon, and she deserved to be there with him.

Lottie blinked, mouth parted. "You want me to go without my girl?"

"It's our honeymoon; let's just have it be us."

She was silent for a moment. "Fine. I'll go without my girl."

I barely had a moment to exhale my relief before Lottie spoke again.

"Do you know that our prenup says you get everything if I commit adultery? It doesn't say anything about you."

"I promised you I would be faithful. I'm not fucking lying," I all but growled.

She found my eyes. "You make me a lot of promises, Grayson...none of them are binding."

My brows twisted. "The prenup was already settled over a year ago."

"We could always get a postnup."

Silence.

That was...insane.

To make this marriage and merger work, Grandfather placed majority shares of Crowne Industries in my name. Lottie received the same treatment. It was all for show. We were puppets. Puppets never think to cut the strings. That's suicide.

But maybe it was a good idea.

My last leash wasn't strong enough to keep me away from Story. Maybe it was time for iron bars. Fucking steel. Or maybe it was a recipe for disaster.

At my silence, Lottie mumbled, "That's what I thought."

"Lottie...I'm not saying no. Can we table it? Talk about it when things aren't so..." *Fucked*.

"Before the wedding, my mom came to me to give me some wisdom...Do you want to know what her advice was?"

The lost, resigned look in her eyes told me it wasn't some mother-daughter girl advice about how to please a man or some shit. It told me I didn't want to know whatever Lynette du Lac had told Lottie. But when Lottie didn't speak for a full minute, I gestured for her to continue.

She stopped rubbing her arm and lifted her eyes to mine. "Be whoever he needs you to be."

STORY

I slept on the cold floor instead of my ashy bed, so when I woke, my shoulder blades ached. I had a brief, painful flash-back to my first nights with Grayson. But this time there was no one sleeping above me to talk to. No one to slip a blanket on me in the night.

I woke alone and cold.

I knew I shouldn't have, but I browsed the internet. I was supposed to be forgotten, right? Except I saw my face splashed on the front page of the internet, bent next to Westley du Lac, a dopey, wide-eyed look on my face. Like I'd been caught. And now I had a name.

Cinderella of Crowne Hall.

I exhaled, falling back to the frigid floor, phone to my chest. They didn't know who I was, didn't even know my name, but they acted as though they knew everything about me.

Gold digger. Whore. Mistress. User.

But others loved me.

Wanted to be me.

They'd managed to contain the papers and major news outlets online, but not everyone could be bought. With a sigh I stood up, getting dressed in the little clothing that hadn't been destroyed.

Upstairs the servants were prepping for the day, and a tray of pastries and sandwiches was set out for us. When I entered, the conversation stopped dead. I knew if I had *any* friends left here, last night had obliterated them.

To them, the only reason Lottie wouldn't kick me to the

curb after what had happened was because I was fucking her husband.

I tried to ignore it, tried to ignore how everyone watched me, and went for a sandwich. The tray was yanked back. All the servants looked at me with cold eyes.

They didn't snicker or laugh, and somehow that made it worse. These cruel acts weren't like what I'd bore upstairs with Grayson's rich peers. These weren't done for amusement. The humiliation was calculated. They were trying to break me down and run me out.

Old Story would have swallowed her voice. Tried to hide. Blend in.

"Do you think I want this?" I whispered.

I was about to go upstairs and attend to the love of my life's *wife*. I'd probably see him. If there was a hell, I couldn't imagine anything worse than what I was currently in.

But the only way I could be free was if my uncle *died*.

I lifted my head, my gaze flitting from one icy stare to the next, and raised my voice. "Do you think I want to be here?"

Everyone stared at me a moment longer, then went back to what they'd been doing. Eating pastries, talking, looking at their phones.

With the time allotted to me for breakfast, I could have gone out of Crowne Hall and gotten something in Crowne Point, but I had so little time with my uncle, so instead I went to him.

"Uncle?" I asked softly as I opened the door, in case he wasn't awake.

"Sabrina?"

I paused at my mother's name. I hadn't heard it in years. He always used *your mother* or *my sister*.

"It's me...Story."

He sank into his pillows, eyes closed, and nodded.

"I was wondering if you had time for a poetry reading?"

"Tomorrow." He opened one eye, locked on me, then closed it. "I'll have energy tomorrow. Promise you'll come back?"

"Promise."

I closed the door quietly, but I stared at the wood. I wanted to press him, to beg him, beg my tired uncle who is dying of cancer to just please read me poetry, but Barn's voice tore through the moment like ripping paper.

"What are you doing?"

I turned, finding her scowl. "I was..."

"Mrs. Grayson Crowne needs her tea."

I looked at my uncle's door, and she tilted her head, eyes slimming. "Of course."

I would quickly give Lottie her tea—Lottie liked jasmine tea made with a flowering bud—and come back down to see Uncle before the afternoon.

I dreaded my walk to Grayson's wing.

Or...their wing.

I knew as Lottie's girl I would have to see him, see them.

I knocked softly on the door, pushing it open with the tea tray. Lottie was already sitting up, but she looked as though she hadn't slept much.

"I brought your tea, Mrs. du—Mrs. Crowne," I quickly corrected. I set down her tray in the spiny silence, arranging the porcelain as I'd done for Miss Abigail. Lottie was wrapped in a silk robe, her hair still in a bonnet, the circles under her eyes dark.

I looked around as I set the tea out.

"He's not here," she said.

"I—I wasn't..."

"Do you know where he is?" She picked up the steaming tea, taking a sip. I finished setting out the items and stood up, eyes on the ground. "He's getting a postnuptial agreement drawn up. I'll get everything. If he so much as puts a finger inside of you, I get everything."

I focused harder on my black leather flats.

I heard the sound of Lottie setting down the tea, the clink of the porcelain on the wooden tray.

"Grayson and I are going to Asheville to visit my family. I need my things packed. Get started."

Asheville? Uncle and I had a poetry reading. I'd barely seen him this morning. The entire fucking point of this hell was to spend as much time with him as possible.

I lifted my head. "I can't leave."

Lottie's lips parted like I'd slapped her. The air between us was toxic, even as the salty ocean breathed.

"You really have no shame," she said softly.

I was filled with it. Consumed by it. Once my uncle died, I would leave this place and hide, try to exorcise the demons I'd summoned during my time in Crowne Point.

"Does Grayson know?" I said the insane thing. The wrong thing. The treacherous, ugly, fucked-up thing.

Lottie stood up, straightening her back. "Does my husband know what I'm asking my girl to do?"

I ground my teeth. Instinctively, before I could stop it, my eyes drifted above the glass wall to the lofted second floor, where his bedroom was.

"Go ahead and cry to him, Story. Who do you think he loves more? The girl he tossed millions at to try and get out of his life, or the girl he's willing to lose it all for?"

Her eyes lingered on mine a moment longer.

"Asheville is warmer than Crowne Point. Pack light layers."

EIGHT

GRAY

Lottie's family lived in an estate in Asheville, North Carolina. It was built in 1895 by Victor Paul du Lac and had been in the du Lac family ever since. The entire du Lac estate originally covered more than one hundred thousand acres, but now it was down to a humble seven.

Spending the weekend with Lynette and Arthur du Lac after my sex tape had just rocked their daughter's wedding had to be at the bottom of the things I wanted to do for our fucking honeymoon. But Asheville had been planned for as long as the engagement.

Lottie and I climbed out of the car first. Behind us, in her own car, Story did the same. Traveling with Story had been fucking hell. Every minute I saw her, I remembered coming into Lottie's hand, picturing Snitch.

Snitch's foot caught on the cobblestone, and without thought, I grabbed her elbow.

She clenched her jaw. "Thank you, *Mr. Crowne.*"

She bit out her safe word. I could see the words in her head. All the shit she wouldn't say. I wanted it. I missed it like fucking *air*.

Call me on my shit.

She eyed the sucker in my mouth, and my grip tightened. I wondered how she was handling everything. While the du Lacs had stopped the video on traditional media, we were all over the internet. After my first scandal, I didn't go online for a month. The only thing that got me through it was poetry.

She said I had a mask...Story was stone. I couldn't fucking read her. It was driving me insane. I wanted to pull her aside. Demand she let me in.

Rip the pain from her perfect lips.

"There's a servant entrance around back," Lottie said, cutting through the moment like a knife. I quickly dropped her, swiping my hand across my pants.

"Follow them to my room and bring me back my house shoes."

Snitch mumbled a "Yes, Mrs. Crowne" and followed two servants through the archway into the home. They weren't dressed in a traditional maid uniform, as Mother would insist on, but in dusty gray-blue uniforms you might see the maids wear at hotels, complete with starched white collars.

"I thought you agreed you weren't bringing her."

Lottie didn't look at me. "She said she wanted to come."

I don't want to believe my wife would lie to me. That I was corrupting sweet, pure Lottie.

But I can't believe Snitch would willingly leave her uncle.

"I still don't see why *you* wanted to bring her."

"Let me get my girl back and I wouldn't," Lottie sniped.

I arched a brow at Lottie. Lottie never sniped. "You don't think it's going to raise questions, cause more drama, when she's here?"

Lottie flexed her jaw.

"I just—"

"You really have no idea all the things that I have to do on my own, do you?" She spun on me, eyes flared. "What's expected of me? Do you think I wanted this? You asked me to have your *mistress* as my girl."

"She's not my—"

"Pumpkin!"

Lottie's glare lingered on me a moment longer; then she swiped it away with a serene smile, turning to her father. Chills ran up my spine.

I knew that smile.

My *mother* wore that smile.

"Daddy!" Lottie returned Mr. du Lac's hug with a stiffness I knew too well.

All warmth drained from Mr. du Lac's body when he turned to me.

"Grayson," he said. I noted how he didn't extend a hand to me, but I wasn't surprised Mr. du Lac already wasn't very fond of me, and punching his son and humiliating his daughter at her wedding...sure didn't help.

I inclined my head. "Mr. du Lac."

Arthur du Lac was tall like his son, with the same hot chocolate complexion as his children, and as with everyone in this world...he had too much goddamn power.

He gave me a stiff smile, then returned his attention to his daughter, as my mother and sister's town car pulled up behind us. My grandfather would join us later, for the holiday only, of course.

Two servants appeared, opening the doors for them. My mother stepped outside.

"Lynette," my mother said, giving a cursory glance to the estate. "Your house is lovely, as always."

Tansy Crowne and Lynette du Lac did not get along. Their rivalry went back decades to when they were teenagers.

"Do we get our own bags or..." my mother asked, taking off her riding gloves and looking around expectantly.

"Of course we don't have the pomp and circumstance of Crowne Hall, but our humble home can manage to get your luggage and take them to your rooms."

Like magic, more servants appeared, chipping at the mountain of luggage for the weekend stay, piled high before the sprawling patchwork green lawn and thousand-gallon fountain that marked their *humble* estate.

We followed the du Lacs inside.

My mother and my sister followed their luggage up to their rooms, and then it was just Lottie and her mother and I alone in their grand foyer.

Lottie took off her sunhat and held it in her hands. Mrs. du Lac narrowed on the action.

"Where is your girl?" Mrs. Du Lac asked. "Your girl should be getting that for you."

Lottie shifted, obviously uncomfortable. "Uh..."

Snitch still hadn't returned. Was she lost?

"You don't know?" Mrs. du Lac arched a brow.

"No, I—"

"She doesn't listen to you?"

Lottie paled. "She listens to me. I just...I gave her the morning off. After traveling, you know."

"You gave her the morning off?" Mrs. du Lac's barely noticeable brow lift let us know that she did not approve.

"Lottie is being humble," I said, wrapping my arm around her waist. "She forgot to mention it wasn't her decision. It was mine."

This was what a husband did. Defend his wife. Stood by her side.

Mrs. du Lac's gaze slowly, deliberately, landed on me. "How thoughtful."

Mrs. du Lac left and Lottie quickly shoved herself off me. Betrayal etched her features, lips parted. She looked like she was going to talk, but then she swallowed and shook her head, following after her mother.

STORY

Lottie had told me to follow the servants and bring her back house shoes, but I was lost. The du Lac servants had taken me inside the home, and that was it. They weren't like Crowne servants with our rigid codes.

The du Lacs were a different breed of rich people. If Crowne Hall was stuck in the Victorian era, then the du Lacs never left the Gilded Age.

"Angel?"

I stiffened at the voice and kept walking, as if that would stop a guy like West du Lac. A moment later, his hand encircled my bicep, and he tugged me back.

"What are you doing in Asheville?"

"I'm here until the Crownes go home."

He quirked a brow. "You've never been to my neck of the woods before."

You never brought me.

I shrugged.

He dropped me and looked around, mischief lighting up his eyes. "I guess I owe you a tour."

I'd always seen West at Crowne Hall, so even when we were teenagers, he dressed nicely, whether it was a suit or expensive designer clothes. Today he wore a cutoff shirt and athletic shorts, as though he'd just been working out.

The sight twisted my stomach.

It was...oddly intimate.

"I'm working." I rubbed the back of my neck. "I'm so late. I can't find Lottie's room."

His brow furrowed, then he gripped my wrist.

"What are you doing?"

"You're in the wrong part of Du Lac Manor. Let me show you, and if I happen to give you a tour along the way..."

I tugged my wrist free. "She's probably out there waiting for me!" I dragged two hands over my face, clammy, stomach filled with knots, as ridiculous tears clogged my throat. Picturing Lottie waiting there had my heartbeat rising. I just wanted to do my job and not give her any more reasons to hate me.

Give *me* any more reasons to hate myself.

His smile dropped, and something like concern filled his face. "How are you doing?"

I paused.

He was the first person to ask me that. Suddenly it was all too much. My throat thick, from the onslaught of emotions. West du Lac was the first person, the *only* person to ask me how I was doing.

He lifted my chin so I was looking into his eyes.

"I haven't been online," I answered honestly.

"That's good," West said. He dropped my chin and took a step back. Allowing me space to breathe.

I wasn't going to cry. I wasn't going to cry in front of West fucking du Lac.

"Why are you doing this?" I asked.

Why are you pretending to care?

West leaned against a window with folded arms, the lush, checkered green lawn behind him. It was dark in this room, a muted dark—the only light glaring from the one diamond-paned window at his back.

"Let me show you Du Lac Manor, Angel."

"I can't leave."

He laughed. "Angel, you're not at Crowne Hall anymore. No one keeps track of the maids. They go missing all the time." I wasn't sure why, but that didn't fill me with ease. It made me feel worse.

He smiled. "You can do anything with me."

GRAY

"You need to wear a suit. My mother wants me to wear a gown." Lottie exhaled, rubbing her right eye. She looked in the mirror, holding up a dress, lips pursed. "This would be a lot easier if I had a girl..."

It was on the tip of my tongue to bring it up, but I knew any mention of Story was bad, would be misconstrued. So I lifted myself up on Lottie's ivory dresser, pulling one leg up. I stared out her window overlooking the acres of patchwork lawn.

It's been two hours and still no sign of Story.

She was probably just learning the layout. Being showed where she'd sleep.

But worry ate at my chest.

I couldn't help but wonder if she was getting fed, if she was sleeping properly. I can't be the one to make sure of those things now, and she *needs* someone to do it.

Story has millions of dollars now. Enough money to sleep like a queen, but she chooses to sleep like a servant. All for her uncle.

She called me Atlas, so then what is she? Story Hale only knows how to sacrifice. She doesn't know how to choose herself.

Lottie lowered the dresses, looking over her shoulder at me. "Don't get father talking about Great-Grandpa; he won't quit until you've heard all about how the estate brought *Châteauesque* architecture to North Carolina."

"Lottie, I've been to dinner before."

Why was she so nervous?

"One more thing," Lottie said. "Try not to punch my brother at dinner."

"No promises," I joked.

Silence passed, but all she said was, "You look kind of like the boy who used to do my homework."

I turned away from the window. "What am I missing?"

A flicker of a smile. "A joint."

An idea popped into my head. It had been years, almost a decade, but I wondered... I pulled open Lottie's drawer beneath me and rooted around until my hand met the small ziplock baggie.

Holy shit.

I lifted it out, pulling out a lighter and a joint. It was probably dry as shit, but whatever.

Her mouth dropped open, and she scrambled to me.

"You hid these in here?" She got to her knees, looking around with her arm. "What else did you hide?" Her eyes found mine from the floor.

I exhaled smoke with a grin. "Cameras."

She slapped my knee. For a minute, the air was light. So of course it fucking shattered like glass.

Outside, I finally spotted Snitch.

With fucking *West*.

"I have to wear a suit?" I asked, tone careful, watching them walk the white stone paths along the fountain.

"I think I'll wear the dove dress," she said. "So anything dark gray..." Lottie continued, telling me what would match, what her mother would expect. Snitch tripped, and West caught her elbow.

My vision blacked.

Lottie's voice faded into nothing.

I stamped the joint out against her windowsill like I used to, absently noting there was still a charred mark.

I didn't realize I was standing until Lottie spoke. "Did you hear me? What are you doing?"

I'm about to go put your brother in the ground.

"Uh..." I rubbed the back of my neck. "Gonna get dressed, go to dinner, I guess."

"We still have an hour before then."

"Then why don't you show me what's changed around here?"

Lottie's face fell a little. "Nothing's changed."

I looked for something to lift the mood, spotting the perfect thing on her bed.

I lifted up a Beanie Baby. "Yeah, you're still addicted to Beanie Babies."

"Only this one." She snatched it from me and shoved it under her pillow. "I don't really like keeping them around."

As Lottie always did, she tried to hide the melancholy in her voice. Maybe I should have let her.

"Why?"

"I always bought them when I felt unloved, unappreciated, unwanted. I guess it's a little pathetic how many I had. It's like a shrine to how little I was loved."

I stared at the pastel-green stuffed animal. "So why keep that one?"

"I bought it the day after you kissed me."

Disgust filled me. I'd been about to leave, for what? To go find Snitch. I rubbed my forehead, feeling like an asshole.

"I'll be better, Lottie."

Sorrow and sadness filled Lottie's features. Worst of all...disbelief. She didn't believe me.

I didn't believe me.

Still, determined not to give Lottie another reason to buy a stuffed animal, I held my arm out to her, and together we headed downstairs.

"So...don't bring up Great-Grandpa?" I reiterated as we descended the stairs.

"Not unless you want to die at the table." Lottie laughed.

I laughed, too, just as Lottie stopped short on the stairs. I nearly toppled us both down. I looked to see what could have made her freeze.

There was a man in the grand foyer, speaking with Mrs. du Lac. He looked like he could've been Lottie's dad's age, with salt-and-pepper hair, but the similarities ended there. His short brown hair was cut and styled youthfully, and he definitely didn't dress like du Lacs. He looked like a pilot or explorer in his leather jacket, dark blue shirt, and darker jeans.

"I thought you were in Bosnia." Mrs. du Lac reached for the man, planting a kiss on his cheek.

"I didn't want to miss Charlie's wedding."

Charlie.

I glanced at Lottie. She stared at him with a look I realized I'd never seen on her face before—anger. Even with everything I'd done, she'd never looked at me like that. I'd received sadness and disappointment.

I looked back at the man as he pulled back on a laugh. "Obviously I failed on that front."

"Oh, well..." Mrs. du Lac trailed off on an awkward, soft laugh, clearly remembering the shitshow that was our wedding. "You're here now. How long are you in town?"

Who was this guy? A photographer? A filmmaker? Some guy who still lived off his trust fund, never quite grasping he wasn't in his twenties anymore? Those were the only people who dressed like that in our world at that age.

"Only a few days, until my visa for Syria comes through."

Mrs. du Lac clicked her tongue. "Is MSF really sending you to a war zone?"

MSF...Médecins Sans Frontières aka Doctors Without Borders.

Doctor.

I gave him another once-over. He definitely came from old money.

"But you'll be here for the Labor Day party?"

"I'll do my best. Is Charlie around?"

Beside me, *Charlie* bristled.

"She's upstairs with her new husband."

His eyes traveled up the stairs, landing on us. Mrs. du Lac followed, eyebrows lifting a little.

"Oh, you're down early," Mrs. du Lac said, then she gestured to the man beside her. "Isn't this a nice surprise?"

A stiff silence passed, one I couldn't decipher.

Mrs. du Lac blinked. "Say hello, Charlotte."

I'd heard that tone used *many* times with my sister, Abigail. It really meant, *What the fuck is wrong with you?*

"Hi, Jack," Lottie said without emotion.

Once again I looked between them as another pause weighed the air.

"Why don't we take this into the next room?" Mrs. du Lac said. "Lottie and Gray, you're welcome to join us."

Aka, you must join us.

Then *Jack,* apparently, followed Mrs. du Lac into the next room. Lottie followed them with her eyes, staying still.

"Who is that guy?" I asked.

"No one," she said, her eyes on the empty doorway they'd just gone through. With a stiff exhale, she descended the steps. Beyond her, West and Story walked by the window.

They were laughing.

Fucking *laughing*.

Lottie reached the bottom, looking up at me expectantly. I took a step, then froze. West licked his thumb, swiping it across Story's cheek. I could hear only buzzing in my ears. Feel the tightness in my chest.

I flexed my knuckles.

He's too fucking close.

"Gray?"

"I'll follow," I gritted.

A look flitted across Lottie's face, but she said nothing.

STORY

After West had given me a tour of Du Lac Manor, I realized the similarities between it and Crowne Hall were as stark as their differences. Each was haunted in its own way.

He opened the door for me and said, "After you, Cinderella."

I tried not to laugh, but failed. I wanted to hate him, but he wasn't easy to hate. He was charming and he was funny. He told me anecdotes about Du Lac Manor, places his uncles and great-cousins had christened with their stupidity. Like the time his great-uncle John tried to piss the farthest and was arrested for indecency, so they had to buy the acreage.

"Did you have a good time?"

Grayson's voice stopped me in my tracks. He stood at the foot of the stairs, sunlight and shadow accentuating a glower hotter than fire.

"Um..." I trailed off.

"Lottie has been looking for her girl," he said, soft and dark.

Oh.

Shit.

I quickly moved to go attend to Lottie, but West gripped my elbow, holding me in place.

"My sister can go without her girl for an hour," West said, laughter in his voice. "She's not entirely helpless."

"Three," Grayson said, his voice cold. "It's been three."

"Oh, well, that changes things," West said, laughing harder.

Grayson zeroed on me. "You're only here because we allow it. Try and make some effort."

Fury and betrayal made a noxious soup in my gut. Each inhale felt like breathing in knives. Yes, he allowed me to stay, but it isn't the greatest benevolence to sleep on the floor to avoid an ashy bed. To be forced to fly to fucking Asheville when I wanted to stay with my uncle, the only reason I'm doing this.

"Thank you for *allowing* me to stay. It's so important I get to stay near my uncle. After all, every minute counts." His brow crinkled, and I swear recognition flickered in his blue gaze.

But I didn't care.

"I should go to *Mrs. Grayson Crowne.*"

I shucked off West and walked by Grayson, leaving them both behind. I swiped at my face, trying to wipe off the heat. For a minute, I'd laughed with West and forgotten my life. Forgotten the darkness.

I heard the footsteps moments later, pounding on the hardwood.

"Hey!" Grayson called after me. I walked faster. "Story, wait! Story!" He spun me around. "I'm sorry. I got..." He tangled his hands in his hair. Absently, I noticed it looked wilder. I hated that I wanted to know what had been on his mind.

"I worry about you," he finished.

Unwanted hope sprang in my chest.

Maybe he still wanted me. Maybe the weight on his shoulders was me.

"It's not your job to worry about me, Mr. Crowne."

He looked like I'd slapped him. Then an icy cold fell across his features. "Why were you with him?"

Why do you care?

Why do you *fucking care*?

I still had no clue why he'd ever broken us in the first

place. But I did know the only reason he'd given me that moment on his wedding was because of his *wife*.

I was starting to think I got us all wrong. He was just like West, a rich boy who believed he was entitled to my love.

I took a breath, then said with an even voice, "What I do is of no concern to you, Mr. Crowne." I turned, not waiting for a reply.

"He raped you!" His yell slammed against my back, echoing off the walls and freezing me in place.

The proclamation seemed to silence everything, even the birds outside, until only dust remained. Lingering in the air and catching the stripe of sunlight piercing the shadowy hall like stardust.

That little shred of hope I had that wouldn't fucking die —ripped out. I don't know how he learned...but I know now why he won't let me go. The *why*—it's always the same with these boys.

I straightened my shoulders, slowly turning. "Thank you for letting me know, Mr. Crowne. I wouldn't have figured it out otherwise."

"Story, wait." He grabbed my bicep. "Just fucking *wait*."

"Why? Why do I need to wait for you?" My voice started to shake. "You left me. The only reason you're paying attention is because you learned another guy dirtied your merchandise."

"That's not—" He exhaled and dropped me. "You don't think that. You don't believe that about me."

I didn't know what I believed anymore.

"Why do you keep hanging around him?"

"Why do you care?" I yelled.

"You know why." His voice lowered to a growl that vibrated and throbbed in my chest.

"Don't," I whispered. I tried to step back, but his grip tightened, holding me in place.

This wasn't okay.

He was supposed to leave me alone. Leave me to hate him.

"You chose to come here," he said, voice fast and furious. "You could have stayed in Crowne Hall with your uncle. You *chose.*"

It was my turn to feel slapped. I bit at my upper lip, my heart racing faster than my lungs could gather air.

Are you allowed to feel betrayal when he doesn't belong to you? Doesn't matter—still burns my chest. How could he believe that?

Finally I spoke. "Does that sound like something I would do, Grayson?"

"Grayson?" Lottie's soft voice cracked the moment. Grayson dropped me, and I took a step back. Lottie looked between us.

Behind her, her mother stood with another man I didn't know.

"I see you've located your girl," Mrs. du Lac said, eyes on me, cold.

I lowered my eyes to the floor.

"Dinner is ready."

NINE

GRAY

Mr. du Lac sat at the helm of the table, Mrs. du Lac at the other end, and sandwiched between them was what must have been the most silent, awkward dinner table in existence.

*Does that sound like something I would do...does that sound like something I would do...*over and over again, Story's words played in my head.

No.

It didn't.

So my lovely, pure, innocent wife fucking *lied*. The lines were drawn clearly by the wedding band around my finger. Yet the protective urge I feel isn't for Lottie. The betrayal coursing through my blood is on behalf of Snitch.

Fuck.

"Grayson, you're so quiet," West said. "I think this is the first time you haven't forced us all to attend the Grayson Crowne show."

I lifted my eyes from my dinner knife. Across the table, at the corner next to his mother and conveniently as far as fuck away from me as possible, was West. He grinned.

I played with the knife in my hand.

He really wanted to do this at dinner?

"How's your eye?" I asked. It was dark, purpling, but not bruised enough, in my opinion.

Lottie knocked her wine to her lap, spilling and staining her dress.

I handed her my napkin.

"Can you not start something with my brother at dinner?" she whispered, and yanked the napkin from my hand.

I settled back into my chair. West's smile had dropped. The corners of my lips lifted, barely. Bitterly.

Silence passed.

Stale.

Jack looked left and right, filling himself in on the silent conversation. "So the wedding looked beautiful."

West laughed.

And the room descended into silence.

Dinner was oppressive. It was dark. All of us in our best clothing, in gowns and suits, eating in sallow silence. I couldn't say for certain if the du Lacs always ate this way, because my mother and Mrs. du Lac had such a deep-rooted rivalry.

"So...MSF?" my mother attempted.

"Jack is a dear family friend." Something flickered in Mrs. du Lac's eyes, something warm. "He's known us longer than Lottie's been alive."

I glanced at Lottie. She was staring at Jack. Again.

"Right, dear?"

Mrs. du Lac tried to get her husband's attention, but it

was elsewhere. He gripped the leg of a maid, who smiled thinly. Mrs. du Lac smiled softly despite her husband's reproach.

I placed my hand in Lottie's. It felt wrong. I was still pissed at her for lying, but I was determined not to be that man.

Jack's eyes flickered to our joined hands as he cut his steak.

"West will be taking Arthur's place soon," Mrs. du Lac said loudly as her husband slid his hand up the maid's thigh. "After the New Year."

"Retirement?" Jack said. "Never thought I'd see that day, Arthur."

"Grayson will step into a more pivotal role at Crowne Industries as well," my mother supplied. "It will be good to have some youth in the company."

"Just two brothers working together," West said, grinning at me.

And at that moment, Snitch came into the room. Though she did as all Crowne servants were trained to do—blend in—everyone watched her. Mr. du Lac stopped showering attention on the maid, turning back to us. He dug into the meal silently.

"Mrs. Crowne," Story whispered. "You called for me?"

Before Lottie could respond, her father spoke.

"Isn't this the girl that turned my daughter into a laughingstock?"

Snitch froze, still bent at a ninety-degree angle next to Lottie's ear.

"I suppose it's a good thing this was always about one thing from the beginning. Crowne Industries. Otherwise I might actually give a shit."

"Daddy, please..." Lottie implored before turning to Snitch. "I... I spilled. I need you to prepare a new dress."

Snitch nodded and left.

I didn't like the way Mr. du Lac's eyes followed Snitch as she exited, tracking her like prey. When Snitch had barely left, Mr. du Lac made some excuse about going to the restroom, pushing out his wooden chair.

"Arthur," I said. "Lottie was telling me your grandfather had an interest in architecture?"

Mr. du Lac paused. "He *was* the first person to bring *Châteauesque* architecture to North Carolina...it's a fascinating story. I'll tell you all about it after dinner." He glanced where Story had gone, and followed.

West and I shared a look.

As he got out of his chair, I started to push from mine. "I'll be back."

"Sure." Lottie smiled and turned back to her food.

I looked from her, to my mother, to Mrs. Du Lac...all wearing that smile as though it were armor. I didn't want Lottie to become them, but Snitch was in the other room.

It's nothing. I'll learn to love Lottie like Snitch learned to hate me. And if I can't, then I'll fucking fake it. I won't subject her to the same ruinous destiny as my mother.

STORY

I edged away from Mr. du Lac.

"You're the girl everyone is making a fuss about," he said.

He'd cornered me in the adjacent bar right as I was about to head up to Lottie's room.

"Mr. du Lac..." I took a small step to the left, and so did he. "I need to go prepare Mrs. Crowne's dress."

"I like it when you keep your eyes down," he snarled. "Maybe we should make the other girls do that."

I stepped back, my back colliding with something hard. I heard a crash, a clatter, and wet seeped into my shirt. A bar.

I stopped trying to play nice and made a dash for the door, but he slammed his hands on either side, dark eyes on me.

"Your wife is in the other room." My hands slipped on the now-wet surface, looking for purchase.

"And?"

Fear pounded in my chest. Do I fight him? And then what? These were the employers you hoped to never have. The kind who saw our submission as their right.

"Get your fucking hands off her."

Relief and something else mixed in my chest at the voice. Westley du Lac had come, and he was not the white knight I'd expected...or hoped for.

When Mr. du Lac didn't immediately respond, West grabbed his father by the shoulder, pulling him off me.

Adrenaline pounded in my skull.

I couldn't recall a time I'd ever seen West look like this. He was always so carefree, but now his square jaw was tilted up, showing a throbbing neck, eyes shadowed and hard—as if he was barely holding back.

"You know what they say about her," his father said. "She doesn't belong to anyone."

Mr. du Lac flung his hand out to me and I flinched, closing my eyes and bracing for the hit.

Moments later, a crash sounded.

Grayson had slammed Mr. du Lac into the wall.

"You okay, Snitch?" His voice was a low, deep growl.

"I had this covered, Crowne," West said.

Grayson either didn't care or didn't hear. I could see the muscles in Grayson's back clench through his tailored dark-gray suit. My heart thumped and thumped and thumped. At West...at Grayson looming so close, eyes murderous.

At being cared for...by both of them.

Mr. du Lac's eyes narrowed. "There are rules—an order to things. Even we follow that. If she's your mistress, you must—"

Grayson lifted him up by the collar, only to slam him harder against the wall.

What rules? What order? I didn't want to ever find out.

"Grayson? West—oh my god!"

We all looked at the same time to see we had an audience. Lottie and her mother, as well as Mrs. Crowne and the man, Jack, had crammed into the doorway.

"What's going on?"

One by one, their eyes landed on me.

I knew they knew the answer. I saw it in their faces, some kind of resigned disappointment. This obviously isn't new behavior.

What is new, is Grayson and West.

"Grayson?" Lottie asked.

Grayson shot me a look. What was I supposed to do?

Slowly, reluctantly, Grayson let Mr. du Lac go and went to Lottie.

His wife.

"Just getting your father a nightcap."

GRAY

Lottie lingered long after everyone had returned to the dining room. The wine stain on Lottie's dress had set and spread. She stared at the broken glass on the bar and ground, a numb expression on her face.

"You saved her. You can't stop saving her."

"You said she chose to come here," I said lightly.

It didn't feel right. Normally I wouldn't second-guess Lottie, but this felt calculated. For the first time, I stared at my wife, uncertain.

I wanted to give her another chance.

Give *us* another chance.

Not turn her into my mother, not become my father. Save us from that fate.

Her eyes lifted, and in them I saw nothing. "You've been talking to her?"

Silence wafted.

"Tomorrow the press arrive for Labor Day," Lottie continued. "Everyone is waiting for you to fuck up again. They want to see if the rumors are true. If she really is the Cinderella of Crowne Hall. If I'm..." She trailed off, and I stopped.

The Wicked Wife.

Shame enveloped me. "Lottie, you're my wife. My beautiful, absolutely *not* wicked wife."

My words affected her, but not in the way I'd hoped. Her throat bobbed, like she'd swallowed down tears.

"I can't stop thinking...If you didn't think you were going to fuck her again, you'd get a postnuptial drawn up."

She didn't wait for me to respond. She turned on her heel, heading into the dining room. It was then I noticed her mother lingering in the shadows. She stood off the wall, coming into the light.

"You know...my husband's family is very open about their mistresses. I had to endure so many women, I lost count."

"Are you trying to imply something, Mrs. du Lac?" I asked.

"Lottie won't have the same life as me."

"No," I gritted. "She won't."

She arched a brow but said nothing else.

Since dinner had been cut short, I went up to Lottie's room—anything to avoid more of her family. I froze in the doorway. Story was there, dropping off a plate of grilled cheese. Her hair was up, messy curls falling around her face. After arranging the plate, she stayed in the room, staring at it silently.

I wondered what was on her mind.

I was fucking desperate for her thoughts.

"Lottie hates grilled cheese," I said. "So either that's not for her, or you really are shit at your job."

She startled and then hurriedly walked to the door without another word.

I grabbed her elbow, catching her. "Why did you bring that?"

I tried to tamp down the anger in my voice, but failed. I'm trying to stop loving her, trying to get over her, and she's making it fucking impossible.

She averted her gaze, looking at the floor.

I grabbed her chin, forcing her gaze. "Answer me."

"Because you hate steak," she spat.

"But why *that*. Why grilled cheese? I'm a Crowne, why would you think I'd like *that*?"

"Am I wrong?" she demanded.

"Fucking say it, Snitch."

"It's your favorite, Grayson."

She yanked her chin and arm out of my hold, and continued on her way.

"You're supposed to hate me, little nun," I said to her back.

"I do."

Then why the fuck are you the only one who knows what I really like?

"My dad used to make me grilled cheese."

She paused in the hallway, partially obscured by shadows. This was how I would talk to her. How I would confess. If we couldn't have our nights, then I could at least have shadows.

"The edges were always burned and the middle not melted enough, but he'd make it for me himself, late at night in the kitchen. It's one of the only memories I have of him that isn't shit."

Her shoulders dropped, and she turned her head to the side, giving me her soft profile.

Even when you hate me, you're still the only one I can count on.

But that isn't how it's supposed to be. I'm supposed to count on my fucking *wife*.

And Story is supposed move on.

Forget me.

"I don't want your grilled cheese, Snitch," I said, voice cold. "Stop thinking about me, forget about me, because I don't give a shit about you anymore."

Her head slashed over her shoulder, glare catching mine. "Poor, sad Grayson Crown. No one's ever been kind to you, so you look at kindness with distrust. I don't think about you, Grayson, I pity you."

She walked away and I wanted her to turn back around, show me her face—show me *anything*.

But she kept walking.

Holy shit.

That glare, those words, that glimpse of the Story that always called me on my shit. It was like a drop of heroin in my blood.

I slid into the chair, gripping the armrest so I didn't run after her, staring at the grilled cheese.

I couldn't fucking eat it.

It was a couple hours before Lottie came back, and by then I'd slid into bed. Lottie sat on the edge, knees to her chest, her gown flowing around her body.

"Why is there grilled cheese?" she asked.

I don't know why I had the urge to lie. I hadn't technically done anything wrong.

"I think someone sent it up for you."

"That's strange...I hate grilled cheese." She crawled to me, lying on my chest, still in her gown. "I'm sorry...about before."

I eyed the cold sandwich. "You don't have anything to be sorry about, Lottie."

I don't think about you, Grayson, I pity you.

Later that night I couldn't sleep.

I stared at the floor, picturing Snitch before she'd crawled into my bed, into my veins. I missed Snitch. Missed her raspy voice in the dark. Missed her in my sheets. Missed her talking with me when I couldn't fucking sleep.

I crawled into bed with Lottie, wondering if she could be that person for me.

"Lottie."

She woke up sleepy.

"What? What is it? Is everything okay?"

"Everything is fine. I just..." It took a minute to work past the mental block. The part that says, *You're a pussy. Roll over. Go to sleep. No one gives a shit.*

"Do you want to talk?" I eventually managed. "I hate steak. My favorite food is grilled cheese—"

She'd fallen back asleep.

I climbed out of bed and went rooting around the one bag I never let the servants touch, grabbing my journal.

Do you write everything in green?

One time Snitch had found this. She didn't know what was inside, the importance of what she'd found.

I can't talk to her. I don't know how she's dealing with all of the new attention, but I can guess, and I know it's probably not good.

I couldn't give her anything but this notebook.

My hopes.

My dreams.

Because, forever, they belong to her.

TEN

STORY

It was another sleepless night, staring at the ceiling. I'm not sure when I finally fell asleep, but when I woke, my lids felt swollen.

That was what I missed most, I realized. Having someone to share the darkness with.

I don't think about you, Grayson, I pity you.

What a fucking lie. He was all I thought about.

I'd stared at the door, picturing Grayson coming to me, as ludicrous as that was. When I heard a creak outside my door, I let myself play out a fantasy that he actually *had* come to me. I told him I would learn to hate him.

I was doing a bad job of it.

But did he have to be so fucking cruel? It was already torture watching him with his *wife*.

I rolled over, and my face smacked into something hard.

A journal.

I sat up so fast I almost got whiplash. It looked like the

one Grayson had in his desk. I held it tightly between my fingers.

Had he actually come last night?

Tentatively, I went to open the leather book.

Love is a smoke raised with the fume of sighs.

I ran my finger across the raised green ink.

This line from *Romeo and Juliet* basically meant passion always gave way to grief, the sighs are one and the same, and my heart ached with the accuracy.

I was deep inside Grayson's soul. Deeper than he'd ever allowed me inside before. It was torture. To be so inside—and so far away from him.

The floorboard outside my door creaked.

"Grayson?" His name fell from my lips before I could keep it in.

I was glued to the door opening, as if in slow motion.

"Angel." West opened the door entirely, leaning against the doorframe.

My heart dropped like a fucking traitor.

Grayson *left us*, I tried to reason with it. I shoved the journal under my pillow, feeling caught.

"What are you doing here?" I asked.

"Wondering if you've given my proposal more thought." He shrugged, as if asking me to marry him was no more exciting than asking me to lunch.

"I haven't, and I won't."

He looked around my room. "We'd make a good pair, Angel."

West was already dressed for Labor Day in a gingham suit that fit his tall, muscular frame perfectly, with no tie on his stark white shirt. It was refined. Southern. Charming like him.

Deceptive.

I scoffed. "You said I was naive for believing in happily ever after. That I could only be a mistress. I won't be a mistress. I won't move from one hell to..."

I think we're both in the same hell, just different wallpaper.

"I won't move to one with different wallpaper."

He rolled his plump lips. "Not a mistress. My wife."

"Everyone would disown you."

"I've always thought it's easier to ask for forgiveness than permission."

I winced at the implication.

"Angel, I—"

"It's fine," I said, trying to brush past it. "I have to go to your sister. Please leave."

I pinned him, and again, surprisingly, he listened. He kicked off the wall. "I'm going. Gone. But...think about it, Angel."

West shut the door, and I stared at it.

He was fucking with me.

They were *always* fucking with me.

I worked the fabric of my bedspread between my thumbs. I thought I could handle a couple of months of this. I'd been a servant for half my life, so what was a couple more if it meant getting to spend the last months with my only family?

I didn't account for what would become of me during those months.

The stains it would leave on my soul.

I fell back flat onto the mattress, shame running cold through my veins.

Maybe Uncle would leave with me.

Maybe he would give up his home.

After all, is it really our home? If it was our home, I shouldn't have to barter my dignity to stay.

I video-called my uncle from bed. He looked wan, weak, and my heart cracked.

"What if I came home and we left? We could go to Scotland like you suggested. We could go anywhere, Uncle."

I had enough money, after all. What was the point of it if I still lived like this? If he was there, and I was here.

I knew his answer before he'd even spoken.

"I've spent my whole life here, Storybook. I can't abandon it at the end."

"Of course."

My words were barely a whisper.

"We'll have a poetry reading when you get back," he said with a smile. "Everything will be fine."

We hung up, and I went to Lottie.

"Mrs. Cr—oh." I broke off as my eyes connected with Grayson.

I nearly lost my breath at Grayson in all white for Labor Day. His stark white tailored suit with matching shirt, the top two buttons undone, showing a glimpse of his perfect golden chest. It was both polished and casual in a way only *he* could pull off.

I could already see the headlines...the trends that would follow, all because Grayson Crowne decided he felt like wearing something.

"Gray—I mean, Mr. Crowne, I didn't know you'd be here. I'm here for your wife's tea."

Did you give me that journal? Why?

All the whys between us piled like thorns until they became briar I couldn't navigate. Why did you choose her? Why did you leave? Why won't you just let me go?

Why do you look so broken every time I see you?

"I thought you were Lottie," he said.

"Not this time," I whispered.

A small, barely-there smile cracked my lips.

Stifling.

I held the tea tray like I had the first time we'd been together. The first time he'd mistaken me for his wife. A sucker stem poked out from his pouty pink lips, and he had a forlorn look in his blue eyes.

"Have you been chewing suckers all day?" I asked softly. His jaw tightened, and immediately I backtracked. "I'm sorry it's not—"

I broke off and braced myself for a repeat of last night, for more cruel and thorny words from him.

"You have to stop doing that, Snitch."

Our eyes caught. The intensity in his blue gaze almost made me swallow my words.

"Doing what?" I whispered.

"Being the only person in the world paying attention to me."

The air froze and a little bit off the walls he'd erected crumbled; through them I saw inside his soul, I saw *Grayson* again.

Grayson Crowne had to be one of the most watched people in the world, but maybe he was right, and I was the only one who really saw him. What kind of twisted irony was that? Because I wasn't even supposed to look at him.

Sharing his gaze was technically forbidden.

"How is Woodsy?" he asked, voice rough, eyes still locked.

"You would know better than me. He lies to me."

He laughed. "He lies to me too."

"Prideful old man," I said.

"He won't take my money. Won't let me pay for his treatment. Anything."

My eyes cut to his. "Must be hard for you. That's the only way you know how to solve your problems."

I'd spoken out of turn, stepped over the line. Instead of looking furious, his eyes ignited.

"Snitch—"

"Grayson?"

We both froze; then he quickly left. Left without saying another word to either of us, shoving another sucker in his mouth.

I stared after him.

It felt like she'd caught us fucking or something, but all we'd done was talk.

I put Lottie's tea down, and as she drank, I adjusted her big straw hat in silence.

I was ripped in two.

If Uncle would leave, I could leave. I wouldn't be here, behind her. I wouldn't be here, seeing him.

"Do you wear lip gloss?" Lottie asked suddenly.

"Uh, no."

"ChapStick?"

"No..."

She exhaled as though my answer was incorrect. I reached for the final touch to her outfit, white pearls. She was classy, elegant, looked as though she belonged at an English summer wedding.

"You can wear mine today." She handed me a gilded, ornately designed tube.

"I don't understand, Mrs. Crowne."

"There will be plenty of press today," Lottie said lightly. "You'll need to look your best. But it should go without saying..." She lifted her eyes to mine in the mirror, barely visible beneath the big visor of her hat. "Stay away from them."

"Of course, Mrs. Crowne."

GRAY

That honesty.

I missed it like air.

Did Story know how badly I wanted to rip that tray out of her hands and rip her to me?

Across the lawn my grandfather approached me with a man who looked only a few years younger. I drank my whiskey lemonade, unsure where the fuck this was headed, but certain it was somewhere bad.

"Grandfather," I said when they approached, inclining my head to the new asshole.

"I thought it time to introduce you to Roger. Or, as you know him, District Attorney Millard."

I shook his hand, eyes cold on Grandpa. "Nice to finally meet."

"We were just discussing his conviction rate."

"Highest in years."

They laughed. I clenched my jaw and focused across the lawn. Story had come out.

All I want to do is snap back at my grandfather. Topple him. Get rid of his influence.

Crowne Industries was always successful, but under my grandfather's tutelage it became a behemoth. Something to be feared. I'm not naive. I wear the last name Crowne but I don't wear the crown.

He's a king, and you don't topple a king without an army.

With a snap of his fingers he could make Story disappear.

Grandfather and DA Millard finished talking, Millard walked away, his threat sufficiently clear.

"Do you know what happens when you keep tightening a string?" I asked. "It snaps."

"You know, your father and I had a very similar conversation years ago. It's always good to know how much you're willing to lose before you start a war, Grayson. He wasn't willing to lose anything."

I lifted my eyes, colliding with his.

"I'm not my father."

STORY

I've only been to parties at Crowne Hall, but the du Lacs came in second place. All the servants were instructed to wear white, and guests were dressed in soft linens and beige, like sand. On the emerald lawn, everyone looked like a still from an old movie.

I blended in with the other servants in their outfits of starched white, and I was pretty confident no one would notice me. Just another servant among the many, there to do her duty for her mistress.

A man to my left eyed me. At first I didn't think anything of it, but as I moved to another spot, his gaze followed me.

Caution crept up my spine. I had my gaze lowered but

still kept an eye on him. Everywhere I went, his eyes followed me. It wasn't lascivious, as when I'd been nearly gambled with Khalid and all the other boys at that table.

This man seemed to be studying me.

I decided Lottie would rather I head inside than attract attention.

"Wait," the man spoke, and I stopped short, too trained to *not* stop. He walked around and came to me, stopping in front of me.

"Do you work here?" he asked.

"I work for the Crownes..."

"How long?"

I did the mental math. "A while."

"Do you live at Crowne Hall?"

His questions were spitfire.

He looked like he was in his mid-thirties and wasn't unattractive—he had that tall, dark, and handsome thing going on. He didn't have a press badge and was dressed in the same soft linen as everyone else, but he had that deep, probing look in his face that made my gut churn.

"Yes," I finally said.

"Do you know the couple?" He nodded at Grayson and Lottie.

I shifted. "Everyone does. If you'll excuse me."

I made a motion to leave again, but he stopped me with another question. "What's your name?"

My discomfort had now morphed into warning.

"Um..." I struggled with the need to always be respectful and the feeling that if I told him, I'd be really and truly screwed. So I just opened and closed my mouth.

He looked at my clothes; then his eyes zeroed on my locket, the one that I couldn't get myself to take off.

"That's a beautiful piece of jewelry. Who gave it to you?"

I slapped a hand over my neck. "My mother."

It had happened in a split second. One minute he was eyeing me, the next he ripped out his phone and snapped a picture of me.

"Hey!" I shouted. I covered my face, but it was too late. He was still eyeing me with that same suspicious look, but then he turned over his shoulder slightly to yell to someone I couldn't see.

"It's her! The Cinderella of Crowne Hall."

ELEVEN

STORY

"What? I'm not—"

A flash so bright it blinded me cut me off. I put my hand up as another one went off right after. I tried to back away, but I fell into another person.

"When did you fall in love with Grayson?" the person behind me asked.

My heart pounded. "I don't...you have the wrong person."

I'd had one job today: stay away from the press.

Guards were trying to break up this impromptu press conference, dragging them away one by one. I was certain they would lose their Crowne family press passes—a coveted item. Only so much press were allowed for each event.

Was it worth it?

"Do you hate Charlotte du Lac?"

"You have the wrong person," I said again, a sinking in my gut. They had the right person.

"Did his family force you apart or did he abandon you?"

It felt like I'd been hit with a sledgehammer in the chest. Suddenly I wasn't fighting to leave, even as the cameras went off, once again recording me at my most vulnerable for the world to see.

I didn't know the answer to his question.

Was that the *why* I'd been searching for all these months? Why we were broken? I tried to search over the heat of the camera, the rapid-fire questions, to the grassy knoll on which I'd last seen Grayson.

Suddenly a hand grasped my arm.

Grayson?

Some primeval part of me recognized him as my savior before I had a chance to stop it. I lifted my head, covering my eyes from the cold autumn sun, trying to block out the glare and see who it was.

GRAY

I was walking to Story before I could think.

"What are you doing?" Lottie's yell stopped me. I turned back. She stood between our parents, desperation racking every nerve in her body, her eyes pleading.

Only moments ago we'd been selling the "couple of the century" bullshit again.

I took another step.

Grayson, are you going after her?

Grayson, do you love her?

Grayson, when did it start?

Lottie held up her skirts, coming to me, eyes pleading beneath her wide-brimmed hat. She stopped before me and dropped her skirts to the grass.

"You will not leave me here in front of all my friends and the world. Not again. Smile, Grayson, and kiss me."

She feathered her hands into my hair, drawing my lips to hers, mimicking. It was dark and ugly, and there was no love.

But she smiled.

Like my mother.

Like hers.

I ripped Charlotte's lips off me, and the paparazzi went wild. Over Lottie's head I could still see Story slowly being swallowed by them.

"Tonight we're consummating this marriage, even if we have to do it in the dark, even if you have to call me by her name."

Lottie kissed my cheek, then walked away, pushing through the photographers as they shouted questions.

I ran to the spot where Story had been, but she was gone.

STORY

I rubbed my chest as West led me back inside Du Lac Manor. "What the hell was that?"

"Have you not googled yourself, Angel?" he asked.

He sat on a windowsill that overlooked the still-going party. West had taken me back to his room. It wasn't like

Grayson's, haunted and hollow. Golden trophies lined his walls. Memories blasted into me, of a younger me who still loved this boy. A boy who'd told her about how he *hated* being forced to play piano.

I stared at the glimmering gold trophies. I'd thought he'd lied to me about everything.

"Why would I?" I said, shaking out of that stupid part of me I still couldn't squash.

I had googled myself. Once. When I was, like, eleven. It was just a bunch of random people I didn't know, dead people, and of course, fairy tales. I guess if you're someone like Westley, you had to do that kind of thing. You needed to know what people were saying about you.

But people don't even know I exist, much less talk about me.

Westley's brow knitted, making me think I might be wrong.

"What?"

"Do you have your phone?"

I shook my head. "The help is trained not to carry their phones while they work." What if they—*gasp*—took a selfie inside Crowne Hall?

West exhaled and handed me his phone, his look telling me I wasn't going to like it. Eyeing West warily, I took it.

He'd already brought my name up on the browser. My lips parted, unable to process what I was seeing.

When you googled my name before, random things that didn't relate to me popped up. Now...now blurry photos from the night of Grayson's engagement party popped up. The video from his wedding. The photo next to West.

Rumors. Conspiracies.

Truth.

And while some had taken to calling me Cinderella, others had taken to calling me a gold digger. A whore.

"What is this?" I whispered, though I knew. "When I looked last, no one knew my name. Now they know my mother's name!" Then my eyes popped as I scanned another blog, dedicated entirely to my fucking *locket*. My head shot up, locking with West. "How do they even know about this?"

He gave me a rueful smile. "You'd be surprised what people find when your life becomes their hobby."

I felt violated.

Confused.

Scared.

I rubbed my chest. "I spent my whole life trying to hide."

"Well, you're at the top now, Story. You can't hide up here. Everyone's always looking up, and when they do, they're gonna see you."

"I'm not at the top. I'm just a girl...a servant."

TWELVE

GRAY

Though many of the press had been removed, the Labor Day party still continued. I knew the rule—continue *as*. Continue as if nothing had happened while everyone was reveling in the scandal. Of course, it had been suggested Lottie and I leave.

So as not to draw any more attention.

Now I sat on the windowsill in Lottie's bedroom, wondering how to fix the ugliness, the black sludge creeping in my marriage.

The door to her walk-in creaked open.

"Lottie?" I looked up. "Lottie, let's get out—"

I broke off. Lottie stood in the center of the room, dressed in a black-and-violet silk robe—she promptly let the robe fall to the floor.

I looked to the ceiling.

"Why are you looking away? I'm your *wife*."

Moments later her soft hand stroked my jaw. I ground

my teeth, focusing on the lofted ceilings, the sound of the party continuing outside.

"I was going to ask if you wanted to get out of here. Go into town or to the lake, like we used to when we were kids."

When shit wasn't so fucked.

"She tastes like me, you know." Lottie's breath ghosted my lips.

That's the dark, twisted irony. Lottie could never taste like Snitch.

It would kill her.

"Our lip gloss is the same," she continued, trailing a hand down my chest.

"She doesn't wear lip gloss," I gritted.

"I made her wear it today."

My eyes slashed to hers just as she pressed her lips to mine.

Barely a kiss.

Just enough to taste the light, glossy flavor. Some expensive flowery shit—not *Snitch*, but if Lottie was telling the truth, it was her today.

"Don't tell me you don't want this. Don't tell me no."

Maybe I didn't give a shit if it was the truth.

I groaned, pressing my lips harder against hers.

"You can call me by her name," Lottie breathed.

The spell snapped, and I broke away.

"You want it," she said. "I can *see* you want it. Why did you stop?"

"Because it's fucking torture!" It was too late to take it back. The damage was done, written on my wife's face. "Shit. Lottie. Wait." I gripped her chin between my fingers. "That's not what I meant. Lottie, you deserve *more*."

She let out a bitter laugh and yanked her chin away,

grabbing her discarded robe from the floor. She tied the robe around her waist and stared at me.

"I'm going to be like them, won't I? The women in my family. The ones who only had sex to procreate or because their husbands got drunk one night and couldn't find a maid."

"I need time. It hasn't even been a *month*."

I could see the words in her eyes, all the shit she wanted to say to me.

Fucking say it.

But when she finally spoke, her words were lifeless.

"Do you think if I dressed up like a maid and we filmed it, people would stop talking about you and her? Probably not, right? They'd just think you had a thing for maids."

"Don't ever say her name again. Don't bring her into this again. Fucking ever. I'm gonna go for a walk."

"Why bother pretending?" I was at the door when her soft voice drifted over my shoulder. "Every kiss you give me, every touch, every look...I know it isn't for me. It's for her."

I stopped short, then kept going.

STORY

It only took until night before I was all over the news. Just an unconfirmed tabloid story, but the story had leaked all the same. The knowledge was like a fault line in my gut as I carried Lottie's nighttime tea up to her.

The door to her—their—bedroom was already partially open.

Lottie sat on the windowsill, chewing her bottom lip,

wrapped in a silk robe. The room was dark, the only light from the window, from string lights twinkling on the night-darkened lawn below.

I wanted to tell her sorry, but instead I said, "I brought your nighttime tea."

I set the tea on a table beside her. Lottie stared out the window, her breath fogging the glass, shoulders slumped.

Whatever I said about today would sound like an excuse. The truth was, it wasn't really about today, anyway. I still hadn't found a way I could apologize for what I'd done.

I'm not sure there is a way.

I think you just have to let them hate you.

"We're leaving soon," she said lightly, softly.

I know. I counted the days until I could see Uncle. Six. Six more days.

Again the words I wanted to say got stuck in my throat.

You're not supposed to be the villain in your own story, but every day I could see my role written clearer on Lottie's face. The longer I stayed here, the further I cemented it...all the things I wanted to avoid.

Villainous.

Ruinous.

Slut.

"Do you have my lip gloss?" she asked.

"I never wore it. Sorry." I handed it to her. She stared at it, then started laughing. Uncontrollably. Until her laughter turned into sobs.

I reached out to hold her, comfort her, I don't know.

In the end, I took Lottie's tea tray, leaving the tea.

I caught him, my ghost of love long past, an hour or two after returning Lottie's tea. He didn't see me or hear me when I came in, so I used that to my advantage. I leaned against the wall, watching him. Watching Grayson Crowne.

He placed what looked like a jar of peanuts on my nightstand. Fluffed my pillow.

And then he just...stayed. Inspected. He fingered the peeling wallpaper, exhaling. His head traveled to my small window, and I wondered what he was thinking.

"The servants' quarters back home are better," I said. "On clear nights you can see the moon."

Grayson jumped. He turned around, eyes wide. Then he blinked, and impassivity washed over his features. He said nothing, moving to leave, brushing past me without a word.

Was he seriously going to leave like that?

"Hey!" I went after him, slamming the door before he could leave. "You left me your journal, didn't you?"

He looked over my head at the now-shut door, still silent, as if I were an annoying wind that had closed the door.

"Did you read it?" he asked softly, eyes still on the door.

"No. And I never fucking will," I lied. "Stop doing this." I shoved him. "You said you would leave me to hate you."

His eyes flashed to mine. "Stay the fuck away from Westley du Lac and I will."

"Who are you to tell me what to do?"

"You're right. Guess it's not my fault you catch the eyes of all the du Lac men."

I froze. Bile and acid rising up my throat. "What are you saying?"

"Just that if you hang out with West, not my problem what happens."

"I'm asking for it, right? I didn't say no, either, Gray. I liked him a lot. I wanted him to call me back after it happened." I stared at him, willing all my hate, my anger, my fear to bleed into his soul.

His jaw clenched and he looked away, looked at the floor.

"You think I need you to save me, Grayson? All you've ever done is hurt me."

That wasn't true.

It wasn't true at all.

But I was so, so hurt now.

"Fuck off. Fuck you. Did I ask you to punch him? That wasn't for me. That was for *you*." I opened the door with so much fury it slammed against the cement wall at my back. "Get out, Grayson Crowne."

I walked by him, not bothering to watch him leave, because I didn't want him to see my tears. Suddenly, I was slammed to my bed. The wind left me as all the time without contact vanished in a second, Grayson caging me on the mattress.

I stared into his icy blue eyes, veiled by wild rose gold hair. I could smell the sugar on his lips. He'd been chewing lollipops, and I could smell the whiskey he'd tried to mask it with.

"Do you know why I gave the dress to you? Why I married her in our wedding?"

Our wedding. Our wedding. Our wedding.

"I don't care." So why did my heart beat?

"Even if that day couldn't be ours, I wanted you to know it should have been."

"Stop," I begged him as tears leaked from the corners of my eyes.

"That I was picturing *you*."

His lips skated mine, a breath away from destruction.

My voice wavered, and when I spoke, I'd lost all strength. "Please."

"And it would always belong to *you*."

When I decide to let you come again. Know it wasn't for you; it was for her.

This scene was eerily familiar. Though his words were sweeter now, he still wouldn't kiss me, still wouldn't touch me. And when he inevitably left me...it would be *for her*.

"Belong to me?" I clawed at the anger taking root like a sapling in my gut. "For me? Which part? The part where you only touched me, only...only..." *Came inside me. Told me you* loved me. "Because your wife gave you permission?"

His eyes flickered with surprise, and I used that to push him off. Grayson moved with me until I was sitting up and he was on his knees, and we were eye to eye.

"Am I finally out of your system, Grayson Crowne?" My voice was shredded.

A cruel, barbed silence stretched between us. Grayson spoke with his eyes, but I was back to being unable to decipher it.

He stood up abruptly.

"Lottie told me about the postnup," I said, standing with him. "She said if you so much as put a finger inside me..." I swallowed, moving on. "That night doesn't belong to me. None of this ever did. When my uncle dies, I'll leave. We can finally write *The End*."

"Story—"

"Please leave, Mr. Crowne."

THIRTEEN

STORY

My uncle died the day before we were going to return to Crowne Point on the third week of September. His funeral was held the first weekend of October. The beach was peppered in a mosaic of fallen leaves. It looked like a fairy tale.

I held in vomit the entire time.

This morning I got my period. I'd had this niggling fear I might be getting pregnant, but then red appeared in my panties.

Blood.

Nothing left to tie me to Crowne Point.

I guess it was the perfect ending.

My grief made me...different. Nauseated. Fatigued. I hadn't talked to Grayson since the Labor Day party, almost a month, but true to his word, not only did he give Uncle a funeral at Crowne Point, but Uncle was buried there.

Occasionally my eyes flitted to him across the leaf-strewn beach. In a black suit and tie, Lottie wrapped around his arm, his eyes down. Red.

A part of me wondered if my uncle's death was ripping him up as much as it was me. And I hurt again.

Because I was back to being alone.

The one person I'd bled with now farther away.

The Crowne Family Cemetery was filled with proud granite mausoleums etched with scrawling poems along their sides. Now my uncle had one, the only non-Crowne ever to be buried there. I can't imagine Tansy or Beryl was pleased. I don't even know how Grayson pulled it off. My heart crunched, knowing how hard it would have been, but he'd kept his promise.

Servants were in attendance, dressed in their finest blacks. Tansy and Beryl Crowne were even there. West had come, as well as his parents. For this brief period on the beach, we were equalized, as only death could.

Then the ceremony ended.

There was a memorial being held for Uncle in the garden, a poetry reading. I went to my room to gather the materials I'd prepared to read, but when I tried to open my door, the knob wouldn't budge.

Why wouldn't it open?

I heard voices.

"Hello?"

Laughter.

My gut sank.

I slammed on the door. "Let me out!"

I repeated it over and over again, knowing it was useless but needing to do something as the last goodbye I would ever say to my uncle happened without me.

I didn't realize I'd fallen to my knees until the door opened and I fell forward onto the cement. I didn't look to see who'd opened it. I ran out to the gardens. They were cleaning everything up and taking down his rose-wrapped photo.

"I feel like I should say something about the clock striking twelve."

I spun on Ellie and slapped her as something inside me snapped. I was fine to take my punishment, because I believed I deserved to be punished. I'd broken a rule, after all, one that we all obeyed.

But for how long was I supposed to sit and take it?

"That isn't very princess-like."

I turned at the voice. All the servants had gathered, and one of them—Andrew held his—phone up.

They'd taken a photo of me slapping Ellie.

The color drained from my face into a soggy wet piece of bread in my gut.

"I wonder what all your fans would think if they knew who you really were."

"You're not supposed to have your phone with you," I said weakly.

"You're not supposed to fuck Grayson," Ellie said.

I looked at them all, those I'd considered family.

"Why are you doing this?" I asked. "Don't you see you're enabling it? When you treat me like garbage, you give them the right to treat us all like garbage."

There was a pause. A breeze kicked up the strewn leaves. For a moment, I thought maybe I'd gotten through to them.

"If you continue to stay here, it will get worse for you, *Cinderella*," Ellie said.

I wiped the snot from my nose. "I'm leaving. Tomorrow morning, first thing."

I walked past them as they snickered.

Inside the hall I could smell everything. Feel everything. Someone had made spaghetti, and grief made me hate the smell, made me want to vomit.

"Excuse me, are you Miss Story Hale?"

I paused at my name, turning to find an older man in a dark suit. I didn't recognize him, but he didn't have the haughty air of someone in the Crowne world.

"Who are you?" I was wary of anyone now, certain they wanted to do something to me.

"I'm Woodson Hale's executor. An estate of his size is going to take a few months to get in order, but he asked me to give you this."

"His size..." I repeated, taking the book. As far as I knew, Uncle had nothing.

"Are you living here?"

"I don't really know where I'm living," I admitted.

I kept looking at the book. It was a collection of all the poems we'd read together, from Dickinson to Whitman to Poe and Byron. His note read, *Would you give a dying man a wish, Story? Write one poem a day for me and share it with the world. Missing me one place? Uncle Woodson.*

"He knew?"

"When you do, please call me."

He handed me a card, which I numbly shoved into my pocket. Distantly I heard him walk away, but I couldn't breathe. All the air sucked out of me like I'd fallen on a steel bar.

"He knew I wasn't going to make it back in time. He knew and he still didn't..." I couldn't get it out. My uncle knew I wouldn't make it back in time, and he still didn't leave this fucking place. He didn't come with me when I offered.

He chose to die here alone.

I finally vomited all over one of Tansy's boutique white rose arrangements. I dry heaved, the noxious smell of vomit and rose mixing. I held on to the wall for dear life.

Were we all ghosts here?

Tied to this awful, horrible castle?

Suddenly, a hand was there, lifting me.

Grayson?

My heart plummeted when my eyes collided with West's warm ones. I'd gotten so used to Grayson always being there.

"Let's go, Angel."

I held on to West, crinkling the buttery fabric of his black suit, my head spinning, as he carted me to the servants' quarters.

We were almost at the entrance when I blinked into the red-rimmed eyes of Grayson.

"What's going on? Story?" He looked from me to West. "What the fuck did you do to her?"

"He didn't do anything."

I tried to push past him, and he grabbed my arm. "Are you seriously going to go with him?"

West ripped his hand off my arm, and they both stepped to each other, as if they were going to come to blows.

I can't take it anymore. It's been a nonstop rollercoaster since that day in the antique room. I feel like I haven't had a minute to breathe. I haven't slept. I'm nauseated all the time. In constant fight or flight.

"I hate you." I shoved Grayson. *I hate that you chose her. I hate that I still want you to choose me, even though I have no right.* "I should've forced him to leave this place. The only reason I ever endured this torture was to be with him, and instead, I *missed his death* because of fucking Asheville. Because I was being your wife's girl."

I gripped the book, my uncle's handwriting burning through the leather, searing my flesh.

His shoulders sagged and he took a step away from West. "Story..."

"I'm leaving," I said. "Tomorrow."

This was how it was supposed to be, but my hand lingered on his chest, his eyes throbbing, my fingers curling in the soft fabric of his shirt.

"Goodbye, Mr. Grayson."

My eyes connected with Grayson's as Westley led me out.

GRAY

My pacing wore the wood beneath my feet raw.

Story leaving?

Fucking leaving. I knew this was coming. This is what I'd been working toward since before the wedding. Getting her out, getting her safe, and trying to give my wife a happily ever after.

I'd fulfilled my promise to her and Woodsy, secured him a nice plot of land on the family cemetery. Of course, it's an eye for an eye in the Crowne family and my mother wasn't going to let Woodson Hale be buried in the family plot without a pound of flesh: a promise.

Never speak to Story Hale again.

Story was leaving anyway.

Leaving.

Fucking. Leaving.

"Grayson?"

Lottie's soft voice called to me. She still hadn't changed out of her funeral attire. A long-sleeved cottony black number that covered her collarbones and went down below her knees. It kind of looked like something Snitch would wear.

I slammed Lottie against the wall, crashing my lips against hers. She gasped against my assault and grabbed me back. I ignored the thoughts in my head screaming it wasn't right. It wasn't Snitch. She had too much gloss on her lips.

Woodsy was dead. I wasn't there for him. I'd been in fucking Asheville, with Lottie's family, trying to fix what I'd broken on Labor Day. If I had just cut our trip short, I would have been able to say goodbye.

I thought I had more time.

I kissed her harder, trying to banish the thoughts.

Be a good husband.

Be a good man.

The harder I tried, the more I failed.

"What's gotten into you?" Lottie gasped as I dove for her neck.

Snitch is leaving and it's driving me insane.

Lottie palmed my cock, but her touch was anathema. Snitch is too in the forefront. Every little thing is compared to her. Her lips. Her kiss. Her tongue. The way she touched.

I took a step back and Lottie blinked at me.

I dragged my hands through my hair. "Take off your clothes."

"Is it really happening?" Lottie asked, but she undid the pearly buttons at the front of her dress.

"Get on the bed."

She stumbled backward onto my black sheets, watching my every movement. I climbed on top of her, and she tried to kiss me. I grabbed her hands, pinning them above her, going for her neck.

"Give me a baby," she breathed against my lips.

Those four words froze me.

I climbed off, running a hand up and down the back of my neck. The quiet was stale and splintery.

"I don't know how," Lottie said after a moment, "but I know this is about her. It's always about her."

Our gazes collided.

"Are we being honest now, Lottie? Finally? Why did you tell Story I was getting a postnup drawn? Why did you tell her you gave me permission? Why are you fucking with her when you already won?"

She looked guilty for a half second; then she stood up. "*I* won?" She let out a sound somewhere between a scoff and a laugh, rolling her eyes. "How am I the villain?" Her eyes were broken and pleading. "What is so wrong about what I did, Grayson? How is it so evil, especially compared to what you've done? What *she's* done?" Her hands scraped at her chest as though her heart hurt. "I *love you*. You're my husband, and she's there, at every turn, trying to steal you away."

"You're *Lottie*..."

Pure, kind, sweet, gentle *Lottie*.

Every time I try to do right, I just fuck it up more. It's like my marriage is a sandcastle crumbling in the wind.

"You never knew me!" She shoved me. "You're just like everyone else. I love you. I'm willing to fight for you. I'll play dirty. That only scares you because you don't love me back."

"Lottie, I—"

"Don't! Don't lie to me anymore. Be honest about it. You don't love me. You won't even try." Her face twisted in agony. "Everything I do is wrong. Is bad for you. She could light the sky on fire and you'd thank her for keeping you warm. If I hung the moon, you'd yell at me for ruining the shadows."

Lottie hiccupped and turned from me. She paused in the hallway, throwing her head over her shoulder.

"I should have realized you'd never want me the day you gave my wedding dress to her and didn't even care enough to make sure I wouldn't see it. My dad does that shit to my mom all the time."

A few moments later I heard the door to the bathroom slam shut.

"Fuck!" I kicked my desk, breaking the wooden leg into splinters.

STORY

West helped me down to my room in the servants' quarters, and I was numb enough to let him. There was that voice in my head telling me to stop.

Stick up for myself.

But I'd already slapped one person today, and my nausea hadn't left, and now I felt light-headed. The servants still refused to feed me. I would've left to grab something in Crowne Point, but I just wanted to pack and get out.

West set me on the bed. "You look like you're going to faint."

"I'm fine. I'm just..." I rubbed my forehead, never finishing.

Every time I stood I got dizzy, like the blood was rushing too fast. Maybe it was lack of food, I don't know.

"I should have just taken my uncle out of here," I said quietly.

"I remember your uncle," West said. "I don't think he would have listened."

"He wasn't the same in the end. Losing his mind. Going on about coins buried beneath poetry and wishes." I exhaled.

He arched a brow. "Coins?"

Grayson's locket glared back at me from my dingy mirror, dangling from my collarbone and glinting atop my black dress from the little light in the room. I was suddenly stricken with an impossible choice. I knew I should leave it behind, leave all memories of this place.

When I wore it, I told myself it didn't mean anything. It was the only nice jewelry I owned.

I never opened it.

What was inside Grayson Crowne's heart?

West put his hand on mine, stopping my frantic packing. "Angel. My offer will always stand."

"Are you hitting on me on the day of my uncle's funeral, West?"

"I'm letting you know you're not alone."

I let out a bark of a laugh.

I was so fucking alone.

"The only person keeping me in this fucking place just died. So you can fuck yourself."

He sat down, ignoring my ire, folding a shirt. "You need me, Story."

"I have money," I said numbly.

Something flickered in his eyes. "In this world...money is useless. You need power. Do you still write poetry, Story? You know I'm taking over the company soon. We run the biggest publishing houses in the East Coast. Do you think about getting published? I could get you there."

West said it lightly, but my stomach went cold. It was nearly the exact same offer Grayson had given me months ago.

"I don't want—"

I broke off as West got off the bed, down on one knee, and reached into his pocket, pulling out a ring. A fucking ring.

"What is that?" Alarm crawled into my throat. "What are you doing?"

"It's a ring. A nice one. Cost a shit-ton."

"You're *proposing* to me on the day of my uncle's funeral?" I put my head in my hands, making a noise somewhere between a laugh and a cry.

West peeled my hands away, and I saw he'd set the ring on my dresser.

"Why do you want this so much, West?" I finally snapped. "I know I can't offer you anything. I don't have a company. I don't have billions of dollars. I'm not some model you can parade around."

He grinned slowly. "I just want you, Angel."

"What the fuck are you still doing down here?"

I looked over West's shoulder, finding Grayson in the doorway. Somehow, he looked even *worse* than before. His hair was a mess, his eyes so red. West didn't immediately let go of my hands. His grip tightened, and he stared at me for a long moment.

Then he stood up and turned to face Grayson. "I think that's a question I should be asking you, bro."

"How'd your jaw heal, *bro*."

Tension oozed like earlier, but thicker and more oily.

"Get the fuck out, du Lac," Grayson said.

West quirked his neck. "I don't think this is your bedroom, dude."

"She's mine. Get out."

West laughed. "Does my sister know you're talking like that?"

"Who do you think you are telling him to leave?" I snapped. "Why are you even here, Grayson?"

His glare flashed to me. "Your uncle died, so maybe I'm here to fucking comfort you, Story."

How dare you? You lost that right. Words got stuck in my throat like chewed gum with the way he looked at me.

West placed the shirt he'd been folding on top of the ring he'd just proposed to me with. "Think about what I asked, Story."

Gray didn't move out of the way for him, and he didn't take his eyes off me as West knocked into his shoulder.

I was so, so tired. I couldn't handle another fight.

"Gray—"

"Truce," Grayson said, cutting me off.

"What?"

Grayson closed the distance between us, still with that burning, intense stare locked on me.

"I don't have anyone else I can talk to, Story. Only you. Only you understand what I'm going through." Grayson fell to his knees, wrapping his arms around my waist, pressing his head to my stomach. "Right now you're Story, and I'm Gray."

FOURTEEN

STORY

Grayson sat on the floor, his back against my bed, taking sips from his flask. It was almost like before, the nights we spent in the dark, the secrets we shared...only now Grayson was on the floor.

"He was like my dad," Grayson said. "The only one that counted, at least."

"Same," I said roughly.

We paused, and he lifted his head, giving me a bone-melting, delirious grin. "That's kinda fucked up if you think about it, Snitch."

I hadn't realized how much I missed his smiles until it blasted me in the heart like that.

He shifted on the floor. "Man. I really was an ass, making you sleep down here."

Another sip.

He raised the flask for me to have some, but I shook my hand. I still felt kind of nauseated, a little weak.

"Everything in my life worth keeping, Woodsy gave me. He gave me the pen. When my dad died, he promised he wouldn't die...obviously lied." He laughed brokenly. "You know what my grandfather said to me at my father's funeral?" Grayson took another drink, and I waited. "He pointed at my half siblings and said, 'You see them? They're your competition now, Grayson. Thank your father for that.'"

I stared at the top of his golden head, my heart once again cracking for the little boy forced to grow thorns around his heart. Why did Grayson always make it so hard for me to hate him?

"My mom didn't have a funeral," I said weakly. "I couldn't afford it."

He slowly lifted his eyes to mine, and I cleared my throat, looking away, looking for anything to change the subject.

"Do you remember when I asked you what you would want to be...you know, if you weren't born Grayson *Crowne*. Do you have an answer for me yet?"

Silence spread.

"I'm not sure it matters, Story."

It mattered to me, even though it shouldn't. Even though all it did was feed the wrong, twisted part inside of me that kept me up at night, wondering if there was a universe where we could be together.

"Yeah," I whispered. "You're right. I'm leaving and..." And I won't need to know anything more about Grayson Crowne. I *shouldn't* know anything more.

He took a long swallow, staring back at my cracked walls. "I don't like it when you say you're leaving, Snitch. I know I'm supposed to let you go. I..." He shook his head, taking a deep draw of his whiskey. "It'd be easier to chain me to the fucking wall."

I stared harder at the top of his blond head, willing myself *not* to do what I was about to do.

I climbed off the bed, sliding shoulder to shoulder with Grayson. If I stared at the wall, it doesn't count.

"My uncle gave me this book of poetry with a note," I said, reaching for the book from my bed. "I called him in Asheville and told him I would leave, take us somewhere... but he didn't want to go. He knew. He knew I wouldn't make it back in time and still said no."

I handed Grayson the book, and he stared at it for so long I thought he would never speak. When he did, his voice was rough and warbled and raw.

"I'm so fucking sorry, Snitch." His blue eyes found mine, gleaming like the ocean at dawn. "For just...everything."

I realized I was looking at him.

I shoved his face away, and he gripped my wrist, keeping my hand pressed to his cheek.

"My wife is supposed to be the one I trust. The one I confide in...so why are you the only one I trust, Snitch? The one I want to tell everything?"

His truth shattered me because...

"I don't trust you anymore, Grayson Crowne. I trust you the least out of everyone."

"Don't fucking say that to me," he growled.

"Why?" I demanded. "It's the truth. Don't you like the truth?"

He went silent. I wanted to know the thoughts that made the muscle in his jaw pop. His eyes dropped to my shirt, and I realized too late why, too late to pull away.

He lifted his locket off my neck. "You're leaving me, little nun."

"Don't call me that." My voice held no power.

He worked the muscle in his jaw harder. "Did you forget because your bruises faded?"

He dropped the locket and grasped the skin beneath it between his thumb and forefinger. I should have pushed him off. I shouldn't arch my neck to the side, arch into the dark possessive look in his eyes as he twists the skin painfully, *bruising*, eyes boring into mine. Dredging up memories of his lips, his teeth.

"You're mine, Story. My little nun."

His voice was so rough, it slid inside me, abrading my blood, until I could taste him in my throat.

We'd kept our distance for so long, and even still, this was barely anything. But I was burning up as his warmth suffused through my body.

"Say it," he gritted.

He twisted harder and I saw stars. Beautiful, *blinding* stars...the kind that blind judgment.

"Yours," I breathed.

He stopped twisting, ran his thumb across the mark. His eyes found my lips and for a second I thought he might kiss me. Then before I could remember all the reasons why I should say no, Grayson was up and against the other wall.

I pressed my hand to my collarbone. What the hell is wrong with me?

"Don't," he rasped. "Let me see it."

The air had shifted.

That thing we'd been ignoring, trying to act like died the day of the wedding, was alive and throbbing. *Grayson*—my *Grayson*—was back and staring at me like he wanted to eat me. Devour me. The only thing stopping him the wall at his back.

"I tried to fuck my wife today," he said. "When you told

me you were leaving...that really messed me up, Snitch. So I tried to get you out of my head."

My eyes darted to his cock. He was so fucking hard. The tapered outline of him was so vivid through his suit pants, and it dredged up every memory of us. Hot... full...*deep*.

I swallowed, throat dry.

"Did it work?" I asked softly, dragging my eyes up.

There was an answer in his eyes I desperately wanted to know, but he wouldn't let me in.

"You should go back to her."

"I should."

My eyes dropped back to his cock, and Grayson's hand fell over the fabric. Stroking. I watched, mesmerized as he grew longer, harder. I *ached*. I missed him.

"What are you thinking, little nun?" His voice was like gravel.

This time it was my turn to keep my thoughts in my head. I'm thinking I want *you*. I want *more,* the way only you can give me. His nostrils flared as though he could read the thoughts in my head.

"Sit up," Grayson commanded.

My heart pounded, breath tight as I did what he said.

"Spread your legs. Keep your clothes on."

I stared at him. The rational part of me that always seemed to take a back seat whenever he was around screamed to fight back.

Disobey.

Don't give in to the asshole who'd left me.

He quirked his head when I didn't listen, veins pulsing in his golden neck. A moment stretched like taffy. I couldn't decide if I wanted him to come to me...or get the fuck out.

But then he started to stand, to listen to me, to *leave me*.

And my legs fell open.

He froze before falling back to the floor.

"Wider," he grated. My groin ached with the stretch, but when he made a sound deep in his throat, I felt like I was floating on air. "Slide your hand beneath your panties."

Maybe it was Uncle's death that led us to this point.

Maybe we were always going to end up here.

"We shouldn't," I said as I arched into my hand. "This is wrong."

"Yeah," he agreed jaggedly, rubbing his cock harder. "Fuck, I can see how wet you are."

Sparky tingles buzzed along the tops of my thighs and the tips of my toes.

"What are you thinking?" he rasped.

I couldn't keep it in. "I miss your teeth."

He licked his bottom lip, giving me a flash of his bright teeth. I felt them on me, and I arched. He released a deep, jagged exhale.

"Touch yourself. Palm your tit." I started to slide my hand beneath my shirt, but he growled: "Over the fabric."

My heart pounded, breath tight in my chest, as I did what he said. I couldn't look him in the eyes. It was too intimate. Too much. So I focused on his shirt, the way the material seemed to tighten across his muscles with each breath.

"Touch yourself the way you like."

"Should I imagine it's you?" I dared to look into his eyes, and they flashed up to mine, then back down. He didn't say anything, but I took the dark, needful look in his eyes as a *fuck yes.*

I fucked myself hard beneath my panties, bruised my tit over my dress. All Grayson could see were the motions. He didn't get anything else, but it felt more obscene that way.

He made a noise in his throat, as if the way I was doing it was wrong.

He rubbed his bottom lip with his pinky finger, and when he spoke, his voice was like iron. "Harder."

I arched on a sigh. It was exactly what I'd been missing. How did he know what I wanted better than me?

"How do you fuck her?" I whispered.

I looked away from him, terrified to know the answer.

Yet some twisted part of me needed to know.

"You want to know how I fuck my wife, Snitch?"

I sucked in a breath. Grayson had come off the wall. He was on the floor with me, arms on either side, caging me. So close but still not touching me. The air between us danced, as though it knew we couldn't touch, so it would do it for us.

"Yes," I breathed.

I could come to the way Grayson watched me, his blue eyes giving me all the focus I'd been denied these past months in concentrate. Drinking me in like he'd just discovered me and wanted to use me all up. I wanted him to use me all up.

"I think about you," he said.

I swallowed air at the confession and was rewarded with a small quirk of his lips. I rubbed myself harder beneath the fabric as he whispered wrong, dirty, forbidden words.

He licked his bottom lip, still watching me.

"I picture it's you in my bed, Snitch. Your taste. Your cunt." He closed his eyes like he was picturing it now. When he opened them, they were raw. Dark. "I need you to come, little nun. I need to hear that perfect gasp you make."

I wanted to touch him.

I knew if I did, it would break this spell.

I was frozen. Stuck. On the precipice with no way to fall.

"Did you forget your first rule of training? You come when I say come." He leaned forward like a junkie locked on a fix. Until his breath fogged my lips. Until I could almost pretend we were kissing. *"Come."*

I came with a violent arch, his name on my lips.

When I came back down to earth, the tender, aching way he looked at me broke me apart, back into splintering grief.

Tears I'd held in all day broke through the corners of my eyes. He brushed them away with the heel of his palm, his hand lingering on my cheek. He looked me up and down.

"Perfect," he whispered.

Grayson stood up, and he helped me to my feet. In less than a second, every ounce of blood disappeared from my head and drained to my toes.

My head throbbed. I wobbled, and the room blurred and blackened.

A brief thought. Grayson Crowne was reaching for me.

He was *holding* me.

"Snitch?" The worry in his tone warmed me.

Right before everything faded to black.

I woke in what looked like a hotel room, but the bright, fluorescent light making halos in my eyes was a dead giveaway.

Hospital.

I was in a hospital—but the swankiest hospital room I'd ever been in. I covered my eyes, hurting because of the bright light, and tried to remember what had happened.

The last thing I remembered was being in the servants' quarters and...

Grayson.

Sorrow and disgust swirled inside me, remembering what we'd done just seconds before I'd fainted. I needed to get out of Crowne Point, away from him. He was a drug I couldn't stop using.

I wondered if he brought me here. It would explain the swanky digs. It was just like the room my uncle had stayed in when Grayson had paid. But this time I was alone.

I hated that I wished he was here.

"Ah, you're awake." I turned my head, finding a woman in a white coat.

I rubbed the back of my head. "Yeah, um, I feel fine, though."

She smiled. "That's good. From what I can tell, you're healthy. It looked like low blood sugar and low blood pressure."

The doctor asked me a lot of questions, occasionally glancing at my chart. When she seemed satisfied, she said, "It's very common with pregnant women. You're eating for two now. You'll have to make some adjustments..."

She continued speaking, and I opened my mouth, then stopped, as a stone fell in my gut.

Finally I blurted, "Pregnant?" cutting off her spiel about diet. "You're wrong. I got my period this morning."

She frowned, then glanced at her chart. "The blood work is here. You likely experienced spotting, which is very common in early pregnancy."

My lips parted, but no words came out.

I'd only slept with one person without protection.

Two months ago.

At his wedding.

"I can do another blood test to confirm, but congratulations, Miss Hale. You're perfectly healthy, just pregnant."

She left, and I sank back into the hospital bed. Pregnant? I couldn't be pregnant. I had to *leave*. Get out. Not become my mother, not die as a ghost like my uncle.

Pregnant.

I exhaled, and my eyes traveled to the door, and my body went cold. Grayson stood in the doorway, holding peanuts.

Grayson dropped them to the floor. "You're pregnant."

Shit.

FIFTEEN

STORY

Grayson rushed to the hospital bed, pulling me so close my face smashed against his shirt.

"You're pregnant," he repeated.

"You weren't supposed to hear that," I managed to mumble. "That was private."

He pulled me deeper into his chest, pressing his lips to my forehead. I was so shocked I let it happen.

I'd been withdrawn from his touch for months, and now his lips were on my forehead. His touch in my hair. Sweet words like satin on my skin.

"You're pregnant." He kept repeating the words against my forehead, carding his fingers through my hair.

You're pregnant.

He didn't say it like I had in my head. With dread. With nausea. He said it as though it was the most amazing miracle.

I pressed my palms to the soft linen to sit up, put space between us, but Grayson stopped me.

"Rest."

"I feel fine."

Discomfort twisted my chest. I needed to leave, not have Grayson looking at me with his soft eyes.

"What else did she say?" He caressed my cheek, pushing the hair out of my face. "Are you okay? Is the baby okay? When you fainted I brought you here. After Woodsy..." I could see the worry raw in his eyes.

Died of cancer went unsaid but nevertheless burned in his eyes.

I looked at him, *really* looked at him. He hadn't changed since the funeral. He'd discarded his jacket and tie but still wore his shirt and slacks. The top buttons were undone, and the shirt was rolled up to his forearms, but it was hastily done. The left forearm didn't match the right one, and his pants were wrinkled.

None of this was his business.

And yet.

He gazed down on me with tenderness, his thumb bruising from cheek to jaw. I splintered. I wanted to lay my head on his chest, wrap my arms around him. Instead I couldn't stop staring at the gold ring on his finger.

I pushed him off.

"I'm fine," I said. "It was just low blood sugar. I don't need to be at the hospital. I just need to get out of here."

Let this horrible day from hell end.

"No one will know you're here, Story. We have a private wing, and I took you in a private car."

"I wouldn't expect them to, Mr. Crowne." I slowly pulled my head from his hands. "I think you should go."

"Story—"

I lifted my head. "I'm not Story, I'm not *Snitch*, I'm *your wife's girl*. Tomorrow I won't be anything to you people."

Gray's eyes flashed dark. Furious. Like our first night together. "You want me to leave?"

"Yes. Forget about me." *Let me forget about you.* "I'm not yours to worry about."

His jaw ticked, nostrils flared, as though he had some argument to that. I stared at Gray, telling him with my glare to get the fuck out of the room. He stared back with that possessive glare, fingers digging into his flexed bicep. As if he was going to fight me on this.

"We need to talk about this. Come up with a plan."

"*We* aren't doing anything. You're not involved. I was planning on leaving. That's still the plan."

All his joy, his love, vanished into a cold breeze. "That's my baby, too."

I threw off the sheets, getting out of the bed with a harsh laugh. "You'd have to acknowledge me for that to be true."

"Easy. Done."

I paused, legs hanging over the bed, not liking how easily that was fixed. If that were true, all our problems would be solved.

"I don't mean while you still have a wife. I'm not going to stay and be your fucking mistress."

I quickly jumped out of bed and went searching for my clothes, ignoring the fact that he had a view of my bare back and panties.

I grabbed my black dress, sorrow hitting me in a wave. Uncle is dead.

Uncle is dead and I'm fucking *pregnant*.

I can't breathe. I can't fucking breathe—

Grayson stepped to me, crowding my space. "Mistress? I haven't touched you. I've barely even fucking looked at you."

His words stopped me in my tracks, suddenly hot in my chest, scratchy in my throat like I was...I was...going to fucking *cry!?* Is this why I was emotional all the time? Because I was pregnant? It was so easy for Grayson Crowne to forget what had happened just hours before.

I blinked, sniffed, looked anywhere but him. "You still haven't let me go."

I let my gown fall and numbly climbed back into my funeral dress. I was overwhelmed, drowning in emotion. I was wearing the dress I buried my uncle in, and I had just learned I was pregnant. Pregnant with a baby I don't know if I should keep.

I couldn't process these emotions, so I just let them sink deeper inside me.

"I won't let my child grow up in the same life I did," I said.

"So you're gonna keep me out of its life?" he growled.

Her, some weird, internal part of me said.

"What about never wanting to have a mistress? To be your father? What about *me?* I don't want to forever be the second choice."

He gripped my biceps, spinning me to him. "You *aren't.*"

"So you're going to leave Lottie?"

"Yes."

Another gong to my chest. If it was so easy, then why have I been living in a fucking hellscape?

"Okay," I whispered. "Let's go tell her."

His eyes clouded. "It's not that simple, Story—"

I put my hand up, stopping him. I already knew the words.

I'll tell her tomorrow.

By the weekend we'll be together.

I'm leaving her.

"If you force me to stay, you're locking us into the very fates you spent your entire life trying to avoid."

For a minute, I thought he might see the light. Shock and sorrow split his features.

"I couldn't figure out why you would break us. Why you wouldn't let me leave," I whispered. "But it was so obvious. You want me all for yourself, Grayson Crowne, but you don't want to keep me. Because I wasn't good enough. Not to marry. Not to have your child—"

He gripped my face, dragging me closer, so tight his thumbs bruised, eyes mad and gleaming. "Is that what you think? That you aren't good enough? *I'm* not good enough. Can you trust me? Can you trust that I won't do that to us? I don't want you as a mistress. I want you by my side forever."

I stared into his blue eyes.

Trust him. Trust him after he'd shattered it forever?

"Then tell me *why*. Tell me why you chose her."

I stared at him, waiting for an answer, a reason for everything I'd done to us. The clock in the room ticked and ticked. I exhaled.

Grayson Crowne had no reason.

I tried to push past him.

"I was trying to protect you," he yelled.

GRAY

. . .

"By breaking my fucking heart?" She swiped at her nose.

"I thought you would leave. I thought you would...I didn't think you would stay."

Her brow furrowed. "That doesn't explain *why*."

She was finally leaving.

I should let her leave.

Why the fuck couldn't I let her go?

The warnings I'd received, the portents of what would happen if Snitch got pregnant with my baby, hung like a storm cloud.

Even though I knew it was best... Every time I tried, I failed.

As she waited for me to form a response, some kind of answer that would make everything I did okay, the minutes stretched on, counted by the beeping of the hospital machines. Finally she exhaled, turning to leave.

Snitch.

Leaving.

Fuck.

"My grandfather was going to lock you up!" I yelled at her back.

She paused, slowly turning around. Distrust clouded her beautiful walnut eyes.

"That's not...he can't do that. I haven't done anything."

But I saw the doubt in her eyes. She knew my grandfather. She knew his reputation. She knew what he could do.

"He knows about your past, what your mother made you do. He gave me a choice, Snitch. Keep you as a mistress, let you go, or he'd cash in some favors and lock you up. I would never..." I exhaled. "I'd never ask you to be my mistress."

She blinked. "How many other lies are you telling?"

"What?"

"How many other lies are you telling, Grayson? I thought we shared everything, but you..." She trailed off, blinking rapidly in the way I knew meant she was trying to stop herself from crying.

I wanted to go to her.

Hold her.

I opened and closed my fist until my nails seared my palm.

"Like you told me about West?" I said it before I could stop myself. "I...fuck, Snitch. I...didn't mean—"

When her eyes found mine again, whatever vulnerability had been there was dead.

"Then let me leave," she said, voice iron. "Let me disappear. I'm leaving Crowne Point. That was your whole plan, right? Break my heart? Force me to leave?"

She shot me a withering, hurt look, then turned to leave. She didn't listen when I called her name. She just. Kept. Walking.

So I sprinted, cutting her off at the door, slamming my hands in the frame to lock her in the room.

She pushed at my chest.

And pushed.

"Get out of my way."

"Do you know how useless power is when you actually have something to lose?" I asked. "That's why my grandfather is so powerful. He couldn't give a shit about any of us, even his own son. My dad died in a car accident on a perfectly sunny December day without any other cars around. Maybe someone was trying to get to Grandpa. Maybe my grandpa killed his own son because he wouldn't listen. Maybe it really was an accident. Who the fuck knows?"

She stopped pushing, hands curling in the fabric of my shirt. She stared at my chest, biting her plump bottom lip.

After a moment, her stony eyes flashed to mine.

"You chose for us," she said. "You didn't give me the option. We could have chosen together, we could have chosen *each other*."

"What would you have chosen, Story?" I backed her into the room. "Jail? Death?"

Her face went blank, eyes flickering. "I...You didn't give me the option!"

I gripped her face, forcing her stare. "I would do it again. Every single fucking time I would take that option away from you."

"Even now? Even after everything?"

"If it means keeping you alive. Keeping you safe. I will always fucking choose that. No matter the consequence."

"So you get to play the martyr. You get to be Atlas."

She pushed at me again, but I grabbed her, pulling her close. I hugged her so tight she couldn't shove me, hugged her until maybe she could feel the truth in my heartbeat.

"I hate you, Grayson Crowne," she mumbled against my chest. "I hate you. You broke us. You did this to us."

I stroked her hair, hoping she could feel the apology in my touch.

For a few minutes it was perfect. Then she spoke again.

"Why is now different?"

She slowly pulled away from me, eyes watery and accusatory.

Why is now different? I've been fighting this thing since the day she kissed me in that fucking room, but it's *impossible*. We're woven together with the red thread of fate.

I took too long to answer, and she broke apart, taking a

few steps back, until the back of her knees hit the hospital bed.

Her hand glanced her stomach. "I wasn't enough to fight for...but my baby is."

"No—fuck. Fuck no, Snitch."

Everything I say is wrong. It's going all wrong.

"What is the plan now, Grayson? Has your grandfather suddenly approved of me? Do we walk out of here arm in arm?"

I dragged my hands through my hair.

I don't fucking know.

I don't have these answers.

For her sake, I hope you wore protection.

If we walk out of here, and they find out she's pregnant, she's in even *more* danger. But I can't let her disappear. I fucking can't.

"I need to keep you safe," was all I managed.

"What about what I want?" she demanded. "You want to lock me away in a tower."

"No—"

"Will I get holidays? While you build your perfect family—the one you care so little about that you keep them around you all the time—will I at least get holidays?"

I scraped my fingers against my skull, trying to find the right words. "That's not what I'm doing."

"We could have talked about this. You said you trusted me."

"I do—"

"But you never told me. You just...hurt me instead."

"Snitch—"

"I almost fell for it again. All your pretty words. But you just want to stash away the mistress, live happily ever after with Lottie. Come visit me for holidays. Give me a nice stipend."

"After everything, you still don't trust me?"

"Why should I when all you do is lie!"

"I tell you the truth. You're the only one I tell the truth to." I gripped her wrist, begging her to see the truth in my eyes.

There was a cavern between us.

A vice grip on my heart.

She looked into my eyes, and I could see she was searching for something.

But fuck, whatever it was...she didn't find it.

"I need you to believe me, Snitch," I said.

Of everyone, I need her to believe me. I need her to trust me. I'd never needed anything more.

"I..." I swallowed the pain in my chest, the voice in my head calling me a fucking pussy. "I can't have you not trust me, Snitch."

Tears welled in her lids; then she shucked me off. "Get out of my way, Playboy Gray."

I was losing her.

I couldn't lose her.

"You try and leave, I will stop you."

There was an icy-cold rush in my veins, and the closer she got to the door, the less I felt, the number I got.

She threw a look over her shoulder. "You can't scare me into staying."

"Snitch, I'm not trying to scare you. I'm trying to..." I dragged my hands down my face. I know this isn't how you're supposed to love. The seeds Snitch planted inside my heart in the dark had taught me that.

This is how my grandfather would handle it.

With threats and fear.

But I can't think past my heartbeat rushing through my ears.

"I will make it impossible," I said. "You will be put on no-fly lists. If you try and cross the border, they'll catch you. If I have to become the Grayson Crowne you thought I once was to keep you here, I will."

Her jaw flexed. "I can fight back now, Grayson. I have the money."

I laughed, but it didn't reach my eyes. "You have pennies compared to me. I'll bleed you dry in a month."

Her fingers froze on the buttons of her high-neck collar.

"Did you forget what you signed, Snitch? Whatever you see, discover, on my property is *mine*."

She blinked. "You said our contract was void."

"Terms to remain—"

"In perpetuity..." she finished. "But that wasn't about a *baby*. It won't hold up in court."

"No." I shrugged. "But you'll have to stay in New York to fight it, and by the time the case is finished, I'll have found a way to secure custody of my child."

A hollow smile flickered across my face.

"You did this to us! You don't get to just come back and decide you want me again!"

"Do you think I want to do this?" I yelled back.

Silence spread between us like bramble, cutting and catching.

"I know you're good," she finally said. "I know there's good inside you. I know you care the most. Why can't you stop pretending?"

I didn't have an answer for her. After all, Snitch was the only one who ever saw any good in me. I don't know if I ever really believed her.

"You don't get to have this, Grayson Crowne. I won't let this be my fate."

My voice was cold when I spoke. "Good luck trying to retain a lawyer. Every big law firm from the East to West Coast is either on our payroll or trying to get on it. No one will touch you."

SIXTEEN

STORY

Grayson gave me a warning the night we made love at his wedding, and I'd never understood what he meant.

Until now.

You'd never trap me, little nun. But I could trap you.

Trapped. Forced to hire a lawyer, when my only experience with them was on bus benches—and something tells me that guy isn't going to be good enough to beat a Crowne.

I figured I had a better chance of getting a lawyer to fight Grayson Crowne if I showed them I could pay up front. I know how the world works, money talks. So I went to Crowne Point Credit Union, prepared to withdraw the money I'd been given and give it to anyone willing to help me fight a leviathan.

The teller's eyes bugged when she saw the dollar amount residing in my account. She went speechless. Story Hale had never had anything more than a little over zero, and now she had millions.

"I..." She blinked. "I think there's some kind of computer error." She picked up the phone, dialing as her eyes remained on the screen.

"It's not wrong. I need to make a withdrawal."

Her gaze flickered to mine, but still she kept her phone shouldered, speaking low.

"How much?" she asked.

I chewed my lip, thinking. Not all of it, just enough to retain the best lawyer possible. "Five hundred thousand."

Her fingers slipped and the phone clattered to the desk.

"You..." She swallowed. "You can only withdraw ten thousand at a time."

"But I have millions in my account."

"It's federal law."

My eyes landed on the pen chained to the desk. *Green.* Why did it have to be fucking *green?*

All these months wondering why Grayson chose Lottie over me. Agonizing. And in the end, it was because he didn't trust me. I was pissed, but mostly because I still couldn't *hate him.*

Protect me? He was trying to fucking protect me?

Grayson Crowne doesn't just set himself on fire to keep others warm, he bleeds himself dry to keep them alive.

So when there's nothing left of him...nothing left to be saved...he's not there to see the ruin.

"Miss Hale?" I looked up, finding another woman in a maroon blazer had appeared behind the teller. She had straw hair and crow's-feet spreading from her brown eyes. When she saw the computer, the same bug-eyed look fell across her face.

"Yes."

"You were inquiring about a large withdrawal?"

"Five hundred thousand," the first teller supplied.

"We're a small credit union, Miss Hale. We don't even *have* that much money on-site. If you want to draw more than that, it will take at least a week. But if I can give you my advice, with this kind of balance, you're better suited elsewhere."

"A week?" I exhaled as my shoulders dropped. "I don't have a week."

They exchanged a look, and I realized distantly what I must look like to them. A desperate woman who suddenly had millions, trying to get it all out.

"If you're in trouble—" the manager started.

"I'm fine. I just need my money."

Silence.

I wasn't going to get five hundred thousand. It was locked away.

"I'll take the ten thousand." I sighed.

They gave me my money, and, dejected, I went outside to an unusually warm Crowne Point autumn day. By some joke of fate, a lawyer grinned on the bus bench at my back.

I still had the card from my uncle's lawyer. It was thick, white stock and felt expensive. He'd told me to call him when I had a new place to live...but maybe he could help me.

After speaking to his assistant, I was put through to him.

"Miss Hale," he said. "Have you secured a place of residence?"

"I..." I trailed off. He sounded so happy I'd called, and I felt awkward bringing up this problem over the phone. A place to live?

I hadn't been back to Crowne Hall, I'd been sleeping in the motel.

"I need help fighting for custody," I finally said. "Can you help?"

There was an audible pause. A car drove by, kicking up wind as I waited.

"I work in estates, Miss Hale. I'm sorry, I wouldn't really know where to start."

He continued to talk, offering platitudes. I murmured responses as I stared down Crowne Point's Main Street, stretching long in front of me. The sun suddenly felt too hot on my back.

He ended the call, and though I was terrified, I was determined not to give up. Because for the first time, I wasn't alone. I had someone else depending on me.

I googled big law firms and found most of them resided in New York. So I took the train, trying to come up with a plan of action. My chest ached, though. I wanted a happily ever after with Grayson. Not...this.

Parallel to me, two girls who looked about fifteen watched me.

"Excuse me," the blonde one finally asked. "Is your name Story?"

My throat seized.

"No," I lied.

They didn't seem entirely convinced, watching me the entire ride there, and even held up their phone to—*I swear* —take a photo of me. I scrambled off the train as quickly as possible.

My first stop was a towering, silver skyscraper. A lawyer I'd read rarely lost a case.

"She doesn't take walk-ins," the receptionist said without looking up.

"I'm...Story Hale," I said cautiously, wondering for the first time if my name would register with someone.

Her eyes lifted, narrowing in interest. She buzzed me in and escorted me to a large conference room that overlooked New York City. The people were ants beneath me. Again, that lung-shrinking fear overcame me.

I was fighting back.

I was using my name.

I wanted to hide.

"Ms. Hale?"

I turned, finding a woman in a sharp black suit and sharper eyes.

"Usually the mistress doesn't come in person," she said.

The word hit me like a stab in the chest, but I powered through it.

"I'm not a mistress. I need someone to help me fight Grayson Crowne. I can pay in cash." I piled stack after stack on the table. "I have more of this."

She eyed it and, without any emotion, met my eyes. "You want to retain me *against* the Crownes?"

I nodded.

She stood up, eyes cold, buttoning her suit.

"We're done."

"But—"

The door slammed.

And that was how every interaction went, up and down New York City, finally concluding with the last lawyer, who said, "Let me give you a piece of advice, Miss Hale. There isn't a spot on this earth the Crowne hand doesn't hold. Whatever fight you have with Mr. Grayson Crowne, give up the idea you can win."

Despair and desperation tore seams inside me.

If you ever need a wish granted, use it.

My uncle's last words rang in my head. I could really use a magic coin right now. I had over twenty million dollars, was the richest I'd ever been, but I'm still trapped, still under the Crowne thumb.

There was only one place I could think of that the Crownes didn't touch, and I hadn't been there since high school.

Don't go there, ever.

That's what Grayson had said to me...but he didn't give me much of a choice. I wasn't going to stay and become my mother.

I sucked in a breath at the rusting, paint-chipped Ferris wheel. October enveloped Crowne Point, the fog even thicker around the metal spokes.

I hadn't seen Grim or any of them in years, but I'd heard rumors of the four boys with no fucks to give and the only power to rival the Crownes in this town. I'd known them back when they were teenagers at Crowne Point High, and even then you didn't approach the four inked and brooding boys unless you were ready to lose something. Didn't matter if you were a teacher.

Now...*everyone* knew the Horsemen.

They run the underworld in Crowne Point.

I couldn't believe I was here. Bargaining with them meant I really had nowhere to go.

How far would I go to save myself? If they wouldn't take my money, like everyone else...then they might ask for more. A contract. A debt. But that would be trading one prison for another...

The Horsemen don't even take on many contracts,

because each contract they marked on their body in ink and blood.

I pushed the creaking gates aside, then came to a complete stop. Gemma Crowne stood in front of Grim, the head of the Horsemen. He dragged his collar down, exposing a new tattoo on his pectoral.

It looked like...scratch marks?

Gemma blanched before turning ten shades of red. "You're evil," she hissed. "Disgusting."

"I like you in red..." He dragged his thumb down her crimson-stained cheeks. "Like your tears more."

She flushed harder, yanking her face away. "Do you think I give a shit?"

Grim's smile stretched on one side, and the dimple in his right cheek popped, eyeing her for what felt like forever.

Then he looked over her shoulder, at me.

"Sweet Storybook." Grim let his shirt fall back into place, lifting off the wall in a fluid motion.

Gemma spun, eyes growing wide when she spotted me. As if shaking out of it, her plump pink lips and bright-blue eyes quickly returned to their haughty, entitled grace. She walked away without so much as a goodbye to either of us.

"See you soon, Rich Girl," Grim called after her. He laughed, the sound like the fog around us.

She bristled, and our eyes locked; then she blinked and kept going.

Did *Gemma Crowne* have a contract? What would someone like her even need?

"Little Storybook," Grim said, bringing me back to the reason I'd come.

I tried not to roll my eyes. He was one year older than me. But I guess he did have that air about him, the one all the Horsemen did. It said they were so much more than human.

"I need your help," I said.

He rubbed his bottom lip, eyes sharp. "I know. I've been waiting for you."

He thumbed behind him to a sign in the window—a rough plastic sign that said *We Reserve the Right to Refuse Service to Anyone.* But it was spray-painted.

I wasn't going to bother asking how he knew I needed help.

"You're not going to help me? I can pay you." Once again I reached into my bag, fisting the cash that I had worked *so hard* to acquire and no one wanted to take. I held it out to him, all but begging him to take it.

His brow arched. "Moving up, Story."

Still, he didn't reach for it.

My hand shook.

"Does this have to do with Gemma?"

He grinned that slow Grim grin that was somehow seductive and sinister all at once.

"There's a bounty on your head. You have people looking for you, Storybook. The princess jumped the castle walls, and the prince is not happy."

Grayson.

"Whatever he's charging, I can double it. Triple it." I thrust the cash in my hand harder. All Grim did was thumb the sign again.

My shoulders sagged.

I knew how this worked. They were going to take me and hold me until Grayson came back for me.

"I *could* pretend I never saw you, if the prince comes asking."

My mouth parted. "Really?"

Grim shrugged like it was no big deal, eyes on his phone. With an exhale, I looked over the abandoned Wharf. At least I had my freedom, if only for a little while longer.

In this world...money is useless. You need power.

West's words blasted into me. What good was having millions if no one would take it? His ring was in my purse... My number was still the same. Was his?

No.

No, I couldn't go down that road.

"Ah, you forgetting something?" Grim called at my back. I turned, finding his dark eyes on my cash. My jaw dropped. Ten thousand just so he and his Horsemen wouldn't kidnap me?

He put his phone away, and all at once his humor vanished. Grim was one of the tallest people I'd ever met, and with his shoulders straight, the shadows at his back seemed to dance along his muscles and make the ink at his neck one with them.

Some say he was called Grim because of his looks.

Those people are stupid.

I shoved my ten thousand dollars at Grim.

He smiled slow, putting the wad into his pocket, before leaning back against the post and returning to his phone.

"Nice to see ya, Cinderella."

His voice seemed to follow me out of the Wharf.

I sat on the warped wood, kicking my legs out into the street. No one drove down this way. No one *came* down here, not unless they rolled with the Horsemen.

I pulled out West's ring, and it caught the light. Why did West du Lac have to be the one to give me this? I stared at his contact in my phone, fighting the urge to dial.

A few months ago, I would have slapped myself for even

considering calling West. Now I was so twisted up in grief, in heartache, in fear, I couldn't think straight.

I held my stomach as if it would protect my baby from my own decisions.

Looking at the facts...West saved me when Grayson tried to gamble me. West saved me from the boat when Grayson left me for Lottie. He'd saved me from his own father. He was there when Grayson married Lottie and left me in the dust.

I thought Grayson was my white knight hidden beneath thorns, but maybe he's always been the rogue, and I had just grown addicted to the pain.

Maybe I misremembered that night with West...

I shook my head.

No.

No, I didn't.

I dialed the number I hadn't looked at in years, refusing to acknowledge why I hadn't deleted it. As the dial tone met me, my eyes were locked on the princess-cut diamond refracting the light.

"Angel." West picked up after the third ring, sounding way too fucking pleased that I'd called.

"Hi..."

"Not that I'm not happy, but why did you call?"

Grayson said I would hate him...and I do. I hate him for forcing me into this. I hate him for giving me no choice.

For making me feel so goddamn useless and powerless. Never have I felt so powerless as I do in this moment, forced to marry the man who raped me to escape being the mistress of the man I love.

Fuck.

Him.

I hate him.

I hate him so much.

I slid the ring on my left ring finger.

Story *du Lac*.

There was a time when this would have felt like a happily ever after.

I swallowed, then said, "Does your offer still stand?"

SEVENTEEN

GRAY

I rubbed the ridges of my broken nose as I came through the large wooden doors. After searching everywhere I thought I might find Story, I was forced to come back to the dark spires of Crowne Hall, empty-handed again.

Everyone thinks Crowne Hall is such a strange mixture of architecture to find in upper New York. Victorian and black but on the whitest sand on the East Coast.

The story goes the first Crowne built it for his wife, a keepsake from old Victorian England. In reality, Crowne Hall was built for the love of his life—a mistress. His wife hanged herself. We've been fucking our wives over for our mistresses since its inception.

Where did I get off even thinking I'd be a good father?

That Snitch wouldn't be better off out of this world, away from everyone...especially me? In my head, when the girl I loved told me she was pregnant, I lifted her into my arms. I didn't fucking threaten her.

I was such a piece of shit.

"Grayson?" Lottie's soft voice called to me. "Grayson, where have you been?"

"I only came back to grab some cash."

Something to bribe the Horsemen with—didn't matter I'd already bribed them. They only spoke in one language: cash.

Lottie cut me off in the grand foyer, just before the entrance to my wing.

Our wing.

Fuck.

"Lottie...not now." I tried to push her aside.

"You look like you haven't slept in two days. Where have you been?"

Looking for Snitch.

I have everyone I know searching for her, but I can't just sit back as she fucking disappears. I've never felt a fear like this before. Where the hell is she? All her clothes are back at the house. I got word she was at the motel, but when I went, she was fucking gone.

In the wind.

I placed my hand on Lottie's shoulder to push her aside. I know she's my wife. I know I should love her and choose her, but Snitch is out there. Alone. I couldn't fucking stay here.

"Grayson...glad you could find it in your busy schedule to join us."

I stopped at the voice. In his iconic three-piece suit, my grandfather stood at the bottom of the grand staircase, watching me. Suspicion wove vines in my blood.

"Why are you here?" I finally said.

His brows raised slightly. "Your wife hasn't told you?"

I rubbed the back of my neck, that familiar pain I was starting to associate with failing Lottie as a husband.

If Snitch ever gave me a second chance...what's to say I wouldn't fail her too?

Before I could come up with the right response, I saw Mr. and Mrs. du Lac behind him, speaking with my mother.

"You have so many homes around the world," my mother said. "I would think you'd be more comfortable there...instead of crammed in here with us."

"Nothing compares to family," Mr. du Lac replied.

"And we'd hate to miss Lottie and Gray's first year," Mrs. du Lac said.

My mother hesitated, but only for a second. "Well, of course you can stay until you find a new home."

I glanced sidelong at Lottie. "New home?"

It took a good ten minutes of Lottie tiptoeing around the subject before I got the story out of her. Du Lac Manor was destroyed. It had been flooded, then the wiring had caught fire. Everything was ruined, her personal possessions gone.

It was hard to grasp.

We'd only just been there, and everything was gone. She showed me the pictures. The once proud and historic roof, now charred and caved in. Stones blackened. All that remained were the impeccable grounds.

"Everything is ruined. Gone. Destroyed."

"Grayson will fix this. Don't worry, dear," her mother said.

Even if Lottie wasn't my wife anymore, I'd known her all my life. Of course she could live here.

But...her mother, who'd all but threatened Story's life if she were to get pregnant.

Her father, a groping drunk.

And *West*? The idea of West living in this house, even if

it was far in the north wing, the one the maids said was haunted, made my throat burn.

It was still too close to Story.

"You're my wife...What's mine is yours."

I glanced at the clock. I'd already wasted ten minutes. The sun would go down soon, and that was another night Story was out there.

"I'll be back in a few hours."

"Are you really leaving me after I just lost my home?" She stared up at me, eyes wide.

If I could just find Story and calm the tempest inside my chest, I could handle this later. I could comfort her. I could.

I don't know how she's managed to hide from me.

But I know it's not good.

Another stale silence passed; then my mother smiled. "Why don't we have dinner, and we can work out the logistics? Will Westley be joining us?"

"He's on his way," Mrs. du Lac said. "He said he had some big news for us. What news can be bigger than this...I don't know."

A look flickered in Mr. du Lac's eyes.

I found Lottie. "I won't be staying for dinner."

"Where are you going? What is so important you have to leave me?"

The mother of my child was missing.

I can't breathe.

My grandfather watched, eyes sharp.

"Later, Lottie. I'll talk to you later."

I wasn't even down the steps when my grandfather's voice stopped me.

"Grayson."

I paused, then kept going. "I'll talk to you later."

"You're married now. You don't get to be a playboy. You need to come into Crowne Industries and do the fucking work."

"Later," I gritted.

"I'm not going to let you ruin this family for some cunt. If you have to learn that lesson the way your father did, so be it."

Ice cold in my veins.

I stopped on the cobblestone driveway, warmed in the golden autumn sun. When I turned, my grandfather was on the last step, only a few inches from me.

"And what lesson would that be, Grandfather?"

He gave me a cold smile. "You won't have anything to risk it for if she's not—"

Years of repressed anger and abuse came to the surface and I slammed my fist into my grandfather's face.

EIGHTEEN

GRAY

I stared down at my grandfather and his bleeding nose.

"If you ever threaten her again, if you even look at her again, I will kill you."

He dabbed cotton at his bloody nose, looking slightly annoyed, as though I'd just let a fly into his office. "Your father—"

"I'm not my fucking father. My father was too chicken-shit to do anything."

I heard the stampede of footfalls, of my mother and others who'd no doubt seen my grandfather fall, rushing over. I didn't have much time left to get this out.

"You asked me what I was willing to lose. So, I thought about it. I'm willing to lose everything—my nice life and the name it came with, the family I've been keeping afloat, my freedom, my wife, you. I'm willing to lose it all, but I'm not willing to lose her."

He pressed the silk cloth to his nose, but his eyes were shrewd as ever.

"So if you try to take her from me, if you even fuck with her, I won't have anything left to lose. But you...." I looked around with a deep exhale. "You will have so much to lose, Grandpa."

He smiled. "There's nothing you can do to me, Grayson. You keep making the same mistake."

I quirked my head to the side, finding Lottie watching me with her parents near the stairway. That was when it hit me.

Strings.

Strings I could tie on my grandfather.

"I'm going to divorce Charlotte. If you try and stop me, I've had a postnup drawn up, and Lottie has signed it," I bluffed, still watching Lottie.

For the first time in my life, my grandfather was speechless.

Slowly my eyes traveled back to his.

"I'll come out and say that video was me. If you so much as look at Story, I'll come out and say that video was me. We'll lose the company. We'll lose everything. This divorce can be painless...or not. I know you had planned on dragging us back into the boardroom after a year of photoshoots while you and the du Lacs worked out the borders on your new kingdom. It would be a shame if it all went to them before then."

"That's insane," Grandfather finally sputtered. "You'll go down with the ship you sink."

I grinned. "But so will you."

"I'm trying to save this family—"

"At the rate you're saving this family, we won't have any family left to save!" I yelled.

My mother landed next to my grandfather. "Have you lost your mind?"

A little bit. Maybe.

"Grayson?" Lottie grasped my wrist.

"What happened, Grayson?" my grandfather asked, standing and adjusting his tie. My mother stood with him, and soon everyone looked at me, waiting. Adrenaline pounded in my skull.

"I'll go get you ice," I gritted.

A chorus of disbelief rang out at my back as I went inside. I tangled my hands in my hair. It could work. This could work. A way out not just for me, but for Lottie—

I stopped short at the sight of wild, curly hair.

"Story?" I said her name aloud, not entirely convinced I wasn't seeing a ghost.

She stopped, then kept walking—faster—heading toward the servants' quarters. I rushed after her, before she vanished into thin air again.

I grasped her elbow. "Story, wait."

She yanked at my grip. "Leave me alone!"

"I'm trying to tell you something."

"I don't want to hear it—"

I spun her to me. "Dammit, Story. I'm *sorry*."

"You put a bounty on my head with the Horsemen!" Her voice raised, but she quickly lowered it, eyeing the open front door at my back, where my grandfather and mother, Lottie, and her entire family still stood.

I wanted to pull her close and hug her. To force that angry face into my chest and caress her back into soothing breaths.

Instead I clenched my jaw. "I was trying to find you, Snitch. I didn't know what to do...you fucking disappeared."

"Nobody would take on my case." Tears brightened the fear in her eyes. "You left me no options. No choice."

She shook her head, looking away at some distant threat I couldn't see. With each word she spoke, my gut knotted tighter and tighter.

She was back.

She was safe.

So why did she keep talking like something horrible had happened?

"I made a mistake, Story. I shouldn't have threatened you."

What was that look on her face? She looked so fucking scared.

"I was scared. Stupid. Immature. Scared." I gripped her hands in mine. "Shit, I don't know how to love one person, let alone two. The idea of you leaving with our baby..." I took a breath. "I went crazy. I lost my mind. It's not an excuse. Can you forgive me?"

Her eyes finally met mine, and I could see the tears she barely kept at bay. Sludge pumped from my heart. I was so fucking worthless.

I'd done this to her.

The mother of my child.

"I'll never hurt you, Snitch. I would never do any of that. I'm sorry. I'm so fucking sorry, Story..."

She was still so quiet. Saying so much with her eyes and yet none of it I could understand. I looked at her hands in mine, thumbed the fragile bones in her palm.

"Do you know I can count on my hand the number of times I've apologized?" I said quietly. "They've all been to you."

"Grayson..." she said, eyes crinkled in pain. "It's too late."

"It's not too late, Snitch. It's not." My chest filled with butterflies. I didn't even know where to begin, how to make up for what I'd done.

We're free. I did it. I'm doing it.

"I have to say, Gray," West said. "I don't particularly appreciate the way you're touching my wife."

My words died on my tongue. The next moments happened in slow motion. A hand slid around Story's waist, drawing her from me, until her hands slipped from mine.

Wife. The word bounced around my brain like a rogue tennis ball, leaving bruises and damage in its wake.

West continued to speak, but I couldn't hear anything past the rush of my own blood.

Vaguely, in the fuzzy perimeter, I saw Lottie's cream heels approach, followed by her mother's very similar ones, and my grandfather's black soles.

Everyone was here, but all I could do was lift my eyes to Story's, look for the lie I hoped to find in the truth.

"Your wife?" I finally said, interrupting whatever bullshit conversation had started.

"What?" Lottie's soft voice. "What is going on?"

"Um..." Story trailed off.

My grandfather started to laugh.

This had to be some kind of fucking joke. Snitch was getting back at me.

"Is this a joke?" Mrs. du Lac asked, smile wavering. "You can't be serious."

"Calm down," Mr. du Lac said, sounding bored.

"*Calm* down?"

"No joke," West said. "It's love."

Story held out her left hand, where a sparkling diamond sat.

"Meet your new sister-in-law," West said.

NINETEEN

STORY

I wondered if Grayson could see the misery on my face as I leaned into Westley.

Everyone started talking over one another, but Grayson stared at my finger. A possessiveness in his stony blue eyes that radiated down the throbbing muscles in his neck.

"You." Mrs. du Lac turned her ire to me. "First you ruin my daughter; now you turn your sights on my son? Have you no shame?"

She took a step to me, muscles tense. I lifted my shoulders, bracing my face for a slap.

"Mom!" Charlotte exclaimed, grabbing her mother's shoulder at the same second Grayson stepped between us. Grayson acted as a wall, a barrier. Behind him, Lottie tried to calm her.

As the world collapsed around us, Grayson stared down at me from his ridged nose. The questions in his eyes throbbed like the anger in his jaw.

"You married him?" he said, so quietly it couldn't be heard above the commotion.

"You married her first."

Grayson was grabbed by Lottie and shoved in the direction of Mrs. du Lac. "Do *something*."

Beryl Crowne was unlike the rest. He watched me quietly, with a look that sent shivers down my spine. Instinct had me wanting to look away. This was *Beryl Crowne*. You don't look someone like him in the eyes if you're someone like me.

His eye was darkening, like someone had just punched him, and all I could wonder was...who the hell had the balls to punch Beryl Crowne, a man known for disappearing anyone who slightly bothered him?

Though my heart pounded, I met his eyes. Instinctively I covered my stomach, and Beryl's eyes went to that.

Grayson stepped in front of me again.

"I'm so sorry, Lynette," Tansy said. "I can't imagine what you're feeling. I promise we'll figure this out." Except Tansy rolled her lips, obviously filled with joy.

Her number one threat had just been taken out by West.

"There's nothing to figure out," West said. "We're married."

Everyone flinched.

Tansy led Mrs. du Lac out of the foyer, Beryl following.

It was just me, West, Lottie, and Grayson.

"What is wrong with you?" Lottie all but breathed.

"Story and I have a history together, sis," West said. "I've loved her since I was a teenager. We're soulmates."

My back itched when he said *soulmate*.

Lottie narrowed her eyes, but on me, not her brother. "I've never heard you mention her."

I swallowed. "He...he was my first love."

A stale silence passed.

Finally Gray spoke. "Is that what you're calling it now?"

My eyes snapped to his, but the click-clack of Tansy's heels drew all our attention away.

"Lynette is lying down before dinner," she said. "All the excitement tired her out."

"Of course," West said. "I'll be sure to check in on her some other time." West's grip tightened on my waist. Gray zeroed on that, the muscle in his jaw flexing again. He tilted his head, the muscle in his neck feathering.

"You're not leaving, are you?" Lottie asked.

"We were only coming to announce the good news."

"Stay for dinner," Lottie said, glaring at me. "I insist. I mean—" She turned to Tansy. "If that's all right."

"We're heading to Asheville. Tonight. You know, it's the honeymoon, sis."

Gray flexed his fist until the knuckles whitened. I focused on anything else.

I had one condition when I married West du Lac: get me out of Crowne Point.

Away from Grayson Crowne.

Away from feelings I can't control.

"Oh...you haven't heard?" Lottie asked.

"Heard what?"

"It's destroyed," Gray supplied, voice like gravel.

"Destroyed?" I gasped.

His eyes snapped to mine. Lottie and West started talking about the events, but the voices faded as I faded into Gray's blue eyes.

There was so much I wanted to say to him, but it was impossible with an audience. I tried to with my eyes. I was mad. Mad he'd pushed me into this. Mad I'd had no choice. Mad at myself for fucking *doing this.*

Mad he had the audacity to apologize.

He didn't get to apologize.

Not when we were still living in the consequences.

Something like recognition flickered in his eyes, and his jaw feathered, with shame maybe, or anger more likely; then he looked away.

"We've been dealing with it all morning," Lottie said. "While you were apparently *eloping.*"

"I guess we'll stay in another house." West looked at me. "How do you feel about Europe?"

I'd only ever been to Europe with Grayson, and the memories rushed through me.

I'm going to mark you everywhere. Would you like that?

It was like Gray knew I was thinking about him, knew he was deep inside me. His blue eyes throbbed and pulsed, leaving me breathless.

I always thought engagement rings were a bit too ephemeral.

His bruise had faded, and now I had a shiny new stone...I covered my wedding band, heart cracking, and his gaze cut to the movement.

I quickly tore my eyes away, back to West. "I love Europe—"

"Don't bother," Gray cut me off, voice icy. "We can't let family stay on the street. Isn't that what you were saying?" He glanced at Lottie.

Silence oozed like sludge. Everyone hated the idea; it was clear in the stiff silence. The only person Gray watched was me.

"I don't think we should impose," I said.

"It's not an imposition."

I wasn't going to stay at Crowne Hall after I just sold my soul to the devil to leave.

"Well, I appreciate the offer," I said. "But I think Europe is more our speed anyway." I hoped my icy tone said the words I really wanted to say.

Fuck.

You.

I'd rather eat glass than stay here.

I looked to West, waiting for him to agree, but then Grayson spoke.

"You know the press will have a field day with this. How do you plan on spinning it? The heir of Du Lac industries marries the Cinderella of Crowne Hall."

Silence drifted as his words settled.

I wanted to scream.

Just let me *fucking leave.*

"I suppose a few weeks of press wouldn't be the worst thing," West said.

"But..." I trailed off.

I could feel the iron bars slamming shut behind me.

I won't stay here.

I'll disappear into the streets if I have to...and live like my mother did, I realized with nausea.

West looked at me. "Let's just go to Europe, Angel. We'll deal with the press."

The point was to get away and eventually disappear. West was a means to an end, not *the end*.

"A few more weeks here and then they won't care?" I looked into West's eyes, ignoring the anger emanating from Grayson. Ignoring the way his muscles tightened when West leaned down and thumbed my cheek.

"They'll forget we ever existed."

That's what I wanted. I could do a few more weeks.

I'd done years.

"Well..." Lottie finally spoke. "I suppose."

"I don't know, Grayson," Tansy said. "Europe seems—"

"It's decided," Grayson said, cutting her off. "You'll move in with us. It's the least we can do for family."

GRAY

Everyone left to gather in the great hall to eat—mother making sure to give me a look, letting me know this wasn't over, that she'd be back for her pound of flesh. Grandfather lingered.

Then laughed.

And laughed.

Until the dark, booming sound echoed off the domed ceiling.

Then it died, and the silence was magnified.

"Is this everything you dreamed it would be, Grayson?" he asked.

I swallowed the emotion in my throat.

"Is this how you pictured it?" My grandfather threw out his hands. "She played you, you fucking idiot. They all played you." Grandpa laughed bitterly. "Oh, but it was so romantic. So *fucking* romantic to sign away our company to her husband's sister. You blew up your world for her, and look what she did? Married a du Lac."

He wore his black eye proudly, the same way he wore the smug *I told you so* curving his lips. For once, I'd had the upper hand. He'd fallen for my bluff...and it didn't fucking matter.

The harder I fight for us, the more I put Story in danger. I got married to save her—and in the end forced her into a marriage to save her from me.

This hell was too beautifully designed not to be fate.

"Are you fucking crying?"

My grandpa gripped my chin, dragging my face to his to examine my eyes. I wasn't crying. I didn't cry. He'd made sure of that years ago, but I was sure my eyes were red with years of unshed emotion.

We were *so close*. We could have left this world. Disappeared into normalcy. Got a fucking house in Wisconsin or something. I don't know.

Fate. Fucking *fate*.

I stared my grandfather back in his red-brown eyes, giving him nothing.

"You were always so weak," he said, digging his thumb into my chin.

My lips broke with a smile. A *Grayson Crowne* smile, Snitch would say. His brow furrowed for a split second. Then he slapped me so hard my ears rang.

I worked out my jaw. "You've gotten weaker, old man."

I shot him another smile, pushing my tongue against my back tooth. He exhaled, like what he'd had to do was a burden.

"Here's what we're going to do. You don't tell anyone about that document. You rip it up. You rip up any other copies. You destroy the files. And you grovel to your wife. Then we act like this never happened, and you keep your cock in your pants. I am not about to watch everything I built crumble to ash."

Grandfather started to walk away.

"And then you kill her," I said. "Oh, sorry, she has a tragic accident."

He paused.

"I think I'll keep those files, Grandpa," I lied. "If anything happens to Story, I'll have nothing left to lose anyway. Keep that in mind if you're ever in the position to book her a car. I think you would have the most to lose if it *tragically* crashed."

He lingered by the column a moment longer, head slightly turned, then smiled. "You can't have her, Grayson. Not even as a fucking mistress. If you do, you'll lose everything, and lose her in the process. Don't forget yourself. The only thing keeping her alive is the one thing keeping you apart." He kept walking, laughing as he said to himself, "Not like his father..."

TWENTY

STORY

We were having some kind of braised small bird. Probably Cornish game hen. Conversation had been stuttering and light. I was seated down the table from West—my new *husband*—and I knew that wasn't by accident.

They isolated me across from Gemma, and next to Lottie. No sign of Beryl.

A stabbing, swift thought pierced me: Grayson would never have let me eat alone. Especially if I were his newly wed. It didn't matter that Tansy Crowne had insisted upon it under the pretense of *girl bonding*.

"Is it weird being served when just yesterday you were the one doling out the dishes?" Gemma asked lightly. She rested her soft, pretty chin on a manicured hand as she waited for my response.

I clenched my fork. It was dirty, I noted, while all the others were polished.

I briefly looked around to see if I could spot the servants. I hadn't banked on living here. The point was to get *out*. That was why I'd tried sneaking in.

Still, it was an improvement. I had the full force of the du Lac family in my corner. Or...I was supposed to.

Slowly, I lifted my eyes, meeting Gemma's. "I actually haven't worked in the kitchen in years."

I kept her stare so she knew meeting her eyes was no mistake.

Her smirk wavered, and she looked away.

I took the moment to lower my fork to my lap, rubbing it in my cloth napkin, getting rid of the crusted food.

"Should we toast the newlyweds?" Mrs. du Lac said, raising her champagne. She was in the middle of the table, across from me. It was the first thing she'd said since we sat down, though her icy, composed glare had barely left my face.

"It's so sudden," she continued. "So romantic."

"Could I get a glass of ginger ale instead of champagne? My stomach is bothering me..." Charlotte said so softly I almost didn't hear her.

"I've always been a romantic, Mom," West said with a laugh.

Her eyes briefly flashed to his. "Mmm." Her attention turned back to mine. "I just thought you were the Cinderella of *Crowne Hall*."

"Mom!" Charlotte gasped like she'd been punched.

I stared at my untouched bird.

"A toast to the Cinderella of Du Lac Manor, then," Mrs. Du Lac said. I lifted my eyes, finding hers. "May she..." Mrs. du Lac trailed off, thinking, and my gut tightened in anticipation. "May she always *get home on time*."

A soft smile drifted across her lips, eyes sharp. I smiled back, refusing to show how her toast had hurt.

I lifted my glass, noting the smudged lipstick, when Grayson's voice drifted down the table. "Should you be drinking that?"

I froze, panic thundering in my breast. I mentally ran through any response I could give that wouldn't sound suspicious, trying to keep my face neutral. Had he lost his fucking mind?

"It's water," I eventually rasped. "So."

"Well, um, no wine for me either," Lottie added. "Since we're trying for a baby and all."

I choked on my water, teary eyes flashing up to his. *Trying for a baby?* Lottie and Grayson were trying for a baby?

Grayson choked on his spit.

"That's wonderful news," both Mrs. du Lac and Tansy said at the same time.

I stood up so fast my chair nearly toppled, and all eyes came to me.

"If you'll excuse me, I need to...I need to pee."

Soft laughter followed me out of the room. I was probably supposed to say something like powder my nose, but whatever.

Trying for a baby.

I dragged my hands down my face as I pushed the swinging double doors open to the kitchen. A small voice in my head said, *You're not supposed to go here anymore.* But the louder one said *trying for a baby.*

I ignored the glares of servants who'd served me an undercooked bird with a dirty fork, heading to the pantry, taking deep, heaving breaths inside.

The pantry was warm and smelled like butter and cookies.

He was going to have a baby.

And I was married to West.

It hadn't felt real until this moment. It was like I was propelled through all of it by flight or fight. In adrenaline-induced instinct. It was all a blur.

West picking me up in...a silver car, I think, or maybe black. Walking up the steps together, or maybe he went first.

I must have said I *do*...I had to have.

Everything just piled on until I couldn't see beneath the weight. First Grayson leaving me, then the wedding, my uncle, the pregnancy...it buried me until I couldn't see, only struggle to breathe.

Now it had lifted.

And it was *blinding*.

Tears welled in my eyes. "Oh my god."

I grasped the pantry shelf to keep from crumbling. I tried to breathe. I couldn't. I was married to West.

What did I do?

I swallowed air as the door opened behind me, then shut. I spun, expecting a servant. Grayson leaned against the door, light shining through the opaque glass at his back.

He dragged his hand up and down his sulky lower lip. "What the fuck did you do?"

I scrambled to mask my face.

I wouldn't let Grayson see me like this. Falling apart. Regretting everything.

"Did," I said, forcing my tone steady. "It's done."

It was *done*.

Another wave of light-headedness.

"I should scream," I said, grasping for control.

"Do it." His eyes flashed to mine. "I'd love to give your *husband* another black eye." He rubbed his lower lip harder. There was an edge to his movements, a gleam in his icy eyes; he looked out of control. "If you think I'm going to let you marry him and take my baby, you're goddamn insane."

He laughed. It was cold. Scary. Filled with something dark I didn't understand.

His eyes flashed; then he took one step, and in the small space it had me pressing my back against the shelf. Above me flour and sugar jostled.

"The servants can hear us," I whispered.

"I don't give a shit. You're my girl, Snitch," he said, voice a low growl. "You'll always be mine. No fucking ring will change that. And I don't like fucking sharing."

"And I do?" I snapped. "I could have left. You could have lived happily ever after. I could have...lived. At least now we're on equal footing. You don't have all the power. For once, it's mine."

"It's always been yours," he said softly, absently, but before I could even think on what that meant, his jaw hardened, and he said, "He's not a white knight, Snitch; he's a snake, an opportunist. He knows you don't love him, but he knows you have no other choice. His parents are going to excommunicate him or worse. So what the fuck is he getting out of this?"

I don't *know*.

Wouldn't it be romantic if all he needed was me? But at least I can say I'm not that stupid anymore. West is getting something...I just don't know what.

He says it's me, but even I don't believe that.

"Yeah. I chose to run away with the villain because my prince wanted to shove me into a tower and force me to watch him live happily ever after with someone else. At least he's honest about it." I shoved him off with both hands. "I need to get back to dinner. To my husband."

"You haven't thought this through, little nun."

I haven't.

I was scared.

Terrified.

"You should worry about your wife, the one you're trying to get pregnant."

"Let me explain what you heard back there. What Lottie said—"

"You don't owe me any explanations."

"I backed you into a corner. Let me get you out."

"Get me out how, Grayson?"

"A divorce, to start."

"And then what? You'll let me leave? You'll leave Lottie?"

His jaw clenched, but he said nothing. I tried to shove him away, but he pinned me harder.

"It's going to be pretty fucking obvious when your stomach swells." His palm glanced across my stomach, and it was like something had come over him, the look in his eyes, the way his words grated with possession.

I hated that he was right. My heart jumped into my throat. Because, oh my god. How do I take back that decision? It seemed like my only choice in the moment. I can't believe I did that.

I've never hated myself more than now.

I'm choked with it.

I want him to choke too.

I swallowed, took a deep breath, and met his eyes,

refusing to let him see how he affected me. I wouldn't give him *any* of the power. He didn't get to know he forced me into this.

"You're right. It will be pretty obvious when my stomach swells. But I wonder who they'll think the daddy is."

Grayson pressed me deeper into the shelves, and above me the flour and sugar fell on us like snowflakes. I licked my lips, and his eyes dropped to them—

The door swung open behind him.

"Grayson." Tansy Crowne's voice wafted like the sweet sugar in the air. "What an interesting place to look for the restroom."

He didn't move off me, eyes burning.

It wasn't until I elbowed him that he finally retreated. He took a step back, past his mother. Ran two shaky hands through his hair, eyes on me, then kept walking.

I moved to follow, but Tansy gripped my bicep. "I won't have my son caught in the pantry with his brother-in-law's wife. You're not a mistress anymore." I noticed the kitchen had cleared out. There were no souls; the flour hadn't even been cleaned off the counters.

I took Tansy's hand off my arm, looking her in the eyes. "I never was."

After dinner finished, we all gathered in the foyer. West had his arm around my waist, and Grayson's glare hadn't left the hand.

"I guess this kinda makes Story your sister, huh, Lottie?" West said.

"*Sisters?*" Lottie and I screeched at the same time. We

glanced at one another, horror writ across both our wide eyes.

Sisters.

I hadn't thought about that implication when I'd dived head first into the shark-infested safe haven that was her brother.

"Think you'll get along with your new bro, Story?" West asked, nodding his chin in Gray's direction. My stomach somersaulted.

"Promise you'll be good to your new sister, Gray?"

Grayson dragged his glare from West's hand, to West. West grinned.

West whispered so only I could hear. "Brother fucker."

I wormed my way out of his grip, and he laughed.

"I think we've all had an exciting day," Tansy Crowne said. "Maybe we should retire."

Lottie looked to her brother. "I guess you're going to sleep....in the guest wing?"

"Story can stay in Gemma's wing," Grayson said, voice cold. "It has the most security. West, you can stay...in one of the guest wings."

Grayson may as well have said, *West, you can go fuck yourself.*

"Excuse me, hi." Gemma raised a hand like she was in school. "I'm not sharing my wing with a servant just because you fucked her a few times."

Tansy exhaled. "Gemma..."

Gemma shrugged.

"I think Grayson is mistaken." Westley grinned in my direction. "We'll be sharing a wing *and* a room. She's my wife."

A muscle in Grayson's jaw twitched.

Despite being in the foyer, Mrs. du Lac held her crystal

wine glass up in the air, waiting for a servant to appear to top her off, as she'd done all through dinner.

"Shouldn't you grab your belongings?" Mrs. du Lac asked, words cold. I scratched the back of my head, realizing where my stuff was.

"Oh. My. God." Gemma covered her mouth, eyes bright and gleaming. "You have to grab your stuff from the servants' quarters." She started laughing through her fingers.

"Gemma Antionette," Tansy chastised, but Gemma kept laughing.

I looked at the floor.

I took a step.

"What are you doing? Are you going to grab it *yourself?*" Mrs. du Lac managed to sound both scandalized, insulted, and delighted all at once.

My heart pounded, absolutely frozen. Every breath was a mistake.

"I—"

"I'll go," Grayson growled.

"Grayson." Tansy swallowed her shocked breath.

"She's got, like, two shirts and a dollar-store skirt. This is fucking stupid."

I watched Grayson head to the servants' quarters to the sound of his mother's protests—to grab my shitty clothes.

My eyes locked with Lottie's. She exhaled, worked her jaw to the side, then looked away.

"Are you going to grab the uniform too?" Gemma called out.

One by one, I took the stairs to the guest wing. West had left me to "go do damage control." It was just me in this dark hallway...and I focused on the hollow sound of my steps, trying not to think of all the times I'd taken them as a servant.

I didn't see him at my back until his arm wrapped around my waist.

I stiffened at first, expecting West.

Then I knew. I knew by his scent, his feel, just *the Grayson* of it all.

"What are you doing?" I asked, trying to worm myself out of his grip, but he tightened his arm. In his other hand he held my meager belongings.

"You shouldn't be taking the stairs alone. You're pregnant—"

"SHHH!" I shushed him, looking over my shoulder.

His eyes narrowed. "He doesn't know?"

"*He's* my husband. What do you think?"

His grip tightened. West actually didn't know, but I was so fucking pissed at Grayson. I wanted him to squirm, even if it was for a second.

We arrived at the double doors to my new wing—*West* and my new wing—when Grayson spoke full volume.

"So then I don't need to lower my voice. No need to hide the fact that you're *pregnant*."

My eyes grew, and I slammed a hand across his mouth.

"No, okay?" I said. "No one fucking knows."

Something flickered in his eyes...possession. His lips were too soft and too warm against my palm, and the dark hallway softened us, reminding me of our nights together. I tore my hand away, but he pulled me back instantly.

It was on the tip of my tongue to tell him to let go, when the look in his eyes froze me. It was like the night of his wedding, right before he'd had to leave me.

"We were close, Snitch," he said. "We were so *fucking* close."

I think my heart stopped beating.

What did that mean?

Behind us, the door clicked open, shedding light into the hallway. I blinked out of the moment, neck hot, and turned to find West...and Lottie.

I swallowed past the emotions. "I thought you left."

Behind them, our new wing was filled with roses everywhere. They carpeted the floor in a velvety white blanket, and the air was clean and crisp.

"You didn't think I was going to abandon you on our first night together?" West dragged me to him, wrapping his arm around my waist. His eyes went to Grayson. "Thanks for helping my *wife*."

Grayson kept staring at me. Like he had a right to stare at me like he owned me. Even with his wife next to him.

"Grayson," Lottie whispered. "We should go."

Grayson kept staring.

"First night as newlyweds." West grinned.

Grayson's nostrils flared.

Lottie wrapped her hands on his biceps, urging him to go back down the stairs.

Maybe I was always supposed to be with West, and Grayson was supposed to be with Lottie. We'd taken a brief detour from destiny.

So why did this feel wrong?

Lottie's hands on Grayson.

West's on mine.

Like we were on the opposite sides of fate.

His jaw was clenched so tight, the muscles dimpled. Eyes still on me, burning that way that said he owned me and didn't give a shit if anyone noticed, Grayson shoved my clothes into my hands.

"Good night."

He turned, and Lottie chased after him.

I exhaled.

For the first time since the courthouse, West and I were alone.

TWENTY-ONE

GRAY

All those roses everywhere. It smelled like a fucking funeral.

Was Story fucking West?

She wasn't actually going to fuck him.

"Gray?" Lottie's soft voice called to me as I rubbed my temples, trying to work out the problem.

"Grayson." Her hands landed on my shoulders, soft and searching as they trailed down my back, around my waist, coming around my hips to my cock.

I tried to shrug her off gently. I probably should've known something was up when Lottie came to bed in lingerie, but I attempted to play it off, and pretend I was tired. I wasn't...I didn't sleep anymore.

What the fuck was Story thinking? That should be *my* ring on her finger. I wanted to rip West's head off. I didn't for a minute buy he was in love.

He looked too fucking smug.

I exhaled.

I know what she was thinking.

It's all my fault.

I did this. I did this to her. To us.

I wanted to tell her everything. She'd called me out for being a liar at the hospital, and I never wanted that to be us. I wanted the truth.

The bloody, raw, jagged truth.

But what was I going to say? Nothing changed. I was still married to Lottie. I still couldn't touch her, still had to keep my distance because my grandfather still held a knife to her throat. I can't guarantee her a happily ever after with me, and I'm not going to break anymore promises. Not with Snitch.

Lottie's hands slid up my thigh. "Grays—"

"Trying for a baby, Lottie?"

Her hand froze.

"You...you *said* you would give me a family."

"I did..." I said, measured.

"And it will make our families happy. They needed that after everything we've put them through, don't you agree?"

I ran a hand through my blond hair. I couldn't disagree.

"Is the idea of having a baby with me so terrible?"

I let out a breath. "Of course not."

Lottie's hand slid between my thighs, to my dick.

"Just pretend I'm her," she said softly.

"Lottie..."

"It didn't stop you the last time."

Lottie's small fingers went for my zipper. "From down here, I bet we kind of look the same."

My muscles tensed, my pulse throbbing up my neck into my skull.

Anger.

Regret.

Disgust.

I gripped her chin. "Lottie..."

I can see it in her eyes. She thinks there's hope for us still.

It's not fair to her. Keeping her on the line like this. Keeping hope in her chest for a flower that's already withered.

Fuck.

If she knew what I'd done.

I wasn't trapped in this marriage, Lottie was trapped with *me*.

"You deserve so much better than this," I said.

"She's fucking my brother, you know?" Lottie sat up, throwing the sheets off us with her. "That's what they're doing. How long are you going to pine after someone like that? She's a gold digger, Grayson. She *ruined* us and she's ruining my family. What does she have that I don't?" she pleaded. "What does she do? You can do whatever you want to me. You can slap me. I'll do whatever you want."

Jesus.

Lottie. Pure. Sweet. Kind. *Lottie*.

I'm ruining her.

I dragged a hand down the side of my face.

I'm ruining them both.

Sticky silence spread. She pushed her tongue into the side of her mouth, looking away, as disdain darkened her eyes.

"Lottie, what kind of marriage would we have if this is how we had to do things?"

Her eyes met mine, and I thought she might speak truthfully with me, but then she blinked and became calm.

"I'm never going to stop fighting for you, for this, for us. I love you...and I have fate on my side."

Fate.

Fucking *fate*.

I stood off the bed. I told myself I would be a good husband. I would love my wife. She's beautiful. Her silky rose lingerie complimented her hazelnut skin, shining even in the shadow—soft, flawless skin that I'm sure only accepted the most expensive product. Her curves are somehow both supple and toned.

Lottie is the definition of beautiful. She's a goddess.

But she's not *Snitch*.

"You love her now," she said, "but will you in five years? You loved me once, Grayson, and I think you can love me again. You just haven't given this a chance. A *real* chance." She took a step toward me, placing her palm on my cheek. "I want to take away that pain in your heart. I did once. If you'll let me, I can do it again."

Something inside me fucking snapped as my wife pressed her palm to my cheek. I gripped her hand, tearing it from my flesh, but I held on to her wrist.

"She's not going to choose you," Lottie whispered. "She'll never choose you, Grayson. She chose my brother. It's over between you. It's finished."

I worked my free hand into a fist, flexing my fingers.

I couldn't believe it was really fucking *over*. But Snitch was *married*.

I dropped her.

"If you would just *try*."

Lottie wrapped her arms around my waist, and once again I had to deny her.

"Lottie, fuck, not tonight."

An ugly quiet grew.

"You know, my mom told me an interesting story earlier tonight. Your father hid Josephine during her pregnancy. No one knew a thing until after the triplets were born." Her eyes found mine slowly. "I bet your mom knew."

If it wasn't for the sadness in her eyes, it might have sounded like a threat.

My wife.

Maybe the most tragic one in all this.

STORY

Moving in as Westley du Lac's wife, in Crowne Hall. I used to dream of my happily ever after with West—he'd sweep me off my feet like a Cinderella.

Now I *was* married, and I was also the Cinderella of Crowne Hall...

I remember Lottie's question on her wedding day. Had fate listened to our wants and given us the most twisted version possible?

West took my clothes out of my hand.

"I can get it myself," I whispered, throat scratchy.

"You're my wife now," he said simply.

My gut did that thing...not a pancake like with Grayson, but a twist. I'd gone into this marriage focused on one thing: survival. Determined not to let the past pretzel its way into the present.

So what if parts of me were still begging to pretty all the dark things that happened between us?

I don't want to be the girl that keeps getting her heart broken.

I took a seat on a soft, buttery leather couch that over-looked Crowne Beach as the sun fell behind the iron ocean. I picked at my bottom lip, focusing on my breathing.

I was married to Westley du Lac.

He stood in front of me, blocking the beach with his jeans. "Having second thoughts?"

I shook my head, placing a smile on my face that felt like someone was stretching my skin with strings. I couldn't let it show in front of Grayson, in front of his family, but was I having second thoughts? That was all I had.

West was supposed to marry me, get me out of Crowne Point. In return, I promised him two months...that was all. Two months. If by the end I didn't love him, he would let me go.

Two months I could do.

In two months I would barely be showing. I wasn't going to be my mother. I would make a safe, happy, beautiful life for my baby. I could handle two months of this. I'd handled much worse. In two months I'd have a full bank account—and freedom.

Was I stupid to believe it? Does it even matter when I had no other choice?

"You promised you would get me out. This is the *opposite* of out. West, it..." I took a breath. "It feels a little bit like you wanted to stay here."

West laughed. "Angel, why would I *want* to stay in Grayson Crowne's house?"

I frowned.

I didn't know.

He sat down next to me, taking my chin in his hand. "Grayson's right. We need to get out ahead of this. If we don't, they'll never stop following."

Shivers raced up my spine at the thought. I was already stalked online...but to be followed in broad daylight?

"We can leave," I whispered. "Somewhere no one cares."

West stood so fast I nearly got whiplash. "Let's go. I'll stash you away on an island, somewhere the paparazzi can only get a blurry picture."

I'd suggest leaving Crowne Point entirely, if you ever want to work again. Maybe try someplace in...fuck, I don't know, maybe Portugal?

Grayson's words from our first night echoed in my head.

Stash me away...an inky feeling filled my veins. "Maybe some place like Portugal..." I whispered.

I told my uncle I would get away, but it wasn't freedom to run; it was just hiding. When I leave Crowne Point, I want to be *free*.

Sensing my disapproval, West sat back down on the coffee table opposite me, legs spreading as he leaned forward.

He gripped my chin, dragging me forward. "You know, Angel, it's easier to get revenge when you're right in front of him."

I ripped my head away. "This isn't about revenge."

But my voice wavered.

I'd liked the look in Grayson's eyes when he saw me with West.

Too much.

I don't know why West agreed to marry me, why he wanted to in the first place. I told him I needed his name, his power. That I wanted to get out of Crowne Point, and I needed someone like him to do it. I refused to sign anything but the marriage certificate.

West hadn't demanded a prenup.

He'd taken me directly to the courthouse.

I had all the cards, didn't I?

I lifted my head. "What are you getting out of this marriage?"

"You, Angel." He grinned.

A part of me felt like I was turning the table on West, and I liked that.

A sick part.

When we were kids, he'd tricked me into thinking he loved me, and had stolen something precious. Now I had the power to take everything from him, because he had fallen in love with me.

So I had to fight that urge. I had to go into this with honesty. It was already a dirty thing we were doing. There had been no god or love in our wedding. I needed to be so *clear, so honest,* to try to keep whatever pieces remained of my soul.

This wasn't about love.

This wasn't Abigail Crowne running away with Theo.

"I don't love you," I said softly. "I'm not even sure I like you."

The humor on his face faded. "I get it, Angel. You're using me."

I opened my mouth...to what? Argue? That's exactly what I was doing. Using him like all those girls had used Grayson.

West stroked a knuckle along my jaw. "I have two months to get you to love me, Angel. Two months to open your eyes to what I see."

I got lost in his warm brown eyes, in the boy I'd loved years ago.

"What do you see?" I asked.

A slow smile speared his plump berry lips. "That we were made for each other."

I jerked out of his touch, heart hammering.

"Are—" I swallowed, trying to change the subject. "Are your parents going to excommunicate you?" Why was my throat so thick? My chest pounding? "I need you to be a du Lac."

West watched me, giving me nothing in his look. After a moment of intense, probing brown eyes, he spoke.

"And you'll get a du Lac, Angel. You know...the du Lac name comes with the du Lac publishing house. You're my wife now, I said I could get your poetry published and I wasn't lying."

"I didn't marry you to get my poetry published," I gritted.

"Why not? You have no problem using me, Angel."

My lips parted.

Another moment of silence passed before he stood.

"I'll sleep in the other room."

My chest hurt. He was being too kind. I needed him to be a villain.

I needed *someone* to be the villain.

Someone other than me.

"West." He stopped at my voice, throwing me a look over his shoulder. "Why don't you hate me?"

His brow furrowed; then he gave me an easy smile.

"I'm hoping it's the same reason you agreed to marry me." I blinked, waiting for him to elaborate. "We're both building our happily ever after."

I couldn't speak, but he didn't wait for my response. He shut the door, leaving me to reel.

A happily ever after with West du Lac? Maybe this was what fate had meant for me all along.

TWENTY-TWO

STORY

Lottie du Lac and I walked hand in hand through Tansy's garden maze, the paparazzi a few feet behind us. Gray and West were at our sides, and occasionally Lottie would break to kiss her husband.

I've lived here for only two days, and in that time Grayson hasn't so much as looked at me.

I watched him. I didn't want to, but I couldn't help it. It was like before, when he didn't look back.

There's a huge weight on his shoulders.

West wrapped his arm around my waist. It was a cool autumn day, with a cold but sweet salty breeze, and the leaves a mosaic of tangerine and citrine. Outside we were the perfect fairy tale. Inside we were off-tune keys, playing the wrong song. We turned to the paparazzi, and West, Lottie, and Gray smiled. I still hadn't quite gotten the hang of the thing, smiling through the lies.

"We were fast friends," Lottie lied through her teeth to some question I didn't catch.

The plan was to get out ahead of it, the rumors that would surely start once everyone got wind that the Cinderella of Crowne Hall had married Grayson's wife's brother. Tansy was the one who'd come up with the spin: Grayson was *helping* us keep our forbidden love secret, but Lottie was the one who made it iron clad: all we had to do was show some of our old texts.

"Story?"

I blinked back, finding everyone's eyes on me.

"She asked when we first met," West said, lips against my ear. I caught Gray's jaw clench.

"Oh, um..." I rolled my lips. "As teenagers."

"You could say we were sweethearts," West supplied. "I always loved her."

More clicks, furious note writing.

On paper, all our stories were so romantic.

Soulmates, all four of us. An inspiring happily ever after.

Gray's eyes locked with mine.

Earlier, when we'd come up with the spin, I'd felt myself sink deeper and deeper into the lie as though I was drowning in oil. I did have those texts with West; we did have a history. It made sense. But I'd never hated myself more than those minutes we shared over a lavender custard breakfast.

"Any babies on the horizon?"

Our heads snapped back.

"Oh, we're trying," West replied, and everyone laughed.

"A picture with the new sisters. You both could be sisters by blood," he said. "It would be easy to mix you up."

Lottie and I let out strangled laughs.

Later we all sat beneath a mosaic of changing leaves, drinking tea. The magazine had changed, but I never would have known had the reporter not introduced herself. It all blurred into a kaleidoscope of questions and pictures.

I snuck a clandestine glance at Grayson, leaning back on his mother's white antique tea chair, his arm draped around the back of Lottie's. How did he do it all these years?

His eyes drifted to mine. I quickly looked away just as the reporter spoke.

"Your style is so unique." She eyed my dark-lace blouse and long cotton skirt. "Are they handmade?"

Gemma's laughter from yesterday rang in my head. I wore clothes I'd had since high school, while the people around me wore outfits that cost as much as a mortgage payment once and then never again.

I had enough money to buy a new wardrobe, but I didn't know where to start, and I wasn't sure I wanted to. I was never frivolous, and now that I had someone else to look out for, I didn't think I should start.

"Oh, I..." I never finished, reaching for my tea. A second later I gasped, dropping the cup to the ground with a shatter. Mine was *boiling*. It burned the roof of my mouth.

I breathed with my mouth open as my tongue throbbed and everyone looked in my direction, waiting for me to say something. Grayson's eyes narrowed as the second stretched without my explanation.

"I, uh...clumsy," I managed.

Everyone moved on, talking about nothing as we were photographed looking beautiful and happy. The broken porcelain lay scattered on the cobblestone as, not even seconds later, two darkly dressed servants came to clean it up.

They paused as they scraped chunks into a dustbin, but not before looking me dead in the eyes.

I watched them leave, dread weaving its way into my veins. I shouldn't be here. The longer I stayed, the more I pushed my luck. The Crownes didn't want me. The du Lacs didn't want me. The servants didn't want me.

No matter my last name, I still wasn't welcome.

After tea we had a momentary respite before the next event, which would include *everyone* in the garden. I ducked where the garden went off path, into the flowers, needing a minute to breathe.

A moment to apologize to my baby for being such a fuck-up. For putting her in this position. I held my stomach and stared at the sky. A bright blue, cold mid-November day. I would get us out of this; she would not live as I had, constantly in the dark.

A crack of twigs had my head snapping to the left. I pushed aside a veil of flowers and found him. It smelled sweet and musky. Grayson leaned against a tree, a sucker in one hand, a joint in the other.

His eyes found mine. A second later, he dropped the joint to the ground, stamping it beneath his shoe.

"You don't—"

"I'm not going to smoke around you." His eyes lingered on my abdomen.

As silence and awkwardness bloomed, my grief flowered. I missed Grayson. Missed talking to him. I was so lost in the pregnancy. Scared.

I didn't know what I was doing.

What to do.

Grayson looked away, and I couldn't take it, being ignored by him.

I cleared my throat. "I'll go. Didn't realize this hiding spot was taken..."

"What the fuck was that back there?" he asked my back.

I paused. "What?"

"Your smile with the photographers. It was fake as shit."

I turned around to face him. "You do it. Lottie does it. West does it—"

"You're not like us, Snitch." He gripped my face, the smell of sugar on his lips mixing with the flowers in the air. "Don't ever smile when you're sad. Promise?"

So taken aback by the abruptness of his touch, the strength in his grip, my words were charred. "I won't if you won't, Grayson."

His blue eyes cracked like lapis lazuli.

Leaves rustled around us like coins.

"I was wondering where—" Lottie stopped, spotting us.

"I was..." I pulled away, for some reason tripping over what I was doing. It wasn't like Grayson and I had done anything. So why did I feel so dirty?

"I was getting a smoke," Grayson finished for me, dropping his hands and then brushing by me as if I were nothing. And like that, whatever had happened between us vanished. The honesty gone.

I stared at the spot where he'd been, sunlight dappling the ground. I urged the pounding in my chest to vanish as he had. I thought Lottie had gone, too, but a minute later her soft voice drifted like wind.

"Why are you back?"

I spun. Lottie's shoulders were down, but her eyes burned.

"Every day I have to watch him love you!" Her voice raised. "His arm is wrapped around my waist, his lips are on mine, his body is in my bed, but his heart is with you."

It was the opposite from my point of view.

Everything he did was for her.

She shoved me, and I nearly fell into the lily pads. I caught the rosebush just in time, scraping open my palm.

Lottie didn't take another step toward me, just stayed there breathing heavily. I held the thorny stem as blood wept down my wrist.

"What would you do if you were me?" she asked. "If you were in my position?"

"I don't know."

She quirked her head like she'd been slapped. "I think you do."

She turned on her heel, going back to the group.

GRAY

Oh, we're trying.

Fucking West.

After a tea time that rivaled Wonderland's in length, Mother had prepared an evening cocktail hour in the garden, and I searched across the cobblestone, looking for the asshole who hadn't been with his *bride* for over thirty minutes.

If Story were my bride, I wouldn't leave her side ever.

Fuck him.

It's like he wants to get punched.

"Grayson." Lottie tugged at my elbow. "You haven't moved from this spot for thirty minutes."

"Are they cutting West off?"

Hurt flitted across her features, but she slowly shook her

head. That didn't make sense. West was set to take over Du Lac Industries soon. There was no way he could marry someone like Snitch without any repercussions.

None of this made any fucking sense.

What the hell was he getting out of this marriage?

"I'm going to make the rounds..." Lottie said softly. "I'll come find you in a little. Please eat something. Your mother has your favorite, steak crostini."

"Lottie, shit, wait—" I broke off. She'd already joined her friends.

I exhaled, gaze wandering to the girl on the terrace as a lighthouse to a lost ship. Everyone here was like a reanimated zombie, going through their final movements before death. But Snitch? She was bright. Alive. Tasting and trying new things.

She was so fucking adorable.

And about to make a fool of herself.

Gemma walked across my path, and I snatched her elbow, yanking her back.

"Hey, what the fuck?" She jiggled her arm in my hold. "Let go."

"Go tell her that's decoration, not food."

Gemma looked at me, then followed my line of sight to where Story was about to pull a garnish off a tower of fresh fruit. Gemma laughed.

"No way." She pulled out her phone, and in the same instant I snatched it out of her hand and threw it to the ground. It shattered.

She snapped her head to mine. "Dick! That was limited edition."

"Go warn her," I gritted.

"Why don't you?"

Because every time I'm within a few feet of her, I can't

decide if I want to pull her to me, lock her in my room and stop her from ever leaving, or force her out of here and throw away the key so she can't ever come back.

I went with silence.

"Let it be noted I'm only doing this because it will be funny to see her face." She blew a strand of rose gold hair from her forehead, then went over to Story.

A few seconds later, Story's gingerbread cheeks deepened.

Better than some asshole socialite telling her.

I dragged my hands through my hair, chest in knots. Fucking West. Did he not prepare her at all for this? She was still dressed in her nun clothes. There was no way for her to blend in, and this was different from some party. These people were *waiting* to crucify her.

"Can you imagine her at Thanksgiving?" Gemma said, sidling up next to me to reach for the rosemary honey vodka spritzers a servant was carrying behind me. "Do you think she'll dress like that?"

Shit.

I dragged my hands through my hair. She needed a girl. And guards. And fucking thousands of things. Thanksgiving? The holidays? She didn't have the wardrobe for that. Was she going to show up like a fucking nun at the most important Crowne event of the year?

I'd love it, but I'd be the only one.

The event organizer called for a photo op, and I quickly walked over to the terrace to join Story before the rest of our group.

Before my wife.

Before her husband.

"Who's going to the doctor's appointments with you?"

"Shh!" Her eyes grew to saucers.

"Is it West?" I continued, unperturbed.

"West doesn't know, so obviously not."

"You need someone to go with you."

"I'm perfectly capable of going on my own."

"You don't have anyone. Not really."

A look of pain flickered across her features.

"I'm the only one who knows." Something about that, knowing it was only I who had this secret, filled me with intense possession. It made me want to keep her more, to keep us safe.

I'd missed sharing with Story, missed our rare connection, and as long as we had this, she couldn't disappear.

"You only have me, Snitch," I said softer.

We only had each other.

"Maybe I'll tell my husband..." Story's eyes drifted to West, heading from across the terrace to join us for the photo. "I could tell anyone. You're not special."

Dark, angry energy filled me at the thought of her doing that. This was for *us*.

So I did what I always did when the pain got too much.

I laughed.

"This secret belongs to me just like everything else about you. You can say you didn't want me to know, but we're bound and tied together by it. It was meant for me."

Something flickered in her eyes, something distant and foreign.

"I want to be there for y—for the baby. I want to be there for the doctor visits."

"You didn't choose me, Grayson. You don't get to choose me now."

I grabbed her bicep, turning her so she faced me.

It was on the tip of my tongue to yell it out.

I did. I did choose you. I will always choose you.

I blew up and will blow up this world for you.

But Grandfather, everyone, *fuck*...Every time I do something for someone else, the only one who remained unscathed was me.

Hell, we had a whole wing dedicated to it.

The one where Story slept.

"You have a bad habit of touching my wife."

I clenched my jaw as she ripped her arm away, wrapping it around West's. I let Lottie wrap hers around mine.

Together we faced the paparazzi for another photo.

TWENTY-THREE

STORY

With my third sucker for the night tucked deep between my lips, I stayed up with Grayson's poetry like an addict. I knew I should let him go...close this book and forget about him, but it was almost like I was asleep with him and he was next to me.

I own all the luck in the world, but none of it belongs to me.

I took my pen, writing alongside his green ink.

Dear Atlas, if my hate for you was a secret, then love would be the reason I kept it.

. . .

I stashed his journal in my nightstand like a beating heart, and pointlessly tried to fall asleep. As the night stretched long and lonely, my thoughts crept.

I don't even know how to keep my world afloat, and there's something growing inside me that will be entirely dependent on me. I don't have any answers. I keep making the wrong choices. I always said I wouldn't become my mother, but she's my only role model. What if she bled into my very being?

I heard the door creak open. I knew he was in the doorway watching me, so I pretended to sleep.

"I know you're awake, Snitch. You're a terrible fake sleeper."

With an exhale, I rolled over, glaring at Grayson. He leaned in my doorway, two bags in his hand.

His eyes wandered my room. "You're not sleeping in the same room as him."

"I have a cold," I lied.

A cocky smile quirked his lips, but it dropped as quickly as it came.

"The fuck are you wearing?" He took in my pajamas, my short cottony pants and loose tank, jaw clenched.

I had hot flashes in the night. Apparently that was a thing that happened during pregnancy.

I folded my arms. "Why are you here?"

"It's night," he said simply.

Anyone could walk in.

A servant.

My *husband*.

Grayson looked around, taking in the guest wing in Crowne Hall.

"Do you keep your windows locked?" He went to the

window, testing it. When it opened, he made a noise in his throat and shut it, locking it.

"We're two stories above ground."

"Doesn't matter," he gritted.

I steeled my voice. "Why are you here?"

"I told you." His blue eyes found mine, somehow brighter in the dark. "It's night."

His eyes throbbed with meaning.

"We don't do that anymore." I looked away. "Go back to your wife."

Instead of listening, he sat on the foot of my bed, placing the bags next to him.

"I brought you peanuts and spaghetti. I wasn't sure if you were craving anything else."

"Just looking at that makes me want to throw up now." It was horrible and true; my favorite foods had turned on me. The smell was invading my nostrils, and I wanted to hurl.

Grayson froze, his hands in the bag, and his face caved. "What can I get you?"

The earnestness, the sincerity in his words, gutted me. How dare he come to my room in the middle of the night and act like this?

"Why aren't you with your *wife*?"

"Because you're—" He broke off on a curse. "I'm trying to be a good man, Story." He craned his neck so he was looking at me, blue eyes staring and beseeching down the length of the bed.

"So be a good man. Go back to your wife."

"She's my wife, but you're carrying my child."

"I don't need you," I whispered.

The Neruda poem "I Do Not Love You" blasted through me. Grayson said he loved me.

But he only loved me as a dark, unwanted thing. In secret. In the cracks.

"You've got to be around six weeks along. You'll start to show soon. How long are you planning to keep this charade up from your *husband*?" He bit out the words.

"Are you so certain we haven't slept together?" I asked softly.

Grayson caged my feet at the foot of my bed, leaning forward until his chest nearly touched my legs, his hair wild and veiling his smoldering blue eyes.

His fingers fisted the fabric on either side of my legs. I felt like he was a second away from crawling up to me or yanking me down to him.

"If he touches you, I'll kill him."

I wanted to say something witty and biting back, about him having *no right* to say those things anymore. But his words, the growl he spoke them with, the look in his eyes... my throat dried. My skin tingled, my gut twisted, the excitement right before I was burned by a flame.

And then he stood up so fast, and suddenly there was an ocean of distance between us.

I looked away. "Does your wife know you're here, in my bedroom, in the middle of the night?"

"I didn't do anything a concerned brother-in-law wouldn't have done."

Brother-in-law.

Was that all we were now?

Fucking siblings?

I tore out of bed. "Leave."

At my demand, Grayson glared and folded his arms.

The smell of spaghetti wafted stronger from this angle, making me want to hurl. Still I pressed forward. I shoved his chest, trying to force him out.

"I've hid behind sheets. Watched you get off your *wife*, watched you *marry her*. I've let you walk all over me. You can stay, Grayson. It doesn't matter to me anymore. I'm going to my husband's bed."

I spun, but he grabbed my elbow. "Snitch, wait."

Some kind of emotion throbbed in his eyes. Something powerful and deep...and secret. He kept so many secrets. I hated that there were things he wasn't telling me.

The ocean between us was too wide.

I wanted to poke and pick at it, but the marinara was overpowering. I swallowed, trying to stop the inevitable.

Oh no. Oh no.

"Let me go." I yanked my arm but he wouldn't let go.

It happened so fast, the rising hurl.

"Let me just expl—"

I vomited all over his expensive pajamas.

GRAY

Snitch covered her mouth. "I told you spaghetti messes me up now." She mumbled through her fingers.

I probably should have been mad, but after watching from the sidelines, my chest was full. I went to the adjacent bathroom, sliding out of my dirty pajamas. I rinsed them clean, hanging them to dry on the marble sink. I grabbed a clean washcloth, running it under warm water.

When I came back, Snitch's eyes grew at seeing me in only my boxer briefs. I sat beside her, but she scurried up the bed.

"What are you doing?"

"You vomited on my pants." I closed the distance she'd made, putting the washcloth to her face. She jerked away, mossy eyes filled with distrust.

"I don't *need you.*"

But I need *this.*

I lowered the cloth to my lap. "Let me stay the night. Let me hold back your hair."

"What about—"

"I'll be gone before the morning." I cut her off before she could say anything more about the wife I kept constantly failing.

This is what a husband—a father—should do.

Silence drifted between us.

"I read you're more sensitive to smells in the first trimester. Sorry."

"Grayson Crowne apologizing," she whispered. "What a sight." Our eyes locked. "You read?" she asked after a minute. "When?"

All I did now was read books. Books and articles. Studies. Anything I could get my hands on.

My thoughts were consumed with the fear I would be like my dad, my grandpa, anyone male in my family. A shit dad. And if it wasn't that thought, it was the reminder that I wouldn't even get a chance to fail.

Snitch would be on her own...and I'd be here.

That was the thought that kept me up the most.

"Fine," she mumbled after a minute. "But you sleep on the floor."

I pushed my tongue into my cheek to keep from smiling.

On the floor.

I settled on the floor, my head on my bicep. "I at least gave you a blanket."

A small, raspy laugh trickled from her bed.

I watched her in shadowy glimpses. She was on top of the sheets, and I could see her bare arm and bare thigh. She turned on her side, and then I could see her face, her eyes.

Sideways.

A view I'd craved every day since it had left me.

Her shirt was loose, soft cotton draping over her breasts. They looked fuller with the pregnancy. It was the most tempting, devious distraction. I imagined running my hands—

"I made a promise to Uncle," she said softly.

I dragged my eyes back to her gleaming, mossy ones.

"But I'm having a hard time fulfilling it. He wants me to write a poem a day."

"Hold on."

I stood up, going into the bathroom to fish through my wet pockets for the green pen she'd given me. The one I couldn't not carry around. When I came back, I handed it to her.

"Try writing with this."

Her eyes widened, and before she could comment on the fact that I still had it, or had it *on me*, I said, "I'm loaning it to you. I expect it back."

She rolled her lips, playing with the plastic.

"I'm leaving eventually," she murmured. "I won't be able to give it back."

The thought of her leaving flashed through me hot. Cold. Hurting my chest.

"There you go again, saying stupid shit." My words were rough, quiet. "When you leave, will you finally do what you want? Be a poet?"

Be *free*.

She went quiet. "You said someone like me could never be a poet, not unless you paid my way."

Snitch changed me. Fundamentally. Chemically.

When I looked up, Snitch was lost somewhere in her head. Before she would have a taken me there, let me wander the twisted pathways with her. But now? I was left on the outskirts.

Silence wafted over us.

A thought popped into my head. "Is anyone going to the doctor with you?"

"I don't have a doctor..." she admitted.

"Let me take care of you. I'll take you to classes. I'll buy you new clothes." I gripped her face. "If you need anything—"

"If I need a horse?" she cut me off.

I exhaled some of the tension in my chest. "Yeah...yeah, if you need a horse." I thumbed her cheek, swiping the smooth skin I'd missed. It was a perfect, quiet moment in the dark. These moments I'd missed.

Then something dark flitted in her eyes.

She jerked her head out of my hold, and just like that, the moment shattered.

"You're *married*," she said. "I'm...I'm married."

"And? I can be your friend."

She laughed. "You could never be my friend." She yawned into her shoulder. "You—"

I grabbed her hand, cutting her off. "Go to sleep. We'll talk about this later."

I settled back on the floor.

"Isn't it uncomfortable?"

It was. "It's not."

But holding her hand in the darkness was worth it.

A few minutes passed, and I thought maybe she'd gone to sleep.

"Have you even had a real friend, Grayson?"

I had a best friend. Her name was Story Hale. But I don't want to be her fucking friend. I want to be the father of her child. I want to be her lover, her husband.

Dudes complained about the friend zone, but maybe if I was lucky, if I tried really fucking hard, I could stay in Snitch's friend zone.

Maybe that's all we could ever have.

"I did. Once."

STORY

I woke up rested and happy, my right hand warm. I looked over—Grayson held my hand. He'd held my hand *all night?* He was asleep at an odd angle. He hadn't even rolled over to fall asleep. He'd just sat against the bed, holding my hand all night.

My chest ached.

Then, like he could sense I was awake, he stirred, and looked over his shoulder up at me. Blinking those beautiful blue eyes awake.

"How are you feeling?"

His voice was soft, eyes softer, and he still held my hand.

My heart cracked.

"It's the first time she's spent time with her father," I said softly, unable to keep my feelings bottled.

His brow furrowed. "She?"

I quickly yanked my hand out of his, feeling too raw and vulnerable.

The first time the baby spent with her dad, and probably the last. I hugged my knees to my chest. Grayson slowly stood, rubbing his neck as though it had a crick in it. He looked too adorable, too sexy, rubbing the knots out as the sun illumined his messy bed hair.

He was still only in boxer briefs, the silky kind he always wore that left *nothing* to the imagination. True to Grayson Crowne, he was completely callous to the effect it had on me.

"The sun is up," I coughed.

He closed one eye into the rays. "So it is."

"What are you doing here?"

He stopped rubbing his neck, eyes digging into me. I didn't like that. I pulled the blanket tighter around my knees, a flimsy cotton armor.

"I'll always be there for you, Snitch."

No you won't.

Anger swamped the sadness in my chest, allowed me to breathe. I threw off my blankets and got out of bed.

"Leave. Go back to your wife."

He blinked like I'd slapped him.

"If you tell anyone—" I said.

His eyes flashed. "Everyone will believe me," he growled.

"You think I don't know that?" I snapped.

He flexed his jaw and turned to leave, as if he was just going to walk the halls of Crowne Hall in his underwear, the way only Grayson Crowne could, but he stopped in the doorway.

He was glaring at me, his anger obvious by the muscle popping in his jaw and the vein in his neck, but he just stayed in the doorway, arms folded. The clock ticked deeper into the morning.

"What?" I finally snapped.

"What is it?" he snapped back.

"Um, what?"

"You don't eat peanuts or spaghetti. What do you like now?" He watched me with an annoyed glare that felt way too much like our first nights together.

Suckers.

I can't stop eating them.

But he doesn't get to know that.

Feeling petty, I said. "French fries, but only from France."

He exhaled through his nostrils. "See you in a day then."

I rolled my eyes. "Grayson, don't fly to France."

"Anything else?" he asked. "Would you like snails, maybe a baguette?"

I jumped off the bed, closing the distance and grabbing his arm.

"Don't fly to France!" I couldn't hold back my laugh, and a smile feathered his lips. For a few seconds, things had gone back to *before. Before* it all got ruined.

But then his smile dropped, and silence crept.

"Would you really fly to France?" I asked softly.

"Always, Snitch."

I lifted my eyes to his. He was already watching me, blue eyes open in a way that made my heart ache.

I realized I was still holding him, and I quickly let go, stepping away, focusing on the floor. On my bare feet.

"Let me know what you really want, Snitch."

"Okay," I said, voice catching on the emotion in my throat.

When I looked up, my doorway was empty.

TWENTY-FOUR

GRAY

Crowne Industries' eastern HQ is headquartered in New York. It's a towering silver skyscraper in the heart of the financial district. My grandfather split his time between California, London, and New York.

His assistants glanced at me when the elevator opened, went back to their work, then did a double take.

"Mr. Grayson!" My grandfather's first assistant rushed up to me. Grandpa had two assistants, an older one with graying hair, Tory, and a younger one.

The younger assistant tended to rotate with the year and newest sexual harassment lawsuit. Tory had been with Beryl for most of his adult life.

"We've missed you," Tory said. "The air around here is..."

Crushing. Demoralizing.

"Different," she provided. "How long are you back for—"

"Grayson." My grandfather's voice cut her off and she froze, clearly not expecting him to have gotten out of his seat.

"Grandfather."

I followed him into his office, past two petrified assistants.

He took a seat behind his massive desk, the New York skyline behind him. I fell into the wingback opposite.

"I've enjoyed the interviews," he said. "You look like quite the happy family."

Silence ticked on.

Smug fucking bastard.

"I can't remember the last time you came to work," he finally said. "If you're coming for my throne, I know you're not prepared to sit on it. What are you going to do? Take it and let the castle crumble?"

"I don't want your fucking throne," I gritted.

He leaned forward, chin on the tips of his fingers. "So why are you here?"

"To bargain. I'll give you what you want. A puppet. I'll take the photos. I'll show up to the meetings. I'll play nice. I'll stop fighting."

"And what do you want?"

"Her alive. Out of this world. Safe. That includes from West du Lac. If anything happens to her, you know what I'll do. We both win. She's gone; I'm here."

"And how do you propose we do that, Grayson?"

"I know you wouldn't have gone through with this wedding unless you had enough dirt on du Lac to fill a fucking graveyard."

He arched a brow. "You want me to go against our new family?"

There was only one person Grandfather ever looked out

for: Grandfather.

"She's gone before Christmas."

"I'll need your assurances. You..." My grandfather tapped his fingertips. "Have a history."

"I'm willing to do whatever you need."

He leaned back, rubbing the salt-and-pepper shadow on his jaw. "It's time to take your place by my side, Grayson, but you've always been weak. Soft." I clenched my jaw as his eyes drifted over my shoulder. "Tory is getting too old to look at. Start by firing her. Then show up for work tomorrow."

I stood up, ignoring the sludge in my stomach.

I put Story in this mess, and I would get her out of it, no matter the cost to me.

STORY

After Grayson left, I stayed in bed, trying to ignore my craving for suckers. It's not *fair*. It's not fair that I crave Gray on a chemical level.

He's in my bloodstream.

Tears bubbled in my eyes, hot and fucking *uncontrollable*. I ripped open my bedside nightstand, determined to smash all the suckers, when my eyes narrowed on the bottle left on top. *Prenatal vitamins.*

When did he manage to leave that? Was Grayson insane? Did he want the entire world to know I was pregnant?

"Angel?"

I slammed the bottle into my drawer too fast, and

caught my fingers.

"Ow, fuck." I grasped my hand, but moments later West was there, taking it into his, examining the throbbing red tip. He thumbed tears that had fallen before I'd slammed my finger, a question in his eyes. I looked away.

"Thanks for letting me sleep in my own room," I said, anything to kill the butterflies in my stomach.

His brow furrowed, jaw tight with some emotion.

"Story Hale, I want you to *want* to be in my bed." His eyes dropped to my lips, and the air shifted, charged.

I swear he wanted to kiss me.

My own eyes dropped to his lips. Lips I'd *never* kissed, not even when we'd had sex. I'd imagined it, imagined what those plump, kissable lips would feel like against my own. Would he be rough? Tender?

His eyes met mine, waiting for something I couldn't give.

My lips parted, but no words came out.

A second later, he said, "I think you're fine." He stood back up, like nothing had happened, but I'd been blown over by a hurricane.

There was a sandstorm in my chest.

West was being too nice, and it made me feel...wrong. Wrong that Grayson had been on the floor last night. Wrong that I'd been craving him. Wrong that I'd just thought about kissing West.

Wrong.

It felt as if I was both cheating on the husband I'd promised I didn't love, and the man I'd promised to hate.

"I wish I could stay and spend the day with you," West said, "but I have work."

"It's fine. I'll just spend the day here." Hiding. Pretending I'm not in Crowne Hall. That this isn't my life.

"Angel...You're a du Lac now."

My eyes met his. "So?"

"They're expecting you in the sunroom. I won't force you to go, but the harder we push, the more they push back."

He checked his watch and, without another word, left me to ruminate on *waiting for me in the sunroom*. No bells on the wall to let me know they needed tea or cucumber sandwiches, but my husband telling me to meet my...in-laws.

In a daze I went to my closet.

I knew what they would be wearing, and none of my *nun clothes* would be appropriate. Still, I pulled out a white lacy blouse and black skirt.

Downstairs, women sat in sateen chaises and chairs around Tansy Crowne. The sun was soft, and it looked like a Victorian painting. I paused in the doorway, feeling like I should lower my eyes and wait to be called in.

"Story," Tansy called for me. "We've been waiting for you."

One by one their heads turned, falling on me.

The only seat available was on a chaise next to Lottie. With knots in my stomach, I took it. They resumed the conversation, ignoring me with an ease only the rich could. They spoke of the impending holidays, of Thanksgiving a few weeks out.

The knots in my gut twisted like a rag with water.

It was black tie and I had nothing to wear.

A servant named Jane, with blonde hair and brown eyes, brought out a tray of fruit with "gourmet" dipping sauce that was basically diluted sugar water. I remember the highly trained chef rolling his eyes every time it was requested.

I reached for a thinly sliced pear.

"Oh, you're not going to eat it plain, are you?" asked Lottie's friend Pipa, tilting her head.

"We can't expect her to know the difference," Mrs. du Lac said.

Around me soft snickers rose.

I dragged the end of my tongue across my top lip.

"It doesn't really do anything. We only make it because you request it..." My heart pounded so loud in my chest it roared in my ears, but I smiled sweetly, as if I wasn't David standing up to Goliath. "But I can't expect you to know the difference."

Silence followed.

Jane looked me in the eyes, and for the first time in months, her gaze wasn't filled with hate. Almost...respect? Then she quickly left.

For the following hour I said nothing, drinking my tea, but a foreign sense of power filled me. Until whispers started up at my back between two gossiping socialites.

"She's the one," one of them said. "The Cinderella."

"I heard Grayson punched his grandfather because of her."

Shock rippled down my spine. Grayson was the one who hit his grandfather?

"Grayson has been working hard," Lottie said loudly, and I wondered if she'd heard them. "He stayed up all night working in his office, and he's gone to work with his grandfather this morning."

My hands shook with my tea. I tried to focus on the beautiful flower blossoming in the amber liquid. He'd been with me all night. In my bedroom.

"They're calling her the Stepsister Slut too," someone whispered behind me.

"*That* makes sense."

I stood, and once again, everyone's eyes came to me.

"I forgot something," I mumbled.

"Why doesn't she just have one of the servants fetch it?" I heard as I entered the hallway.

I can't do it anymore. I can't hide who I am. I can't hide my baby. I'm not going to have her born to someone like me.

Sitting next to Lottie.

Lying.

"Story?"

No.

Not *now*.

I kept walking, ignoring Grayson.

"What's wrong, little nun?"

"Go away."

He grasped my arm, spinning me. "Something's wrong."

How did he know? How did he always fucking know?

"Everything is fine. Go away."

His thumb applied the slightest pressure above my elbow. Something weighed on his shoulders. I could see it in his heavy lids. The suit he was wearing was all wrong, not Grayson.

"What's wrong with you?"

His brows rose. "Me?"

The soft laughter from Tansy's solarium drifted to us.

"Did you hit your grandpa?" I asked.

Grayson was the only one I could ever talk with. Who was I going to talk to about poetry and my uncle? West? Who was I going to worry about my pregnancy with? Once again, Grayson and I were tangled in secrets.

Maybe he wanted to tell me everything, like I wanted to tell him.

Or maybe that was wishful thinking.

I pulled my arm from him.

"He threatened something that didn't belong to him," he said. His blue eyes traveled a slow path down my face to my collarbone, where his locket lay, the one I couldn't take off no matter how hard I tried.

I took a step back and his hand shot out, gripping the locket, holding me in place.

"Let me go."

"I will," he said, voice rough.

His fist curled tighter.

"Was there no scenario where you didn't marry her? Where you and I lived happily ever after?"

The minute I said it, I wished I could take it back, but in that moment I wanted nothing more than to know how I lived happily ever after with Grayson Crowne.

More than being pathetic.

More than anything.

He gripped the locket, eyes pinched. On me. "There was."

"Why didn't you choose me?" I asked. "What does she have that I don't?" The words tumbled and fell from my mouth, jagged pieces of my already broken heart.

His eyes slashed to mine. "I'd do anything for you."

"Except leave your wife."

His jaw clenched, as if he was holding something back. Finally he said, "I would do what I had to do to keep you and the baby safe."

I shoved him off, walking to my wing. I was so weak. So pathetic. I rubbed my forehead with the palm of my hand, trying to think clearly even though every time Grayson was around me my thoughts clouded into white fog.

A hand snatched my wrist. "I'm getting you out of this world, little nun."

I looked over my shoulder at Grayson. "You had that chance. You're not the man I depend on anymore."

"You can't honestly tell me you trust West?"

No, I don't, but I *could* say, "I don't trust you, Grayson Crowne."

He reeled. "What? You'd trust him over me?"

I swallowed. I don't know who to fucking trust. I'm in a bed of snakes, and they're all begging for my wrist.

Grayson was the one man I trusted above all, and he'd shattered that trust.

I tried to yank my wrist but he held on tighter, blanching the bone.

"You realize how ridiculous this is, right? It doesn't add up. He's a snake."

"What's so crazy? How someone like him could want to give everything up for someone like me and then actually go through with it?"

His shoulders tensed so much I could see the muscles twerk in his golden neck.

"Or why someone like me would go back to someone like him? How pathetic and weak I am?"

Something flickered in his eyes. Regret maybe. The emotion clouded and muted in this shadowed hallway.

When he spoke, his voice was his signature stone. "Both."

I pulled at my wrist again, furious. He dragged me to him, my hands slamming against his chest.

"Did he hire you guards?" he demanded. "Get you a girl? Get you anything? You're still wearing your nun clothes."

"I'll hire them myself," I all but spat. "I'll get everything myself."

He looked at me with pity. "You only have a couple

million dollars. Some of which I'm sure you're allotting for the child—*which you don't need to do*," he added the last part, giving me a dark, possessive look that went straight to my gut.

Of course I needed to do it.

I couldn't trust Grayson, as much as my heart said I should.

"A full-time bodyguard costs anywhere from fifty to five hundred dollars an hour," he continued. "Ours are thousands. We employ only the best ex-special ops. You can't have someone watching you twenty-four seven, which means you'll need at least two, but I want you to have ten."

"Ten," I gasped. "I'm not some princess."

"That was my low number," Grayson said. "At least a million for them."

"A million?" I blinked. "A million dollars? That's almost all my money."

"Not including room and board, food, airfare, etcetera."

"Being rich is so expensive," I whispered.

He pushed a curl from my face, behind my ear, jaw clenched tight.

"Let me hire them if your fucking husband won't do it."

I liked the way he said *husband*...his usually apathetic voice catching on a snarl. It fed something wrong inside me.

"No," I whispered. "I'm not getting in debt further."

"I'm not going to ask you to pay me back," he growled. "And I'm not going to sit back and let you get hurt."

I used both hands and shoved him, shoved him so hard I stumbled a few feet backward into the hallway.

"Fine. I'll ask West."

His jaw twerked, and when he spoke, it was through clenched teeth. "Fine."

TWENTY-FIVE

GRAY

The sun hadn't even cracked the horizon when I was heading out for work.

"You're going in to work a lot," Lottie's sleepy voice called to me. "Are you going to be back before sundown tonight? It's only a few weeks before Thanksgiving—"

"Will your brother make sure Story is ready for the holidays?" I asked the thing that had been sticking in my side like a thorn.

Lottie's face dropped. She worked her mouth, before shaking her head. "No, I doubt he realizes what she needs to be prepared for."

I cursed.

She'd be eaten alive.

"I'll be out late," I said.

I was in the foyer when a weak voice stopped me.

"Mr. Crowne."

It was a servant with blonde hair and brown eyes.

Before Story, I would have had her fired for even daring to talk to me, let alone look me in the eyes. But I paused.

She looked away.

"If anyone finds out I did this...I don't think how they're treating Story is right."

That piqued my interest, and I joined her in the shadowy corner.

"You should know," she said quietly, "that a few months ago, a servant named Ellie stole a picture when she came to dress Miss Hale. I heard she sold it to a newspaper."

I quirked my jaw. "What picture?"

"I—" She looked over her shoulder. "I don't know. They said she made her sign something. But she said it's coming out tomorrow. Please don't tell anyone I told you. If anyone finds out...I'll be like Story."

Before I could ask any more questions, the woman dashed off, running down into the servants' quarters.

I should have gone into work, but I spent the morning calling every outlet I knew, until I found it. The one about to decimate her.

It was *mine.*

It was my fucking secret.

The headline was a photo of Snitch with the title *The Real Cinderella Killed Her Mother.* She held the photo I'd taken of her, the green ink fresh next to her stony glare.

When my mom died, I wasn't sad. I was relieved.

This place wasn't safe anymore. The walls I'd built had eroded. I had enemies on all sides, and they were going after Snitch.

If Story wouldn't let me take care of her, I would do it secretly. Our love is a precious thing. Only safe in the dark. In the cracks. In the places people cannot reach and harm.

There's only on way to stop a story from printing.

Give them something juicier.

STORY

I don't sleep anymore.

I stay up, writing letters to Atlas, thinking about Grayson even though I keep trying to hate him.

When there was a knock on my door early in the morning, I wondered if I was dreaming.

Then West opened the door, leaning against the frame. "Go on a date with me, Angel."

"I thought you worked during the day?"

"Today I was supposed to settle some final things with Crowne Industries over the marriage, but..." He laughed. "They're busy."

I furrowed my brow, confused, and West pulled up his phone, coming to me.

GRAYSON CROWNE, PLAYBOY PRINCE: VIRGIN.

I must have stared at the headline for over a minute. A full-page print about how Grayson Crowne was a virgin before he married Lottie.

"Never saw that coming," West said.

I swallowed. "Right..."

"Anyway, today is a shitshow, so I can take you on a date."

"How, um..." How was Grayson handling it? The comments were horrible. Some were nice. But so many of them were cruel. Every mean thing I know he'd called himself secretly. "How are the Crownes reacting?"

He stared down at me, eyes narrow, as if he saw the real words in my head. Then he smiled.

"The entire house is in lockdown," he said softly. Again, I felt like he was saying something else. "Beryl has come back. I heard him yell a few choice words...I think Tansy has locked herself in her room."

I swallowed, my heart cracking for him.

His lip lifted higher. "I don't know about Grayson. I think I saw him downstairs. Maybe you want to go check?"

I scoffed, looking away. "Why would I want to do that?"

I swear I heard him laugh. "So a date then?"

"I guess..." I didn't want to go out with West, not because I didn't want to, but because for the first time, I didn't actually hate the idea of it. "I just need a minute to get dressed."

"Sure thing."

He left me alone, and it only took five minutes to get dressed in a dark, high-collared lace blouse and knee-length skirt.

Downstairs.

Fuck.

I picked at my nail.

I really wanted to see if Grayson was okay. I don't think I could go the entire day without knowing how bruised his eyes were.

I tore open my door, seeing just a glimpse of him would do. Like before, when I used to watch him.

I stopped short on the stairs. Ellie was on her knees before Grayson, crying.

"Please, Mr. Crowne. *Please.* I have nowhere else to go. My life—I...please."

"You'll manage," he said.

Ellie ran off, tears in her eyes.

The first night with Grayson blasted through me.

He was wearing another three-piece suit. It looked impeccable on him, tailored to his tall, lean frame. The charcoal color was timeless, and his rose gold hair didn't have a strand out of place. He was perfect. Cold.

And he wasn't *Grayson*.

"Who are you?"

He tensed at my voice, then turned to face me, jaw flexed.

"What happened to the Grayson that donates his shoes? The one that made sure my uncle's wish came true? You just..." I looked away. "I'm starting to wonder if that Grayson ever existed, or if you were always that man who threatened me at the hospital."

I was slowly watching the Grayson I knew dissolve before my eyes.

"I came to check on you..." Because I was worried. Because I'm a fucking idiot. "This was a bad idea. My husband is waiting for me."

"If you mention your husband one more fucking time—"

I spun. "You'll what? Threaten to send me away? Get someone off in front of me? Marry her after you fucked me? Threaten to *lock me away?*"

He worked his jaw to the side.

"You don't care about me. You never did. You're just bothered by the idea of West touching something you thought belonged to you."

His eyes grew, his lips parted.

Grayson pounded to me. "Get it through your fucking skull, Story. I don't give a shit about that. He hurt you. He's continuing to hurt you. I let it happen. I'm supposed to protect you." His words were strangled and raw.

I don't know why they bothered me so much.

I guess I wanted him to be a little bit irritated by the prospect of me sleeping with West. The same way it *ate* and *ate* at me imagining him with Lottie.

"You want the truth? No one wants this baby but us. If I have to stay married to Lottie to keep you safe, I will."

"How fucking chivalrous of you, Grayson."

I shoved him, but he grabbed my elbow, thrusting me against the stair's railing, yet throwing his hand behind me so my back was cushioned.

"Let me go."

His jaw clenched. "You shouldn't have said anything. You should have kept walking. Shouldn't have let me know you were here."

"So let me go."

His hand at my back fisted the fabric of my shirt, ripping it from my skirt.

"I don't want you anymore, Grayson."

He laughed, dark. "Liar."

"See how much of a liar I am when I'm in West's bed tonight."

His eyes flashed to mine. Wild. Filled with something I knew I shouldn't poke at. He dragged his free hand through his hair, and some of his perfect coif came undone. I liked it too much when the first strand fell across his blue eyes.

"I could fuck you against these stairs right now. I know you'd let me. You always let me." His hand at my back slid beneath my shirt, flesh against flesh. "Come inside you." He was possessed, tumbling into this fantasy. "You're already pregnant."

Another secret. A dirty, dark secret.

I whispered back, soft. "But when I have the baby, it will be *his* name on the birth certificate."

Grayson froze, fingers digging into my flesh, eyes slowly locking with mine.

"Say that baby is his and see what fucking happens, Snitch."

"Are you threatening me?"

"I'm trying to warn you. I've been on a very thin leash since the moment you walked into my life. I'm trying to be good." He slammed his other hand on the railing, caging me. "Trying to be decent. Trying to become the man you saw in me. But if you say that West is the father of my child..."

I knew I shouldn't goad him.

"You'll what?"

He exhaled a jagged sigh and stepped back.

"Maybe I'll go back to my wife and fuck her. Come in her cunt. Get her fucked up with me the way you used to like."

My stomach twisted at the image. "Go for it. I don't give a shit what you do anymore, because you're right about one thing. Somebody can come in me without worrying. But I think that's a privilege reserved for my husband."

He grasped my arm, yanking me to him. "I don't share, Story."

"I don't share *either*." I shoved him off. "You might not have been my *first*, Grayson, but you were my first everything else. My first kiss. My first blow job. My first orgasm. But you won't be my last."

He looked like he'd just been punched in the gut.

"So take a good fucking look, Grayson Crowne. Everything you do with Lottie, West gets to do to me."

TWENTY-SIX

STORY

I turned sideways in the mirror, running my hands over my barely rounded belly. It was just a slight bump, barely noticeable, but it made my heart race all the same.

Thanksgiving with the Crownes.

It was hard to believe I'd already spent the month of November at Crowne Hall, but the calendar didn't lie.

I practiced my fake smile again. It still felt stiff and awkward.

I exhaled, dropping my hands to my side.

I'd only ever experienced it as a servant. Thanksgiving was a prelude to the holidays. With extravagant, opulent traditions, beautiful gowns, and way too much food. Like many, the Crownes broke the turkey wishbone, but their tradition looks nothing like what you'd imagine. *All* guests break bones, dressed in their ballgowns, laughing beneath chandeliers as the paparazzi took gilded pictures. Whoever breaks the biggest bone must do a lucky kiss with their date, to be displayed on all magazines across America.

Once, someone smuggled in a huge bone to try to cheat. They thought they could end up on the covers and become an overnight celebrity. It had happened before.

I decided my one goal this Thanksgiving was to avoid winning.

Avoid kissing my husband.

Avoid being spotlit even more.

The door opened behind me, and I spun, nervous it was West. Ever since we'd come close to kissing, it had been different between us.

"Miss Abigail?" I gasped.

Abigail Crowne stood in the doorway, dressed in the cutest knee-length black maternity dress with matching boots and hat, showing off her slight bump. I was so used to looking away that I averted my gaze.

She laughed. "You're married to a fucking du Lac, and my last name is Hound. I think we can look each other in the eyes."

I slowly lifted my gaze. Abigail always had a hollow look in her eyes, like all the Crownes, really. Now she had a smile on her face and not a sneer.

"You're pregnant," I said.

"What gave me away?"

She turned, showing her little bump.

In the few weeks that had passed, Grayson had kept his distance, and West had been...perfect. He only held my hand, not even a kiss on the cheek.

The only thing marring this was the internet.

Maybe we'd spun the story, but I was still gossip fodder, and there are always a few people you can never truly convince.

"Why are you here?"

"I guess you could say...I'm your girl for the day."

I choked on my spit. "I'm sorry?"

She held up a hand. "Don't expect me to get on my knees or bring you tea or anything. I'm just going to give you a desperately needed makeover." She arched a brow at my chosen outfit for the day: a high-collared white lace blouse and black skirt.

"I might not live in this house anymore, but I will never kneel."

A moment passed; then she turned on her heel.

When I didn't follow, she threw her head over her shoulder. "You coming?"

"This is Tansy Crowne's *wing*." I whisper-hissed as Abigail led me into the sprawling, opulent part of Crowne Hall that demarcated Tansy's personal wing. I hunched forward, hiding behind Abigail as if that would save me.

Abigail led us through two grand arches carved with intricate molding into a brightly lit room. She walked us up stairs that overlooked the ocean on one side, with scowling portraits at our shoulders. We went past a bed made neatly with pastel satin pillows and into a walk-in closet bigger than my room in the guest wing.

This was Tansy Crowne's dress room.

Famous.

Photographed.

Insured for millions.

Ball gowns hung along the wall, spotlit and beneath pristine glass cases.

"She's going to kill me," I said. "This is how I die."

"Let me tell you something about Tansy Crowne," Abigail said, completely ignoring the fear in my voice. "She has more dresses than Jesus had wine and only keeps track of a few. As long as you don't disturb those..." She gestured to the ones beneath glass. "She'll *never* know you're wearing one of hers."

"We were always taught that Mrs. Tansy has all of her dresses catalogued and the rooms are heavily watched."

She laughed. "Of course you were."

She went to one wall, typing in a code in an electric lock. Out of the wall sprang a closet, and Abigail disappeared behind the silk and satin and glitter.

"This one."

Abigail popped her head from behind the pull-out closet. She held the dress up to my body, then shook her head, tossing it to the ground. Liquid gold fell to the floor in a heap as Abigail disappeared back behind the pull-out closet.

"No, *this one*." Abigail held another beautiful gown up to my body.

She came to me, holding it up and staring at me with wide red-brown eyes. "Well?"

"What?"

"Get dressed."

Abigail must have been a few inches shorter than me, but I felt miles smaller than her. I took it cautiously.

"Are you back?" I wondered aloud as I shimmied into the green material.

Had the Crownes allowed Abigail back—and why did that give me hope?

But then Abigail laughed. "Hell no. A special holiday dispensation has been made. Every other day of the year, I don't exist to these people. My mother doesn't even know

I'm pregnant. Oh!" she said suddenly, and I froze, worried I'd ripped the fabric or something. "You have the Nutcracker Masquerade and Christmas Eve and Christmas too. Do you have something for that?"

I shook my head.

"So you probably don't have anything at all for the holidays?"

Another shake of my head. She exhaled, blowing a strand of curly brown hair, and headed to another wall, typing in another code. The wall popped out like the last one.

"So, um..." I focused at the satin buttons on my side. "You're still excommunicated?"

"Of course. I broke off my engagement and eloped with my *bodyguard*."

I dropped my hands, giving up on the beautiful green dress to say what was really on my mind, "I don't understand. Why do you have to lose everything just because you loved someone you weren't supposed to?"

"Because forcing us to love who they choose is how they stay on top. My grandfather always told me *you're either for this family, or you're against it...*" She pulled out another dress then her eyes popped on me. "You look like you need to sit down." She came to me, sitting me on a sateen chaise, before returning to the closet.

"I think it's time for a few insider tips that no one will tell you, not even Gray, because he has no fucking clue what it's like to be a girl in this world." She rifled through more dresses, choosing her favorites. "Tansy Crowne's compliments are not compliments."

"I knew that one." I smiled wanly.

"It doesn't matter what century it is, you are not equal. You're expected to know that. Watch out for snakes because they *do not* look like snakes, and they will prey on you."

"I knew that one too..." I whispered, and Abigail appeared from behind the wall of dresses with a soft look. She went on about what color lip to wear to what kind of breakfast and lunch, what shoes to wear, what not to wear to what party. How to cross my legs, how to smile for paparazzi, how to angle my chin for photos, what not to say, until the advice started to blur into one.

"A Finsta? A what?" I suddenly felt overheated.

"A Finsta is just a secret Instagram account. Everyone in our world has one, and the rules are you *do not* share out of our social circle. Can't have a prince of Dubai's cocaine and cunnilingus habit made public or the First Daughter's tits all over social media."

Abigail thumbed through more dresses, speaking casually. Meanwhile, I struggled to stand.

"I don't think I can do this," I said. "They talk about me online. They think they know me. And some of them...they do."

Abigail laughed. "Hoo boy, I think I understand why my brother called me."

Her *brother*.

"Your brother?" My heart pounded, fingers shaking as I buttoned up the side of my dress. "Your brother is the reason you're here?"

"Oops, was I not supposed to say that?" She rolled her eyes, clearly not upset about spilling the beans.

"Listen," she continued, not giving me a minute to think about what she'd just said. "The first secret they learn is the most violating."

Abigail Crowne was the most infamous Crowne. She'd been the center of scandal after scandal, even more so than her brother. If you searched her name, her naked body was the second thing to pop up.

At least Grayson's body had somewhat hidden mine, so no one had seen me naked, but her? Everyone had seen her.

"I've hidden my whole life," I said. "I don't know what to do now that everyone sees me."

She sat beside me. "Just remember to wear your CROWNE."

"My what?"

She laughed. "It's a stupid acronym our mother had the nanny teach us as children. Cross your legs, Remember to smile, Own the room, Wear your best, Never apologize, and Eat your vegetables." She paused, knuckle to chin. "The last one really only applies if you're five."

She smiled. "But really, I'll impart a lesson that took me my whole life to learn: be honest with yourself. Then whatever they say can't hurt you. We're all so busy trying to be what everyone wants us to be, or what we think we should be, so we shit ourselves worrying they're going to discover the truth, who we actually are."

She spun me around, a smile on her face.

It was the most skin I'd shown in years. My shoulders. My breasts. My knees. My hair.

"No one is going to recognize you."

I touched the soft green chiffon. "Should I be on the lookout for any pumpkins?"

TWENTY-SEVEN

GRAY

"You keep staring at the door."

"Just wondering when Abigail is getting here."

Lottie kissed me on the cheek, and I jerked away like I was burned.

Everything you do with Lottie, West gets to do to me.

Hurt marred her face.

"I...think I'm getting sick."

Lottie stared at me with another question in her eyes I knew she wouldn't ask. Then she gripped my hand, affecting her own smile. Empty.

"Maple glazed turkey?" A servant wearing a feathered headdress atop his regular black-and-white uniform asked. *Feathers imported from the finest birds of Africa,* my mother would boast.

One time, a magazine did what my mother would call a hit piece on us.

"The Crownes aren't just harmlessly oblivious, they're a

symbol of a larger problem, of those who stubbornly continue the ignorant, tasteless, and traumatizing traditions..."

How dare they try to take away our traditions? she'd said. *We'd been doing this as far back as the eighteen hundreds. Where would it stop? Next they'd come for the very stars on the American flag.*

Interesting enough, after that article came out, the Crownes started the biggest Native American college scholarship in the country. Now that's all anyone talks about come Thanksgiving.

Through the massive arched entryway draped with autumn leaves, Story appeared. I dropped the turkey I'd taken, the glaze streaking the marble floor.

"Grayson? Are you okay?"

Maybe it was just in my mind, but I swear the room went hush as Story came through. Paparazzi snapped furious pictures. Lottie followed my line of sight, and a moment later she exhaled.

I looked away, but Story was burned in my retinas. Her *bare* shoulders. Her pushed-up breasts and cleavage for miles. Her long, slender neck. Everyone was going to look at her tonight. She stood out among the women wearing muted colors of gold and brown, the men in dark suits. For once, she allowed what I saw in her every minute to shine through.

Exquisite. Unique.

West and Story were clearly headed our way as Abigail passed by in a deep-red ballgown that would make my mother's head spin.

"Abs. Abby. Hey."

Abigail stopped, turning around. "I'm in the middle of something very important."

I narrowed my eyes. "You have that look on your face."

"What look?"

"The one that says you're about to do something stupid."

Her mouth dropped. "That's—what—have you been talking to Theo?"

I threw an arm in Story's direction. "What the fuck did you dress her in?"

"She looks hot, right? Vintage Chanel can do no wrong. It fits her well and brings out the color of her eyes."

I glared. "I didn't ask you to make her look *hot*. I said *presentable*."

Theo stepped between us, dragging my sister back against his chest. "Chill, Gray. I'd hate to have to punch you in the face for making your sister cry."

Her dog, Theo, wrapped his arm around her stomach possessively, eyes on me. I was about to make some comment to him about staying in his fucking place, but then Gemma and her fiancé, Horace, Story, and West joined us, and my attention went elsewhere. West, the idiot, wore a tall, traditional pilgrim's hat.

"I'm not going to cry." Abigail scoffed at Theo as Lottie wove her arm into mine.

"I see you're getting fat with married life," Gemma said to Abigail.

"I see you're staying fat," Abigail replied. Gemma rolled her eyes but smiled.

I can count on my hands the number of times my siblings and I have been together without disdain and fighting, and it was...nice. Odd, but nice.

A servant appeared, offering a silver tray of stuffed mushrooms. As everyone took one, Story's face totally changed. She looked like she was going to hurl.

"Are you doing the wishbone with Horace later?" Abigail poked Gemma, obviously knowing how little Gemma wanted to kiss her fiancé. Horace, on his phone, raised his eyes at his name but went back moments later. Gemma made some comment to Abigail, but I kept my eyes on Story.

She stared at the floor, working her lower lip between her teeth.

Was she also sensitive to the smell of mushrooms?

"Story and I can't wait to bone later," West supplied.

I ignored West's attempts to rile me up, focusing on Story, who looked about two seconds from vomiting. Without another thought, I smacked the mushrooms off the server's plate. They went flying, a few spongy pieces sticking to the matte white walls.

Silence followed, everyone looking at me as Story quietly vomited into her napkin.

"What the fuck, Gray?" Gemma finally broke the silence.

I shrugged, sliding back into my chair. "I really hate stuffing."

"Since when?"

Story's and my eyes connected. I swear I saw thanks, but I wasn't going to look into it.

STORY

Cross your legs, Remember to smile, Own the room, Wear your best, Never apologize, and Eat your vegetables.
"Are you wearing your CROWNE?"

I jumped, finding Gemma watching me, brow arched.

I rubbed my neck. "Possibly."

She picked up a cranberry tart, pausing before her plump pink lips to say, "You forgot the most important one."

I mentally went through the list again, panicking. *Cross your legs, Remember to smile, Own the room, Wear your best, Never apologize, and Eat your vegetables.*

Had I apologized?

"Eat your fucking vegetables." She laughed, dropping the tart into her mouth. "Welcome to our royally dysfunctional family, I guess."

"I'm not—I'm just...I'm..."

Gemma made a *tsking* sound. "You're forgetting your O."

Own the room.

Gemma wore a flowing gold gown with intricate leaves embroidered in the tulle, a color like many others in the room. Other than Abigail, I was the only one *not* in gold or brown. And I was the *only* one in green.

I didn't blend in.

Anxiety made intricate knots in my chest.

Gemma lingered, not quite looking at me but not totally ignoring my presence either. It was weird. Gemma Crowne had laughed with me. Had acknowledged me. And now was standing next to me, around paparazzi, in a place where we could be photographed.

"So...how do you know Grim?"

Ah. Now it made sense.

Her clear blue eyes lingered on me.

I shrugged. "I just do."

I knew him the way everyone who isn't rich knows everyone in Crowne Point, the way I was learning everyone who was rich knew everyone. We were a small town. You're involved in people's business even if you wished you weren't.

She looked like she wanted to press, when really I wanted to press how someone like *Gemma Crowne* knew Grim.

"Are you, um..." I swallowed, remembering the tattoo, but also stuck feeling like it still wasn't my place. "Okay?"

She shrugged. "They have the best drugs."

That made sense, more sense than a guy like Grim getting inked for a fucking Crowne, and a girl like *Gemma* taking that dark contract.

They'd have been bound together forever.

The Horsemen provided everyone with drugs, but a Crowne usually didn't buy them themselves. I know, because I knew the servants who did.

"You haven't told anyone you saw me there," she said after a moment.

I arched a brow. "How do you know?"

"Because no one told *me* they saw me there."

"I was trained to keep Crowne secrets. Old habits die hard. I'll catch up, don't worry."

We laughed, but mine died in my throat as a servant passed. She offered me a plate of hors d'oeuvres similar to the one Gemma had received, but mine was clearly rotten, fungus spreading across the cheese. When I looked closer I saw...glass. Shards of it embedded in the cheese balls.

"They're really good," Gemma said, raising her own and lifting her chin at my deadly one.

I don't know if I would ever dream of a day when Gemma Crowne talked to me like an equal, but if I did, it would make sense it would be like this. While she ate delicious food and I had to be careful not to swallow glass.

I had to bear this quietly. It wasn't like I could turn to

Tansy Crowne and say her servants were treating me poorly. No one believed I belonged here. They would simply shrug and say, *Well dear, it's not like they're wrong.*

Gemma placed her empty napkin on a tray and I put my balled-up, uneaten food next to hers as a different string rhythm started up, more hurried and excited.

"The dance is starting. At the end, we might even get a marriage proposal. Can you imagine?" She rolled her eyes at me.

Gemma Crowne was joking with me.

I'd watched this dance so many times, but I'd never *participated*. The Crownes had been doing it as far back as when they'd first immigrated to America. Back then, only women who'd come out in society danced, and only men looking for a wife joined in. It was an elaborate proposal.

We all lined up, our partners opposite us.

West was in his ridiculous pilgrim hat, and he grinned and shimmied at me. I tried to hide my smile in my hand.

"What are you wearing?"

The voice stopped my smile cold.

"You're not supposed to be on this side," I hissed. "The men go over there." Gray had lined up next to me, apparently completely ignoring the fact that all women were supposed to be on one side.

"What are you wearing?" he repeated as the song struck up a folksy dancing chord, and all the women, plus Gray, took our first step.

"A dress," I said. I took a step forward with the rest, linking arms with West. Lottie was next to her brother, watching us carefully, and I made sure to keep my eyes on West. I had enough on my mind trying to do the dance anyway. It was a simple two-step dance. Step, link arms, spin. Step, switch partners, spin.

"I can see that," Grayson growled as we spun. "Why does it show your shoulders and tits?"

I glared. Was he really doing this as we danced?

"Because it's not 1802," I hissed on a spin. "I'm also showing some ankle, Father Gray."

West spun, and then I realized in horror as we switched partners, and almost everyone went to a same-sex dancer, that it wouldn't be the case for me. My arms linked with Gray's.

My eyes were wide.

His were triumphant.

I looked over my shoulder at Lottie and West.

"If you stop now, it will be a bigger deal."

I ground my jaw, going along with the dance. I stared anywhere other than his chiseled jaw, his pouty pink lips. The face I'd been deprived of, the heady smell I was getting drunk off. My mind spinning with *Grayson, Grayson, Grayson* as we did the final steps.

"What are you even doing dancing?" he growled. "You're pregnant."

"I'm pregnant, not dying. I can dance at a party. You don't get to tell me what to do anymore, Grayson Crowne."

"That's my baby inside you."

"Is it?" I smiled at West, acting as if Grayson and I were only talking as friends would.

He was supposed to let me go, supposed to let me spin into West for the final dance, but he held on, pulled me closer.

"You really need to stop saying that," he growled.

I looked over my shoulder at a waiting West.

My eyes collided with Grayson's. "Or what?"

His grip tightened, bunching the fabric at my waist before he let me go.

I spun into West, finishing the dance.

"Did he propose?" West quirked a brow, tilting his chin at Grayson.

"I don't know, did Lottie?"

"She did," West said. "It's gonna be a weird Christmas."

My lips quirked. It was getting harder and harder not to laugh and smile around West. He was always so carefree, and I needed that. Grayson was opposite me, jaw clenched so tight I bet the muscles screamed.

When the dance finished, everyone clapped like some Victorian mating ritual had finished and then went to go watch the turkey be carved. West walked a few paces ahead of me, and I lifted up my skirts to walk down the stairs.

Suddenly, Grayson was at my side, linking arms with me, helping me down the stairs.

"What are you *doing*? People are staring."

"Let them stare. I'm not leaving you. You're pregnant."

"How many times do I have to tell you I can use the stairs?" I shoved him off just as we reached the floor.

I linked arms with West, anything to get away from the look in Grayson's eyes. A few seconds later, Mrs. du Lac and Tansy joined us. I could still feel Grayson's stare on my neck, hot as the sun. What was wrong with him? We were in public.

"Are you wearing *vintage* Chanel?" Mrs. du Lac asked. "That's very beautiful," she continued. "I think I recall Tansy wearing something similar, years ago."

I chewed the corner of my lip, heat rushing up my neck as I felt Tansy eyeing my dress. Abigail swore she wouldn't notice so long as it wasn't one of the dresses from the glass cases.

"It..." I coughed. "It was a gift."

"That's a very kind *gift*," Tansy said.

"Yup."

I just said *yup* to Tansy Crowne and Lynette du Lac, perhaps the most elegant women in existence. I opened my mouth to come up with something better, but instead ended up looking like a fish.

"Would you like some wine?" Mrs. du Lac held out a glass of wine, and I searched for a reasonable reason to decline it.

"I..."

Grayson snatched it out of her hand. "I'd love some, thank you."

Mrs. du Lac smiled at me and Grayson. "You're very welcome, Grayson...Well, good thing we have the second glass. You really have to try it, Story. It's the best vintage. Tansy really outdid herself." She reached for a second glass, handing it to me.

Something felt really, really *off* with the way she watched me.

Once again, I was out of excuses to say no.

Grayson snatched the second glass, as he drank the first in one gulp. "You're right, Lynette. This shit is dope."

Lottie's audible inhale was the only sound; she grasped Grayson's forearm, mouth parted.

"Are you unwell?" Tansy asked Grayson. *Crowne code for: Are you high?*

I saw Mrs. du Lac reach for yet *another* wine glass and quickly said, "If you'll excuse me, I need to go...pee."

I turned, lifting up my skirt, and quickly heading toward the bathroom.

Goddamn it.

How hard is it to say powder my nose or something—

"How are you enjoying the party, dear?"

I froze at Tansy Crowne's voice. She'd *followed* me? I

slowly turned to face her. The bathroom was only a few feet from me, its dark oak door taunting.

I slowly turned around. "It's...fine."

She worked her diamond pendant between her fingers, watching the party. "You should have taken the money and left."

"I don't want your money."

"Hmm..." She rubbed her throat. "You know, he promised me he would never talk to you again. What promises has he made you?"

My heart fractured, but I wouldn't let her see. "He doesn't...we don't—"

"Lilian!" Tansy turned from me on a smile, waving at a woman with hair like a beehive, leaving me in the dust.

Tears were hot in my eyes.

Stinging.

I don't know why I was even surprised. It was exactly the thing Grayson Crowne would do, but I could feel it. Hot and itchy in my lids, scratching up my throat. I was going to cry.

So then it happened.

The worst possible thing at the worst possible time.

Grayson Crowne.

"Snitch."

"Go away," I snapped, refusing to turn.

Grayson gripped my elbow before I could run away, spinning me to him.

"Let me go."

I needed to get out of here, to the bathroom, and lock myself in until I could get control of my face. I *never* cried in public.

What the fuck is happening to me?

"I need to talk to you. You need to tell me what the hell

you're going through. I've had to look like an idiot, like, three times today!"

"This is my first time being pregnant!" I snapped. "I don't know what the fuck to expect!"

I shoved him off, but he wouldn't let me go.

And so the tears fell.

GRAY

Tears welled in her eyes, big fat ones that rushed down her pretty hazel cheeks. Alarm rushed through me. Story Hale didn't cry. She might get watery eyes, but she quickly wiped them away.

"I am fine!" Her face scrunched in anger. "Don't think because I'm crying you control any of the situation." She circled the air around us with her finger as more tears blurred her eyes. "What the fuck is happening to me?" She dragged her hands down her face.

Story's hands barely muffled her sobs, her shoulders racked up and down. I couldn't just sit here and watch this. I dragged her to me by one shoulder, anchoring her to me with my arm.

This was fine.

This was barely a hug.

"What are you doing?" She tried to shove me off.

I held on tighter, forcing her face into my white dress shirt. "Just let me do this."

It was nothing. Friends hug. They comfort each other. Story and I might be in a weird, no-man's-land of hate and love, but we could do this.

Eventually she stopped resisting, melting into me, into the hug. Her tears wetted my shirt, until she stopped crying.

I pulled back, one hand lightly on her shoulder.

I swiped her cheeks clean with both thumbs, her jaw clenched tight.

"Why are you crying, Story?"

"Why can't you keep your promises, Grayson?" she rasped.

I paused, her words hitting me like a fucking arrow I wasn't prepared for.

"I'm trying," I said. "Really fucking trying."

Her brow furrowed, and I dragged my thumbs down until I touched the corners of her pretty plump lips, wondering if I could taste the salt on them if I kissed her right now.

"You're kind of cute when you cry," I said, voice grating like sandpaper.

Her glare slashed to me, but it was soft, vulnerable. "Shut up."

I bit my tongue from smiling. "You've been away too long. You forgot. You can't talk to me that way, Snitch."

"Someone needs to call you out on your shit..."

"And that's you?" I dragged my thumb a millimeter to the right, tracing her bottom lip—

"There you both are." Mrs. du Lac's voice cut into the moment, and we spun. She stared at both of us, an unreadable expression on her wrinkleless hazelnut face.

"It's time for the lucky kiss."

We followed her back to the ballroom, where all the guests were lined up to break bones for our morbid tradition.

I wondered if Snitch's heart pounded as hard as mine did.

Had Mrs. du Lac overheard?

"You know the rules," my mother said. "Whoever pulls the bigger one has to do the lucky kiss."

The bones snapped in unison, the crack echoing in the air. It came down to just West, me, and some loser I didn't give a shit about with the biggest bones, so we all lined up to break the final bones.

My heart pounded.

Sweat beaded my brow.

This felt like life or death.

We broke, and West held his up, triumphant. I stared at my puny bone, gut sinking. It was like it happened in slow motion. West wrapped his arm around Story's waist, dipping her like she was a dame in an old movie. She gripped his shoulders. And then...they kissed.

TWENTY-EIGHT

GRAY

I dropped my bone to the ground as the paparazzi's cameras flashed.

I saw red. I saw black. Beyond the bright, burning spots blanketing my vision, West was kissing Story.

He was kissing her.

He was kissing my fucking girl.

I didn't realize I was heading to them until Lottie gripped the fabric at my bicep.

"What are you going to do?" she asked.

Beat his face into the fucking floor.

West and Story came back up, and she blinked, looking flustered as he laughed with the room and paparazzi continued to take photos.

"There's press everywhere," Lottie said.

I don't give a shit.

Maybe I had been deluding myself. *Was* she fucking

him? The idea drove me absolutely insane. I couldn't think beyond it.

I zeroed on West's hand on her waist. It isn't the tight grip driving me mad. It's the way Snitch touched her lip, with the dopey, blurry look in her eyes. That's *my fucking look*. *My* fucking lips. She's *my fucking girl*.

Fifteen minutes passed as they took paparazzi photos. I picked the skin at my thumb absently with my pointer finger, zoned in on them.

Be a good man.

Pick.

Honor your vows till the very end.

Pick.

Even if it kills you.

Pick.

Lottie left to go join her friends, but I stayed until Story excused herself, heading to the towering pecan fondant cupcake nightmare my mother had had specially designed for this.

I followed.

Feeling more like a predator than a man.

She reached for a turkey cupcake, and I stepped behind her body, acting like I was going to reach for the cranberry tarts just beyond her. She stiffened as my body came into contact with hers.

"Are you fucking him?" I growled into her ear.

"He *is* my husband," she said without looking at me.

I wanted to bite her.

Mark her.

If West fucked her, he'd still see *me*. All over her.

I stepped closer, pressing her into the table, jostling the tower of cupcakes.

"What are you doing?" she whispered, looking over her shoulder.

"Did you forget, little nun?" I dipped my head so my words vibrated against her neck. "I told you your sounds were mine."

I stepped closer until my thighs caged hers. It was already crossing the line coming to talk to her. What was one more step?

Her words were breathy. "I didn't forget. Maybe I just don't fucking care anymore."

I wanted to sink into her, into her soft skin and softer curls. Something about crossing lines, about being a good man, about not being my father, swirled around and got lost in her scent, one I hadn't smelled in too long.

"Bad nun. You're lucky you have my baby in you...I'll be gentle with your punishment." My teeth grazed the side of her neck. She lifted a hand as if to push me off, and I took it, slamming it back on the table, covering it with mine. "Keep your hands on the fucking table, Snitch."

"Can he make you scream the way I do?" I ran my hand up and down her bare arm, the pads of my fingers tracing her goose bumps. "Can he make your eyes roll back like I do?" I whispered against her earlobe. "Can he make you come the way I do?"

Her head fell back on my shoulder, and my chest collapsed. I lost focus. I lost sight of everything. The game I was playing vanished.

Goose bumps—fucking goose bumps—sprang up on my arms. This is *my girl*. When our eyes locked, there was only raw emotion. I trailed my knuckle from her shoulder up to her cheek.

"There's my girl." The words slipped from my lips.

And then she blinked and shoved me off. She looked

left and right, seeing if we had an audience. I grabbed her bicep before she could leave.

Don't fucking kiss him again.

It was on the tip of my tongue to growl it.

Those are *my* lips. Lips that ensnared me. Enslaved me. Of all the things fucking *West* could be doing, it's his lips on her that drive me the most insane.

Her nostrils flared as fury rose in her eyes. *Fuck,* I wanted her to do something—*say* anything, but she only pushed past me, presumably to go back to West, to continue to take their damn *lucky kiss* photos.

———

I felt like I was possessed as I watched West and Story get their photos taken on the second floor. I couldn't think or reason. I was just pure emotion, pure instinct. Rationally, I knew I had to stay away from her.

It was the only way she could be happy.

But West's hand was on her waist, wrinkling deep emerald with his tight grip.

Her head was on his shoulder, curls falling in tight spirals down the dark fabric.

"They look good together. Maybe I was too quick to judge."

Lottie was with me, but I couldn't stop thinking about Story. The bright golds and ambers in the room suddenly seemed rusted. I smelled the smoke of the tapered candles that had burned out and hadn't yet been relit by a servant.

West and Story faced each other for another fucking kiss.

My heart stopped.

Pretty sure.

I had reasons for keeping my distance, great fucking reasons. They all seemed pretty inconsequential as West's red lips collided with hers.

"Grayson!"

I snapped out of it. Lottie placed her hand on mine, and I realized I'd been picking at my lip. That was the copper taste in my mouth.

"Do you want to go back? I think we've well put our time in."

"Why is your mother up there?"

She followed my line of sight. "I don't know? Probably giving some kind of interview about her *lucky* son. Grayson? Let's go back."

I didn't like the look in her eyes. I didn't like how close Story was to the two-floor staircase. One misplaced foot and she could go tumbling down it.

Mrs. du Lac took a step toward Story, and I saw the clandestine heel she slid beneath Story's ankle. She didn't so much as look at Story, and if I hadn't been paying attention, no one would have noticed.

That was all I needed to see. I was running up the steps, ignoring Lottie calling at my back, sprinting until my lungs gave out. I yanked Story's wrist, pulling her violently toward me just as Mrs. du Lac lifted her foot.

Story fell into my chest, and I anchored her. Safe.

Then the paparazzi turned their attention to us.

Story looked at me, eyes wide. "What the hell are you doing?"

What could I say?

Your mother-in-law was about to trip you down the stairs because she suspected you're pregnant with my baby?

"Gray." Lottie's voice was at my heels, harsh. "Let her go."

My heart wouldn't stop pounding. If I'd been a second late, Story would be at the bottom of the staircase. Reluctantly, I let her go.

"She looked like she was about to slip," I explained.

"You saw that from how many feet away?" Lottie asked.

If I explained what I saw, I'd have to say *why* I knew Mrs. du Lac had done that, and spill the beans about Story.

I wiped my hand across my mouth as Mrs. du Lac dragged her sparkling gold champagne to her lips, a warm smile on her face, attention elsewhere. Suddenly I wasn't so sure.

Maybe I *hadn't* seen what I thought I saw.

Mrs. du Lac walked away, disappearing into the crowd.

"Let me go." Story's raspy yet firm voice pulled me out of the moment, and I looked down, realizing I still clutched her in my arms.

Let her go.

The rational voice in my head repeated it, but I couldn't. I couldn't fucking let go. It felt right to hold her against my chest, to wrap my arms around her and protect her from this fucking world.

"Grayson," Lottie said in an insistent tone.

Paparazzi were furiously flashing photos, and our guests were taking their own. I knew I was feeding into the gossip we were desperately trying to kill.

It was like ripping off skin, but I released her. The distrust in her eyes was a shard of glass in my heart. She looked at the floor, cheeks heated, and quickly moved to leave.

"Story."

She kept walking, disappearing into the crowd.

"Are you planning on getting her a bodyguard anytime soon?" I said, focusing my adrenaline on West. "A girl? It's been almost a month."

A slugging, torturous month.

West grabbed a champagne bottle meant for a table off a passing server's tray and patted my arm. "Don't worry, Crowne. I'm her husband. Why don't you focus on my sister?"

I ground my jaw as West poured champagne from the bottle into his mouth.

"Do you even give a shit that your wife is being gossiped about all over the fucking internet?" I'd seen firsthand how dangerous that shit was with my sisters.

West shrugged. "She's a big girl."

I grabbed him by the collar. "Are you keeping track of the death threats?" I'm sure she was getting more than what I saw. I could only keep track of the public ones, and those were a lot.

West laughed. "You sound worried."

"I am. She's the fucking moon, and there are people out there who will snuff her out for no other reason than to bring her into their dark."

West leaned closer, so when he spoke, only I could hear. "You know, I don't know why you're so obsessed, Crowne. I already took her virgin cunt. She was so tight too."

Was he really going to brag about his rape? I fisted the fabric between my fingers and bit my top lip so I didn't pound this asshole's face into the marble.

"But she was always so eager to please." Even though I was still holding his collar, West poured champagne into his mouth, a mocking gleam in his eye.

All right.

I quirked my neck, then swung.

"Grayson!" I heard Lottie calling for me to stop, but I was on top of him in a flash, pounding into his face until the blood from my knuckles mixed with his.

I think Lottie continued to yell at me.

I'm sure she did.

But I was too far gone.

I didn't stop until Lottie ripped us apart. I stumbled back and West laughed. He was fucked up. He hadn't fought back, and that twisted inside me.

I didn't feel bad.

I felt...discomfort. I had pummeled his face until it shone with blood, but I didn't feel any better, and West just laughed.

"What's so fucking funny?" I asked.

"I won." He laughed harder through his bloody teeth.

"West, just go," Lottie implored. "Please, just go."

West grabbed another bottle of champagne. "Happy Thanksgiving, bro." He disappeared out the kitchen doors, chuckling.

"You don't think it's fucking weird?" I turned to Lottie. "He hasn't been cut off. And he just up and married Snitch when—" *When she got pregnant,* I almost said. "After our marriage. He's a fucking snake. This whole family is."

"This whole *family*?" Lottie's mouth dropped—fully dropped—and tears blurred her wide brown eyes.

I realized what I'd said—what I'd implied—too late.

That my wife was a snake.

I raked my hands through my hair.

"Lottie, that's not..." I rubbed my forehead. "Shit."

I was messing everything up. I'm losing my shit. I know what I saw. I know what her mother did. I don't know what the fuck West meant by he *won*, but I know it's not fucking good.

And the one person I could have confided in, is now the one person I can't tell anything.

Lottie's lips were scrunched, her jaw tight, like she was about to explode with something. But after a moment, she exhaled.

A soft, serene smile came over her lips.

"The only one who has a problem with this marriage is *you*," she said.

She turned on her heel, leaving me in the aftermath of paparazzi and eager spectators. I didn't realize my mother had joined me in the mess until her too soft voice drifted into my ear.

"You swore to me you would let her go."

I jerked my head, finding her staring at the crowd, working her diamond pendant between her fingers. She slowly found my eyes.

"Do I need to dig that man's grave up?"

I recoiled. "Mom—"

"I'm trying to *protect you*. This world has taken my husband. My daughter. I won't let it take you."

"She'll be gone before Christmas," I gritted.

"Good."

TWENTY-NINE

GRAY

Hours after the party, I lay in bed, staring at the ceiling.

I'm the reason we're all in this fucking mess.

I alone.

"Grayson?" I lifted my eyes, finding Lottie.

She had changed from her soft golden gown into a Crowne Hall maid's uniform.

"What are you doing?" I croaked.

I had no words, but Lottie didn't wait for them. She approached me, eyes downcast, and fell to her knees before me.

"Did you ever fuck her in her uniform?" Lottie asked.

I dragged a hand across my lips. Now I can't stop picturing it. Fucking Snitch in that dark uniform. Getting it as fucked and messed up as we were.

"Lottie, this is fucked up."

Lottie dropped to her knees, small fingers going for my zipper. "Has she ever sucked you off?"

The memory of Snitch's lips on my cock blasted through me, making me hard.

Can I kiss you like this?

Lottie's lips met my cock. "How does she suck you?"

The way only Snitch can. As if she can't get enough of my cock, like it's her favorite fucking treat. With an addicting combination of innocence and bottomless lust in her walnut eyes that make me want to watch her for hours.

You were my first everything else. My first kiss. My first blow job.

I threw my head back on a groan at the memory of Snitch's confession and Lottie took that as encouragement, sucking me harder.

I promised on our wedding night that I would be Lottie's husband. A good man. A man who loves his wife. A man who only thinks about his wife.

I could come like this, in Lottie's soft mouth.

Except as Lottie sucked me deeper inside of her, I thought of Snitch.

Maybe this was all I'd ever get again. All I *deserved*. A twisted, dark facsimile of my addiction. My wife and I could pretend this was an okay thing to do.

Everything you do with Lottie, West gets to do to me.

But if West put his mouth anywhere near her cunt I will rip his throat out.

FUCK.

I grabbed Lottie by her bicep, and dragged her off the floor. The veins in my neck throbbed like my cock, and my voice was raw and warbled.

"Go change."

My heart pounded; sweat beaded my neck.

She shrugged me off with violence. "I saw you watching her. You haven't stopped watching her."

I pushed the hair out of my face.

I needed air.

I needed to get out of this bridal suite that was becoming a coffin.

"Are you leaving again?" Lottie asked.

I looked back at her, in her fucking maid's outfit, but she didn't want my response. She just shook her head and disappeared up the stairs.

STORY

"There's my Angel," West said when I returned with the ice.

I sat down, pressed it against his swollen, bruising face. We sat in silence, the ice melting cold through the fabric. I'd barely had a second to breathe all night, jumping from one drama to the next. Now that I had a moment, my mind wandered.

Did my mom ever feel this way? Put in an impossible position. Keep my dignity or deny my baby a father. Give her a father, live in shame.

Pretty sure I know what she chose.

I don't want my baby to have the life I had. A mother who sold her pride. A father who didn't acknowledge you in public, if at all.

I glanced at West, who was staring back.

When I eyed a new book on the nightstand.

"What's that?"

West pulled away from the ice, reaching for the leather-bound thing. He handed it to me. It was a book of poetry.

"I seem to recall you and your uncle reading Keats every Thanksgiving."

"You remember that?"

"You were mine before you were his, Angel."

Every time he spoke like that made it harder to remind myself the reason I was here: to fucking leave.

"What are you getting out of this marriage, West?" I asked. "You already know about me. My cards are on the table."

"If you'd let me kiss you, *really* kiss you, without some fucking tradition as our chaperone, you wouldn't be asking that question."

I lowered the ice seeping through the cloth, wetting my fingers. I *can't* let him kiss me. I...I liked it too much.

"You never wanted to kiss me before." I looked down, fiddling with the ice.

He lifted my chin with his knuckle, forcing my eyes to meet his warm ones.

"I was afraid."

Afraid?

"West du Lac isn't supposed to love a servant, Story."

I felt the wrinkle in my brow. Then what changed? Before I could ask, West spoke.

"I want to get you a bodyguard."

"Why?"

"I am fucking worried about you, Angel. You're the moon, and some people out there want to snuff you out for no other reason than to bring you into the dark."

I blinked, not expecting such...nice words from him. It almost sounded like when we were kids. He caressed a knuckle down my cheek. He leaned closer, as if he would kiss me. When I didn't move to kiss him, he didn't go any further.

"Story Hale, do you think you could ever stay with me?"

I dropped the ice and it clattered to the floor. "What?"

"You're it for me. I want more than a few months. I want to have babies with you. I want to have a life with you."

Babies.

A life.

"I..." I stood up. "The ice. I need to get more."

I don't like West. West is a means to an end.

I kept repeating it as I went to the kitchen to gather ice.

I grabbed a cloth, filling it with more ice. There's a part of me...a part I promised to erase, and it won't stop scraping at my chest with the words *what if?*

What if I really let West pick up the pieces?

Grayson's cold voice drifted over my shoulder. "We have servants for that."

I startled and the ice fell out of the cloth with a stuttering clunk into the sink. I turned, facing Grayson, locking with his piercing blue eyes, gripping the sink for support. My heart thumped. The air suddenly thick. Muggy. Hot.

"What are you doing?"

"Getting ice. For my husband. The one you beat up."

"You're getting him fucking ice?" He leaned against the doorframe, arms folded, one leg propped behind him.

I went to the freezer, trying to ignore Grayson, but it's like trying to ignore a storm. It breathes and consumes your air.

"I'm sorry I'm not the black-and-white person you want me to be. For three years, he was my best friend before he was the guy who raped me. I loved him. He did something awful, but I didn't stop loving him, even though I knew I should, even though I wanted to. You should understand that."

"Are you comparing me to him?" he growled.

"I'm saying I don't have the answers you want. I can't make myself stop feeling something just because I know I should."

"Do you still fucking love him?" Grayson stepped closer until only a sliver of darkness separated us.

I was assaulted with Gray's features in the dark, the messy, bedhead blond. His cruel features softened in the shadows. I missed him at night. I missed *us* in the night.

Before, I'd always been alone, and now that I'd had someone to share the loneliness with, I was bereft without Grayson.

I was afraid it was impossible to love *anyone* after Grayson Crowne. But after what he did to me, he didn't get to know that.

"Yes," I lied.

His eyes narrowed. "You're lying to me, little nun."

"You should go back to your wife, Grayson Crowne."

"You should go back to your husband, Story Hale."

But when he took a step to me, I didn't move. Tingles rose along my shoulders, little needle pricks.

Wrong.

Heady.

An excitement you get when you know you shouldn't do something.

Love is a smoke raised with the fume of sighs.

I spun away from him, facing the sink. Silence spread and spread. I stared at the porcelain as the ice melted.

Then I felt him. The hard packs of his pecs and abs, pressing into me, forcing my gut to bite the sink. We both breathed together, jagged and hot, his exhalations warming my neck, as if we were riding the high of the tension that had been threading between us for *months*.

Then he gripped my thighs, dragging his hands up and down. Feeling. Digging. Bruising.

My head fell forward as a sigh escaped my lips.

"Tell me whose baby is inside you. Tell me who fucking owns you."

"It isn't *you*." I lifted my hand, flashing him my ring. "It won't ever be you."

He tangled his fist in my hair, jerking my head back so I had to watch when he ripped it off my finger, tossing it to the ground with a clank. His blue eyes locked with mine as if he wanted me to feel the pain in them. Then he pulled my finger to his lips before I could speak, biting it.

A gasp tore from my lips, and then my senses came back.

I tried to shove him off, but he pressed me harder against the sink. His hands slid up my thigh, under my shorts, feeling the curve of my bare ass.

He froze when he realized I was without any panties.

"Dirty little nun," he groaned. "Tell me to stop."

"Why?" I gritted. "So you can feel good about yourself? When really you're forcing me to hold all of our sins?"

The muscle in his jaw popped. All the air in my lungs vanished as he slid his hand out from under my shorts and over the fabric. I swallowed a whimper.

I'd wanted him to go under...what the fuck is wrong with me?

"My wife just sucked me off before I came to you," he growled. "Does it turn you on knowing you're getting sloppy seconds, Snitch?"

His grip in my hair tightened, forcing me to arch. I swallowed my groan, refusing to give him anything even as my legs turned to jelly.

"Because you're fucking *wet*, little nun." He licked my ear. "I think it does. Do you like the idea of cheating on your husband?"

He only cupped me over my shorts...yet my vision blurred.

"Do you like cheating on your wife?" I hissed back. "You're the one with a hard-on." My eyes flashed, darting to his hard cock. I licked my lips and let my thighs fall open just a little. He grinned.

He released his grip in my hair and dropped to his knees. The sudden loss of him was so stark I gripped the sink to keep from slipping.

He slid his hands up and down my thighs. He was so gentle and soft, lingering on my bare knee, thumb achingly tender.

I probably should've known that his words would be harsh.

"You're gonna let West touch you now, huh? That was the deal, whatever Lottie does to me, West does to you." His hands stopped just beneath the crease in my groin, pressing the skin until it blanched. "This is fucking mine."

Then he bit, hard.

Some twisted part of me said this was fine.

It was just a bite.

"Let him touch you." His voice was softer now, deeper, his eyes half-lidded. "He'll see, Snitch. You're mine. You will *always* be mine." He dragged his thumb across the wound. "I bet if I pushed aside these whore shorts of yours, I'd find a wet pussy."

Our eyes locked, a second splintered into thousands. I shoved him off with my knee.

"You'll never know. Fuck yourself. Touch yourself. Get off on the idea of me. Because that's all you'll ever get again, Grayson Crowne."

His eyes flashed. "Fuck a thousand men. Marry a hundred thousand. Leave. Run away. I'll find you."

And yet *he* wouldn't ever marry me.

"You want me to tell you the truth? I hate you." I meant it, too. "You only fucked me because your wife told you to. You promised your mother you would never talk to me." His eyebrows shot up, but I kept going. "I hate you, Grayson Crowne. I hate your lies and I hate *you.*"

I hated him.

For tossing me away.

For never letting me go.

For not having the courage to keep me.

Something broke in his eyes, but he hid it too quickly. "You haven't even begun to hate me, Story."

"No, *you* haven't even begun to hate me, Grayson Crowne—"

My voice faded into nothing as icy-cold fear seized my gut. Blood dripped down my thighs. Not a lot...but enough. Had he bit me too hard? Then I realized my shorts were stained red.

"Is that blood?" My voice rose in fear, all of the earlier fire dead. "Why am I bleeding?" My voice got higher and higher.

"Hey. Hey." Grayson stood up and gripped my cheeks between his hands, pulling my eyes to his. "Everything is going to be fine. You're my girl, Story. I won't let anything happen to you."

THIRTY

GRAY

At the private hospital, I hadn't let go of Story's hand. She seemed to be deep in thought but hadn't spoken a word. This was my fault.

Again.

I wasn't good for her.

"I'm sorry I called you the bad B-movie version of James Dean," she blurted.

I raised a brow. "You didn't call me that."

"I did in my head."

More silence. More me wondering if she'd lost our baby, if I'd caused it.

"I'm sorry I—"

"Snitch?"

She lifted her head, and I leaned forward, thumbing her lip. Her breathing slowed. That calmed me.

"You can go," she whispered. "You've done more than enough."

Annoyance flickered, but all I said was, "Do you want me to go?"

She shook her head, and it eased the tension in my gut.

More seconds passed. I stroked her chin, holding her hand with my other.

"Maybe she's..." Snitch started. "Gone and this will all be over and you can go back to how it should be."

"Is that what you think I fucking want?" I growled, my grip on her chin tightening.

The doctor came in at that exact moment, so she didn't have to answer. But it ate at me. Did she think I didn't want this?

I wanted to clear all the obstacles in her way. In *our* way. But each day it became clearer and clearer... *I* was the obstacle. My life. My fucking family. Me.

As the doctor began to tell me to leave, that this was only for family, I stood up.

"I'm the father."

Snitch glanced at me, a look in her eyes I couldn't decipher. I stood by the bed, tall, shoulders square, one hand above her, letting everyone know they'd have to go through me to get to her. Even the doctor.

"What's wrong?" Snitch finally asked the doctor, voice thready. I squeezed the chair above her head.

She smiled. "Nothing. Bleeding during the beginning is perfectly normal."

I exhaled. Normal.

Normal.

As the doctor talked about how her pregnancy was progressing and what she needed to do, I listened, committing to memory everything.

When she left, I looked down and found Snitch staring at me.

I took my seat next to her bed wordlessly, eyes still locked. I grabbed her hand. This felt routine.

Normal.

I wanted that.

"You should go back to your wife," she croaked.

I flinched and dropped her hand. Barely perceptible. But I knew Snitch would notice, notice how I'd been slammed back to reality.

"I've been thinking about that," I said after a moment. "I see no reason why I can't be there for you."

She blinked out a scoff.

"Am I supposed to just let you go, Snitch? Let you live married to my brother-in-law with my baby. How the fuck do I do that?"

"You did this to us. All I can think is that I wasn't good enough to marry. I wasn't good enough to have your child—"

I gripped her face tight, but not enough to bruise. "Stop saying that. This world is not meant for you, Story Hale. It's not meant for our child."

She's perfect. She's innocent but has miles of depth. She can't be bought. She's everything they want to destroy.

Then as easily as I had been trained to do my entire life, I mopped my emotions away and sat back, shoulders straight, and said, "I have a proposal. I'll be there for you. Take you to the doctor. Do everything you need. Be everything you need."

She stared at me for so long, her mossy eyes gleaming under the fluorescent lights.

"West can be that for me."

I saw black. Fucking *West* taking care of my child? I didn't realize I was clenching my jaw until the muscle ached. I leaned forward until I could see the flecks of green in her stony hazel eyes.

"West can never be that for you."

"How is this going to work? You cross lines, Grayson. *We* cross lines. It won't work."

Snitch wanted to be free, to not hide. To be with me, I'd have to hide her, hide the baby.

I couldn't give Lottie a happy marriage. In the end, I had wed her as she cried under her veil.

But I would do this, I'll give Snitch a happily ever after.

Just without me.

She would live far away from Crowne Hall with its darkness and ghosts. She would live someplace sunny and bright.

I will fight for her.

I will save her.

From me.

"We'll just be friends."

STORY

I laughed, but it was choking and hollow. Grayson Crowne and I had never worked as friends.

"What?" He gripped my face. "Why are you laughing?"

"We can't be friends, Grayson."

"Why?" He seemed genuinely upset that I'd pointed out what should have been so obvious. His brows caved.

I can think of a billion reasons. Because I like it too much when you say you're the father. Because I'm trying to build a life, a good life, a *respectable* life for our daughter, and with you I'm...bad, shameful.

"You know me," he said, voice raised. "I know you. You

know the darkest parts of me. You know what makes me bleed. Isn't that friendship?" he demanded.

I couldn't speak.

"I want to hold your hair back when you have morning sickness," he continued. "I want to satisfy your weird cravings. I want to rub your feet. I want..." He broke off. "I can't be your husband, but I'll be your everything else. I'll be your protector, your guardian. I'll make sure you're cared for. You always have everything you need. I'll be your best friend."

It was so, so tempting. I wanted to give in to him. Let him be there for me. But he *couldn't* be there for me, not really. We were once again in the dark. Hidden. A secret.

I looked up at Grayson, the ninety-degree angle of his chin, the determined, concerned way he listened.

And my chest sank.

My diamond ring glared back at me—I'd barely had time to grab it off the floor before Grayson rushed me here—and his wedding band glimmered under the fluorescent light.

I felt protected and safe...by someone who didn't belong to me.

We didn't belong to each other.

I couldn't let my child be born into that.

"You can't give me everything I need," I whispered. "It's impossible."

He balked. "I'm Grayson fucking—"

"Crowne," I finished.

For some stupid, irredeemable reason, I still needed the one thing Grayson Crowne couldn't give me.

Grayson Crowne.

His blue eyes cracked. "Let me fix what I broke, Story."

My heart filled and broke at the same time. Only months ago, I'd been in the same position.

"Let me stay with you during the pregnancy. Let me get you through this safely, let me get you out of the position I put you in, let me *save you*, Story. I won't be able to live with myself otherwise."

Tears were hot and scratchy in my throat.

I wanted us to be different.

I wanted to aim for a happily ever after.

But this was all I would ever get with Grayson Crowne. A goodbye.

"I want you to have your happily ever after, Story. Out of the shadows. You and our child." It sounded like a love confession, but at this point, I knew better. I braced for the crushing blow to follow.

"I'll get you out. I'll get you away."

"Away." I choked on the word.

So he can live happily with Lottie.

"You said you would have to be tied down. You said you couldn't ever let me go. Why is now different? Every time you try and let me go you *fail*."

"For you, Snitch, I'd handcuff myself to the bed."

"Grayson, I'm not joking."

A small, sad smile. "I'll never let you go, Snitch. I'll always be there. You just won't see me."

I felt broken and dead.

I sighed a jagged, cutting sigh.

He thumbed the edge of my jaw. "Just give me one thing."

My eyes found his.

"I get to be in the delivery room."

I paled. "What? No. I...I don't even know what I'm

going to do yet. I might give the baby up." The thought made me sick.

It just felt right to keep it.

But it was also wrong, right? Because what kind of *life* was it to bring a baby into this fucked-up family with no love and all the wrong kinds of affection. It was exactly what I'd grown up in. A mom who didn't know how to say *no* to the men who always left her. A dad who wouldn't recognize me as their child.

Grayson physically tensed.

His jaw.

His neck.

His shoulders.

But he just took a breath, and said, "You'll still have to have the fucking baby, Story."

And with those words, the elephant stomped into the room. I was going to show soon.

I got sweaty just thinking about it.

Grayson gripped my face tight. "Fuck, let me be there, *please*. No games, no contract, no bullshit. Be my friend."

All the air in my lungs left. Vanished. I can't breathe.

My eyes met his.

"Friend," I repeated, skepticism pricking my tongue, but I whispered, "Okay."

No sooner had I rasped my acceptance, than his eyes darkened, the lids drooped. His grip on my jaw tightened as his eyes dropped to my lips. Grayson pressed his forehead so tight to mine I thought it might bruise.

"Just friends," he rasped.

He lifted his head.

"Nothing changes," he said, standing straight, leaving me to deal with the aftermath of that forehead touch. "Tomorrow we'll come back and see the doctor together."

"*Tomorrow* a Corrosion of Crownes arrives."

"A what?"

"Crownes from all over the world are descending upon the Hall for the Holidays, and you want us to just slip out and go to a doctor's appointment without being noticed?"

Ignoring me, he grabbed my phone and said, "Get dressed. I'll take you home."

"What are you doing with my phone?" I asked as he left the room.

"Adding my number. I should have done it months ago."

He shut the door.

I slowly got dressed.

I could be friends with Grayson Crowne. I could do this.

But it wasn't until we got back to the midnight-darkened spires of Crowne Hall, that doubt sewed its way into my blood. Grayson got out of the town car and opened my door for me.

"Are you still going to want to help me if I stay with West?" I asked.

He paused with the door. "What the fuck does *West* have to do with this?"

"He's my husband."

He angled his head, bending so he could see me clearly and I had a good view of his piercing eyes.

"And I'm going to fucking fix that. I'm going to save you. Get you out."

Irritation wove in my veins. Save me? Why am I the only one who needs saving?

A black town car pulled up behind ours. Almost on instinct, we took a step back, blending into the great black shadows of Crowne Hall. The driver got out of the car and opened the sleek black door, as Grayson had done for me moments earlier.

A woman bent her head, getting out.

"If you save me from West," I whispered, "then I should save you from Lottie."

"It's not the same. You're trapped."

"I'm not trapped."

Grayson scoffed, as though what I'd just said was the most ridiculous thing.

I can leave any time.

Right?

But I couldn't stop thinking about West's proposal. His *real* proposal. Grayson was offering me a goodbye, and West was offering me a life.

"My mistake," I said softly. "I know you chose her. But if you're not trapped, Grayson, then neither am I."

In my periphery, I saw he'd snapped his head to mine, but I watched the woman who'd just arrived. Her hands were warmed in a fur muff. Her dress long and flowing behind her. Her auburn hair in ringlets down her back. It was minutes past midnight, and she looked ready for a ball.

Josephine St. Germaine.

The bastard Crownes didn't arrive with the rest of the cavalcade, and neither did their mother. They always arrive the night before, because for one month out of the year, they slide smoothly alongside the other Crownes, as if they were always a perfect fit.

Josephine saw me watching her, and her red lips tilted ever so slightly. Then she turned back toward the hall, dipping her chin and heading inside Crowne Hall.

"Are you going to tell your wife?" I asked, eyes on Josephine disappearing inside the Hall.

"Are you going to tell your husband?" Grayson countered.

My eyes wandered back to his.

"Just friends," Grayson said again.

"Friends," I echoed.

The very first Crowne had just arrived for the holidays.

The late Charles Crowne's mistress.

THIRTY-ONE

STORY

I woke up to more texts from Grayson than I could count.

How are you feeling?
    Did you have morning sickness?
    What do you want for breakfast?
    Snitch.
    Answer your fucking phone.
    What do you want for breakfast?
    I'm coming over if you don't answer your fucking phone.
    I'm coming over.

That last one was sent less than five minutes ago, so I quickly sent a reply that I was *fine* and he was insane, and I went to shower.

Today was the first official start of the holidays. In

less than an hour, the first round of Crownes would arrive. Cousins, aunts, all the others twice removed. They would be shepherded to corners of the house, and servants would be expected to unpack and cater to their whims.

I dropped my head against the tile as water ran down my back. The farther away you got from wearing the title of Crowne, the *worse* your behavior. It was like they were all trying to compensate.

I turned the shower off and wrapped a fluffy towel around my body. This mirror never fogged, and a weird part of me missed swiping it.

I guess I had rich people problems.

I also had more pregnancy problems...I think. I was unusually *horny*, and my entire body ached with it. I left the bathroom to go get dressed, not only for lunch but for my doctor's appointment.

I stared at my empty closet as my stomach caved in. I was missing my dresses, the ones Abigail had stolen from her mother. All that remained were my original nun outfits, as Grayson liked to call them.

My towel fell to the floor. I walked into my closet and ripped off an empty hanger, throwing it to the ground.

I had to buy the Crownes presents, every single one of them, including cousins I didn't know the names of.

I ripped another velvety soft hanger off the softly lit walls. Empty. All. Empty.

I dropped to the floor amid broken and empty hangers, focused on breathing, on not passing out. I knew who'd taken them.

The servants.

They were still trying to drive me out.

I needed to buy a whole new wardrobe. I'd need to

somehow hide all of it so the servants didn't see, or I'd just keep losing money.

I'd have nothing when I left. I wanted to save the money for my baby. Nothing for a new life...

A sound startled me out of my thoughts. I looked up, finding West watching me. He was in a burgundy suit with a dark-blue bow tie that somehow worked, in a way only a rich person could pull off. And I was...naked.

I was fucking naked.

I hurriedly reached for my discarded towel.

"How long have you been standing there?" I asked, scrambling to my feet.

"I knocked. Thought I heard you. Sorry, Angel." His brow furrowed at the mess I'd made in my closet.

"I..." I held out a finger, as if I'd find my point. "I, uh..."

"The servants are fucking with you," he said easily. He bent down, picking up my discarded hangers, the pearls that had come flying off their handles when I'd broken them.

"West, you don't—"

"I want to help. Let me help."

I couldn't just sit and watch him clean up my mess, so I got down on my knees as well. Together we cleaned up the rest of my panic attack.

"Thanks," I said, once everything was piled up. "How did you know? About the servants?"

"I've seen plenty of servants fuck with each other back at the manor."

We were still on our hands and knees, facing each other. Wet hair had fallen across my eyes. One of my hands held my towel together, and the other kept me righted on the floor.

"They'd been nicer lately. I guess I just thought...I don't know I hoped they forgot about me."

"Firing one of them quiets them for a little, but in the long run, pisses them off," he said.

I wrinkled my brow. "But I haven't fired anyone."

"Angel..." He laughed, trailing off like I was missing something important, then West pushed my hair behind my ear. "Have you given any more thought to my offer?"

His offer...to give him a chance? A *real* chance?

"Don't let me interrupt." Grayson's icy voice pulled me out of my thoughts. I jerked my head in the direction of his voice, finding him in the doorway.

His eyes flamed, taking in me and West, on the floor, West's hand resting on my cheek. I felt like I'd been caught by a lover.

I stood. "What the hell?"

"Oh right," West said, getting to his feet. "Grayson is here. Something about...breakfast."

"In my closet?" I exclaimed, holding my towel tighter.

What was he doing? We were supposed to sneak out later to go to the doctor's. Key word being *sneak*.

Whatever fire had been in Grayson's eyes died, leaving them stony blue-silver. He rubbed the back of his neck, calm. "You were holding everyone up. That's fucking rude."

"Almost as rude as barging in on a woman changing?"

Grayson's jaw clenched like he wanted to say something; then with eyes like cut stone, calm, arrogant Grayson Crowne returned. He turned on his heel and left.

West raised his hands, backing out slowly.

Just friends. Just *friends*. I repeated it to myself over and over again. I could be friends with Grayson Crowne. He needed a friend. He didn't have any friends, not really.

I needed a friend.

I didn't have any.

I can do this. Just *friends*.

But when I saw Grayson Crowne in his dark gray suit, his hair messed like he hadn't slept, I knew I was fucked.

GRAY

Downstairs we held an informal reception for the first of my relatives who'd arrived in the morning, complete with live orchestra and brunch. It was the season for Meyer lemons, and my mother was throwing a fucking fit that we couldn't use them in everything on account of that small bother it would kill my wife.

I was grateful. Grateful I didn't have to eat a reminder of Snitch every five seconds.

Snitch was with West, who kept his arm around her as they talked with my aunt. My aunt Hetty always smelled like cigarettes and perfume, and was always somehow, someway, in need of money.

Hetty shoved her glass to Snitch.

Snitch took it, holding it with a furrow in her brow. My gut twisted in anger as I tamped down the urge to shove my aunt out of my fucking house.

Instead I grabbed the glass from Snitch and gave it back to my aunt.

She blinked, wide-eyed.

"Are you in the habit of pawning off your trash onto my guests?"

"She's...a servant?" Hetty looked at the way Snitch was dressed, confusion in her eyes. Abigail was supposed to get her more dresses. She'd come downstairs in a nun outfit. And, fuck, I missed those outfits.

I pulled out my phone, quickly texting, *Why are you dressed like a nun?*

Story pulled out her phone, and when she saw the text, her eyes widened; then she quickly put it away.

I quirked my neck to the side. I did not like that.

So I texted her again.

And again.

Her phone vibrated until everyone looked at her.

"Do you need to get that?" Lottie asked.

Snitch shot me a look. "No."

Lottie wound her arm around mine, her wedding ring glowing brighter under the chandelier.

Just friends.

Friends who freak the fuck out when their friends don't respond to their texts.

That's normal.

Maybe this morning was an overreaction. I feel outside of my skin when I'm not around her. It's not new that I don't sleep. What is new is the reason. I lay awake now thinking about Snitch. Worried about her. I don't like that I can't see her.

I wasn't sorry I showed up in her wing. I probably should be, but I'm not. When she didn't respond, I started thinking of worst-case scenarios. What if she was passed out again? What if she was bleeding? And on and on, all of them worse than the next, until my heart felt like it was going to burst through its chest.

The fact that she's pregnant with my kid just...I'm getting twisted thinking about it.

It doesn't feel right leaving her alone.

Snitch made some excuse about getting more to drink. I slid out of Lottie's grasp, eyes on her. "I'll be right back."

I followed her to the champagne tower.

"Is your phone broken?"

"I never thought I'd regret the day I gave Grayson Crowne my phone number," Story said, reaching for a scone. "This doesn't seem like very *friendly* behavior, Grayson."

"Friends check up on each other. Where are your clothes?"

Snitch paused. "Gone."

"What do you mean 'gone'?"

"It doesn't concern you."

I gripped her bicep, forcing her to face me. "I said I would help you with anything, Snitch. Day or night."

She shifted. "What happened to *keeping it a secret*? I was supposed to meet you secretly. Now what?" She looked over her shoulder, where West was consumed by the uncle who could start a five minute story and somehow take an hour to finish.

"You didn't answer my texts, Snitch."

"Well now we can't go to the doctor. If we're both missing it will look suspiciou—"

She broke off as I wiped a bit of the jam from her lips, licking it off my thumb. She followed the movement with her eyes. It was like the beginning. When I could kiss her only in pieces. In stolen moments.

"We should get you new clothes, Snitch," I said, voice rough. "But nothing like the ones my sister got you."

"What kind of clothes would Grayson Crowne approve of?" she asked, voice quiet, raspy.

Fuck.

I'd missed that voice; it said some of her walls had fallen down. I'd taken it for granted. Snitch had put up so many walls...so many thorns around her heart.

For a moment I pretended we were in a world where I could speak truthfully, and I looked her up and down.

"I like you best in nothing."

Her eyes widened as West wrapped his arm around her waist. "Fuck, I thought he would never finish his story. What are we talking about?"

"I need new clothes..." she said.

Her eyes burned into mine while I still pictured her naked. Wondered what her tits looked like now. If they still fit in my hand.

Friends don't picture their friends naked.

Story swallowed, her throat bobbing as though she saw into my mind, saw the dirty, dark thoughts.

"Great idea," West said. "Want to go now?"

"Now?" Story swiveled to West. "Can we skip brunch?"

I ground my teeth. Every time she turned away from me to West, I wanted to rip her to me. West tilted her chin up with his knuckle, and I fisted the drink in my hand.

"We can do whatever we want, Angel. I'm not going to let my wife go without some damn clothes."

Angel. Wife.

I took a deep breath through my nostrils.

Don't punch the brother-in-law.

Again.

"But..." She glanced at me. I saw the worry in her eyes, the uncertainty. No doubt wondering how we were going to get to the doctor's.

That was the least of my concerns, the easiest problem to solve.

West arched a brow.

"Sounds great."

She shot me a look as West carted her out of Crowne Hall.

My grip tightened on my whiskey.

I want to be the one to take her. To provide for her. To give her everything—

Crash.

"Grayson!" Lottie gasped.

I looked at my palm, the pieces of glass now embedded in it from the flimsy crystal glass my mother insisted on using.

A few of my distant relatives looked over, no doubt hungry for some gossip to sustain them. Lottie grasped my arm, taking us out of the hall.

She held my bleeding hand in her palm.

"It's fine," I said. "I've had worse."

"I'm worried about you," she said.

About *me?*

"Lottie—"

"You don't want me. I get it. But someone needs to take care of you, and she can't." Before I could respond, Lottie continued, "Stay here. I'll go get you a bandage."

THIRTY-TWO

STORY

It was like no clothing store I'd ever been to. For starters, no one else was there. Just a suede couch and spotlit mirrors surrounding us. I didn't even see any clothes.

I turned to West. "How do we...shop?"

His lip quirked up a little, in on some secret I didn't know. Then they appeared, the women—or *clones*, I should say. All dressed in the same form-fitted eggplant uniform with their hair pulled back in a tight bun, the only difference among them their hair colors. Blonde, brunette, and darker blonde.

"Mr. du Lac," said the blonde one, who appeared to be their leader by the way she stood at the tip of the triangle. "Good to see you again."

"We need daytime, nighttime, evening wear." He rubbed his forehead, sparing me a glance. "We need everything."

The changing room was as large as my bedroom, with a

couch and table. Nothing like the cramped cubicles I used to change in. The women came in with me and helped me get dressed, the same as I had done for years with the Crownes and Lottie.

The first outfit they slipped me into was a satin number similar to the one Abigail had stolen for me. When I came out, West's eyes narrowed on my bare shoulders, on my chest. He turned to the woman behind me with a smile.

"Perfect."

I shifted.

It didn't feel like me at all, and a spearing thought stabbed me: Grayson would have hated it.

We did this for over an hour. Without showing any emotion, the clones stripped me and dressed me, stripped me and dressed me, until we finally found one. It was a camel dress with a straight neckline that covered my collarbone and capped my shoulders.

They were getting ready to send me out, and I stopped them.

"We don't...we'll just set this aside. I like it."

They ripped me out of that camel dress, and I was thrown into another one West liked. Then they tried on jacket after jacket. At least it was winter and the jackets would cover me.

When we finally finished, my heart was in my throat.

"We'll take it all," West said.

The blondest clone smiled. "We'll get started on tailoring."

West opened his wallet.

"I have money. I can pay." I was sure a wardrobe like that would cost at least in the hundreds of thousands, but I did have the money now.

West gave me a look like I'd just slapped him in the

face. He handed a black card to one of the girls, and she disappeared.

Then it was silence.

I swallowed the lump in my throat at being cared for. At *West* being the one to do it.

"Why are you being so nice to me?" I asked quietly.

"I'm trying to win you back, Angel." He wrapped his arm around my waist, dragging me closer. His other hand came to my neck as he dipped his head, shadowing our faces.

"How am I doing?" he whispered against my lips.

Butterflies sprang in my stomach without consent.

"Um—"

He crashed his lips on mine, cutting me off.

I was so surprised I didn't push him away.

His lips were warm and soft, and he gripped my neck with just the right amount of pressure. I realized this was the first time I'd ever kissed him, *really* kissed him, not for show, not for some stupid tradition.

It was like I'd fallen into some twisted, dark Victorian novel. Kissing this rogue for the first time as my husband.

My gut twisted, though. It hurt. Something sliced with each clever swipe of his tongue, because I felt like only *Grayson's* lips should be there.

And it felt like I was cheating on myself, on a promise I'd made the day he broke all of ours—

West broke the kiss suddenly, searching my eyes, a wrinkle in his smooth, chestnut brow. Then the wrinkle vanished as if he'd answered some question as two black cars pulled up to the curb. I fixed on them, a question in my eyes.

West pushed aside my curls. "I'll meet you back at the house. Emergency at the office."

He opened the door for me, ushering me into the car. After I was seated, he kept the door open, lingering, humor in his eyes that made my gut flip. It was...brutal.

"I don't mind you thinking about him."

"W-what? I wasn't thinking—"

"I like a good chase," he cut me off, slamming the door.

West drove away in his car, my gut gnawing.

That was wrong, but maybe it was the *wrongness* that gave power to the butterflies in my stomach

My driver turned to look at me over one arm. "To New York, Mrs. du Lac?"

I wrinkled my brow. "New York?" But the moment the question left my lips, I'd answered it. That was where the ob-gyn was.

I'll take care of it.

And somehow, Grayson had.

I sank back into the leather as the matte black partition rose between us. I lifted a hand to my lips.

What was I doing? I don't want to make these mistakes again. I don't want to be the person who went back to the men who hurt her. The girl everyone is screaming at in the horror movie.

I'd just kissed my husband for the first time, but was on my way to meet the father of my child.

THIRTY-THREE

STORY

Since the ob-gyn was in New York City, it was a bit of a drive to get there. I stared out the tinted window at the pretty lights donning the trees decorating the medians.

This was supposed to be a friendship.

I couldn't help but think...friends didn't drive in two separate cars to a private, sworn-to-secrecy ob-gyn.

Friends.

The car came to a stop, and I was ushered inside by Grayson's security. I had sunglasses on and a hat, the collar of my coat pulled. I looked like the girls I saw in magazines. Magazines that photographed Abigail and put Gemma and Gray on the covers.

Grayson and I couldn't be seen together, not until we were in the room. My gut sank deeper.

Friends.

We were friends.

I pushed away the icky feeling that I was a thing to be

hidden. Something to hide in the dark, in the cracks, in the places people didn't want to see.

I was his friend.

He was helping me.

And then I would leave.

I would come out of my hiding place for good.

As the elevator dinged and I stepped into a luxurious room that looked more like a penthouse than a doctor's office, I ignored the part of me that said...*you've said that before.* Over and over, I said I would leave while instead I became like glue.

"I'm—" I started to speak to an auburn-haired young woman behind an oval desk taking up half the room.

"We know who you are." She gestured for me to take a seat.

The place was eerily empty.

On purpose, I'm sure.

I pushed past it.

Did she know me?

The Cinderella of Crowne Hall.

Or...The Stepsister Slut.

It ate at me. I didn't know who they saw me as now. Who *I* saw me as.

Only a few moments later, another woman dressed in pale lavender scrubs came out of a door. She saw me and smiled. "Mrs. du Lac."

Oh right, I was her now too.

I stood up off the soft couch, grasping my purse and following her, but pausing at the receptionist.

"Can I take one?" I pointed at a porcelain bowl of suckers. She nodded warmly and I took one, following the nurse into another well-decorated room. Still no sign of Grayson. I was beginning to wonder if he was really going to show.

They directed me to get changed.

I pulled on the nicest, softest hospital gown I'd ever worn, then sat on a pale lilac leather patient's bed.

When the door creaked open behind me, I assumed it was the nurse returning to get my vitals. Grayson shut the door behind him with a soft click.

His brows caved. "Why do you look so surprised?"

I thought maybe you weren't coming back.

I shrugged. "No reason."

He came to me and pushed aside my hair, eyes searching, a look in them I didn't want to read.

"What's with the sucker?"

They're my need for you incarnate.

Both satisfying yet leaving me with a deep, aching Grayson-shaped hole in my stomach.

"Skipped brunch," I rasped. "Remember?"

He looked to the side, brow furrowing. "I should have brought you something."

That's when I noticed his hand was bandaged. I gasped, grabbing it. "What happened to your hand?"

It was a moment before he responded. He just stared at me, a look in his eyes that had me holding my breath.

Finally he said, "I guess I held on when I should've let go." Before I could think on that, he continued, "Did you get the clothes you needed?"

I nodded.

"A husband should take care of his wife." He said it more to himself than me.

I swallowed, throat suddenly thick. He kept staring at me with an intensity I couldn't read, never taking his hand off my forehead, thumbing the skin in a way that made my heart stutter.

"Did you ever start writing poetry, Snitch?" he asked quietly.

I thought to my secret letters.

I wanted to tell him. He was the only one I ever told anything.

But the miles of distance between us were too wide to cross.

"Um...no."

His mood turned dark. "Just be a fucking poet, Snitch."

"Oh, it's that simple?" I snapped back.

He leaned closer, glare sharp. "Yeah, it is."

I scoffed. "I could suck, you know? You could be encouraging suckage. You've never even read anything I've written."

"Doesn't matter," he said instantly, matter-of-factly.

I looked away, folding my arms. "It's kind of the only thing that matters, Grayson."

He went silent in the way I knew meant words were running through his mind. I couldn't read them now, but I wanted so badly to know them.

"I already know the world should listen to you," he said. "How you say it is irrelevant."

My eyes cut to his, breath froze in my chest as the door opened behind him. This time it was the doctor. Grayson stepped away, but he kept his hand above my head, gripping the examination chair as she put my legs in stirrups.

"Oh, what's this?" Her pointer finger glanced Grayson's bite, and her head lifted above my legs, eyes finding mine.

My cheeks flared. I heard Grayson's fingers above mine curl in the leather.

Do you like the idea of cheating on your husband?

I coughed. "I...um...."

This is fucking mine.

I scratched my head, refusing to look at Grayson, having no way to find an answer.

Let him touch you. He'll see, Snitch. You're mine. You will always be mine.

"It's probably a cat," I managed.

Her eyes grew. "Do you own cats? It doesn't look like a cat bite but...this is deep. We should get you started on antibiotics and scanned for—"

"We don't own cats." Grayson exhaled his annoyance.

"Oh." She stood up. "I'll...go get the ultrasound now. Are you ready to hear the heartbeat?"

I nodded, sinking into my shoulders, wishing the world would swallow me whole. When she'd left the room, I smacked Grayson as hard as I could.

His eyes darkened. "You're really pushing the whole 'carrying my baby' thing."

"Why did you say that?"

"I pay her millions to keep her mouth shut. You'd rather have her think a cat bit you than I did?"

"Yes." I sank against the leather, folding my arms tighter.

His jaw twerked, neck strained so hard I saw the muscle jump. He stared ahead. Was he pissed? I was the one with a reason to be upset. Now the doctor not only knew I was knocked up by someone other than my husband, but we liked it weird.

The next ten minutes passed in stony silence until the doctor and the technician came back. They squirted slimy, cold gel across my stomach. I kept thinking this was never going to work. It wasn't even thirty minutes into this and Grayson and I were arguing.

And then it happened.

It was faint, but it was there, the heartbeat.

"Whoa," I breathed.

I turned to see if Grayson was watching, but my gaze collided with his.

That moment was what fairy tales were made for. Maybe a happily ever after with Grayson would never be possible, but for a second, everything faded away save for the soft, aching look in his eyes. The warmth in his smile.

Grayson Crowne was happy.

And so was I.

We finished up, and then it was time to talk to the doctor, ask her any questions I had. I *did* have questions, but none I wanted Grayson Crowne privy to, especially if we were trying to keep this thing friendly.

I eyed him. "Can you leave?"

He furrowed his brow. "I'm here for everything, Snitch."

I worked my hands in my lap. "I have questions I don't want you to hear."

"*Everything*, Snitch."

I glared. Somehow his jaw got sharper, and he had that look, that Grayson look, and I knew arguing with him was going to take hours. We would be late for the beginning of the holidays.

"Fine," I grumbled. "I'm feeling a little bit...more—"

"Hungry?" Grayson prompted. "Nauseated? Are your ankles swollen?" He turned to the doctor, hand held in my direction. "Fix that." He sounded pissed at her, and the doctor frowned.

"No," I glared at him. "Horny," I whispered quietly, wishing I could melt into the leather patient chair.

It was so quiet the silence buzzed. Grayson looked like I'd just thrown a pie at his face. He swallowed, closed his eyes, and rubbed a finger through the wrinkle between them.

Then she spoke. "That's perfectly normal, as is sex—"

"She doesn't need to know any of that." He cut her off, turning to me, tone frigid. "You're not having sex."

I blinked. "I might be."

Our glares clashed in a stalemate.

Did he think I was just pining after him? That I'd lit a candle and closed up shop in my vagina because Grayson Crowne ruined me? I mean, *yes*, but he didn't get to know that.

The air was frostier than outside, and I lost myself in his blue glare, forgetting we had an audience until she cleared her throat.

"Well, you should know, if you were worried about hurting the baby. I know some people are, and sex is perfectly safe during pregnancy."

I turned to her. "Thank you."

I felt his tension. I felt it all the way to the car, until he snatched the door away from the driver, opening it for me.

"Get in," he growled.

I bristled, hating him for barking orders at me, but also liking that he cared enough to open the door. I slid in, and he kept his hand on the door, bending over so he caged me in my seat.

"Slide over," he said.

"We're taking separate cars..."

He bent farther, until his breath warmed mine. "We *were* taking separate cars."

THIRTY-FOUR

GRAY

I worked my bottom lip between my thumb and forefinger over and over until it bruised. It was stifling in the car, even though we sat on opposite sides.

Friends.

We're fucking friends.

Friends talk about this shit.

Friends do not think about what the other friend was doing, where her hand was, if her legs were spread or back arched—

Fuck.

"Has that problem of yours resolved?"

Snitch lifted her eyes to mine. "My problem?" she questioned. Then, realizing what I was talking about, she scoffed. "Not yet."

"Yet?" I gritted, working my lip harder.

She looked away, folding her arms.

In my world, where morals and dignity were rarer than

diamonds, I only ever wanted to be loyal. To not be the man my father was. It should have been so fucking easy. *Tell yourself not to do something—don't be that guy.*

But I want her.

That want stretches my loyalty like fine lace.

"You gonna have *West* help you out?" I asked.

She jerked her head to mine. "What's it to you, Grayson Crowne?"

I dragged my thumb across my lower lip. There was no answer I could give her that wouldn't betray the truth.

The car jostled, hit some fucking pothole.

I didn't realize I was on the floor, hands on her thighs, until it was too late.

Her eyes grew.

"It's fine. It was barely a speed bump." Her words were that sweet, quiet raspy breath that I lived for. I could still remember falling asleep to it. Now I just stayed awake, listening to the silence, wondering—hoping—she didn't do the same.

Fuck.

This was such a bad idea.

"Grayson."

"Did West get you something for the Nutcracker Masquerade?" I asked, sliding my hands beneath her dress.

Her breath hitched.

With her clothes on...I could pretend. Pretend what I was doing was still okay, that I wasn't a cheating bastard. That I hadn't become everything I'd strived against.

"Little nun?" I pressed, finding the bruise on her thigh, pressing into it with my thumb.

"N-no."

I slid my thumb to the crease in her groin, rubbing the sensitive flesh just before the trim of her panties. Her lips parted silently. I see it in her eyes, the need, the bottomless desire that ensnared me in that antique room.

I want the word to fall from her lips.

More.

I'm falling into her mossy eyes, forgetting everything, every promise I've ever made to anyone but her.

"What do you want, little nun?"

Her lips opened and I waited for the word, about to fall over a cliff, when the car jolted to a stop.

My grip on her thighs tightened. "Don't worry about your dress, Snitch."

The door opened to the bright winter day, and I pulled away.

THIRTY-FIVE

STORY

Back at Crowne Hall, it was white and cold. I stared at the pearly sky, wondering if the snow would finally fall, when Grayson took my arm, wrapping it around his.

"Oh my god, I can walk up stairs," I said.

He made a noise in his throat but said nothing. He helped me up the steps, his hand warm on my arm, his presence strong and safe.

I wanted to scream.

Stop being so fucking perfect. It's impossible to hate him like this.

To let him go.

I have to go back to Westley. The man I kissed before you.

We stopped just outside the towering wooden doors that marked the Hall's entrance, but neither of us made a motion to open or knock to be let in.

Grayson looked down at me from his ridged nose with

the same look he'd had in the car. It's dangerous. I was so close to begging for *more*. It made me forget all the reasons I have to leave.

"Do you think it will snow tonight?" I asked. "My uncle and I used to watch the first snowfall. We'd watch the snowflakes and talk about the weird things poets did. Like my favorite poets would spend weeks, months, sometimes years, away from their lovers, and I used to read their love notes and letters...but *that* was something I couldn't do with Woodsy, because it was way too dirty."

The longer Grayson and I stayed outside the massive wooden doors, the more time seemed to push us to go inside. I could feel fate on our heels again, a runaway boulder.

"You want love letters, Snitch?"

His voice drew me back to him with fervor, it sounded like my heart, shredded and torn. But also hopeful, as though he could feel the boulder, as though he knew that this was our only time before we had to go back.

"I want so much more than love letters," I whispered. "We should probably go inside." I turned but he grabbed my bicep.

"No. Wait...just wait."

"We're already so late, Grayson. They're all waiting for us. Your family, my..." My *husband*.

Fury and something else, something too much like heartbreak, splintered his blue eyes. "My grandfather owns every one of those people. Every one of them is a vote against..."

"Against?" I pressed.

His eyes burned. "Us."

Us.

"What do you mean *us*?"

"Never mind." He dropped me and shook his head. "You're right. We're late."

He was closing his walls, building his thorns. Fate was almost upon us. I had to get it out. All the things I needed Grayson to know and hear and just listen to. The things only he could.

"I'm scared," I said. "I'm scared I'm gonna do something wrong. What if I do something wrong?"

His eyes pinched, and he tilted his head, giving me that deep, probing look only Grayson could. The one that said he saw right through me.

"I shouldn't be a mother. My mother shouldn't have been a mother...but you would make a great father, Grayson." He really would, he cared so much about his family. Grayson Crowne's biggest secret wasn't that he was a virgin, it was the notorious playboy prince, known worldwide for being callous and imperious, loved his family and would do anything for them.

A small smile. "No, you would make a great mother, Story."

It was fainter than a blurry Polaroid, but it was there, the image of Grayson and me, and our newborn. A happy family. A happily ever after. And no sooner did the picture come, did it vanish with his next words.

"I'll be there for you, Snitch. I'll hold your hair back. I'll get you ice chips. Let you scream and hold my arm until you break the skin." He stopped off, staring off somewhere I couldn't follow.

And then what? What comes after, when the delivery is finished? He'll go back to his wife and I'll disappear.

"June..." That was my due date. "Almost a year to the day when this all started."

"It's hard picturing you gone from my life, Snitch." He

had the same look in his eyes as he had in the car, at the doctor's office. I don't know what it meant, but it made my gut tighten and throb.

Then he said, "Mistletoe, Snitch."

I lifted my eyes.

It was like every stolen moment over the past months had been leading up to this second. We had a leak slowly eroding the moral line between us, and now that hanging flower above us was the final drop.

The moment in the car. My uncle's funeral. Hell...just every time we found ourselves alone together, something popped, something very *un*friendlike.

I stepped closer as Grayson's lids dropped.

"I've missed your blush, Snitch," he rasped. "Missed the way your cheeks heat up like glowing amber. You know, it's so subtle. It's like another secret just for me."

As if on command, my cheeks heated.

He dragged his thumb down my cheek with a barely-there smile. "There it is."

Bad. Wrong.

But I don't care anymore.

I angled my chin.

Then the doors behind us opened.

Grayson and I stepped apart as Tansy Crowne, Josephine St. Germaine, and Lynette du Lac filled the space between us. Gemma and her fiancé were behind them, and behind them, Gray's wife and West.

My husband.

"Just in time," Tansy said.

Behind us, a caravan of town cars was pulling up the

round the cobblestone driveway. *The holidays.* The remaining Crownes had just arrived.

The snow globe Gray and I had been building all day with sugar glass slowly fell apart around us, crashing to the floor.

Tansy Crowne, accompanied by a murder of servants at her back descended the white marble steps of Crowne Hall.

West came to me first, wrapping his arm around my waist as he had earlier. "I thought for sure you'd beat me."

"I..."

Gray didn't stop staring at me, even as Lottie came and took his hand.

If Gray and I had just stuck to the plan, we wouldn't be getting caught like this. How do we even begin to explain why we were out here together? My car was supposed to take me home, but instead I was with Gray.

This was getting more muddled each day.

"We're under the mistletoe," Lottie said softly.

Both Gray and I lifted our eyes. Mine burned—it was like the pretty evergreen leaves were made with fire.

Lottie stood on her tiptoes for a kiss, and Gray returned it.

I turned from the sight, to West. "Mistletoe."

The word came out robotic.

West arched a dark brow, but he tightened the arm around my waist and pulled me close.

"This would have made for a more romantic kiss," West said. "I should have waited."

"Should have waited?" Grayson repeated.

I ignored the way his growl made me feel and leaned in for West's lips, letting the kiss happen. My eyes remained open, as did Grayson's. As he kissed Lottie and I kissed West, Grayson watched me.

No, he bruised and burned me with his gaze.

My heart felt like a violin bow used too much. Over and over again it played the same hideous melody. I wondered if the song hurt Grayson as much as it did me.

"What a perfect pair of pairs," Mrs. du Lac murmured.

THIRTY-SIX

STORY

Crowne Hall during the holidays was a haunted, beautiful thing. With Swarovski icicles dangling from the balconies that glittered in the winter sun. A stark white twelve foot Christmas tree jutting up two floors and icy garland along the bannisters.

It was a winter fairy tale, but it was more akin to being invited to the ice queen's castle.

I remembered setting this up as a servant. The painstaking hours we spent hand-cutting lace snowflakes, polishing the icicles, being reprimanded when the air didn't smell of fresh gingerbread in one hallway and peppermint in the other.

"What the hell was that kiss?"

"You're supposed to be talking to your cousins from Luxembourg," I mumbled.

"What was he talking about, *another* kiss?" He grabbed my bicep. "Did you kiss West?"

I rolled my shoulders back. "Yes."

His eyes were locked on my lips. "Don't kiss him again, Snitch."

My chest pounded. "Or what?"

He stepped to me, clasping my lower lip between his thumb and forefinger. "You've forgotten so much, little nun. These are my lips."

My gaze darted around the twinkling foyer. Anyone could see us.

I was about to move, step away, but then his next words froze me.

"It's been too long since I've kissed my little nun." The possessive, dark look in his eyes turned tender. *Longing.*

I swallowed a sigh that scraped down my chest.

I missed his kiss.

I ached for it.

I tried to step away, but his touch turned bruising, holding me in place by my lips. So I violently yanked back, gasping at the sharp pain.

"You don't get to tell me who to kiss anymore, Grayson," I said, holding my bottom lip. "You're supposed to be my *friend.*"

"If you didn't want me to own it, then you never should have fucking kissed me," he growled.

A ripple slid up my spine and twisted my gut. Sparks and tingles and something *wrong.* I breathed like I'd run a marathon, locked on his lips. Looking for any distraction, I took off my coat. Gray's jaw clenched, taking in the outfit West had picked out.

"What the hell is that?"

"A dress."

He dragged his hands through his hair. "This isn't you, Snitch."

"You're one to talk. You've changed, Grayson, or should I say, *Mr. Crowne*."

His jaw twerked.

"What the hell is it to you how I dress and who I kiss, anyway?"

His eyes darkened. "I'm the father of your child."

"So you get to tell me how to dress?" I met his eyes with a glare. "You were next to me on that porch. Are you going to tell me that you don't kiss your wife?"

"If I do?"

"Whatever Lottie does to you..."

I sounded petty.

I hated that I sounded petty.

"So if I fuck Lottie in the ass, you're going to let West fuck you in the ass?" he demanded.

I froze so I didn't flinch. "Yeah. I am."

He stepped back, examining me. "You have thorns around your heart now, Snitch."

His words hit me like a punch to the chest. I swallowed, trying to work past the emotion.

"And you have secrets burying yours, Grayson."

Grayson worked his jaw back and forth. Across the room, I spotted West coming to me, through with talking to one of Grayson's great-aunts.

"I want to tell you everything, Snitch," he said, "but I won't make anymore promises I can't keep."

What the hell am I supposed to do with that?

I swallowed. "I don't care. I won't let you in. Ever again."

I didn't trust my words.

Grayson dragged his pinky across his lower lip, an action I now knew meant he was barely holding himself back.

"I don't care if you hate me forever. I'll cut myself on you. I'll bleed. You're worth it, Story Hale."

"You said you were letting me go!"

"I—fuck." He looked away, dragging his hands through his hair.

"Damn, Angel," West said as he got to me, weaving his arm around my waist. "I like this dress on you." He pressed his lips to my cheek.

It felt wrong and my gut tightened.

But I liked the look in Grayson's eyes, as though he was two seconds away from punching West in the face and tackling me to the ground.

I thumbed my locket later that night with more desire than to open it and see what was inside. I felt like if I opened it, I would end us for real, though.

This was all wrong. I was supposed to be moving on, not tangling myself deeper into his briars.

My phone buzzed.

Are you asleep?

I climbed up, sitting against my headboard, pulling my sheets with me and staring at the message the entire time.

Am I asleep?

I started typing out a response, then quickly deleted it and tossed my phone to the bed, breathing like I'd just run a marathon.

Space.

We need space.

A second later my phone vibrated again.

I know you're awake. I saw you typing.

I put my mouth to my hand, fighting the urge to pick up my phone.

Though still in my bed, my thoughts go out to you, my Immortal Beloved.

And with that, I crumbled.

"Beethoven," I whispered, even though he couldn't hear me. I picked up my phone, lids heavy, body heavy.

Exhausted.

I'd been fighting this invisible force inside me from the moment Grayson and I collided in the antique room. Every molecule wanted to go to him.

Just give *in.*

At night...it was easier to stop fighting. Ignore the reasons why I had to fight. So I sent him one of my favorites from Zelda Fitzgerald to F. Scott.

I love these velvet nights. I've never been able to decide ... whether I love you most in the eternal classic half-lights where it blends with day or in the full religious fan-fare of mid-night or perhaps in the lux of noon.

I waited in the dark for his response. My phone vibrated.

I can't be clever and stand-offish with you: I love you too much for that. Too truly. You have no idea how stand-offish I can be with people I don't love. I have brought it to a fine art. But you have broken down my defenses. And I don't really resent it.

I knew the letter instantly, remembered the day I'd read it even. Vita Sackville-West to Virginia Woolf. Remembered wondering if I'd ever find someone to love me that way. I held my phone with both hands to my chest, staring out at the inky star-speckled sky.

Love.

His poem had said *love*. It wasn't like we were saying the words aloud. We hadn't even written them ourselves. It was nothing more than showing a friend something someone else had read.

So why did it feel like we were expressing something that was deep?

Buried.

I typed my next words, bleeding, bleeding.

If only I were a clever woman, I would tell you that you are the greatest marvel of all ages, and I should only be speaking the simple truth...You are not only the solar spectrum with the seven luminous colors, but the sun himself, that illumines, warms, and revivifies! This is what you are, and I am the lowly woman that adores you.

Juliette Drouet to Victor Hugo.

My phone vibrated within seconds.

My love has made me selfish. I cannot exist without you.

Keats.

He said love again, or...Keats did. My heart pounded and pounded in my chest as I wrote out my response, but before I could, my phone vibrated.

I miss you in my sheets, Snitch. I miss you on the floor. I fucking miss you. The longer I spend without you, the more I wonder if you'll really have to chain me to the fucking bed when you leave. Or maybe...I'll follow. Would you like that?

The phone seemed to grow brighter the longer I stared at it.

Grayson.

That was only Grayson.

Each breath I took was stuttering and rocky. Without a poem to hide behind, I wasn't sure what to say. How much to reveal.

I had it on the tip of my tongue.

I miss nighttime with you.

I miss sleeping side by side with you.

I miss seeing your crooked nose in the dark, the way your lips curve when I say something too brazen.

I miss the secrets you'd whisper in the dark, only for me.

Do you share them with her?

Could you really leave her...could you really leave with me? Aren't we too far gone?

But in the end, I said nothing.

Because, in the end, he was sleeping next to her.

I kept the text open, staring at his words as my fingers drifted to his mark on my thigh. I pushed down, imagining Grayson's growl urging me on.

Harder.

Sparks.

Fire.

Grays—

My mind came to a stuttering, screeching halt as my eyes landed on my now-open door.

I scrambled up my bed, grabbing the sheets as I went. "What the hell are you doing?"

Grayson was in my bedroom, bedhead hair wild and falling over wilder eyes. How long had he been there? What had he seen?

He either didn't hear me or didn't care. He walked straight to my nightstand, and then, eagle-eyed, looked at me, zeroing on my hand, my phone. He grabbed it, turning it over, as if inspecting for damage.

He studied me, his eyes searching. I held my blanket to my chest, flushed and embarrassed. Had he come all this way to gloat? He was married, he had all the power, he wasn't even *here*, and still I caved.

But all at once, he exhaled. Deep and long, as though something seriously heavy had been crushing his chest.

He dragged his hands through his hair, blue eyes pinning me. "Answer your fucking phone, Snitch."

He tossed it in my bed, leaving without another word.

THIRTY-SEVEN

STORY

The next morning I woke to another text.

When I am with you, we stay up all night. When you're not here, I can't go to sleep.

It was the poet Rumi. A smile came to my face, but I quickly squashed it.

Grayson was sending me love notes, even if we weren't acknowledging that's what they were...they were love notes. Like the ones my favorite poets used to send. My heart thumped, just as the door to my room burst open.

I pulled my sheet up to my chest, as one by one, servants dressed in black tore into my closet, ripping out my clothes, following each other out of my room like a line of ants.

My questions died on my lips. At first, I thought the servants had officially snapped and given up hiding their hatred for me. Then West came into the room.

"What's going on?" I asked, still watching the servants carry my things out of the room.

"Apparently this wing is being fumigated."

The way he spoke alluded to his disbelief.

"Fumigated? Just this one?"

"I'm being moved to the north, and you're being moved to the south."

I pushed my cheek with my tongue. "That's... interesting."

A servant came out of my closet, carrying the one dress I'd picked myself. Forgetting modesty, I dropped my sheets and dashed after him. I snatched it out of his hands.

"I need *something* to wear today."

He eyed me coldly and kept walking.

Hours after Grayson left, the sun had risen, and I still sat in my pajamas, thinking. Grayson had poked at so many of my wounds.

A soft knock on the door had me lifting my head. I mumbled something about coming in, and West appeared, fully dressed for the day. I had some kind of appointment with the du Lacs and the Crownes, a tea date at the most exclusive tearoom in Crowne Point, probably in the East Coast.

Seeing me in my pajamas, he raised a brow.

"I've been thinking...I don't want to go," I said. "All this press isn't a good idea. It doesn't feel right."

I want to eventually go back to who I was.

Blending in among everyone.

Just me, Story, not Cinderella, not anyone.

This was never supposed to be part of it.

West frowned. "Angel, have you not looked online?"

Not since I saw the last trend, a person who discovered how my mother had died. Everyone was having a field day with that. Cinderella's mother was supposed to die silently, peacefully, with roses atop her grave.

Not with track marks in her arm.

I felt exposed. Violated. I wanted to pretend it wasn't happening.

"Not recently," was all I said.

He loosed a deep exhale that settled like lead in my gut, then came to sit beside me. He pulled out his phone, and all he did was search my name.

I stared at the results in dismay.

The STORY of How the Slutty Stepsister Stole Cinderella's Spot

On one major news outlet, there was a picture of me, blown up in my maid's uniform, sandwiched between West and Grayson. It was a bad picture, blurry, and I was frowning. In the corner, there was a picture of Lottie in her wedding dress.

I flipped through the slides, finding the story. There were even more pictures, current ones, taken at Crowne Hall. I blinked, stunned, when I saw ones taken of Grayson and me in the kitchen right before I went to the hospital.

The servants.

I used to wonder what it would be like to be them, the women dressed in white, to be seen. It turns out I am no less a ghost. I'm talked about. I'm on every search engine. But no one sees me. If anything...I'm more ghostly now.

Story Hale.

Everyone has a conclusion about me but no one knows me.

I found West's eyes in dismay. "I thought the plan was to get out ahead of it?"

"These aren't my publications. You're my wife, Story. I

wouldn't let them print that." He closed the website and went to a du Lac publication.

The Real Fairy Tale of the Cinderella of Crowne Hall

"In a few weeks, no one will remember this."

"A few weeks," I repeated.

He smiled at me, then stood up. "You have a date with the Crowne women today. That's all anyone will talk about."

It was starting to feel like quicksand. The harder I fought to get out of this world, the deeper I sank.

GRAY

My grandfather was standing by the window when I came in, and that should have been my first warning that something was off.

When he heard me, he didn't turn around to speak.

"I'm surprised you even came in today. I guess I...misunderstood your level of affection for her."

At the mention of Story, my muscles tightened, but I played it cool. I came to his side, putting my foot up against the window he had someone wash twice daily.

"Or maybe you haven't heard?" He tilted his head, one peppered brow raised at his desk. The grandfather clock in his office timed the seconds of our chess match in a slow, burning *tick-tock*.

Eventually, after the minute hand ticked for a second time, I got off the window and went to see what the hell had him looking like a cat with a canary.

The STORY of How the Slutty Stepsister Stole Cinderella's Spot.

What the hell had Snitch gotten herself into that she was already on the cover of some magazine, and how the fuck had I missed it? I got all the papers delivered before they released.

I pushed the magazine along Grandpa's glossy desk, swallowing my rage.

This wasn't a hit piece.

It was an assassination.

"Are you wondering how you missed it?" Grandpa asked coolly.

I dragged my thumb across the top of my bottom teeth, refusing to answer. By my grandfather's slow smile, I could tell my mask had slipped a little.

Fuck.

"You couldn't bargain your secrets this time, Grayson. It's a new print. A du Lac and Crowne joint venture."

Du Lac and Crowne joint *propaganda.*

"We had a deal." I ran my finger across the ink before slowly lifting my eyes to his. "Are you trying to start a war?"

"You're smarter than this, Grayson." He exhaled. "Let me spell it out for you: she's a liability. To us, to the du Lacs. It isn't just a throne on the line; it's a fucking kingdom. Neither of us plan to lose it over Helen of Troy."

"You fucked up, Grandpa. I probably would have lived my entire life as your puppet if you'd left her alone."

"We used to be kings, Grayson, but do you know what my father left me? A tourist trap and a whore to look after. Do you know what your father left you? Debt, another whore, and three bastards. I spent my life rebuilding our kingdom, spent years grooming you to be a king. Years wasted because of another fucking whore. We're owed a dynasty. Our names should be written in stone."

I headed for the door. Somewhere, Snitch was having tea with the du Lacs. After this kind of article, she would not be safe. My muscles ached with tension to go to her.

"You have no idea what I gave up for your spoiled asses," he said. "So you could live pampered. Protected. You don't think I've loved? You don't know how quickly you can lose it all."

"Yeah," I gritted, turning around. "I do."

He narrowed his eyes. "I know a bluff when I see it. You'll never let that little piece of paper see the light. You've lived like royalty your entire life."

I worked my jaw as rage rose hot up my spine. "Maybe."

"We're close, you know. I've enjoyed working with you, Grayson. We don't have to be at odds. That girl will be what she was always meant to be: expendable. There is nothing you can do to stop it. Do you want to be the playboy virgin prince for the rest of your life, or do you want to join me? Do you want to rule?"

THIRTY-EIGHT

STORY

At least thirty Crowne women sat at tables all around the elegant tearoom. Servants circled us like sharks. Whenever a scone was eaten, another one magically appeared, and there was never a dirty plate.

Outside, a mob had formed. I couldn't see their signs, but the mob was big enough that the street had been blocked, and dividers had been put up to keep the crowd sectioned off.

"No vintage Chanel today," Tansy remarked.

"Your outfit is lovely," Mrs. du Lac said. "Is it new?"

Their comments drew me away from the window, and I fingered the hem of my brown jacket. Beneath it I'd worn the camel dress I'd picked out for *me*, some kind of flimsy armor against this day.

"Yes, Mrs.—" I cut myself off. It was still so hard to get used to looking everyone in the eyes and calling them by their names.

A plate of fluffy minicakes in pastel of greens and pinks and blues, dotted with candy pearls, were stacked in the middle of the table in tiers. And I wanted to vomit. I was starting to get "morning" sickness just about any time of the day.

"Is everything all right, dear?" Tansy asked.

For a moment, I thought I'd stumbled into an alternate universe where someone gave a shit about me.

But they were talking to Lottie, who stared at the cakes with a green look on her face.

She swallowed and lifted her warm eyes. "Fine, I was just wondering if I smelled lemon."

"Lemon?" Mrs. du Lac practically tore the paint off with her voice. "There better not be any lemon in these."

The cakes were swept off the table as quickly as they came, to be replaced with something chocolate. Chocolate I could do. Chocolate smelled divine.

The trill of tinkling porcelain and soft laughter became our melody. It didn't matter I was drinking tea with them. I was surrounded by women who wouldn't hesitate to ask me to warm theirs. Mrs. du Lac, Tansy, Gemma, Lottie, and Lottie's friends, Aundi and Pipa.

Though Josephine St. Germaine sat next to Tansy, Tansy made no motions to include her in the conversation. Josephine may as well have been eating at a separate table. I realized, I hadn't seen her children yet. Her triplets should have joined her for the holidays by now.

My eyes connected with her jewel-toned ones. I think I was the first one all day to acknowledge her presence. She smiled softly and I smiled back.

"Story." Tansy's voice cut me out of the moment. "You remind me a lot of your uncle." I couldn't tell if that was supposed to be an insult—you never could with Tansy. "Not so fond to put him in the family plot, but then promises must be kept."

I choked on my tea and it burned my throat.

Maybe Tansy meant it as jab, to hurt me, remind me her son had thrown me away. But it had done the opposite. I grasped the table, vertigo assaulting me.

That was why he'd promised never to talk to me?

For my uncle. For me.

The conversation continued around me as our tea was refilled, our macaroons and chocolates replaced, and I heard nothing. Not until Aundi.

"I don't care what that article said," she whispered, her laugh low enough that Tansy couldn't hear. "He will always be Playboy Gray."

"Right?" Pipa whispered. "Anyone who knows him knows that was a fucking joke. He's *Grayson Crowne*. The only thing he cares about is his cock."

"He feels the most," I blurted. "Grayson Crowne feels the most out of everyone." I realized too late I'd spoken too loud when the room fell to a hush.

Shit.

The only one who didn't glare was Gemma.

"So, Story," Aundi said, voice saccharine. "I wonder, now that you have such a romantic history with West, if you'll remember the cute bet he and I had? Do you remember anything about that?"

They watched me with twinkling eyes.

I clenched my tea to keep from shaking.

"Pipa and I were just wondering if it had anything to do with your marriage."

"Actually," I said, voice raspier than I'd hoped. "I don't really think about you at all, Aundi."

Her smile dropped, the vicious glare she'd been hiding

now front and center. My heart hammered, and I was two seconds away from dropping my tea to the floor. I set it down, stood, and made some excuse about needing the bathroom.

I'd already gone three times, but whatever.

I wandered around the tea house for a good thirty minutes, needing air.

For a few moments, I just stood in front of the window. I pressed fingers to the cool glass, staring outside, picturing flakes falling along the private beach. It would snow soon...I could feel it.

I could make out some of the signs from the window. It looked like they said Cinderella, and my gut dropped.

I quickly turned to go back to the table.

I live in one of the most beautiful lies in the world. Crowne Point is so small, you can walk from one side to the other, and yet it has the most wealth per capita of any city in the world, and the biggest wealth disparities.

Oh, and everyone here who *is* wealthy got that wealth from the Crownes.

You get used to growing up in the sphere of royalty they cultivated, because that's how they wanted it. You forget it's not normal, the twenty-first-century noblesse oblige. They plant fairy tales in your head while you shine their shoes—

"He told the world he was a virgin." Lottie's voice stopped me short. "I know he did. For her. What if he'd gotten wind of today's story? What secrets would he have told then?"

Grayson spilled his own secret? For me? Why?

I placed my hand against a lavender wall, knowing I shouldn't eavesdrop, but unable to stop.

"But everyone *thinks* he lost it with you, sweet pea. You have a rich husband," Mrs. du Lac responded. "You have *the* rich husband, Charlotte. Cheating is a part of it. Your children will become like him. They will take. They will be owed."

Cheating.

I stumbled back. Hearing it from her lips made it real. I'd done so much to not be the person my mother raised me to be. Instead I'd become someone who cheated on two people instead of just one.

Quicksand.

Sinking deeper and deeper.

I had to get out of here. What the fuck was I doing? I pushed to the front of the restaurant, until I was outside in the wet cold, salty bitter wind blowing against my cheeks.

"It's her!"

I lifted my head at the shout. Outside the tearoom, people shook homemade signs, faces twisted in vicious sneers. Now that I was closer, I could read their signs.

Team Lottie

Step Sisterslut

On the other side, the signs read differently.

We love you, Cinderella!

Sides? People were picking sides?

"It's definitely her! Stepsister Slut!" They jeered at me.

I stumbled back, tripping on my heels as a tomato flew through the air, hitting me in the face. I wiped the sticky wetness out of my eyes, surprised at the throbbing that followed.

Glass.

They'd shoved glass inside the tomato.

Then the crowd broke through, rushing toward me.

THIRTY-NINE

STORY

My ankle hurt, but I could probably walk on it. The problem was the *sea* of rabid fans between me and the street. They'd divided and conquered the narrow shop into factions, with one small strip of no man's land between them. I'd managed to hide from them, but then my phone rang at the worst possible time.

"Where are you?" Grayson's gruff voice demanded. "Ping me your location."

"I can't talk," I whispered.

"Where are you?" His deep growl stopped any rebuttal I had.

"I'm..." I looked around. "By the tearoom, but hidden between the bookstore and the garbage."

"Stay there and ping me your location."

He hung up, and I prayed no one had heard.

I should have hired guards.

I should have asked West to hire guards.

I never imagined I would be someone worth attacking.

But it was a fucking bloodbath. I'd already witnessed four fights break out between different factions, and a few others between those who were supposed to be on the same side.

There were at least two hundred girls. Some of them were clearly Team Lottie, some were on my side, and most simply hated anyone who had the balls to claim Grayson Crowne.

Then there was a shout.

"It's Grayson Crowne!"

I looked up and saw him, walking like the untouchable god he was, down the narrow strip dividing the factions, toward *me*.

The crowd grew wilder, thirstier.

"Team Lottie!" they called.

"Grayson!" hundreds called.

He looked like a movie star in his dark suit, his tie undone. A rock star. A god.

When they finally saw whom he was coming toward, the warmth vanished. He didn't care, eyes locked on me. Even as the crowd turned violent and they surged toward him.

He got to me, bending down, just as the crowd surged. Plainclothes bodyguards appeared, creating a shield around us.

"Are you okay?" Grayson asked, unperturbed by the girls screaming inches away, only blocked by a wall of muscled bodyguards.

She's a liar.

A cheater.

Team Lottie!

"Grayson, everyone can see—" He cut me off, lifted my

chin, ignoring the calls of the crowd. So soft and gentle, examining the cut beneath my eye where the glass had hit.

Though his bodyguards bulwarked us, we were literally dividing the mob on either side. Girls screamed and pushed. Their hands and signs were like rolling tidal waves threatening to break through.

"Are you, Snitch?" His voice was so soft. "Okay?"

Our eyes locked and the madness faded away, the cries of *Team Lottie* disappeared. He licked his thumb, cleaning away the blood on my lip and beneath my nose.

My heart pounded.

This wasn't okay. None of this was okay. Gray Crowne was not someone my heart could pound for.

His thumb lingered. Pulling at it, pulling down my lip to expose my bottom teeth. That ache. That tingle, that ripping at my heart. That uniquely *Gray* feeling. The one that shouldn't but *did*.

"Answer me, Snitch."

Why. Why do you care?

"Yes." Voice soft. "My ankle hurts, but other than that I'm fine."

His eyes narrowed, and his thumb kept rubbing.

"Please just let me go. Everyone is watching. Did you see the papers? They're going to write even more stories—"

"I *can't*."

Pain, anger, anguish, as if he physically couldn't. It was enough to seize my words, my breath, as I stared into his eyes.

At that moment, someone chucked a wooden sign over the fortress of bodyguards. As it was about to hit my head, Grayson's other hand shot out, fingers still grasping my chin, and caught it.

His sweet eyes turned feral.

He tossed the sign to the ground so hard the wooden handle snapped. Then he stood up, turned around, and bent down.

"Get on my back."

"Everyone can see—"

"Get on my fucking back, Snitch." It was a growl, a command.

Reluctantly, I climbed on as everyone took pictures.

FORTY

STORY

"How is your ankle?" he asked after moments of silence.

"Fine. You can let me down now. At this rate, you'll carry me all the way home."

"Are you uncomfortable?"

"No..."

"Then shut up."

Grayson rubbed his thumb in circles on my thigh as he walked us home. It was such an absent touch, I'm not sure he realized he was doing it.

"Grayson."

"Hmm."

"Why did you promise your mother you wouldn't speak to me?" He tensed but kept walking in silence.

"I want to hate you," I whispered. "I'm trying really hard. Why are you making it so hard?"

After another ten minutes, I put my head on his shoulder—to avoid strain, I told myself. Not because I missed him, because Grayson's shoulder was warm and smelled of home. The sun was setting and the air seemed pregnant with snow, but still it wouldn't fall.

"I'm not even your *wife*," I wondered aloud. "I'm married to someone else. Why do they care so much?"

"You might not be my wife, Snitch, but you'll always be mine. They see that."

My breath hitched, and for the rest of the way back, I didn't say a word.

We arrived at Crowne Hall, and Grayson took us through the gates, but he didn't go inside, and he didn't let me down. We went around the Hall, to the beach.

"Grayson," I said quietly, softly, not wanting to break this spell. "You carried me all the way to your beach, Grayson."

"I guess I did," he said. Still, he didn't put me down.

His grip tightened on me.

My heart squeezed...maybe it meant he didn't want to let me go.

But in the end, he slowly lowered me off his back.

I stared past the cold sand to the slowly darkening sky.

When I spoke next, my throat was like cotton. "I always wondered what it was like to be on Grayson Crowne's private beach."

He blinked, looking around. "I shouldn't have brought you here."

I tried to hide the sadness in my eyes, the way my face fell.

A second later he said, "It's too cold."

He slid out of his jacket, draping it over my shoulders.

"I'm already wearing a jacket," I pointed out, voice barely a whisper.

It was only his jacket, so why did it feel so wrong, clandestine, dirty? The things those girls had shouted at us. I went to stop him, but his hand shot out, covering mine. My eyes met his, searching.

"Don't fight me on this, Snitch. You'll lose." He tugged the jacket tighter, eyes pinched, then stepped away.

"You walked me miles home," I said. Grayson looked out at the frosty ocean. "You could've just put me in a car."

He shrugged. "I haven't worked out today."

"Is that really why?"

His head whipped away from the ocean, eyes colliding with mine so fast I swallowed my breath.

"You're the mother of my child, Snitch. I'm not putting you in some car." He looked so insulted I couldn't speak.

Whoa.

Hearing him say it out loud drenched my body in goose bumps. *Mother of his child.*

"I don't know if I can do this," I blurted. "I don't know if I can be a good mom."

His hand came out as though he was going to push my hair from my face, but it froze, and then he lifted the locket from my neck.

"That's impossible...You care too much."

"Are you scared?" I wondered.

Hope flowered. Was he as uncertain as me? Did he feel it too? That jagged, crippling shard of fear.

The thing that made me bleed.

"Am I *scared*, Snitch?" He blinked, looked at me like I'd just asked him if I had two heads. Insecurity bled into me. Of course *Grayson Crowne* wasn't scared.

"Every goddamn minute. I only have my dad and my grandfather as examples...and I don't want to be anything like them."

I was about to tell him, *No, you won't; you could never be*, but he continued before I could.

"You're the only person I ever cared about protecting, and I did a shit job of that."

"You did a great job," I whispered. Without him...where would I be?

In response he licked his thumb, then dragged it across my bottom lip. My heart stopped and restarted, shocked. All Grayson did was look at his thumb, at the blood he'd wiped away, and shake his head with a self-deprecating smile.

"That outfit doesn't look like something West picked out."

I tried to hide my smile. He'd noticed.

"I picked it out...Well?" I asked. I ran my hands down the silky material fitted around my hips. It was almost like my old clothes, but better material, and a little bit sexier.

His eyes flared, his jaw tightened, and a half second stretched into a millennia. My fingers froze on my hips, gut throbbing with the look. His eyes locked with mine.

"You did good, Snitch." His voice was like the crashing wintry waves: shredded and raw.

Then Grayson fell to one knee.

He took my ankle in his hand, pushing at the swollen skin. "Does it hurt?"

On one knee, looking up at me, it was almost as if Grayson was proposing. My brittle heart cracked for the future I would never get.

Did it hurt?

"Just a little," I whispered.

His eyes ached, too, but he lowered my ankle. He didn't immediately stand up, just stayed on his knee.

"Grayson?" I asked quietly.

He thumbed the bone at my ankle. "You know, Crownes never get to propose. Not really. We're told who we marry, and then a public proposal is planned with plenty of paparazzi. Or we stage one and leak it to the press. "

He slid a hand up my leg, underneath my dress, pausing at the curve beneath the knee. I swallowed air as heat climbed up my leg from that one spot and eviscerated my gut.

"You asked me once about my wedding, but I never asked you." His eyes burned. "What kind of proposal would you want, Story?"

Any.

Any kind of proposal, if it's coming from you.

I tried to pull away, but his thumb and forefinger were a possessive bruising grip, keeping me stuck in the sand, stuck in his gaze.

"Stop." I swallowed. How could I have so little air when the beach was breathing it?

The wind whipped the sand around us.

"I don't want you leaving Crowne Hall..." he said, thumbing the bone.

I sucked in a breath, lungs paralyzed. I know I shouldn't want to stay with him, shouldn't want *anything* to do with him. But...

"What?" I finally managed.

His eyes found mine, burning. "It's too fucking dangerous. Don't leave without a guard. Don't go out at night."

Just like that, whatever spell he'd put on my heart shattered.

"That sounds like a curfew, Grayson," I whispered. "Are you trying to give me a curfew?"

I didn't let him respond. I shoved him away, putting

space between us. Grayson stood with easy grace, following me.

"You can't lock me in here."

"The hell I can't—"

"You're supposed to let me go."

"You think I don't fucking know that?" he yelled. "It's all I've been trying to do since you crashed into my goddamn life."

I mashed my lips as the ocean breeze grew angry, magnifying our silence.

"Friends don't get their friends' husbands kicked out of their wings. Friends don't give curfews, friends don't send friends poetry—"

"So you did get my last text," he cut me off.

I rolled my lips to the side. "As if Grayson Crowne has never left anyone on read?"

He smiled a little, like a teenager caught with a girl in his room.

I missed that.

Fuck, I missed his smile.

That's the problem.

I stepped back. "No more poetry. No more of this. We're supposed to be *friends*."

He grabbed my elbow. "I'm your friend, Snitch? That's it? That's all this is?"

It's what it *has* to be. He's married to Lottie. He wants to be married to Lottie. Every action has proven that from the very fucking beginning.

I looked away.

"What if we could be more?" he asked.

As if fate heard us conspiring against it, Lottie called through the frosty winter breeze for her husband.

"Grayson? Is that you?"

Behind Grayson, Lottie gripped the gates of his private balcony, leaning ever so slightly over it to try to see us in the dusky twilight. The inky spires and turrets of Crowne Hall jutted into the frosty twilight.

"Don't write to me, Grayson. Don't protect me. Just... *don't*. You don't get to hold on when you refuse to fight for me, when you *never* fought for us."

He grabbed my wrist as I tried to walk by him, eyes blazing like there was something he wanted desperately to say.

But he let me go.

GRAY

"It really was you on the news," Lottie said the minute I got inside our wing. "You carried her. You *saved* her. You rescued her. You're her *savior*. You should have just taken a mistress. I could have handled that."

"Should I have abandoned her there? Like you did?"

Lottie's lips parted at my words. After a moment she said softly, "I don't understand why you hate me so much. We were friends before we fell in love. The only answer I can come up with is...because I'm not her."

I ground my jaw, going to my desk to grab a sucker.

"It was a du Lac publication, Lottie," I said, rooting around my drawer for a sucker. "This situation never would have happened if that article wasn't published."

"You think I did this?" she asked my back.

"I know your father has someone on the inside. If not you, then who? Who has the most to gain?"

"You do. You think I did this."

I turned around. The wind blew like a soft scream against the windowpane. She stared at me with open brown eyes. I wanted to believe her, wanted to believe the woman sleeping in my bed wasn't capable of this, but every bad thing happening to the woman I loved was either traced back to a du Lac or my grandfather.

Or both.

Lottie laughed when I didn't deny her.

My eyes narrowed. "Are you drunk?"

She laughed harder. "Drunk? Am I *drunk?* You're so fucking blind, Grayson Crowne. Blind to anyone but her. I get it. You need...*something.* A reason. To hate me. Will it make it easier when you fuck her then? It's all crazy, psycho bitch Lottie's fault."

She stood up, looking absolutely miserable.

"Do you know what they say about me online? I'm a cunt. I'm..." She took a deep, rocky inhale. "I'm a frigid whore. *Wicked.* All because I had the audacity to marry you. Why is this my fault? Why should I have to lose my family and friends? You should. You're the reason we're like this. I didn't do anything. I didn't change. I still love you."

She stared at me.

"How long have you been plotting this, Lottie?"

She didn't speak for a minute.

"Did you try to divorce me?"

I blinked. "What?"

"My mother warned me, but I didn't want to believe it."

I worked my bottom lip between thumb and forefinger as remnants of the man I wanted to be clung to me with claws. The man I *thought* I should be. Every minute I watched Snitch with West, it became clearer.

To be a good man, I'd have to be bad to someone.

Living in the gray was dragging all of us down.

"Yeah," I rasped. "It's true."

Lottie stumbled backward. "You know we *can't* divorce, Grayson. There are too many jobs, too many lives, just too *much* riding on this marriage."

It was a moment before I responded, and even then all I could say was, "I know."

"You would have given up *everything* for her. Your inheritance. Your company. Your home. Your family. *Everything*. Why?"

"I love her."

She bit her lip. "I think I hate you."

I nodded.

It was the least I deserved.

"You've broken every promise you made to me, so I'll make one instead. I won't let you divorce me. If this is what we are...fine. You'll at least treat me with the same respect my fucking mother got. You won't choose her in public."

"I wanted to be nice," I said, voice lifeless. "I wanted to be good. You were my wife, and I didn't want to be..."—*my fucking father*—"a dick. I want us to be civil, because we're trapped in this hell together, but I don't want you to get confused. She comes first. She comes first, second, third. You could try for a thousand fucking years, and you wouldn't even break top ten."

"It must be nice being so in love that every horrible thing you do is just *romantic*." She chucked a box at me that I barely caught. "When you go to your mistress tonight, give her this. I thought after today she might need it."

I tried to hide the suspicion in my voice.

"What is it?"

She laughed, but it was bitter. "Do you think it's poison

or something? Please, give me more credit. Of course, I'd have a *servant* do that, wouldn't I?"

She left the room and I fell to the bed. I opened the soft satin box, pulling out a pastel-green plush animal.

Fuck.

I bought them when I felt unloved, unappreciated, unwanted.

FORTY-ONE

STORY

The first snow of the season fell later that night. I stared outside as the soft flakes blanketed the beach in a soft powder, my thumbs swiping across my stomach. Abigail's Finsta lesson was still fresh in my mind...I could be anyone I wanted to be on the internet. I didn't have to be Cinderella. I didn't have to be the Stepsister Slut.

I didn't even have to be *Story*.

I already know the world should listen to you. How you say it is irrelevant.

Grayson's sweet words tumbled around my skull.

Maybe I wasn't ready for the world to know who I was.

Maybe I never would be.

But I could make an account, and I could share my poetry. I could share everything, all the words I couldn't say to Grayson because we no longer slept beside one another.

I made an account and typed my first letter.

Dear Atlas, you were meant to hold up the world, is that why you can't let me go?

I'd barely finished making my first post when there was a soft knock on my door. My heart jumped into my throat, and I shoved my phone away.

My Atlas himself leaned against the frame, head down so his messy blond hair covered his eyes. He had a bottle of whiskey in one hand and a sucker in his mouth. I hated that I both loved and worried over the sight.

"I bought this to share when Woodsy died." He held up the bottle of whiskey, which looked expensive. "Obviously... it's inappropriate now."

"You shouldn't be here," I said.

"Truce, Snitch."

I needed to say no.

We had to stop doing this.

It made it so much harder to think about leaving. It made it impossible to look at him as a friend. It made it harder to hate him when he turned off his affection.

He shook the bottle slightly, lifting his head just enough so I could see the smallest smile play on his rose petal lips, enough to crack and crumble my defenses.

I nodded slightly.

He sat on the floor, resting against my bed. It was almost as though we were in high school and he'd snuck into my room.

But I had a husband, he had a wife, and I was pregnant with his baby.

We both stared out the window as snow fell harder and harder.

"I've been wondering for a while...You haven't stopped calling me Snitch, but your voice is soft. It sounds like a term of endearment."

He was quiet for so long I thought he wouldn't respond, but then he took a drink of whiskey and said, "You're *my* Snitch, you spill all your secrets to me. You're the only one who does that."

My heart stuttered and stopped.

"Or, at least, you used to."

I didn't know what to say, so I just stared at him, trying to get my heart to stop hammering.

"Even if you can't open up to me...don't be anyone else's snitch. Just be mine. I want all your secrets." His eyes flashed to mine, burning. "Promise me."

I licked my lips. "I'll give you mine if you give me yours, Grayson Crowne."

He traced the glass bottle with his thumb, as if considering my proposal. "I have an answer for you."

"An answer?"

"What I would be if I wasn't CEO of Crowne Industries."

"You do?"

He nodded slowly, carefully. "A hero for my sisters. A good man. A good father. I want to be that man. I'd like to be what you see in me."

The way he spoke, it sounded like he knew it could never come true.

As Grayson unburied his heart, pieces of mine that I'd tucked in thorns broke free.

"I have a card from my uncle's attorney," I whispered. "I don't want to go to his reading. Then it makes it real...but it will be read soon. Within a few months. He doesn't have any property. I was going to give him money. I can't imagine what they're going to give."

He slowly lowered the drink from his lips, eyes on the window. "What if he has something to give you?"

"Then the bank will probably take it. That's what happened with Mom...No, he doesn't have anything for me. He said all he had for me was a coin. My uncle was losing his mind toward the end," I whispered. "Talking about wishes and coins buried beneath poetry."

He lifted his head, blue eyes locking on mine. "Coins?"

I nodded. We were silent for a moment, then Grayson reached into his pocket. Gold flashed in his palm. *Coins.*

"I don't think he was losing his mind, Snitch."

They weren't like regular coins, they were etched with lace-like detail, and the lace patterns were all different.

I'm so fucking *stupid*. I should have known the minute my uncle spoke of a coin what he was referring to. I leaned off the bed, trying to get a better look.

"That looks like the coin West threw down when you gambled me."

"I didn't gamble you," Grayson growled. "I've known everyone at that table since I was in fucking diapers, and they're all shit at poker. Gambling addicts with the easiest tells."

I tried to stop the way my heart grew at the confession. "What are those?"

He shoved them back into his pocket. "It's hard to explain if you didn't grow up like me, with archaic rituals and Victorian bullshit."

"Try me."

"There are only five of them. I have all but one—mine." With his arms on his knees, the bottle in his hand, he stared out the window. "They're a specific kind of currency in our world, tied to our bloodlines, and just about the only thing we honor. Families save them for years to force anything from marriages to mergers. That's why it was so weird when West used one on you...but now I understand," he growled the last words. "When you use a coin, the person has to obey or challenge."

"That night, West asked if you wanted to challenge..."

"He was asking if I wanted to start a war." He shot me a wry grin. "I considered it."

There Grayson went again, making my heart beat without consent. I looked away, but despite my best efforts to tamp it down, hope sprung in my chest.

"Want to know something dumb? I've been saving them for so long because I have this hope I can use them to barter my way out of this world."

"That's not dumb," I said softly. "So then, you can use them for anything? Can they be used to reverse fate?" I attempted to ask the last question lightly.

"Snitch..." That was all he said for at least five minutes. His voice was so soft and tender, I wanted to curl up in it. "If I could have reversed our fate, I would have. I know my grandfather, and I know the du Lacs. They wouldn't hesitate to challenge."

"That's not what I meant. I don't..." I stammered, tried to backtrack.

His eyes met mine, voice stone. "I'd go to war for you Story, but I won't let you be a casualty."

And as though he'd just asked me the fucking weather, Grayson looked away, easily asking, "So, you have it now? Woodsy gave it to you?"

I think I'm having heart palpitations. "No..." I cleared my throat. "I didn't think it was real. He said it was buried beneath a poem. I still have no idea what that means."

He frowned.

I jerked my gaze back to his. "Wait, you said you're missing yours. Did you give *yours* to my uncle? Why?"

My heart pounded, waiting for his answer. He could

have left this world years ago. Instead he'd given the most valuable thing he owned to my uncle.

He stared into his whiskey a long time before he answered. "At the time, it was the only one I had. And it was the least I could give."

This was such a bad idea.

"Get up here, Grayson."

GRAY

"Get up here, Grayson," she repeated.

I stared at my reflection in the glass. I missed her, my girl, my Snitch. Regardless of right and wrong. I set the whiskey down and stood up, taking a second to just stare down at her.

She stared back with those wide, mossy eyes.

Not breaking our gaze, I climbed into bed until I was in the center, then I slid down on my bicep, sharing a pillow. That *feeling*—the tight, ripping one I got every day, every minute I'm away from her—quieted. I could breathe again. The only thing left was an ache in my muscles from the urge to pull her closer.

It was almost like we were back in my bed, and she was going to fall asleep, and I would wake up to her.

Dangerous.

It took every ounce of willpower not to drag her on top of me.

"It's been a while since I've seen your face like this," I said.

Sideways. Softened in shadow. Looking at me in a way

only Snitch could. I couldn't resist running a hand along her naked shoulder.

Fuck.

It must be the whiskey.

"You have four coins," she whispered. "What if I found my uncle's, and you had all five?"

"No one has ever had all five at once," I said. "It's basically a fairy tale. Maybe we really could reverse fate..."

She sucked in a breath.

The gold locket I gave her glinted in the dark. I lifted it from her breast, trying to ignore the hard swallow at her throat.

"Have you looked inside it?"

She shook her head. "I...I can't."

Probably for the best.

I'd been grief drunk when I put the item inside, a part of me unwilling to let her go forever. Now, as fate had made our destiny clear, it seemed too cruel to open it.

"I've been writing poetry," she whispered. "In your journal."

My grip flexed on the locket, trying to rein it in, but my heart beat faster. Alongside my words Snitch wrote hers.

"What are you writing?"

She was silent.

Fuck.

Her shorts revealed the swells of her ass, and all I could think about was whether she still carried my bruise.

"What happened to your little nun nightgowns?" I rasped.

"I get hot at night," she said, breathy. "I think it's the, um..."

She swallowed.

Pregnancy.

God, when she talked about my baby inside her I get way harder than I have any right to be. It fueled some primeval, caveman instinct in me. Story with *my* child.

"I'm still missing it," I realized sadly. "All these things are happening to you."

"You took me to the doctor..."

"I've never even held your hair back. I've barely satisfied your cravings. I'm not being the man you need me to be, Story. I've never felt more like my father than I do now. Trying not to be him."

"Every day I feel more like her," she said quietly.

I still hadn't taken my other hand off her, tracing my thumb along her pulse. It pounded and throbbed against my thumb. I worked the sucker in my mouth, trying to focus on that, not how much I wanted to pull her locket, pull her to me.

"You never told me what you crave now."

She looked at my lips and rasped. "Suckers."

My groan ricocheted through my chest.

Fuck.

Fuck.

"What?" Her eyes grew in that innocent, exclusive *Snitch* way. They got big as walnuts, and I couldn't help the twitch of my lips. I slid closer until I could taste her sweet breath.

"Now every time I have another sucker, I'll think of you." *Wonder if you're thinking of me.*

Her lips parted.

"Well..." she said, and I closed my eyes, listening to how her voice got raspy with lust. It had been too fucking long.

"That seems fair," she finished.

"Fair?" I gritted.

"For months, all I've tasted is you on my tongue."

My eyes popped open, and Snitch was locked on me. As if in slow motion, she tugged on the sucker stem until I released it from my lips, then popped it into her mouth.

"Lemon?" She sounded surprised.

I couldn't decide if I wanted her to give it back or keep it. My heart pounded like an ocean in my ears. If I wasn't hard before, I was rock-hard now. My grip steel on her locket.

My eyes were stuck on her pouty lips. "For months, all I've wanted is you on my tongue, Story."

Slowly, I lifted my eyes to hers.

Throbbing. Pulsing. She slowly withdrew it from her mouth and pushed it between my lips. A burst of lemon hit my tongue, followed by a noise that didn't sound quite human leaving my mouth.

Fuck.

Fuck. Fuck. Fuck.

I missed the taste of her.

"I miss the taste of you," she whispered.

Then, as if she realized she'd said too much, she blinked and tried to roll away. I kept my grip on the locket firm, biting into her skin.

"Let me go."

"You miss the taste of me?" I pulled harder at the chain. "What else do you miss, little nun?" I searched her eyes. Her tongue darted out to wet her lips.

"Grayson..." She said my name in a raspy, husky sigh that I wanted to breathe. Swallow. Consume. "I've been thinking a lot. About who I want to be. What kind of mother...Even if by some miracle you did leave Lottie, that doesn't mean we'll be together."

"What if I could win you back?"

"This is a bad idea. I don't want to talk about this—"

She tried to roll away again, but I grabbed her bicep, pulling her close.

Giving into the insanity growing inside me.

What if I did it? What if I took down all the obstacles in our way? My grandfather, my mother, the du Lacs, my *wife*. What if I created a safe place for Story? What if I built us a happily ever after?

"I don't like this distance between us, Story," I said. "I don't...I've never cared about what anyone thought of me, but I want you to look at me like you did before."

"Don't do this to me." Her eyes watered and, instinctively, I reached to wipe a tear away.

She gripped my hand, stopping me.

"I can't get you off my mind. When you're here, you're the only thing that exists. I'm bleeding everywhere. And you were the person I used to bleed with. What the hell am I supposed to do now? Snitch I...I'm bleeding alone too."

Her grip lessened as tears fell down her cheeks. I swiped them away until her skin shone.

"What would Grayson Crowne have to do to win back Story Hale?" My voice grated like sandpaper.

"Whatever you do, it won't be enough. There's too much."

"I can do anything."

"Let the servants look you in the eye," she challenged.

"Done."

She blinked, surprised. "You'd have to eat steak every day for a month."

I swiped my thumb across her lower lip, fighting the urge to push it between her teeth. "Easy."

"A lifetime supply of spaghetti. Once I'm...not so averse."

A smile flickered on my lips. "Done."

"You'd have to be honest," she said with a quiet rasp. "With everyone. Let them know you donate your clothes. Tell them the truth about who you are. You're a good guy. If you embraced it...maybe this place wouldn't be so suffocating. So...so haunted."

I frowned, lifting my eyes from her lips to lock with hers.

"Stop lying to me. Unbury your heart. Don't keep me in the dark any longer. I can see it in your eyes. I can see the weight on your shoulders."

I paused.

It was on the tip of my tongue to tell her everything.

How I'd tried to divorce Lottie.

How I was trying to get rid of my grandfather.

But in the end, what if it all amounted to nothing? What if I pulled her into a promise that fell apart at our feet like last time?

"I don't want to break any more promises with you, Snitch. Not with you. I can't promise you forever...yet"

Pain and anger crackled in her eyes.

"Then why are you in my fucking bed?" She shoved me, but I gripped her wrists.

"Get off. I'm not going to be your fucking mistress."

"I'm not sleeping with my wife, Story. I should be, but I'm not."

She paused, brow crinkling, then her elbow nearly hit me in the face. I pinned her to the mattress, but she didn't stop fighting.

"You're a fucking liar, Grayson Crowne. I carried the bloody sheets! You taunted me with it. *Does it turn you on knowing you're getting sloppy seconds?*" she mocked darkly.

"I didn't sleep with Lottie." I pressed her wrists into the

mattress. "Do you want to know what our bedroom looks like, Snitch? It looks like you."

"Stop." She attempted to knee me, and I slid my leg between her thighs.

"I can't get hard without Lottie pretending to be you. Our marriage bed is a twisted, dark, fucked-up thing. You slid into it the same way you slid into my veins."

Her lips parted, and my eyes dropped to that, to the angry way she swiped her tongue across her bottom lip.

This was the closest we'd been in too fucking long. I flexed my grip on her wrists, trying to ignore Snitch hot and writhing in anger beneath me.

"Lottie isn't even in the same fucking universe as you. You're all I think about. All I dream about. All I care about. All I'll ever want. I might be married to her, but I'm lost in you."

She shook her head, spirally curls flying beautifully —*distractingly*—across her face.

"I owe Lottie so much," I said. "I owe her a family. I owe her a heart. I owe her so much that I can't give her, because you already own everything."

She froze, walnut eyes wide. Then she shook out of it.

"Friends aren't supposed to hear this. Friends aren't supposed to get excited over hearing this."

Excited.

I lowered my head until our lips were separated only by the moonlight.

"I'm not your fucking *friend*, Story."

"You said—"

"You were the only person I wanted to be good for, Story. I wanted to be a good friend. I wanted to be a good husband."

"So *be* a good husband," she beseeched.

"You didn't let me fucking finish."

Our breathing was ragged. Ragged like my willpower. Ragged like the shreds of my dignity and soul.

"I want to be a good husband, Story, but I want you to be a bad wife more."

I slammed my lips against hers.

Fuck.

Story Hale is my heroin and I have missed this high.

STORY

My mouth opened on a gasp as *Grayson* flooded into me. A vital, missing part of me had come back to life. I can feel again. I can breathe.

Just as I was about to dive into the inky black waters of my desire, he broke the kiss.

"Fuck. *Fuck.* Sorry."

There was just a sliver of starlight between our lips, the most fragile connection.

I knew I should push him off, but all this time I'd been deprived of him. His lips. His taste. His *soul.*

He exhaled, about to turn his head, and I gripped his shirt, fisting the fabric, needing that thread of connection to stay. Grayson's gaze flickered from my hands, back to my eyes.

My lips parted, but I didn't know what to say. I don't know what tomorrow will bring. I just have this *bleeding* need inside me.

So I settled for his name.

"Grayson," I whispered.

"Little nun," he groaned, tangling his hands into my hair, thrusting me hard against his lips as our bodies collided once more.

I dragged my nails around his waist, back, biceps—anything—before knotting them in his hair. I wanted his hair messy. I wanted it ruined. I never wanted to see it in that perfect coif again.

His hands slid from my wrists, tangling into my fingers, pushing our entwined hands into the mattress. His erection throbbed against my thigh, but it was his kiss that Grayson focused on.

I could feel them—all the words he didn't say, the secrets he's still keeping, the apologies he never gave—on his lips.

On his worshiping lips and punishing tongue, in his desperate bite, I felt the words. Bleeding into my chest. Clinging to our lips.

Grayson is a poet, but his lips are his pen, and his kiss is his poetry. And I'm frantic for it.

"More," I begged.

It felt like he's holding himself back. Holding *me* back.

"More."

This time I bit him, dragging out his bottom lip between my teeth, eyes open so I could watch the look in his blue gaze change feral.

He pinned me to the bed, and I bit harder. I can feel him throbbing between my thighs and it spurred me on. I dragged his bottom lip out with my teeth. Grayson bruised his forehead to mine as my teeth bruised him.

I released his pouty pink lip with a pop.

For a moment, everything was still, the only sound our breathing.

"Perfect," he rasped.

Then he pushed off. The sudden loss of him was ice cold. He left me alone on the bed, adjusting his hard-on as he towered over me.

His rose gold hair was messy and wild—everything I'd missed.

Thoughts tumbled like a rockslide into my head: *What did I do? He's leaving again. Abandoned. Forgotten—*

Grayson leaned over and caught my bottom lip like I'd done with his. "I will get us out of this with some *shred* of our souls intact, little nun."

And then he left.

FORTY-TWO

STORY

I don't remember falling asleep. I must have...because one minute it was dark, and the next it was light. My head ached with lack of sleep, and I felt disoriented by the sun.

I want you to be a bad wife more.

I jolted up as last night blasted back into me. I dragged a hand over my forehead. Oh my god.

Oh my *god*.

I wanted it. *I* pushed *him*. I would have...would have... Only Grayson saved me from making a terrible mistake.

What is happening to me?

A knock on the door sounded.

"Um..."

I felt naked and caught, like I was still with Grayson.

"Come in," I croaked.

The door creaked open, and West stood in the frame. He held something behind his back. What looked like a white dress box.

"What's that?"

"An apology."

The confusion must have shown on my face, because he said, "You were attacked."

I looked away as more of last night tumbled into my thoughts.

What if we could be more?

"I didn't expect you to be there, West," I said lightly.

The waves sounded softer this morning, lighter.

"I didn't..." he started, then stopped.

He exhaled through his nostrils, looking away, working out his square jaw.

I stared at him. I don't think I'd ever seen West at a loss for words. He was always someone who had the last word, who knew exactly what to say and was confident with his quips. Now he stared at the dress box, something making his jaw flex.

His eyes collided with mine. "You were never...I never wanted you to get hurt, Angel."

The intensity behind his brown eyes unsettled me.

"It wasn't your fault," I said.

He worked his jaw, as though he was about to say something. Whatever it was...he decided against it. He came to me and placed the box in my lap.

I fingered the peach satin bow.

"You didn't have to do this..."

"You didn't think I would leave you without a dress for the Nutcracker Masquerade?"

Tansy Crowne's Nutcracker Masquerade happened two weeks before Christmas. A white tie masquerade party, and like every Crowne party, women spent months preparing their costumes. I had nothing...but Grayson had said he would get me a dress.

West nudged me out of my thoughts with an envelope.

"More?" I asked, taking the envelope.

He nodded for me to open it.

As West sat beside me, I pulled out starchy plane tickets for *one* to...*Scotland.*

I lifted my head, eyes colliding with his.

"I promised I would get you out, Angel."

"I guess I just thought..."

"That I was fucking with you?"

We'd been here for so long I was starting to lose track. The days blurred into one. It seemed like the perfect ending. For some reason, my uncle had wanted me to go, and now West was offering me an out as well. I should take it. This was the place for a free Story Hale.

"Why Scotland?" I asked.

Again, some emotion flickered behind his brown eyes, but all he said was, "Have you been?"

I shook my head.

"It would be a good place for you." He pulled my hand into his and moved the ring on my finger around. "Do you remember the first time we met?"

"You came up to me at a Crowne party I was serving." He'd been so charming...he stood by me the entire night, making me laugh.

"That wasn't the first time, Angel."

West looked at my hand, thumbing the glittering diamond.

"You were moving in to Crowne Hall. You didn't know the rules yet. You came up and you asked me where the servants' quarters were."

He smiled, in on some secret. My lips parted, horrified.

"No I didn't. I wouldn't do that."

He was totally grinning now, pearly white teeth stretching his hazelnut cheeks.

"You asked me to throw away your trash," he said. "No, you *told* me to. You handed me a bubblegum wrapper, and then you just left."

I vaguely remembered the time in my life when I wouldn't have thought twice about giving a du Lac my trash. When it wouldn't have filled me with horror. The learning period after I moved in, when Grayson kicked over my bucket because I'd dared to clean while he was awake, or when I'd looked Mrs. Tansy in the *eyes*.

West fixed me with his gaze. "I'd never had to find the garbage before."

"Sorry," I mumbled.

His brow furrowed at my words. A few seconds passed as he played with the ring on my finger.

"My time with you is almost up. Have you thought anymore about what I asked?"

"I..." I trailed off.

Despite my best efforts, I was starting to feel something for West, but we were sitting on a bed where I'd only just locked lips with another.

I wasn't supposed to want a future with either of them.

"I haven't been a good wife, West...I'm..."

"In love with Grayson Crowne?"

I coughed. "No."

West stood, giving me his hand. "We're late for breakfast. Again."

With the table so filled with Crownes and du Lacs, it was

easier to blend in, because the Crowne extended family *needed* to stand out. Every five seconds someone was making a toast. West held my hand and refused to let go. He would set down his fork if he needed to raise his drink again.

"I think our cook is learning a new recipe for the steak," Tansy said with a tone I knew meant *He's taking too long.* "I apologize for the delay."

"I'm sure it will be worth it," one of Grayson's great-uncles said. "I know steak is your favorite, Grayson."

"I hate steak. Not eating it anymore," Grayson said. "But I'll eat it every day for a year if the right person asked me."

I coughed on my eggs.

"Uh..." Grayson's uncle trailed off.

Grayson pinned me with his gaze as he spoke, and my neck heated. I suddenly wished I was wearing something a little less thick.

Tansy smiled as though what Grayson said was a joke, then faced her in-laws. "Everyone settled, I assume?"

"I think our wing is smaller than last year," one of Grayson's twice-removed cousins noted.

Tansy smiled thinly, expertly maneuvering the conversation to this year's masquerade.

Everyone was dressed down for breakfast, and by dressed down, I mean in designer jeans and one-of-a-kind sweaters and jackets. Grayson's black zip-up fit him in a casual, sexy slouch and I hated that I wondered about the softness.

West dragged my gaze away with his finger, lifting my chin up to meet his warm brown eyes, leaning so his lips were against my ear.

"Do you like it when he watches, Angel?"

Grayson's cold voice drifted down the table. "Look me in the eyes."

It *felt* like he was talking to me. An audible pause followed, and I followed the eyes of everyone to what had them so stunned.

Grayson had spoken to a servant.

I tried to jerk out of West's grip, but his hold turned bruising.

"West, everyone—"

"Is watching Grayson now." He grinned, leaning closer, like he was going to kiss me at the fucking table.

"Grayson..." Tansy's light-as-a-feather voice warned.

"I think it's time we stop having the servants walk around with their fucking tails between their legs."

One of Grayson's aunts coughed. "I think, I...read something about a blizzard this weekend."

Grayson stared at me as he spoke, and the heat in my neck rose. My heart pounded as West locked on my lips.

"What if they look?"

"So what? I'm your husband."

West pressed his lips against mine, kissing me deeper than before, harder. My lips parted on a gasp. My eyes stayed wide open on the table, darting around to see if anyone would turn from Grayson.

Don't kiss him again, Snitch.

Grayson's warning played over and over again on repeat.

When West pulled back, Grayson was watching, jaw clenched.

"If this is how I have to have you, Angel. For now it's okay."

West stressed *for now* with a growl.

I stood up so quickly the plates on either side of me wobbled.

"I need...air."

"It won't blizzard for the party," Tansy said with certainty.

"You can't control the weather, too, Mother," Gemma said, voice fading as I left the hall.

This was bad.

This was wrong.

Something twisted was growing between all four of us.

I'd barely left the dining hall when the servant from inside stepped in my path. I think his name was Jared. I exhaled.

"Listen, can we do the whole bullying thing later?"

"No—I...I wanted you to know there are servants on your side, Story. We loved Woodson, and we don't think what they're doing to you is okay. It's gone too far. And, for the record"—he looked over his shoulder, probably having been away from his station for too long—"I didn't want that photo out there. I don't know how Mr. Crowne stopped it; I'm just glad he did."

Jared started to walk away.

"Wait. What photo?"

He stopped. "Ellie took a photo of you from inside his wing. You..." He rubbed his neck. "You said you were happy your mom died or something."

I wanted to press him, but he quickly left, and I know he'd already stayed longer than he should have. So, I left the hall, head buzzing.

Outside it was snowing soft flakes, and the maze called to me. I'd always wanted to wander it, and with my mind and heart the way it was, it felt right.

Firing one of them quiets them for a little...

The conversation I had with West came rushing back. I never fired anyone, but *Grayson* had, and at the time, I thought it was because he'd been turning into someone else. All this time, for *me*.

He told the world he was a virgin. I know he did. For her.

The words I'd overheard Lottie say twisted in my mind as I went left and right in the overgrown emerald hedges. I wanted to believe there was no way Grayson would do that...tell the world his most guarded secret.

He fired Ellie for *me*. He sold his secret for *me*.

I thought it would be easy to hate West. I thought it would be easy to hate Grayson.

They'd done horrible things to me.

Instead I'd ended up hating myself.

"You shouldn't be out here in the cold."

I spun. "Grayson."

"What are you doing here?"

Ignoring me, Grayson slipped out of his jacket, draping it over my shoulders. It was almost like the first time he'd given me his jacket.

Without another word, he turned to leave.

"Did you fire Ellie for me? Did you stop a story from coming out?" I demanded of his back. "Did the servants leak my secret? Is that why the entire world knows yours?"

He paused.

"You did. Why?"

He slightly turned his head so I had a view of his angular profile, his perfect jaw, soft lips, and crooked nose.

"That was my secret, Snitch. You gave that to me."

I shoved his back. Grayson spun around, blue eyes

alight with some emotion. He walked to me, forcing me to take steps back until my back slammed into the prickly hedge. There was only a whisper of cold air between us.

He ran a tender hand along my jaw.

I couldn't move.

"Lottie loves you," I said, desperate for something to eat the silence.

"She does," he agreed, still tracing that hand down my cheek.

"West loves me."

His hand froze. He clenched his jaw. He took a step, pressing me farther into the hedge, arching over me until we were shadowed by his massive height.

"When he kisses you, do you think about me, Snitch?" he asked quietly.

Yes.

Always.

"I saw the way he kisses you...my little nun doesn't like it sweet. Are you that desperate?"

I swallowed, voice rough. "This is where we're supposed to be, Grayson. Everyone wins."

His lips were on my neck, hot, soft. "I love my name from your lips."

He trailed his other hand from the arch of my neck, along my shoulder, down my arm, to the exposed skin of my wrist. I swallowed a sigh.

"Grayson..."

He either didn't care, or he was done talking. His lips were a sultry, teasing whisper at my neck. Not quite a kiss, but not leaving the flesh. He swirled his touch along the bone at my wrist and made my gut *ache* for more.

He moved even closer until we were practically one. He was hard on my hip, and my heartbeat sped. I wanted him. I couldn't *stop* wanting him, but I didn't want to be this person.

"I hate you," I whispered.

His smile stretched along my neck. "No you don't."

"I'm leaving. You're letting me leave. You're just my friend."

"No I'm not. I'll never be just your friend."

I squirmed to get away, and he gripped my chin, whatever game he was playing vanishing like the sun above us into the lacy winter clouds.

"Seriously, Story. What would I have to do to win you back?"

"I'm married. You're married—"

"I don't care. I'll be with you even if you're married. I'll love you if you marry all the men you meet. I'll love you if you join a convent. I don't fucking *care*, Snitch." He grabbed my face with both hands. "Let me love you."

I tried to shove him, but he was too strong. "You've broken my heart too many times."

"I won't force you to stay, Snitch. I won't lock you in a tower. But I'm going to follow."

His words made my blood freeze. "What?"

"I'll follow you. To the sea. To the moon."

I bit my lip to stop the smile. "You kind of sound like a stalker."

A smile flickered and died on his lips. "You've reduced Grayson Crowne to this. A lowly stalker." He slid his hands underneath the jacket he'd given me, hands roaming my body like he'd been starved of it. My rib cage, my hips. All places ...innocent...friendly...right?

"You said you wouldn't..." I breathed. "We wouldn't."

"What?" He shot me a wicked smile. "I'm not kissing.

I'm not doing anything. I'm just touching you. Friends hug. I can touch you like this, right?"

"You said we wouldn't. Not..." My words died when he slid his palm between my thighs.

"Friends touch." Gray pressed his lips against my neck. "I can't stop picturing you getting fat with my baby. I heard chicks get wetter when they're pregnant. Is it true?"

His teeth scraped against my earlobe, the pain sending delicious tingles down my spine.

"What is your pussy like now, Snitch? Does it still get wet for me?"

"Friends don't talk like this," I said jaggedly.

"Good friends do."

The wind blew, rustling the leaves, enough sound to break me out of it. I shoved him off.

"We're friends," I said, wiping my brow. "We're supposed to be friends."

"Friends?" Grayson growled. "I'll be your fucking *friend*, Story. I won't touch you." He traveled his hand down his abdomen, gripping his hard cock over his jeans. "I'll stay away from you. Go on, go back inside." He jerked his head toward the opening of the maze.

I was frozen.

Transfixed.

I couldn't see anything save the hard, tapered outline, and that made it worse. Made the memory of him ache inside me.

A cocky, cruel grin speared his pink lips. "Sure you don't want to touch me, little nun?"

I wanted to touch him so badly. I wanted to feel him.

"You..." I swallowed, watching him palm and work himself. "Your wife...someone could hear."

"Who the fuck cares? I'll fuck you right here until you

scream so loud everyone comes to make sure you're not fucking dead."

He fucked himself harder, faster. My thumb came to my bottom lip.

"Oh, little nun, you want this bad."

My eyes locked with his.

"Get over here," he commanded.

Go back, the sane part of my brain said, the part barely clinging to the idea I could still leave Crowne Point.

I moved to him. In a trance.

The minute I was within reach, Grayson grabbed my wrist and thrust my hand to the waistband of his jeans. I met the deep, hot ridges of his eight-pack.

But no further.

If we were going to do this, I had to make the decision.

He continued to work himself, and the movement rubbed the hem of his jeans against my palm. Each rough scrape eroded my willpower. I slid the tips of my fingers down, brushing coarse hair.

His half-lidded eyes and clenched jaw, the look that said he was about to tear me up, made my heart pound. Almost as much as the feeling of him as I lowered my hand more.

"Friends help friends," he rasped, with a wicked smile spearing his lips.

Then I felt him. Hot. Hard. Iron and velvet and *Grayson.*

The humor in his eyes vanished into brutal lust.

Oh god. It was wrong.

It was like he saw the words in my head, because he sandwiched my hand beneath his, trapping me over his cock, in his jeans.

"Friends help friends, little nun."

He palmed himself like he'd done before, but now he used my hand as sinful friction.

Slowly at first.

Then faster.

Harder.

His breath grew rockier, mine shallow, our eyes locked together. I forgot the wrong of it, losing myself in his icy eyes. He swiped his tongue across his lips, and I leaned forward, wanting to taste him.

Needing it. Grayson made a frustrated sound in his chest. Like he wanted it too.

Neither of us went the final millimeter.

Our breath fogged the air. The vision of him steamy. Muggy.

"Tell me what you're thinking," he growled.

I couldn't. It was too damning and vulnerable. Every nerve in his body was coiled, veins like lightning on his neck, his cock steel and throbbing. I knew he needed to come, but he was waiting on my words.

"Fuck," he gritted. "Snitch, please, just let me in."

"I want to kiss you," I whispered.

Then it happened, his groan I could feel in my legs, and sticky *hot*. He dragged my lips down with his thumb, as if picturing kissing me as he came, or maybe fucking my mouth.

Or both.

Then it was just the ragged sound of our breath.

Silence passed in what felt like forever, his come coating my hand as we stared into one another. His eyes were too dark. Too muddled. But I could taste just a sliver of him by the thumb he kept on my lip, and I was strung out.

I pulled my hand out, sticky and covered in his come.

Emotions twisted in my gut. Bad...wrong...so why did it feel so right?

He lifted my chin.

"Friends help friends clean up, Snitch," he whispered soft, coaxing.

The spell shattered.

His grip on my chin tightened before I could break away. The look in his eyes darkened and he spun me around, my back against his chest, my ass against his cock.

"You're not done, little nun," he growled in my ear. "Fuck my come up inside your cunt."

FORTY-THREE

STORY

I knew that if I did this, we were crossing a line neither of us could come back from, but I told myself as I slid my hand under my skirt and beneath my new soft-as-sin lace panties, that it was fine...My new thick double-breasted dress jacket covered me. Grayson couldn't see anything.

His blue eyes were dark, eyelids heavy. "Fuck it up inside you, little nun."

He made a sound deep in his throat as though I wasn't doing it right, as he had the night we first started spiraling into our demons.

But unlike that night, his hand covered mine over the fabric.

He moved his hand with mine, telling me how to fuck myself.

His lips at my ear, biting. "How does it feel?"

When I didn't answer, he bit hard on the lobe.

"W-wrong."

His teeth slid down my neck. "We're not doing anything *wrong*, Story." He put his other hand to the hedges. "I'm not touching you."

It *was* wrong—so, so wrong.

He was at my back.

His presence a heated shadow.

His lips at my neck. Not kissing me.

I wanted him to kiss me.

I knew all I had to do was ask.

He wanted me to snap first.

"Go back to your husband, Story." He scraped his teeth along the curve of my neck. "Take him inside you. Take him inside you when you have my come inside you."

Flutters rose up and down my back at his words.

"Do you like that, the idea of taking him inside you when you're filled with my come? When I go back to my wife, I'll be all clean."

I tensed at the idea and his laugh followed like fireflies in the night. He worked his hand harder over my skirt, forcing me to get off on my worst fucking nightmare.

Always torturing me.

"You don't like that, little nun?" he teased. "Say the word, little nun."

His hot breath and his teeth on my neck were a sinful temptation.

I was heady with it. Eroding this razor-thin line between us further. One step away from it dissolving.

So he couldn't *see* me.

So what?

I was fucking his come into my body.

"Say the word and I'll get my cock covered with you, Story."

He nipped the skin at my neck, as if finally giving in a

little himself. A small mark. A bruise barely noticeable. Except it lit thousands of fires inside my body.

More.

"More," I begged.

He groaned against my neck like he was just as swallowed in the fantasy as I was. He bit harder and I exploded.

My head fell against his chest.

He pushed the hair out of my eyes.

"My girl," he said softly. "You are still the most beautiful, perfect creature when you come."

"What are we doing?" I whispered. "We're becoming everything we don't want to be. You're hiding me from your wife. You're lying to her. I'm cheating on my husband. I'm having another man's baby."

"*Another man?*" he growled. "Is that what the fuck I am to you? Just some asshole who knocked you up? I'm *yours* the way you are *mine*." He quirked his neck to the side, as if fighting the rage crawling up his spine. "What are we doing? You could never cheat on your fucking husband with me."

He bit off the word, his grip on my waist becoming a vise.

"Get this through your head, Snitch. When you're with him, you're cheating on *me*."

FORTY-FOUR

STORY

I rushed out of the maze, Grayson at my back. I ignored him calling for me, ignored him all the way back into Crowne Hall.

"Story, wait!"

The Crownes had moved from breakfast to a light cocktail brunch in the library. I'm sure they were wondering where we were. Both of us...missing.

"Story!" He grabbed my arm.

"Let me go. They'll be wondering where we are."

"I don't give a shit."

I yanked at my arm. "We can't do that again."

"Stop fucking saying that."

"I have your—your—"

He grabbed my waist with both hands. "My *come*."

"There you are, Angel."

I shoved Grayson off. West came to us, and I could feel Grayson's eyes on me. My skin was hot and itchy, and my chest bruised from my pounding heart. I wrapped my arm around West's, letting him lead me away from Grayson, into the library.

"I'm sorry," I said.

He glanced at me, brow raised, and if I didn't know any better...I'd swear his eyes were filled with humor. "What for?"

I don't know. Nothing. Everything. In the end, I didn't respond.

In the library, Lottie held Grayson's hand, but he stared holes at me. Lottie was talking about some book she'd had trouble finding, by an author she couldn't remember.

"Story could help you with that, right, Angel?"

"Um..." I trailed off.

"I don't see why," Grayson said.

"She's quite the bookworm," West supplied. "And sisters should be close."

West was enjoying torturing me.

I know he was.

"Oh...well, I guess," Lottie said.

This was so wrong and fucked up and morally repugnant on all sides. To be talking like in-laws while her husband's come was inside me. While he stared at me like he knew, like he wanted me to *know* he knows.

West slid his hand from my waist, down to the curve of my ass. He dipped his head down, so he could whisper against my ear.

"Where were you, Angel?" He slid his palm lower, under the curve of my ass. "What has your skin so hot?"

When you're with him, you're cheating on me.

My gut flipped, eyes on Grayson.

I stepped back. "I-I need a drink."

West's laughter followed me to the mimosa tower.

Josephine stood next to the tower, one hand on her shoulder, the other holding her sparkling drink. I grabbed a water.

"I'm Story," I said, realizing we hadn't talked. I don't think I'd seen *anyone* talk to her.

"I'm Josephine." She smiled. "You'll have to forgive me. I would have introduced myself earlier, but I'm not allowed to speak unless spoken to." She shrugged as if it was the simplest thing to say that.

I blinked. "What?"

"You're the servant girl, right?" she asked. "Story?"

She hadn't said it with derision as everyone else had, so I nodded.

"I'm sure there's a lot you don't know about this world. There was a lot I didn't know." She grew wistful, then smiled again, and moved to leave.

"Wait. What don't I know?"

She studied me beneath her thick, black lashes, maybe wondering if she could trust me. Then she kept walking.

"Please." I stepped in her path. "No one talks to me either...what don't I know?"

"That's a very long conversation."

"Then just tell me, why can't you speak unless spoken to?"

Josephine cast a furtive, sideline glance to her left. Tansy Crowne was watching us.

"Being a mistress isn't cheating with some guy's husband. It isn't like the world you know. It's a title. It's a sentence. When you become a mistress, you give up the life you know. We do get one thing. The mistress always gets the holidays."

"Why do it?" I whispered.

"It was either that or die. I had triplets to worry about. I'd already lost one child to them."

I covered my stomach with my palm, and her eyes dropped to that. "They tried to kill you?"

"The Crownes do not abide bastards." She took a sip of champagne. "But really, anything that would destroy their way of life. You don't get...this..."—she waved to the enormous ballroom—"by allowing people like us to change things."

My heart cracked. "Grayson could help. I'm sure he doesn't want his siblings—"

"Grayson Crowne and my children are not siblings, Story. He, along with his *real* siblings, have never spoken a word to them."

I blinked. That couldn't be true. I tried to remember past Holidays, a time when I'd seen Grayson speak with the bastard Crownes.

I came up blank.

"Is it also forbidden? Is that why they're not here?"

She shook her head. "They'll be here soon, and they'll be ignored like me. If you manage to have your baby—"

"I'm not—"

"You'll get a prison in Scotland...I mean, a castle. And you'll be forced to watch your children grow up to become the people who murdered their father." She sighed. "At least my master loved me. He made me his mistress to save me. But he couldn't save me from everything. From rituals dating back centuries."

I shuddered at the memory of the wedding night. "I'm not a stranger to archaic rituals."

Josephine paused, a distant look in her eyes. "I see myself in you, Story. Be careful. Whatever you think you know, or have seen, I can guarantee it's only the tip of the iceberg."

I opened my mouth to ask more questions when a hand wrapped around my waist.

"You've been over here for a while," West said. "Your conversation looked riveting."

I stared at Josephine, wanting to keep talking to her. It was a tsunami of information, and I felt like she had all the answers to questions I didn't know needed answering.

Josephine smiled. "Just girl stuff."

She walked away, mingling with the crowd in silence. West's eyes fell to me, and I placed a hand on his chest before he could speak.

"West, I'm going to get some air."

He grinned. "In the maze?"

I opened and closed my mouth like a fish, then mumbled something incoherent and dashed off, stealing away into a linen closet.

I fell against a pile of soft sheets with a deep exhale. My head swam with everything I'd learned and done, but this closet smelled like clean cotton and was dark and I could *breathe*.

Then the door opened, followed a second later by its closing and then Grayson's voice.

"Lottie, can we do this later?"

"You were gone for thirty minutes. *Everyone* noticed." Lottie's voice followed.

I froze, unsure if I should speak up.

I felt cheap and wrong, as though it were months ago, and I was back behind the linen watching one of their private moments. They stood next to the door, bodies muted in the darkness, and they didn't see me in my pile of sheets.

"You're a horrible husband," she said. "You promised you would be good but...You're worse than my father. You're making a fool of me. It's like I'm your mistress, not your wife. Don't speak unless spoken to."

Grayson dragged two hands through his hair, the pain in his eyes tearing lines down my heart.

I was watching Atlas dissolve into pieces.

I knew how much it meant to him to be good, and I was the reason he was bad. Me.

"You know what I want, Lottie," he said. "You know."

She curled her fist. "I'm not letting you divorce me. I don't care that you tried. I don't care."

She opened the door, slamming it shut.

Grayson stared at it, scraping his hands through his hair, muscles in his back tight, neck corded.

"You tried to divorce her?"

FORTY-FIVE

STORY

Grayson spun, eyes wide.

"Story—what—" He broke off, rubbing his jaw, looking around the small closet like someone else was going to pop out.

"You tried to divorce her? When?"

I stared at Grayson, waiting for him to say something—*anything*—after what I'd just heard.

Silence spread.

"Right after I learned you were pregnant," he finally said. "My grandfather asked me what I was willing to lose. And I thought about it.... Everything but you. My fortune. My family." He paused. "My wife."

He let that linger.

"I...would lose her if it meant keeping you safe. So I did...only you came back married to West, and everything changed."

I wasn't sure if that filled me with happiness or sadness.

I went with anger. I tried to push past him, and he grabbed my arm.

"Let me go."

"I'm done letting you go."

I tried to yank my arm, but he dragged me to him.

We were so close.

"Why didn't you tell me the truth about being a mistress, about your family, about this, about *everything*?"

"Why do you think I pushed you away?" he yelled. "I tried to get you out of this world. Away from us. Away from *me*."

I clutched my stomach. "Am I in danger?"

He ground his jaw. "If they find out about you...yes."

My chest bottomed out.

Fear.

Raw, breathless *fear*.

"Why didn't you tell me? Why are you *always* lying?"

"What good would it have done, Snitch?"

"I could have—" I broke off, mashing my lips together.

What could I have done that Grayson Crowne couldn't?

He brought my head into his hands. "This is my weight to bear. I'd rather you were safe and happy and away from me, than with me and unhappy like everyone—or worse, dead."

"I would have hated you less," I whispered.

His thumbs dug into my cheeks. "You should hate me more, little nun."

"You want honesty from me, but you keep so many secrets. This whole time you had this huge fucking secret. How many others are you keeping?"

"What if I failed, Snitch?" His brows drew and he looked away, like he was *embarrassed*.

Seconds ticked on, the wind howling.

His grip never loosened.

"I wasn't going to give you a hope for a future that I can't guarantee. Put you in danger and make promises I couldn't keep. I did that once before, and I won't do it again."

I tried to force the armor around my heart to stay locked tight, but each word he spoke pried it apart. West was offering me the future I'd been scraping at. Out of Crowne Point. Away for good.

"Is there hope now, Grayson?" I whispered.

His jaw was clenched so tight the muscle popped.

Then he nodded, so slowly I wondered if he didn't want me to know.

It burned my chest.

"Your family will never accept me, Grayson. They'd rather kill me. We just keep knotting the thread further and further. There's no hope for us, Grayson. None at all."

"Don't say that."

"You fought. You fought so hard. It doesn't matter. No matter what we do, we'll never be together."

Even though I knew, deep in my marrow, Grayson and I wouldn't be together, there was still this part of me that wouldn't stop poking at the idea. It was a dream and a hope. You can't shake those, they exist like their own shards of glass, cutting you with the image of happiness.

But now I finally saw.

It would never happen.

Ever.

I fumbled with the locket at my neck. Ready to open and end this thing between us once and for all, when his hand came to mine.

"Stop."

My eyelids burned. "Let go of my hands."

"We're almost there, Snitch."

"We'll always be almost there, Grayson. Don't you see?"

"I know you don't trust me." He spoke like the words were smoke burning his chest. "I'm your shard of glass now."

He thumbed a tear at my cheek that I didn't realize had fallen.

I wished I could tell him otherwise, but he was right.

"But we're almost there, little nun."

GRAY

Later that night, as the sun set on the ocean, I gripped the papers in my hand until they wrinkled. I could be a hero for my family, or I could be a good man for Snitch.

But I couldn't be both.

"Grayson?"

I lifted my head at Lottie's soft voice. She held her left arm with her right hand, her silk pajamas wrinkled. She looked like she'd had less sleep than me.

"I...I need to talk to you about something. I'm..." She exhaled a shaky breath, hand on her stomach; then her eyes zeroed on the document in my hands. "What is that?"

I stood up, gripping the postnuptial, then handed it to her.

Lottie held the papers, staring at them for a while. "Is this what I think it is?"

I nodded.

She looked back at them, going quiet. "You're handing me papers for a future, so why does this feel like the end?"

Because once my grandfather saw this, I'd finally have leverage to get us out.

"It's for her." She gripped the papers, wrinkling them. "It's *always* her. They won't let you get away with this, Grayson."

"They won't have a choice."

She sat on the couch overlooking the winter ocean. "Do you know why I hate Christmas? It was the one time of year my father's mistresses could come to Du Lac Manor. My mother had to play good hostess and act like what was happening wasn't a knife to the soul. For most, Christmas is the happiest time of the year. For us, it was the darkest."

My chest twisted, and I fell beside Lottie. Christmas had always been the darkest for me for the exact same fucking reason. I'd first promised myself I'd never be my father next to the tree, as I watched my mother hide her pain.

The waves crashed on the wintry sand as I watched my wife, saw a life that had seemingly been mapped by fate since the beginning.

She turned to me, eyes bright and earnest. "You need more time. I'll give you time. I'll give however long you need."

"Lottie, I love her. I'll never stop loving her."

"You would give me everything? Even though all of it is going to go to my *brother*?"

We would be out of this world—*both* Snitch and I. West du Lac could jack off into a pile of money like Scrooge McFuck for all I cared.

I'd finally have my girl.

I sat beside her, pulling her hand into mine. "We'll be

free, both of us. I'll take all the responsibility. You won't leave this marriage with a scratch. No dark holidays. None of that."

"I'll never be free," she muttered.

"Lottie." I gripped her face. "What is going on?"

There was *something* on her mind. I couldn't believe she was happy in this marriage, happy with Snitch always between us.

She yanked her head out of my hands and reached for the discarded papers. She put them on the glass table in front of us, scribbling her name.

"There." She thrust the papers into my lap. "Let me know when I should expect my divorce."

"Lottie..."

"It won't work," she said. "Whatever you're trying to do, it won't work. Your grandfather won't let you give everything up; my parents won't let you leave me. We're stuck together now. None of this will work. People like us don't get to choose our fates, Grayson."

Maybe she was right. Maybe all this would be for naught. But I reached for my green pen, and signed my name next to hers in green ink.

Hoping that fate would listen.

Despite what I'd just signed, I would be faithful to Lottie until my marriage dissolved. I wouldn't start a life with Snitch with stains on our souls. I knew that was as important to her as it was to me. I would build us our perfect happily ever after.

Even if I had to burn everything to the ground.

FORTY-SIX

STORY

When the door pushed open later that night, I knew it was Grayson.

"Come with me, Snitch. No games. It's snowing and we haven't visited Woodsy."

"It's midnight..."

But I was already getting out of bed.

We walked through the shadowy hallways of Crowne Hall, out into the gardens where Uncle was laid to rest. Grayson laid his jacket on a snow-dusted bench for me, and we stared at my uncle's mausoleum as the snow fell.

Around us, poems were etched in the granite tombs. Up the walls, beneath the names, some mournful, others joyful.

"Woodsy and I used to come out here a lot," Grayson said.

"It feels emptier without him," I said.

"Yeah."

Grayson pulled my hand into his.

I wanted a world where I could hold his hand.

In public.

"What are you thinking?" I asked.

He craned his neck slightly, the sharp ninety-degree angle of his jaw and the slope of his plump lips catching the moonlight.

"About how much damage I've done to my family."

"Grayson, you care about family more than anyone. You would never do anything to hurt them."

A look flitted across his eyes.

Hurt.

Pain.

Why? Thorns were back around his heart, and I couldn't get inside...But then, they were around mine too. Silence was soft as the falling snow.

"You said you wanted to leave Crowne Point. Is that still true?" He thumbed the bones on my palm.

I swallowed hard. "West gave me plane tickets."

He tensed but said nothing.

"I should probably want to leave this world. It's never been kind to me. Now everyone knows my name and they gossip about me."

Grayson continued to thumb the bones in my hand, something on his mind he wouldn't let me read.

"You really haven't slept with her?" I asked quietly. I'd spent these months distrusting everything about him.

He shook his head.

"But you *said*. You said you fucked her. She sucked you off."

"I lied."

"Why would you lie to me about that?"

"I thought if you hated me...it would be easier."

I could feel the pain in his words, and it tugged the wire around my heart.

He leaned forward, brushing the snowflakes out of my hair

"Why are you acting like it's the end? That look in your eyes always means you're about to do something bad."

"You know me so well, Snitch."

I think I know him best of anyone.

The look in his eyes was too intense; he was too close. I knew I should shrug out of his touch, but I leaned closer until I could taste the sugar on his lips.

"Would you want to be with me if I wasn't Grayson Crowne?" he asked.

"I told you...Grayson *Crowne* is my least favorite thing about you."

"Tell me more about what you'd need for a happily ever after," he demanded.

The wounded part that still hadn't healed from all the times he'd abandoned me said to lie or move away, but my heart was beating from the way he watched me.

"Fight for me! I asked for it in the hospital and you never did."

"I am fucking fighting for you. That's all I've been doing since the day you slammed into my goddamn lips."

I rolled my eyes before I could stop it, turning away—he gripped my shoulders, yanking me back with violence.

"Don't roll your eyes. Don't fucking leave, Snitch. Keep going."

"I want you to care! I want it to tear you up inside the way it does me whenever I see her on your arm."

"You think it doesn't?"

I shrugged in his grip.

"I'm barely holding it together, Snitch. Every time he

even looks at you, I want to punch his face to the floor and drag you to me." He wrapped his arm around my waist, pulling me until I was flush against his side.

"Fuck you." His lips were a deep growl against my ear. "Kiss you." Soft now, coaxing on my earlobe. "Mark you." His teeth grazed my ear. "Let the world know you're *mine.*"

I swallowed a breath, fighting the tingles between my thighs, the urge to fist my hands in his shirt. He pulled back, suddenly serious.

"But I tied this knot. I made this bed. I'll get us out of it. No more stains on our souls."

I looked away, anywhere but him. "It's too late, Grayson."

"It's never too late, little nun. I'm going to build us that happily ever after, even if it takes until we're ninety. I know you don't trust me anymore...but I'm going to fix this."

My chest cracked with the desire to believe him, but I'd already done that. So many times I'd fallen into his beautiful lies. I wouldn't do it again.

"You..." I swallowed, tried to blink out of the heat rising up my chest. "You don't get to just decide you want me again and everything is perfect. Things are different. I'm married—"

"So fucking what? Do you fucking love him?"

"I don't know! He's offering me forever, and all you've ever done is offer me...promises of a future that break in my hands. He married me, Grayson. And you married her."

"You have no idea what I've been doing. What I've done. What I will continue to do for you."

"Then *tell me.* Don't keep me in the dark any longer. Don't lie. If you lie to me again—"

"Tomorrow I'm forcing my grandfather's hand."

Tomorrow.

That sounded too good to be true.

Suspiciously like a happily ever after.

"How?" I didn't like how he was speaking, the darkness in his eyes. "Grayson, *how?*"

He looked away. "I don't want to lie to you again, little nun. But I know if I tell you, you'll try and stop me."

Panic crawled up my chest. "Then don't do it."

He gripped my cheeks between his palms. "I'm not letting you go anymore. You can't stop me. I'll marry you, Snitch. We'll finally be free to love and start our family in the way we've always dreamed."

"I-I..." I stuttered, frozen between *needing* that dream to come true, and being deathly afraid of whatever Grayson was about to do. "I don't know if I'm ready."

"Run away with me, Snitch. Be my wife. Be *mine.*"

"I can—"

"Don't say you can't."

Grayson crashed his lips against mine.

The snow froze in the air, the world melted away, and all I knew were his lips. He tangled his hands into my hair, pulling me closer.

We'd been denying it for so long and giving in was stardust in my veins. His groan was whiskey down my throat, rough and sweet. His grip was iron, and I could feel the restraint even as he dragged me closer.

I sighed into his mouth. *"More."*

I felt the faintest quirk of his lips against mine.

A smile.

He slanted his mouth, diving deeper, giving me more. More tongue. More teeth. More *Grayson.* Before I realized it, my hands were fisted in his rose gold hair, my thigh across his. He pulled back, a dark, needful look in his eyes, as though he was two seconds from laying me flat to the bench.

"You are it for me," he said roughly. "You will always be it for me, Story Hale."

"How do you know? How do you know we're not just bad? I'm..." *I'm kissing another man...in love with another man...* "I'm a terrible wife. Maybe we would be bad together."

"All I've done with Lottie since day one is fuck up my marriage. I'm the worst husband. But I know I would be great to you. I know I would, Snitch."

"Maybe we're just bad people," I whispered.

"You would be the best wife, Snitch."

"How do you know?"

His eyes dropped to my lips, jaw tight.

"Because I wouldn't have to keep restraining myself. I'd have what I want. She'd be in my bed every goddamn morning."

My eyes popped as he dragged me back to him, pressing his lips to mine for a slow, delirious kiss.

"You would be a good wife," he said softly, pulling back. "We would be good together. West will never be it for you. We're soulmates, Snitch. Face it."

He kissed me again. Brutally. Roughly. Until my thoughts swam with the flavor of him. Until I was strung out anytime he pulled away for a breath.

Then he finally broke away, leaving me on the snowy bench. Leaving me to watch him walk back alone to his snow-dusted castle of Crowne Hall.

Soulmates.

FORTY-SEVEN

STORY

The night of the Nutcracker Masquerade was one of the
worst blizzards to ever hit the East Coast. Snow and sleet
slammed against the windows as though they were mad at
something.

I should have listened to fate's warning.

Grayson and I were going off course.

I kept wondering...what had come over me? My uncle
had told me to live with dignity. Before, I'd abandoned
dignity for shame; now, I'd sacrificed it to be shameless.

Not even Tansy would listen to the warning. As the
chandeliers flickered and the wind howled through the
halls, she made it clear: anyone who did not make it to the
party would *not* be invited next year. Canceled flights and
snowed-in streets were not acceptable excuses.

Two unopened dress boxes lay on my bed, wrapped in
ribbons of different colors: deep emerald or peach.

Grayson or West.

Two men promising to build me a happily ever after... and I trusted neither of them. The morning paper lay next to the boxes, a photograph of West, Grayson, Lottie, and me captured a few nights before.

While he was holding Lottie close, and West was holding me close, our heads were turned to each other. The chandelier glimmered behind our portrait.

We're soulmates, Snitch. Face it.

All this time I've been hating Grayson, he'd been building us a happily ever after.

But my trust for him is now wrapped in thorns.

I don't know how to just...unravel that.

I opened West's first, lifting the silky peach lid. It was beautiful, a stark white. Looking in the mirror, I held the pink-and-white material against my skin, trying to picture the woman who would wear the low-cut neckline, the short tutu, the matching mask.

It was beautiful.

And once again...not me.

I set it down and went for Grayson's.

Simple yet elegant. The lacy skirt fell below the knee and sparkled even in my low light. A green ribbon tied at the waist and fell to my shins. This was me.

The mask was even more beautiful.

Nutcracker Masquerade masks weren't simple lace and ribbon. They were usually made with sparkling diamonds and gold—real diamond of course—and mine was no exception.

I dropped it to the bed.

It would definitely garner Tansy Crowne's ire. I would be the *only* one not in a mask, but tonight I couldn't hide. No matter the consequences.

I wasn't sure how I'd explain changing my dress to

West. He'd been nothing but perfect from day one of our marriage.

Still, I slid into the lacy material.

The finishing touch was a ribbon in my hair. The box had come with a silky white ribbon to match the dress, but I took the green one off the box, and tied it in my hair.

It fell to mid back.

A knock sounded on the door and my heartbeat sped up.

I opened the door, trying to keep my face from falling when West smiled back.

"That's not the dress I expected."

"I bought this one myself," I lied.

Why am I lying?

It's not like West and I have anything.

West smiled. "Well, tonight you really are my angel."

"And you are?"

He pointed to his mask, a beautiful bronze with circular wired ears. "The mouse king, of course."

"Of course."

He caressed his knuckle down my bare face. "Forgetting something?"

My stomach twisted, but I shook my head. West arched his brow, but only held his arm out for me.

"Ready?"

In the end, the only people who'd made it to the party were those who'd already been in Crowne Hall, so the ballroom was dotted with various Crowne and du Lac family members—and one socialite who *had* managed to brave the storm, refusing to miss a Crowne party.

Even Abigail and Theo hadn't made it.

It was an ominous party. The few of us lingered like forgotten stage props in the massive ballroom, with no music, and the chandelier flickering overhead, threatening to die, all while Tansy forced us to act as if everything was perfect.

"There's a legend in my family," Grayson's low, grating whisper sounded close to my ear. "This masquerade was established so my ancestor could dance with his true love without consequence."

I stared forward as Gray spoke, stared at the marble floor like everything was fine. West was next to me, Lottie was next to Gray, but the howling wind was our secret keeper.

"You could get in a lot of trouble for a dance, back then," he continued. "Imagine what would happen if they kissed."

Images of Grayson and I kissing, a dirty secret hidden behind his mask, flooded my brain without consent.

"Angel," West said. "You're looking at the ballroom floor like you want to fuck it."

"Am not." I gasped, turning to West.

West's lips lifted. "You're blushing. What are you blushing for?"

I pressed the back of my hand to my cheek. "Um. It's hot in here."

"I want to dance with you, Snitch."

I could tell by the way Grayson's low, sultry voice seemed to caress my ear that he'd turned, was looking directly at me. But I stared at West, focused on his smile, as Grayson made my heart slam against my chest.

Pound.

Thump.

"I want to dance with you...but not behind masks."

"Clara and her prince!" I jumped, startled, feeling caught. The socialite pointed at my and Grayson's outfits.

I looked at my sparkling white-and-green gown. "I-I'm just an angel."

"*My* angel." West wrapped his arm around my waist.

Lottie grabbed Grayson's hand. "And *we* are Clara and the Nutcracker."

Grayson removed his hand from Lottie's. Lottie paused, slashing her eyes to the floor, mouth parted. She marched off to the opposite side of the ballroom to join her mother.

The socialite's mouth stuck in a confused grin.

When Grayson and Lottie were together, their costume made sense. But somehow, when Grayson stood next to me, we also looked like Clara and the Nutcracker. I wanted to burrow into a fucking hole.

Grayson focused on me, heat rising to my neck.

Soulmates.

I made some excuse to West about getting a tart just so I could get away. The servants were still on the premises, of course, so the ballroom was decorated beautifully and still had towering cakes and sparkling ciders fit for hundreds of guests. I'm sure they'd spent hours on it.

"I hope you're happy with yourself."

I jumped, startled.

Lottie had taken off her pretty diamond-and-lace mask, and her face had lost some of its color, the pretty hazelnut drained.

"You know what they call us? The Golden Sisters." She laughed. "Do golden sisters fuck each other's husbands? Should I fuck yours?" She made a face, realizing what she'd said. Then she pointed at me. "You couldn't even marry someone for me to fuck. Bitch."

She shoved me off but stumbled again. I gripped her arm.

"You know the messed-up thing? I don't even want to fuck anyone else... I don't understand what I did wrong. I've done what I'm told to do. I did everything I was told to do."

She stumbled again and I reached for her elbow. "Let's go sit down."

She shoved me off. "You're not my girl anymore."

"I'm not helping you because I have to, Lottie."

She glared at me. "There's no going back from this. You're supposed to love him. How could you let him do this?"

"What are you talking about?"

She laughed, but it was breathless, weak.

"He didn't tell you? I guess he doesn't share everything with his *mistress*."

The snow slammed harder against the windows. I let her go, and she fell to the floor.

"I think you need some water. Or coffee."

"Fuck you, whore."

I took a step back, heart in my throat, and kept going. Kept walking until Lottie's glare wasn't so bold.

Then I was grabbed.

"Grayson?"

Grayson dragged me backward.

"Grayson, people will see."

He ignored me, pulling me out of the ballroom, walking so fast I tripped over my feet. He dragged us past jewel-colored eyes peering out of their metal-and-lace masks. Dragged us until we were alone in a hallway.

"Grayson—"

He spun on me, his height seeming to grow in the shadows and howling wind, blue eyes wilder beneath his gold mask.

"I need to know tonight if your happily ever after includes me," he said.

"I don't know, Grayson. I can't—I'm not ready."

He nodded like he was expecting it, expecting me to deny him. "I don't give a shit. You can have time later. Go grab whatever you need. We're leaving tonight."

My heart pounded.

Leave with Grayson.

Leave *tonight*.

"Can't we—can't you—why do you keep doing this?" I shoved him.

He frowned. "What?"

"Everything is on your timeline. I won't do it."

He gripped me above the elbow, thumb bruising, pulling me so my back arched and I was forced to feel the ache in his bruising eyes.

"You said you wanted me to fight for you," he growled. "So I'm fighting. We're leaving tonight. You can have all the time you need when you aren't surrounded by fucking sharks. You can hate me out of Crowne Point. You can hate me for decades."

He ripped me to him by my arm, crashing his lips to mine as the snow slammed against the windows. His other hand found my waist, anchoring me against his body. Our tongues collided as the chandeliers above us sizzled, and he kissed me until I couldn't breathe.

Until I tangled my hands in his hair and forgot to care.

He pulled back, biting my bottom lip softly, gold mask glinting under the flickering light.

"Wake me up every morning in my bed with a slap to my face," he said low, "but be in my fucking bed. I am done letting you go, Snitch. We leave tonight."

He released me and I stumbled, my legs jelly.

"If your heart is caged by thorns now, I'll spend the rest of our life together ripping them out."

My heart cracked, and I looked at the window, completely white with angry snow. "Tonight?"

He nodded and headed down the hallway, but he paused, throwing a look over his shoulder like he'd forgotten something. With two fast strides, he had me against the wall, slamming his lips against mine until all that held met up was his weight on my body.

He pulled back, exhaled as if a rock had been lifted from his chest, and walked the way he'd been going.

"Wait!"

He paused, turning around.

"Lottie said something to me. She said you were giving up everything. I don't want you to do that. Nothing that makes you *you*, Grayson. I know how much your family means to you. I know how much you want to be a hero for your sisters. I know how much you want to be a *good man*."

He looked away. The flickering chandeliers cast a shadow on his gold mask, put his blue eyes in darkness.

"You said no more broken promises, so promise me, Grayson. I won't be okay with it. I..." I didn't know what I would do, but I wouldn't let him get away with it. "Promise me." I raised my voice louder than the howling wind.

He lifted his eyes. "I promise."

FORTY-EIGHT

STORY

There were only a few things I wanted to bring, and they were all tied to Grayson: the notebook, the pen, and my locket.

"Where are you going, Angel?" West's voice stopped me just outside the ballroom. With it, guilt grew strangling vines inside my chest.

I turned and faced him.

West has been nothing but kind to me. Am I really about to abandon him without word? He looked at me with the patient quirk of his lips I'd grown accustomed to.

"I..." I broke off.

West held out his hand. "Dance with me?"

"There's no music." I stated the obvious, but I took his hand.

He led me into the ballroom, out to the empty dance floor. As the chandelier flickered above us, the howling wind was our only melody.

His hand found my lower waist and pressed me close to him.

I looked around the ballroom, anywhere but West.

What if Grayson is lying?

West doesn't deserve this.

Or does he?

"What are you thinking, Angel?"

"Um...just that the holidays are a lot nicer than antici-pated." It wasn't a total lie. Servants had always known the Nutcracker Masquerade—and the holidays in general—to be insane. The Crownes kept multiple doctors on staff for the event to keep quiet and deal with the inevitable drug overdoses.

This was nothing like I'd imagined in the servants' quarters.

Actually, so far all the parties I'd had to attend hadn't been *that* bad. Compared to being gambled, to being aban-doned on a boat, they were almost...tame.

"This isn't the holidays, Story. The holidays haven't even begun. It would have started tonight, but..." he eyed the blizzard.

What the hell did that mean? The holidays started weeks ago. I opened my mouth to question, when my atten-tion was grabbed elsewhere.

Lottie stumbled near the white-chocolate-and-gold-leaf fountain.

"I think your sister had too much to drink," I said.

He laughed.

I looked at him. "What?"

"You don't need to pretend you give a shit about my sister with me, Angel."

I blinked at the cruel words. "You can be very callous sometimes, West."

He tilted his head at my words, a smile barely quirking the side of his mouth. "I'm starting to think you like that about me, Angel."

Grayson came back into the ballroom. He didn't see me. He looked like he was on a mission. I watched him as he grabbed his grandfather and took him just outside, as he'd taken me only moments before.

West dragged my gaze back. "I hope you're not falling for the same trick, Angel."

GRAY

"I'm leaving tonight."

My grandfather exhaled. "How many times do we have to do this? It's...getting repetitive." I handed him the papers. "What is this?"

"It's the copy of the postnup with both Lottie and my signatures, as well as a notarized statement from me that I was the one in that video. It's now in West du Lac's inbox."

He was silent.

Then he laughed. "I always thought I was the greedy one in the family, but look at you, Grayson, throwing your entire family to the wolves for your own happiness."

I swallowed past the heartburn in my chest. "I gave you every opportunity to avoid this."

It was one more broken promise. Story would forgive me.

Even if it took a decade.

She would.

"Your mother will be on the street. Your sister will lose

everything she knows. Her fiancé. Her life. Her safety—oh, so a part of you does care." He laughed at the look on my face.

"You left me no other choice! You could have let me leave, could have let me cancel my wedding. I gave you so many fucking chances. Whose greed put us here?"

"Everything I've ever done was for this family. I was going to make us untouchable."

I clenched my jaw. "If it wasn't for you, we wouldn't need any of that!"

"I gave you the keys to a fucking kingdom."

"You gave me a lock to a fucking jail." I took a deep breath. "I know you've been working with Mom. With my wife and father-in-law. With damn near everyone."

He tilted his head, smile growing. "Is that right?"

"You still lost. Enjoy poverty."

I turned, searching for Story. We were getting out of this house. Tonight.

"What you want is impossible," my grandfather said to my back. "All you've done is fuck us. All of us. She'll never be safe. You don't get to run away from power just because you decided you don't want it."

"I'm not running away," I gritted.

The ballroom was plunged into darkness as a scream sounded.

"Lottie!"

FORTY-NINE

GRAY

All around us, flames flickered to life as the servants rushed to light hundreds of candles.

I pushed my way through the crowd gathered around Lottie.

"We need a doctor!" Mr. du Lac yelled, looking around the ballroom filled with CEOs, socialites, and financiers.

Gemma laughed. "I guess this is what you get for calling doctors the working class."

"Gemma Antoinette," my mother hissed.

"I already told her if she doesn't take it easy she could lose the baby," Mrs. du Lac said. "You shouldn't even *be* here."

Shocked cries of "Pregnant?" rose out.

I stared at Lottie and she stared back.

Pregnant?

Fucking *pregnant?*

"We don't typically announce it until the last trimester."

Mrs. du Lac patted Lottie's head, held her hand. "Our pregnancies are very rough."

"She's pregnant?" I spun at Story's voice.

She took stuttering steps backward, eyes locked with mine, growing wider with betrayal. Heartbreak.

Looking left and right.

Mouth opening and closing.

"Wait!" I yelled for Snitch.

"Let her go, Grayson," my mother trilled, bored. "She's leaving before Christmas, anyway, right?"

I shot my mother a harsh, furious glare, and she met it. A fucking rare time Tansy Crowne didn't hide behind smiles. In an instant, her face was back to serenity.

"How does your mother know I'm leaving—h-how do *you* know?"

Story took another step back.

"I was working with my grandfather—I was trying to get you safe, Story. It was before. Before—wait!" I shouted as she took another step back.

"Don't—get away from me."

"Wait! It's *not mine*."

She paused on the outskirts of the ballroom. I could see the thorns of distrust in her eyes. I'd barely pushed through them yesterday.

"Are you accusing my daughter of being a whore?" Mr. du Lac said. "Not all of us have your proclivities, Grayson."

Said the groping drunk.

"Proclivities?" my mother said, voice rising with each syllable. "Have you stopped reading the newspapers, Arthur?"

"It's yours, Grayson," Lottie said weakly.

I slashed my glare at Lottie. "There's no fucking way that baby is mine."

"Grayson, dear..." my mother spoke in her soft, bell-like voice, which I knew meant to *shut the fuck up, we're in public.*

"Isn't this great news?" My mother tried to pivot. "A baby...how many months along?"

"Four," Mrs. du Lac supplied.

My mother crossed an arm across her chest, her chin on her hand. "You must be due around June, then? A summer pregnancy. How delightful."

Almost a year to the day when this all started.

I dragged my hands through my hair.

Willing what she said to be a lie.

No.

Fuck.

No.

"I know what you're thinking." Tears surfaced in Lottie's eyes.

Mrs. du Lac patted a cloth on Lottie's forehead. "You need to rest."

"I haven't slept with anyone. That night...our wedding... I pushed it up inside me."

I think the room stuttered to a halt. Then I heard my sister cover what sounded like a cough, or maybe a laugh.

If this was true, then Lottie had conceived on the same night Snitch had. Nausea made knots in my stomach as the knowledge hit me like a fucking boulder to the head.

No fucking way that was true.

I stared down at Lottie. "You are not pregnant with my child."

I lifted my head as the shouts of Lottie's parents dulled to a buzz, pushing through the ogling crowd. "Story!" I called for her, over and over...but Snitch was gone.

Fuck.

"You're going to leave your sick and pregnant wife?" my grandfather questioned. "Even your father wasn't that cruel."

I paused.

Then kept going.

FIFTY

STORY

Pregnant.

The wind howled as the blizzard slammed harder against the windows.

His wife is pregnant. His *wife* is pregnant. It's been staring me in the face for so long. Lottie is the girl in his dreams. Lottie is the one he loved. Lottie is the one he married.

To Grayson, I would always be the girl behind the girl.

Foolish me for thinking Grayson Crowne would ever love me in the light.

I walked down the dark hallway, forgetting why I'd come. The wind howled as I passed the wing I'd stayed in with West.

I wanted to exorcise Grayson Crowne from my body.

From the very beginning it was always about one. Fucking. Thing.

Her.

Getting him back with *her.*

So why do I feel like I'm breaking, I'm cracking? Little pieces of me chipping off with each step. The gold decorations glinted hauntingly in the dark.

Grayson kept doing these things because I keep letting him. Our relationship isn't built on trust, it's built on my allowance of his fucking lies. I'm a pushover.

I let him walk all over me.

He promised he wasn't touching her. I'm taking his promises like broken glass and they keep cutting my hands.

I almost fell for it.

I almost became the girl in the tower. Because everything had seemed to be falling into place. One of the artfully decorated trees caught my eyes, the glimmering metallic bulbs shining too bright in the darkness.

The mistress always gets the holidays.

"Angel?"

I stopped short at West's voice, as though I'd been ripped out of a dream. I turned to find him carrying a candle. We were just outside the antique room...I struggled not to fall.

He still wore his bronze mouse king mask and the candlelight flickered against the bronze. He lowered the candle to my face as he approached me.

"You don't look very good, Angel."

I swallowed the lump of emotion in my throat. "And you would know?"

"I pay closer attention than you think."

A heaving, deep ravine of sadness caved in my chest and threatened to destroy me. I lunged for West, standing on my tiptoes, wrapping my arms around his neck.

He anchored my lower waist and dragged me flush against him as our lips crashed together.

"We haven't consummated our marriage," I said.

FIFTY-ONE

STORY

I shoved West into the antique room, and he stumbled back. West looked around at the cloth-covered antiques, more eerie in the screeching wind.

I could feel it around us.

A ghost.

A memory.

An entity.

I eyed the spot I'd taken Grayson's virginity, where I'd given my soul forever. The beautiful ornate rugs he'd pulled off the wall still lay on the ground, frozen in time. This place was a snow globe that needed to be shattered.

I'll ruin them.

Good.

A vision of Grayson's wolfish grin blasted into me, shotgun shells of memory shredding into my soul. I stumbled. West grasped my elbow, peering down at me, warm brown eyes twinkling behind his mask.

"What is this place, Angel?"

A graveyard.

I pushed West toward the rugs. At first he was a wall, unmoving, but then he let me. His intense stare didn't let up the entire time. He had questions in his eyes I couldn't answer, and more emotion than I was prepared to deal with.

I gripped his massive shoulders and tried to shove him down to the rugs.

I'm bruised.

Black.

Broken. I wanted to desecrate this room. The piece of me that wouldn't let Grayson go—

"Hey, slow down." West gripped my cheeks.

His brown eyes searched, *probed.* Every pause, every breath, I breathed in Grayson, and my lungs cracked with the betrayal.

"Are you going to fuck me?" I snapped.

West blinked, brows furrowing. He let me push him to the floor. I climbed on top of him, fumbling with the button at his trousers, fingers shaking. West's hand overcame mine, helping me, guiding me.

His free hand slid under my dress, up my thigh.

Slow.

Easy.

A direct contrast to my furious, fumbling movements.

"No panties..." I could hear the grin, the lazy smile in his voice. "Since when do you not wear panties, Angel?" He gripped my flesh, fisting and bruising my ass. I froze, our eyes locked.

Dirty little nun. Do you always sleep without panties?

"K-keep the mask on," was all I said.

I popped the button on his pants. He was iron-hard, bigger than I remembered. Thicker than Grayson, I think, if it was possible. I dragged his pants past his roped thighs, my fingers trembling as I climbed atop him.

My costume felt too much like a nightgown.

"Story," West said softly.

Story.

My name from his lips felt intimate, wrong. He's supposed to call me Angel with a mocking, humorous lilt.

"Don't call me that," I whispered. "Just...don't."

"Story, slow down—"

I fisted his cock, and he broke off on a hiss, head falling back.

"Fuck. Story. *Fuck.*"

West was hard at my entrance, and I swallowed air at the fullness. Everything burned. My thighs. My eyes. My chest.

West grasped my chin. "Slow the fuck down, Story."

He gripped my thigh, bruising my chin with his free hand, forcing me to freeze as he split me in two.

To feel a moment I wanted to rush past.

Tears burned my lids. "I don't want to slow down. Don't make me slow down. *Please.*"

His eyes cracked.

No.

I can't see vulnerability in West. I needed him to be what he always is. Callous and cavalier.

I tried to yank my chin away, but his grip tightened.

"I want to make you come, Story," West said. "Don't want this to be a repeat of last time—"

The door creaked open as West's words slashed at the tender skin of my heart. My gaze jerked to the side, to a shadow that hung in the doorway.

Messy rose gold hair. Deep blue eyes. Old and new memories intersected.

I always wondered what you'd kiss like now.
You're my first...first...

My eyes flickered back and forth, from my first cruel prince to my last.

The roles had switched. Now Grayson hung in shadows, leaning in the doorway, arms folded, leg propped. My heart seized as I watched him, waiting for him to act

Waiting for him to rush in and rip me off West.

To attack West.

The waiting was *torture.*

"West. Please," I whispered, eyes still on Grayson.

Grayson wasn't moving and that was more terrifying than if he'd come and ripped me off West. It was...ominous.

"I can't have this be a repeat, Story," West said. "Tell me what you like now."

I feel like I'm on the verge of something. Every dark, suppressed, fucked up emotion swirling a spell inside me. All the things I pretended don't exist. Grayson. Grayson and his pregnant wife. Grayson and the love I can't rip out.

The very shadows hung, waiting to drop for us.

I can't breathe.

I want to break us, destroy us.

My eyes were still on Grayson. "It doesn't matter."

I flickered my gaze to West, beseeching, but he'd followed my eyes to the doorway and was staring at Grayson. If I didn't know better, I'd say West looked hurt. For a split second, his pain poured inside of me like bleach.

I felt caught.

Frozen.

Twisted.

A bitter laugh left his lips. "I guess it doesn't."

Then we slammed together.

I opened my mouth on a silent gasp. My eyes connected

with Grayson's as West filled me. West hissed a curse. I kept my eyes open, locked on Grayson. Grayson didn't move, a stone in the corner.

I hated that. I want him to hurt like me.

West tangled a fist in my hair, ripping my eyes back to his.

"You want to make it hurt for him, Angel?" West whispered, so low only I heard.

Before I could think, be disgusted, be *anything*, West flipped me, so I was on my knees. He knotted his hand tighter in my hair and dragged me back in an arch, slamming harder inside me.

I let out a gasp.

Grayson *still* didn't move, but his eyes narrowed.

West's lips came to my neck. "That's not very convincing. Put on a show, Story."

FIFTY-TWO

STORY

West bunched my dress with his free hand, fisting the fabric to my hip until we were obscenely exposed to Grayson. A taunt. A challenge.

I couldn't breathe.

From the fullness of West.

From the emptiness in my heart.

"Is this what you like, Story?" West whispered against my flesh. "Is this what will get you off? When he watches me fuck you?"

Grayson still hadn't moved and it's driving me insane. I knew Grayson had insane self-control, I've known it since the beginning, but I want it to *snap*.

All he does is watch, dragging his pinky along his bottom lip.

Sometimes I watch you. I know you don't see me, and you don't think anyone is watching.

This moment is a dark mirror of our love, of every

moment we'd shared together. I spent years watching Grayson. Years loving him with a broken heart.

"Bite me," I demanded.

For the first time, Grayson took a step, and I can see it, picture him ripping West off me. I feel fire in my veins.

West's teeth grazed the dip between my shoulder and neck.

I want you to bite me harder.

No. No, no, *no.* Grayson slid deeper into me.

My breath left me on a sharp gasp, eyes never leaving Grayson as West worked himself inside me. The sound of our slick sweat, of West's groans and the howling wind, is a dark melody.

West slid his thumb to my clit, and shocks of pleasure I couldn't control fall from me in whimpers. I liked the way Grayson clenches his jaw, the fist he made. I want him as broken and unhinged as me.

West licked my ear. "Why don't you call him over? He can fuck your ass while I fuck you."

The image assaulted me in hot flashes. *Wrong.* So why am I burning up? I'm starting to think he's doing this to fuck with Grayson. Or maybe me.

"Stop," I whispered. I'm losing control.

I groaned, dropping my head as West fucked me, staring at Grayson's blue eyes gleaming through his mask.

West pressed harder on my clit, and for a blinding second I think I might actually come, but then he stopped.

It's not enough.

None of this is enough. I need more. I need the man in the corner. This is all wrong. I feel the agony in Grayson's eyes. See it in the throbbing vein in his neck, the muscles rippling in his clenched fist, his twerking jaw.

Why don't you come to me? Why don't you rip him off me?

Grayson tilted his head like he sees the words in my eyes.

Did he think he *deserved this?*

Tell me something. A secret. Anything. Something no one else knows.

The harder I tried to banish them, the more the memories rush like whispers I can't unhear. Grayson hadn't left the wall, but he's closer than ever. Whispering words and stroking me with his blue, blue eyes. Somehow he's still inside me.

"Your pussy is fucking magic, Angel."

Grayson's eyes flashed to West for the briefest moment. Murderous. Deadly.

"I'm gonna come," West gripped my waist, and I'm pulled out of the stony, gleaming blue eyes in the dark. "I'm not wearing a condom."

You'd never trap me, little nun. But I could trap you. So say your fucking word.

Grayson took a step. I zero on his fist, flexing and unflexing. When I speak, my eyes are locked with Grayson's.

When I fuck you, Story—really fuck you—you're mine.

"I don't care."

I care.

I don't want his come inside me.

But that dark, twisted agony in Grayson's eyes is the first time I've felt anything since leaving Lottie's room.

It hurts.

It feels like a punishment.

It feels like a reward.

West tensed at my words.

Then I know he's coming, first by the strangled groan, and then I could feel it.

Put on a show, Story. Put on a show.

I focused on Grayson as the words leave my lips. "Fill me up until you leak down my thighs, West."

Grayson dragged his pointer finger along his full bottom lip.

Then he smiled.

He fucking smiled. Not the Grayson Crowne smile, not the bright one that makes my chest full. This one is... dangerous. Crooked. Predatory.

My chest bottomed out. What do I do with that?

I can't think past the throbbing in my skull, the pressure in my gut, the aching in my thighs I didn't let West sate. Past Grayson.

As West came inside me, I can see words in Grayson's eyes, see them in the aching determination creasing his brow. From the first time he'd whispered them in this room to every time after, they slide deeper than West inside me. Curling around my heart and locking forever into place.

You're still so goddamn perfect, you know that?

I had to look away.

Focus on the rug beneath my hand.

This moment never belonged to me.

The fate wasn't mine.

I stole something forbidden.

West finished, sliding out of me, and my tears fell like dark pearls in the shadows.

I wanted to exorcise us.

I wanted to *destroy us.*

I should've known; when you desecrate, you don't banish—you empower.

"Angel..." West pulled me to him and I tore my head

away, only to have him rip it back, anchoring me. For a minute, the world around us vanished as West thumbed the tears away. Tenderness burned in his eyes, something he wanted to say.

Then he kissed me.

This kiss was like none we'd shared before. It was furious and punishing, and it consumed me. The wet heat of his tongue, swiping and claiming every of inch of me. The power of his mouth, swallowing not giving me an inch to breathe—

West was ripped off me.

Grayson.

FIFTY-THREE

STORY

The air in my lungs vanished, all the power and confidence I'd felt gone. I thought Grayson would leave. I thought we would end it here. What kind of person stays after witnessing that?

My heart wouldn't slow down, because I already knew.

Grayson grabbed West by the collar, jerking him to his feet.

"Done watching?" He smiled at Grayson.

"You know, I made a promise to Story that if you touched her, I'd kill you." Grayson pressed his thumb into the vein on West's neck. I couldn't look Grayson in the eyes. He was a blurry Polaroid, sharply tailored pants and a sharper jaw, a fist so tight I could see the veins bulging.

"Feels kinda like you're gonna fuck me, Crowne. I might have worn our girl out, but I'll be generous. You can suck her off my cock."

A caustic, callous laugh fell from Grayson's lips, which I knew meant he was a second away from losing it.

West was going to get himself killed.

I lifted my eyes to see them shadowed above me. It was like a perverted fantasy, with West still exposed and Gray so close. Some lascivious mythical Greek painting.

Sharp chin to sharp chin, lips so close, two gods warring and about to collide.

"If you touch her again. If you *ever fucking kiss her*"—he growled the words so low I felt them inside my bones—"I will end you."

West swiped his tongue across his red lips, eyes dropping to me. "But there are *so many* places I haven't kissed her yet."

"Her lips are mine, du Lac, but I might let you jack off to the memory of them—"

"Who the fuck do you both think you are?" I cut him off. "I don't belong to either of you."

Both their eyes dropped to me as I quickly stood up and started to leave. This was a mess. This was not how it was supposed to go. Me on the ground, stuck between these two men. Again.

"Angel—"

"Snitch, wait—"

They said my name at the same time as they grabbed me. West held one wrist and Grayson the other, stopping me just as I reached the door.

"Let me go." I yanked, but they held my wrists firm.

"Shouldn't you be with your wife?" West taunted Grayson. "The one losing her child?"

"Lottie's losing her child?" I lifted my head, so stunned I forgot I was about to look into the sun.

Grayson was staring at me, his blue eyes *searing*.

I quickly looked down.

"She's not losing her child, and it's not my baby," he gritted.

Lies.

Liar.

West scoffed. "Women in our family have difficult pregnancies. She's not supposed to have any stress for the first and second trimester. Has there been any stress, Grayson?"

More shame slammed into me.

All the men around me know how to do is lie.

I yanked my hands out of their grip, turning to West. "How long have you known she's pregnant?"

West ignored me, eyes on Grayson. "You're going to stay here while your fucking wife could lose your child?"

A silence followed West's words, and none of us moved.

My two princes standing on either side of me like titans.

The way Grayson had looked at me was still stuck in my head. I slowly lifted my eyes, wondering if he was still watching me.

Bad idea.

Grayson dragged a knuckle across his lower lip, his narrow glare fixated on me. I clenched my thighs and was grateful my dress hid it.

West was the first to speak, the first to act.

He casually buttoned up his pants as though he hadn't just fucked me in front of Grayson, adjusted his mask, and gave me his hand. "Come with me, Angel."

The sliver of vulnerability was back in his brown eyes. Maybe I should have gone with him...or maybe I should have just *left*, but I couldn't take my eyes off Grayson, even if it would destroy me. All I wanted to know were the thoughts that made him rub his lower lip.

"I'll meet you in the ballroom," I rasped.

His hand stayed outstretched a moment. Then he stood upright, shoulders square.

"You sure you want to do this, Crowne?" He turned to Gray. "I think you have a lot more to lose now."

Grayson's eyes flitted to him, something unsaid, but landed back on me.

West laughed when he left; it was bitter and choking and nearly stole all the oxygen in the room.

Then the door slammed, locking us in silence.

Follow him. Leave.

Grayson bent down until we were eye to eye, still dragging that knuckle across his lip. So close, the sound of our breathing was no longer drowned out by the howling wind. I could feel my power slipping, draining like smoke through a fan into him.

"Go fuck yourself, Grayson Crowne."

He grinned, that same smile he'd worn only moments before, then gripped my hair, tearing my face to his. "You shouldn't have done that."

FIFTY-FOUR

STORY

I tried to yank my head away from Grayson, but his grip was iron, and it only burned my scalp.

"I had a plan, Snitch. I had a really good plan." His voice was raw, warbled. "I was gonna get us out of this clean. Or..." he growled. "As clean as we could get."

"I don't give a shit about your plans and your promises. Whatever Lottie does to you, West does to me."

His eyes seemed to burn darker. Then he thrust me against the window sill. It was like he couldn't hear me. Grayson grabbed the collar of my dress, ripping it across my shoulder. His lips found the spot West had bitten, kissing slowly, easy, without any hurry.

"I thought we might get out of this without burning everything to the ground," he said as we kissed. His words were nonsense to me, but his lips stoked fire.

Then he bit.

Fucking *hard*.

I gasped, slamming my hands against the window.

I felt cold on my neck, wet trickling down from his teeth.

"You have no idea what the fuck you've done," he said against my skin. "But I don't fucking care."

"It's done. It's over. I broke us. Let me go." I tried to elbow him off, and his grip slipped from my hair to my wrist, slamming it back against the window.

In contrast to my fast, furious, and angry emotional movements, Grayson was calm. How could he be so calm after watching me fuck another man?

I don't understand.

I'm burning up inside.

"You're mine." Lips to my neck, he slid one palm between my thighs, thrusting a finger inside me. "You'll always belong to me."

I resisted the urge to melt into him, but as he slid another finger inside me, my vision blurred, my thoughts fractured.

"That's not something that changes. Run away. Leave me. Get *fucked* by every man in every continent." He growled the word *fucked* as he fucked me harder, like he wanted me to hear it, hear the sloppy sound West's come made as he fucked me.

Some distant part of me said to stop this, but I had missed Grayson's touch, been deprived of it for so long.

I couldn't fight. I couldn't give in...I was boneless.

He gripped my abdomen, keeping me up, forcing me to stay pressed to him as he used me like a doll to fuck another man's come inside me.

It was a twisted punishment, like he knew I hated it. Hated West inside me.

I think he hated it too, but he continued to fuck it up inside me.

"Your soul will always be *mine*."

He spoke with his teeth at my shoulder, fingers now thrusting faster as he fucked me. The sounds harsher than the howling. Sloppy. Cruel.

It was like Grayson couldn't decide if he wanted to rip it all out of me, or push it farther inside me and punish me.

We're locked on this brutal and forbidden ballet, forced to spin and spin and spin for an empty audience of our own sins.

Maybe if I gave into this moment, I could end that crushing desperation wreaking havoc on my soul. My life.

My head fell back on his shoulder, giving in.

He smiled, his lips stained with me, like rose petals that had been touched one too many times.

"My poor girl," he said, voice a low sultry lullaby against my skin. "You didn't even get off." His lips were just beneath my ear, warm, seductive, intoxicating. He slid the hand sticky with West's come up to my clit.

A jolt of pleasure fluttered through me, and my eyes fluttered shut.

"Keep your eyes on me," he growled.

They popped open, into his deep blue.

His lips were so close.

I arched for him, and he pulled away just as I was going to meet his mouth. Teasing. Torturing.

"You want to kiss me, little nun?" Grayson slid the hand from my hair down to my ribs, between my thighs, replacing the one currently working me senseless.

He pressed harder on my clit and I gasped, searching for him. Our tongues touched feather-light, *too brief*, before he pulled back.

He grinned. Mean.

"Then don't give away shit that doesn't belong to you." He held up two dripping milky-white fingers.

"Open your mouth," he gritted.

"No fucking way," I breathed. "I don't want to taste that."

Further solidify what I'd done.

Grayson pried my lips apart with his fingers, shoving them into my mouth, forcing me to taste it.

"Then you shouldn't have fucking done it."

He crashed his lips into mine, tongues tangling as the storm raged on. He finger-fucked me, making me come into his mouth as he swallowed the taste of our sins. Because even if you couldn't see him, Grayson Crowne was never someone to make you go alone, especially into darkness.

As the last aftershocks of the orgasm hit me, Grayson pulled away, dragging my bottom lip between his teeth.

"You owe me new sounds, little nun," he growled, biting my lip. "You gave mine to him."

He released my lip with a brutal pop.

"First, I'm gonna fuck his come out of you. Then, I'm gonna fuck your ass. I've waited too goddamn long." He crushed his lips against mine swiftly. "No use waiting anymore."

FIFTY-FIVE

STORY

"Get on the rugs."

Grayson stepped off me. Without his heat, the window was icy cold, and shame assaulted me. I slashed a glance at the rugs.

A sharp, stuttering breath left me. "There?"

Where I'd just attempted to desecrate my love for Grayson? I stepped back, rubbed my chest, trying to stop my beating heart. He pressed his hand over mine, pushing me back toward them, ripping open the fly to his tailored pants in the same breath.

"It's—"

"Wrong?"

Grayson slid down my body, pushing up my torn dress, kissing every inch of skin as he did. Wet and tender, careful yet sloppy kisses along my rounding stomach. My thoughts abandoned me, but Grayson kept me grounded, held me up by the arch of my back with strong hands.

From the ground, his eyes found mine, his voice was deep, vibrating in my chest. "I've wanted to do that since the day I learned you were pregnant."

Tingles rose along my skin like the softest touch.

"Your wife could be losing her child." I whispered my fear aloud. He dragged his hands along my ass, teeth grazing my inner thigh. I struggled to focus.

Teeth.

Grayson.

More.

Then it was gone. I opened my eyes, dazed, as Grayson stood again. Before I could decipher the look in his eyes, he tangled his fist in my hair, ripping my mouth to his.

"There is nothing redeemable here," I gasped against his lips. "If this was a fairy tale, we would be the villains."

But I kissed him back.

Deeply.

Losing myself in him as he dragged us down to our knees, forgetting my shame, until we were soft on the rugs.

"I wanted to give you a beautiful happily ever after, Story." He was calm as he spoke, calm as he pulled off the rest of my dress.

I was ravenous for him.

I tugged on his jacket.

I ripped at his pants.

Needing *more.*

"I wanted to make your life perfect, because you deserve perfect." He kissed my shoulder tenderly, lazily. "I wanted to build us everything. I always thought the worst thing was becoming my dad. But I know better now."

Our clothes lay discarded. A thousand thoughts tried to push into my head—*wrong, shameful, bad*—but they all vanished at the sight of him, one I'd been deprived of for months. His chiseled body golden even in the violent storm.

If it was possible, he swallowed my naked body with more hunger than I did him, jaw clenched, tongue pushing into his cheek. I pressed my hand to his muscled chest, dragging it down to his eight-pack. He gripped my wrist, and I paused—then he tore me to him, and our bodies collided.

"Worse than becoming my fate, is running from it, is losing you." He wrapped his arm around me, an anchor against his cock throbbing against my stomach. "I would break every law, every rule, every moral code to be with you, Story Hale."

He slammed his mouth against mine.

Hot. Brutal.

Every part of him bruised and plundered and stole. His hand gripping my ass, his tongue searing mine—months he was making up for in seconds. I gasped into his mouth and he swallowed it. I could only let Grayson use, explore, and take.

A soft pressure circled the entrance to my ass. I jolted away from his lips on a gasp. He kissed my jaw, never breaking contact.

"Still haven't had anyone in your ass, little nun?" he asked against my neck, still teasing my ass. The slamming snow behind him was glittery in my blurred vision.

I shook my head. I couldn't speak. The air in my lungs stuck in my chest.

Grayson made a sound in his throat; then before I could think, he spun me so I was on my knees. He ran a taunting, teasing hand up and down my spine. He knotted my hair around his fist, dragging me back so I could see him.

"Why not?" His breath fogged my lips.

"I—"

I broke off on a groan as he slid his pinky slowly, so slowly, inside my ass. His mouth quirked on a crooked smile.

"Why not, little nun?" he asked again.

"Because I—"

He pushed deeper inside and grinned when I broke off on another groan—but then he pulled out and I felt bereft, empty. He circled around me, teasing and thumbing me, eyes watching, drinking in every soft whimper.

"Why not, Story?" he asked softly.

"You know why not."

The muscle in his jaw feathered at my answer, blue eyes cracking.

His grip tightened in my hair. "Say it." As he spoke, he pressed his thumb against me, stretching me so much more than his pinky had, and I swallowed air. "Say it, Story."

"Because I want it to be you," I gasped.

Our groans melded together as he slid deeper inside me. I got lost in his blue eyes, in his fingers digging into my tailbone as his thumb rocked into me.

He thrust deep inside.

Deeper.

Deeper until I couldn't breathe.

Then he kissed me.

Devoured me.

Tongue stealing my breath as he fucked his thumb harder into my ass.

Suddenly he pulled away, taking heavy breaths like he'd just run a marathon.

"What?" I blinked, feeling as if I'd come out of deep water. "What's wrong?"

He let out a breath of a laugh, eyes heavy lidded. Predatory. "Little nun..." He slid his tongue across his top lip, and I wanted to lick him.

"Fucking trouble," he finally said, rocking his thumb slower inside me. "I wanna fuck your ass, but you're way too tight." He thrust in again, eyes dropping to my parted lips. "You need way more than this. You need lube and shit."

I closed my eyes on a groan. "Grayson, you're the worst virgin in history," I breathed. "You're supposed to have that on a key chain. Or a couple of samples you got one time in Vegas."

I felt him freeze; then his finger slipped from my ass.

I couldn't help it. I whimpered.

He rose up behind me like a shadow, a predator. Thighs caged either side of me; his cock throbbed between my parted legs, hand still in my hair.

"Jokes," he growled into my ear. "I missed your jokes."

I was blind with my need for him. I arched my back, trying to arch into him. His hand dug into my hip and he pushed into me just a little, and a small whimper fell from my lips.

"I like your ass from this angle, little nun. You want me to fuck you this way? From behind?"

"Any way." I begged, looking over my shoulder at him. "I want you any way."

He ripped me up by my hair, forcing me to arch against his chest.

"You already got fucked, little nun. I can feel him inside you." His eyes flashed, wild and dark. "Sure you're not finished?"

I tried to shake my head, but his grip in my hair was too tight.

"Say it."

"I'm not finished."

"Watch," he growled. "Look at my cock in you. Watch me fuck him out of you."

He pushed inside me, and if it weren't for Grayson's burning, bruising, and unrelenting grip in my hair, my head would have fallen forward. It was sparks and tingles and fire in my chest and veins

And it was torture.

Grayson kissed me softly and tenderly as he slowly entered me, never all the way in, never all the way out.

"More," I begged.

He laughed against my neck, kissing me wet and hot.

Not *biting*.

Not what I need.

And he knew it.

"Did he feel good inside you, Story?" Grayson taunted.

I gasped at the knife-sharp pain, the memory of West slamming back inside me twisting with the pleasure of Grayson's thrusts.

"Did he hit that spot you like?" Grayson asked softly, *too* soft.

He thrust harder, deeper, but still not enough. Just so I *knew* what could have been.

"No, he didn't," he growled. "Not even my little nun knows the things that make her scream."

"Grayson," I gasped. "*Please.* I need *more.*"

He thumbed my chin tenderly. "You're so beautiful when you beg." His touch turned vicious. "He's all over my fucking cock, Snitch."

"I'm so—"

Grayson slammed his lips against mine, cutting me off with a brutal, bruising kiss that left me winded.

"Shut the fuck up." His eyes crackled and popped as he thrust. Harder, deeper, but still not enough. "I don't ever want to hear those words from your lips. Not about this."

Pain broke through his eyes.

The game vanished.

"He's all over my cock," he gritted again, thumbing my lip tenderly while saying words that eviscerated me in the way only Grayson Crowne could. He bent forward, until I could taste his breath on my lips. "Should I make you suck him off me?"

My eyes grew at the idea.

He laughed. "You don't like that idea, little nun? Then you better come so fucking hard you're the only thing left." His words turned to a dark snarl and he bit my bottom lip. A strangled groan fell from me just as he pulled away. He seemed to focus on that, eyes zeroing. Animalistic. His own lips parted, sparkling with his saliva.

I wanted to lick it. Lick *him*. I reached for him and he pulled farther away on vicious smile.

He continued to thrust at the same ruthless, calculated rhythm. His hand trailed down from my chin, lingering on the swell of my abdomen. Restraint made his grip iron.

My thighs ached, my entire body throbbed.

Dangling on the precipice, but never allowed to fall.

"Grayson." I wrapped my arms behind me, encircling his neck. "*Please.*"

He froze, as if coming out of a trance. "What? Do you want me to stop?"

My heart cracked. Even after everything, he paid attention to me.

I dragged my nails down the back of his neck. "Fuck him out of me, please, Grayson. Do it for real."

It was shameful and hideous and it should have

disgusted him, but he groaned like I'd just swallowed his cock inside my mouth.

"My little nun..." He licked a blaze of fire up my neck. "You were made for me."

He groaned and thrust harder.

In and out.

But his bite still wasn't enough.

His thrust still wasn't enough.

He was holding back.

"Please. More. Give me what I need."

Grayson flipped me to my back, eyes burning, jaw clenched.

"Story...I..." He looked away.

I pressed my hand to his jaw. "What?"

"I don't want to hurt her." His brows drew together.

"You're worried about hurting the baby?"

My heart broke a little.

Because of course Grayson Crowne was worried about that.

"She said we couldn't hurt the baby. Give me *more*."

I wrapped my legs around his waist and dragged my nails down his back. His groan only heightened my need.

He went a little harder, but not enough. Not Grayson.

"Please." I scraped at his shoulders. *"More."*

His jaw was clenched, nostrils flared.

There was something in my chest.

A truth I was keeping secret.

Because even if this moment never lasted, it would always be true.

"I've missed you," I whispered. "I love you. I need you. Only you can give me this."

He groaned, dropping his head to my shoulder, then

rolled his hips, thrusting harder and faster at exactly the speed I needed.

We were a chorus of repressed desperation and need.

It started at the perfect spot between my thighs, growing until the throbbing was mind-scattering, until I couldn't breathe or think in anything but *Grayson*.

"Give me what *I* need," he rasped, pulling my hair back, biting my neck. "Give me those beautiful sounds. Let go, Story."

He went harder, faster, eyes burning, studying and drinking me, each thrust like the careful stroke of a violin. My mouth opened on a whimper, a gasp.

"More," he demanded with a powerful thrust.

I came undone.

For those two point five brilliant seconds the world stretched on into forever like melted taffy.

For those two point five brilliant seconds, everything was perfect and whole.

I cried his name on a broken scream, the room blurring. All I knew was *feeling*. Him throbbing inside me, his groan against my neck, lips wet and hot, sucking and biting.

I arched into it, into him, until I came into stardust.

When I came back down, he was watching me. He anchored my head with both of his hands, watching me tenderly, still hard inside me.

"You will be the death of me, Story Hale." He kissed me brutally until I was breathless. "But I will die over and over again if I could hear that sound one more time."

He pulled back, lips still pressed to mine.

"What if it's fate, Grayson?" I whispered my fear. "What if we're not meant to be? We keep trying to beat it, but what if it's *fate*?"

He smiled against my lips. "If our fate is forbidden, then I'll live as a fugitive."

FIFTY-SIX

GRAY

Story lay on my chest and I carded my fingers through her hair, listening to the sounds of the blizzard dying outside. Somehow the world was burning down around us, but for the first time in months, I could breathe again.

Story pushed off, sitting up. "What just happen can't happen again."

"Fuck that."

I grabbed Story by her hair, pulling her back down to the rugs and beneath me. I crushed my lips to her, kissing her until she melted back into me, her body listening to my touch.

When I pulled back, it took a few seconds for her to blink her eyes open, a hazy look on her face.

I ran a knuckle down her jaw.

"Stay the fuck here," I said softly. "I'm going to kill West."

She blinked out of her delirium and grabbed my arm. "Wait."

"I should have killed that fucker at my wedding, Story."

This was all my fault...I'd pushed my girl to the brink of destruction. But not again.

Never again.

"This has nothing to do with West. It's *us*. You lied to me. Again. I keep letting you. You're getting rid of me to live happily ever after with Lottie. I almost fell for it. Stash away the mistress. Come visit me for the holidays. Give me a nice stipend."

"After everything, you still don't fucking trust me? I didn't sleep with her, Snitch." I gripped her face until my thumbs blanched her skin.

How the fuck did I get her to believe me?

"It's not my fucking baby."

Snitch started to stand again, and I grabbed her arm, forcing her down.

"You still don't trust me."

"I saw the come on her thighs on your wedding night. Lottie isn't conniving, Grayson. She's broken. Because *we* broke her."

She reached for her locket, trying to undo it, and I slammed my hand over hers.

"What the fuck are you doing?"

"This is where our thread ends. Just please forget about me."

I pushed my tongue against my canine as a dark laugh stuttered from my chest.

Forget about Story?

"Story Hale, you crashed into my lips and into my life. You took my virginity. You took my heart. You are the only woman I have ever had sex with, and the only woman I ever want to sleep with. *You.*"

A look flickered across her eyes; her breathing came short and sporadic and she tried to break away, tried to shove me off, but I held her by the wrist so she couldn't run.

"Don't tell me you don't fucking trust me. You bleed with me."

"I can't breathe. Let me go."

"Did what we just do mean nothing to you? Every secret we share, is it nothing? Look at me, Story."

She yanked on her wrist. "Let me *go.*"

"No!" It bellowed out of me, louder than the wind, louder than any word I'd ever said. Scratching at my throat and lungs.

She fell back down beside me, shoulders slumped.

I let her wrist go, studying her, waiting for her to speak, afraid to touch her and spook her.

"Tell me what the fuck I have to do, and I'll do it."

"I believe you," she whispered.

"Then why won't you look at me?"

Slowly her eyes locked back on mine, her breathing labored. "We're ruined," she whispered. "We're broken forever."

STORY

"What the fuck are you talking about?" He stroked a hand down my face. The look in his eyes too soft. Too sweet.

"Even if you didn't sleep with her, I slept with him. I slept with West."

I was the *only one* in this twisted, fucked situation who did that.

Grayson smiled.

Not the *Grayson Crowne* smile, the *Grayson* smile. The one that made me feel like the sun had shone just for me. I wondered how he could be smiling at a time like this.

When he spoke, his words were gentle. "There you go again, Snitch, saying stupid shit." He dragged my lips to his. "You're my girl, Story."

Tears I'd held at bay for months finally fell. I tried to hide them in my shoulder, but Grayson pressed me against his chest, holding me as sobs wracked my chest.

I pushed off, swiping the tears away.

"It's not my baby, Snitch."

I pressed my palm to his cheek. "I love you, Grayson. I will always love you Grayson Crowne."

He grasped my wrist, holding it in place. "Don't. I'm not letting you go, Story Hale. I'm never letting you go again."

"Can you live with yourself if you walk away like this, Grayson? I'm not going to make you choose between me and your wife, between which of your children to abandon."

"I'm not asking you to choose. I've chosen."

"All you've ever wanted was to be nothing like your father."

We'd tried so hard to avoid this.

But fate had other plans.

"I don't care. I don't fucking care, Snitch."

"You won't leave your *pregnant* wife for me, Grayson. I know you. And I... I don't know if I can let that happen. We've been trying to fight fate for months, Grayson. At every turn it's obvious we're not supposed to be together."

"I told you, Snitch. Even if it takes the rest of our life, I'm not letting you go."

"There's too much debris between us, Grayson. We're broken glass and thorns."

And then, like a burning sign of our infidelity, the lights turned on. The antique room stuttered into clarity.

"Power's on," I said, just so I had something else to say.

"Snitch." Grayson grabbed my arm. "We're still leaving tonight. I'm going to find Lottie, and I'll figure things out, and in an hour you'll be here. Waiting. Promise me."

I can't make Grayson choose between me and his wife. I can't make him choose between which of his children to abandon. What a horrible, impossible decision. All Grayson had ever wanted was to be nothing like his father, and now he would have to decide...me or Lottie?

In the end, Grayson would always lose.

"Fucking promise me!"

"I can't let you give up everything, Grayson."

He gripped my shoulders. "Promise me you'll wait, dammit."

"I promise," I said weakly.

He stood up, got dressed, but he didn't leave. He stared down at me, jaw clenched.

"Do you not trust me to wait?"

He dragged his hands through his hair. "Every time we get close, something snatches it away. I want to run with you. Run out of this fucking place right now."

"I don't want our life together to be running and hiding," I whispered. "I want it to be more. And you could never live with yourself if you abandoned your child."

I could tell he wanted to say more by the way the muscle in his jaw feathered, by the veins throbbing in his fist.

Yet all he said was, "One hour."

I pulled on my ripped dress when he left, lost to my own thoughts.

I think we tried so hard not to be the people we feared we might be that we became something even worse. What demons will we summon not to succumb to those we fear live inside us? What darkness will we give in to, what parts will we dirty and tarnish just to keep a little piece pure?

Because of every betrayal I'd experienced after entering the Crowne world...today was the worst. I betrayed myself. I betrayed the promise I made to myself the day West betrayed me. I wanted to be like the people I read about. I want to be someone who doesn't make mistakes. I wanted to be powerful and empowered

"Damn, Angel. You didn't even wait an hour."

I blinked out of my tears. West was standing in the room, and I don't know how long he'd been watching me.

"West. How long have you been there?"

"Are you gonna call me a rapist again? Or maybe you wanted to call me *Daddy*?"

FIFTY-SEVEN

GRAY

When I got to Lottie, she was awake in the room she'd slept in before we'd started to share my wing, and she'd changed out of her costume into pajamas. She sat up when she saw me.

"I'm asking for a paternity test. Or you could just stop this right now and tell everyone the truth."

She blinked rapidly, then glared. "I would expect nothing less from my husband and the father of my child."

"Can you blame me? I don't remember us having sex, Lottie. Want to remind me when the fuck that happened?"

She clenched her jaw and shot me a glare, and I prepared for an argument. Then suddenly she threw her head in her hands.

And cried.

I shifted, rubbing the sharp pain in my neck as Lottie cried harder.

"You came on my thigh and..." she said through her hands.

"And what, Lottie?"

Her eyes met mine, shiny and shamed, angry.

"I pushed it up inside me." She swiped away tears. "I haven't had sex with anyone else. A paternity test will show that."

I couldn't move, couldn't breathe, couldn't fucking blink, could only stare at Lottie as the room caved in on me. The dying wind was suddenly howling again.

"What the fuck is wrong with you?" I finally managed.

"The girl is supposed to do that, you know? She's supposed to do that for me, but you hired your mistress."

I bit my jaw until it ached. "Charlotte."

She looked away and bit her bottom lip, working the flesh for a good two minutes.

"My mother used to tell me stories of how my father doted on her during her pregnancies. I thought you would start to love me again...I never thought you would divorce me," she shouted. "What you did, *no one* does. It's not fair she gets to have everything. She gets *you*. She gets a *healthy* baby. She gets *everything*, and I did everything I was supposed to do!" she screamed. "It's not fair!"

Color drained from Lottie's face with her scream, and her eyes went cross.

"Calm down."

It came out harsher than I intended, because she flinched.

The air was sticky. Spiny.

"If you don't calm down, you could lose the baby," I said, softer.

Her eyes slashed to mine. "Wouldn't that solve everything?"

I ground my teeth together. "How long have you known?"

"A while."

"You've been dealing with it on your own?"

"I know you don't love me, Grayson. I was afraid of how you would react."

I dragged my hands down my face.

Angry.

Threatening.

"If—if I knew...if you told me what you did...I might not have been so..."

Her brow furrowed, and she looked away. "But you would always look miserable."

Silence wafted.

"Is this why you've been so..."

"Insane?" she supplied.

"I was going to say persistent."

More tears filled her eyes.

I could feel my own lids, hot and burning. Was this fate? No matter how hard you fight, the stage resets itself, forcing you back into your position.

"I don't know who I am anymore," she said, voice hoarse. "I've been trying to be someone else for so long. That night, my mother came to me. She told me more than a few things. Like, if I didn't get a baby from you, I was as good as forgotten."

I sat beside her and dragged her hands into mine. Trying to apologize for everything I put her through even though I knew there would never be enough words or actions.

"I'm so sorry." She broke into tears. Deep, heaving tears. So when she spoke, I could barely hear above the sobbing. "I-I know you don't love me. I know you won't ever love me.

I know what I've done is unforgivable. I started picturing myself. A laughingstock among our peers. *Poor Lottie, must be something defective.* You wouldn't love *me*, so I thought I could become *her*."

"I haven't been good to you, Lottie. I've failed you. I won't fail our baby."

She looked up, blinking through her watery eyes. "So you'll abandon her?"

"No," I said instantly.

Fuck.

Shit.

Fuck.

Snitch was waiting for me, to run away, to leave.

I dragged my hands through my hair. She exhaled and dropped her shoulders. I couldn't leave Snitch. I *wouldn't*.

I stood up.

"Are you going to her?" she asked.

"I have to."

Lottie nodded, fisting the sheets. "Can I stay here, in my half of the wing until I'm cleared to travel? I won't bother you. It will be like before, like I'm not even here."

"You can stay here as long as you need."

She worked the sheets harder between her fingers. "I lied, I can't take that back, but...I do love you, and I'll always be there for you, Grayson. Always."

"Don't you want your own happiness, Lottie? I want that for you. I want you to have a man who deserves you. I'm not him."

"I don't get that," she mumbled. "Fate made that perfectly clear."

"You said I wasn't your first. There must be someone else out there."

Her eyes clouded.

"Are you hoping I'll admit I cheated on you?" she said darkly. "I'm sorry, but neither of us are that lucky."

"I'm hoping I can help both of us."

"He's worse than you, Grayson. To him I'm only ever going to be Charlie, an annoying little girl...a mistake. A shame he wishes he could erase. A secret that would ruin him."

Charlie?

"I won't fight you on the divorce. I never thought I'd be pregnant and divorced, but anything is better than this." She lifted her eyes, meeting mine. "But I know I'm not the only one who grew up with the stories they masked as fairy tales. We're kings and queens, and kings don't divorce queens. Not without war. Not without death," she rasped. "Does she know how much you're giving up?"

FIFTY-EIGHT

STORY

"Well, if that was really your plan, you probably should have fucked me a few months ago, Angel. Made this a little bit more believable."

I stared at him. "How long have you known?"

"Pretty much as long as we've been married. You're shit at keeping secrets."

I fell back against the wall. West gave me a sad, pitying look as he came to stand in front of me.

Behind him the night grew darker.

"Let me tell you what happens next. We get divorced. You won't ask me for shit. You won't take anything. If you go to the press with your story, or the cops, or who the fuck ever, no one will believe you. They might have before. What with...the way people are now, always canceling shit on Twitter." He made an annoyed face. "But now? You were my wife. Why would you have married your rapist? And you took all those loving photos with me. Hell, you just fucked me in a closet." He held up his phone and pressed play on a video.

I felt ill.

So ill.

"And you got pregnant." He put his phone away and shook his head, smiling. "You don't look very good right now, Story."

I think I'm going to throw up. "Why?" was all I could manage.

"Did you think I was just going to let you get away with it?"

"Get away with it?" I balked. "With *what*?"

"You called me a fucking a rapist," he yelled. "I'm about to take over my father's company. I can't have you trying to hashtag me and ruin that."

The snow slammed against the window.

Always a cut away from bleeding out.

This is what my mother meant after all. I was bled out; there was nothing left of me to take. There was always a part of me that thought West must have *some* angle. I just couldn't figure it out. It was staring me in the face.

It all made sense now, all those little things that never added up. Why West was so gung ho for me, why he took me to the court house instead of insisting on some giant wedding as those in his position always had, why he never faced any consequences.

They were all steps leading to this cliff.

It was just like the first time he stole into my heart. Every nice action, every sweet moment, was because he had something to prove, something to gain.

And just like the first time, I really didn't believe that was the only reason.

"All of this?" I asked. "All the things you did and said,

from the very beginning, were just to get back at me? Did you ever once love me?"

A look flickered across his features.

He thumbed my chin. "Do you care?"

Yes. I wanted to know if there was more to West du Lac than darkness. But I wasn't going to let him know.

"You're evil."

He laughed. "I haven't done shit Grayson wouldn't do. You're fucking my sister's husband. What do they say about glass houses?"

I mashed my lips, biting them until I tasted blood.

Because it didn't matter. He was right.

"I'm a shitty person," I said roughly, quietly. "But so are you. I'll divorce you. I'll stay quiet. You'll never see me again."

And I could forget all those times I wondered if there was more to West du Lac.

He laughed. "I'm not done with you, Angel." He pushed the hair behind my ear, tangling it in his fist and drawing my face closer. "I'm taking you as my mistress, and that baby will be mine in name. No one will ever know about you and Grayson Crowne, not officially, nothing past unsubstantiated rumors."

What?

Why would he want that?

"Why do you need my fucking child? Why do you need *me*?"

"I think you're starting to feel for me, Angel. We just need time."

I could only speak in stuttering breaths. "Y-you don't love me. If you loved me, you would remain married to me, not divorce me and make me your fucking mistress. You wouldn't threaten me."

"Like Grayson married you? You should know better by now, Angel. There's only one reason I was ever allowed to marry you."

I looked away as hot oil burned through my veins.

"We can live happily ever after, just not as man and wife."

That was what finally did it.

Why I didn't just slap him but punch him in the nose.

He wiped the blood off, then looked at his hand like he'd accidentally run into a branch.

"Are you done?"

I spat in his face. "I'm worth more. You could lock me in a tower with you for a thousand years and I'd still hate your guts."

But something in my chest worried at my words.

It had taken only a couple of months for me to fall for his mind games.

His eyes flashed dark at my words, his smile gone. "But you'd belong to me, Angel. You're mine. For as long as I want to keep you."

I'm not his.

My heart doesn't even belong to me anymore.

Right?

"Grayson will never let you take his child, and I won't either," I gritted. "I'll never be your fucking mistress, West. There's nothing you can threaten me with. You could tell the entire world I'm a whore, and I still wouldn't be your mistress."

"You need me."

I laughed, but when his grip tightened, my gut dropped.

"The du Lacs don't care about bastards," he said. "No one will think twice if you have mine."

"So are you supposed to be my knight in shining armor now?" I hissed.

He grinned, but it was mean. "Call me whatever the fuck you want. I'm your only shot at keeping you and that bastard in your belly alive, Angel."

Fear drenched me like acid.

Not for me, for the baby.

I shoved West off, standing up and putting distance between us. I trusted Grayson when he said he would take care of us. He'd already done so much for us; he'd always protected us.

He would look after us.

He would free us.

West had done nothing but trap me.

"No one is on your side, Angel," he said softly. "I've never seen the du Lacs and Crownes work together so well. We spent *years* working on that marriage. No amount of money could stop their bickering...but when you entered the scene? A decades-old rivalry vanished in an instant. Imagine what they'll do when they find out you're pregnant. Be my mistress and that all changes. You don't have to fight anymore."

I felt like I was going to be sick. "I'm not falling for your tricks anymore, West."

I was nearly out of the hallway when West's voice drifted back. "What about Grayson? Would you do it for him? I thought you loved him."

I paused. "What?"

It was almost exactly what Lottie had said.

"How do you think he's getting you both out of this?"

"He forced his grandfather's hand," I said, but my heart was a knot.

West laughed. "How did he do that, Angel?"

Silence ticked on.

"It's so romantic," West said. "He gave up everything for you. He blew up his entire fucking world right in my inbox. Pretty good early Christmas present."

He held up his phone for me to see, but I didn't understand. It looked like some kind of contract—that much I understood. I was familiarized with it from Grayson.

"What is this?"

"Uh, the short version?" West put his phone back. "While you run into the sunset, his family crumbles to ashes, and I'll take his kingdom."

My heart bottomed out.

I'll move the earth for you, Story. *I'll make the sky fall.*

His family would be on the street.

"Are you going to make him choose between which child to abandon? He can't have both, Angel. Not in this world. If he runs away with you, my family will make sure he never sees Lottie again."

You're either for this family, or you're against it.

Abigail's words to me on Thanksgiving spun in my head, mocking. This was always the end. Even she couldn't avoid it.

I could feel it, the chains of fate locking into place.

"You can run off with him. Go live somewhere. Forget about Lottie and her unborn child, about the family you just destroyed." His lips curved as he watched me imagine this future.

All Grayson Crowne had ever wanted was to be a good man, a good person for his family.

I swallowed. "Or?"

"Or we leave Crowne Point tomorrow."

FIFTY-NINE

GRAY

A rock lifted from my chest when I found Story waiting for me. A dark part of me thought she'd be gone, that fate would have gotten to us.

I ran to her and grabbed her hand, refusing to waste another minute.

"The blizzard is letting up," I said.

"What about Lottie?" she said. "Your child?"

"I'll come back once I've settled you." I pulled her to the door.

"Is there going to be something to come back to, Grayson?" she asked.

I stopped. "What?"

"You promised me no more broken promises. You said you wouldn't give up everything."

"Who told you?"

"West."

Rage crawled up my spine. "West was here?"

"He wanted to talk. Is he lying? Are you about to give up everything? Destroy your family?"

"I told you, Story. If it means keeping you alive, keeping you safe, I would do whatever it takes, no matter the consequences."

She nodded.

I expected her to yell.

Scream.

The silence was more disconcerting. "Why aren't you upset?"

"You don't get to be Atlas anymore, Grayson Crowne."

STORY

Grayson's eyes narrowed. "What did you do?" When I didn't immediately respond, Grayson raised his voice. "What did you do, Story?"

"I'm staying with West, but I have a plan—"

He grabbed my arm, dragging me to the door.

"Stop!" I scraped at his hand. "Let me go. Listen, I have a plan."

"We're getting out of here."

I used all my strength to break out of his hold, slamming both hands into his wrist. With heaving breaths we separated.

Grayson reached for me again, and I stepped backward.

He looked wild and unhinged.

"I'm not letting you stay with West, Story!"

"I'm not letting you throw everything away, Grayson!"

He looked left and right, grabbed the nearest antique—a

vase—and chucked it against the wall. It shattered. "My family isn't worth it! They don't care about you or us, Snitch. You're going to throw away our happiness for that?"

"Your family treats me like garbage. You think I don't want to see Tansy Crowne scraping by to make ends meet like I had to? See Gemma wear off the rack? I've been watching you, Grayson. I watch you when you don't think I am, and I see how this is ripping you apart."

He looked away like he was ashamed. I know if I let Grayson destroy them, he would never forgive himself.

I knew that, which is why I wasn't hurt this time. It was the reason I'd made my choice so easily with West. Maybe we were each other's glass shard, and we should walk away.

But fatal flaws are fatal for a reason.

"Do you think I can't protect you?" he demanded.

"You protect me better than anyone."

His blue eyes cracked.

He dragged his hands through his hair.

I stepped to him and placed a palm on his cheek. "I have lost so much. I lost who I was. I lost what made me *me*. I'm not letting that happen to you. I can't take back what I did...It's there. Sludge in my heart. A stain in my soul. But we don't have to sink into that stain. That's the easy way out."

Hiding in our demons. Saying because we did something bad, we have no choice but to *be* bad.

"I want to be good. I want to be good with you. I don't want what we've done to be our future."

I threaded my hands through his golden hair. "I want everything for you, Grayson. The way you want everything for me."

He looked up. "You *are* everything, all I need."

I thumbed the single tear that had fallen from his eye when he'd come to get me. "Then why were you crying?"

He jerked his head out of my grip, turning away and giving me his back.

Grayson Crowne didn't cry, even in front of me.

I waited for him to collect himself.

When I turned around, all emotion was gone, and I was faced with Grayson *Crowne*.

"I could force you," he growled.

"You could..." I said. "You could put my name on no-fly lists."

His face collapsed as he realized what I was implying. Back to what had started all this. He paced back and forth, dragged his hands through his hair.

"Goddamn it, Snitch."

"We'll take them down from the inside. I'll get West to trust me, you get the coin—"

He tugged me back to him, glare harder than I'd ever seen before. "There's a cost to using a coin. Every time you use one, you're giving power to the person you demanded a favor from. They can't take back the favor you demanded of them, but they can demand something else, something darker. There's a *reason* no one has used five coins. That's an insane amount of power to give someone. I'm not putting my faith in fairy tales. Not when it comes to you."

"This is our last hope for a happily ever after Grayson, a *real one*, don't you see? I'm not putting my faith in fairy tales, I'm putting it in you. In us. In trust. If it's not real, we'll figure it out—together. West cares for me, and we can use that—"

"You want me to let you fucking seduce him?" he snarled.

I saw the fear in his eyes, and I realized I needed to show him *why* this time was different. I wasn't leaving him.

Not really.

"I'll kill my grandfather," Grayson said, nodding to himself like a light bulb had just gone off. "I'll kill West. I'll kill—"

"I *finally* understand the weight on your shoulders. I know you want me." I stepped to him and grabbed his hands. "I *know* you don't want to let me go. I'm telling you, *you won't lose me.*"

His jaw clenched, eyes shadowed with distrust.

"We have something they don't have. Something they don't see coming. Something they can't steal."

His brows drew deeper together as he waited for me.

"Trust—I don't have to be by your side for you to own my heart."

He dragged me closer, pressing my hands to his chest.

"You own it, Grayson," I whispered against his lips. "You owned it before I even knew you'd taken it. You owned it when I hated you. You owned it while I was married to another man. You could be a thousand miles away and it would still be yours."

I kissed him.

Trying to let him see the truth of my words on my lips.

He kissed me back feverishly, as if he was trying to change my mind or maybe glue me to the spot with desire. I pulled away on a breath, and he tried to pull me back.

"Grayson."

He ignored me, dragging me back, thrusting his tongue into my mouth.

I shoved him off, taking a few steps back.

"Let me shoulder some of your weight, Grayson. Let me carry that world with you. You didn't fight this hard for your family to give it all away to West du Lac. Let's cut our thread. Choose where our fate ends."

Grayson exhaled, running both hands through his hair.

"I don't want you to have to choose between your children. I don't want them to grow up like you did. Vying for love like it's a competition. I don't want us to be on the run our whole lives or have our relationship ruin everything it touches. Do you think we can have that?"

"I will give you anything, Snitch," he gritted.

"So then give me your trust. We'll get that happily ever after. You said you wanted to be a hero for your sisters. A good man. A good father. We just need to fight fate a little while longer. But...together this time."

He eyed me. "Can you tell me you don't love him? Can you promise me you won't, Snitch?"

"Do you trust me? Because I trust you, Grayson. I trust that we can do this and get through to the other side. No matter what happens. What he puts me through. What he does to me. What I have to do. What you have to do. Where we end up, what happens to our souls in the process. We'll find that happily ever after as long as we stay truthful to each other."

Another long, soul-crushing stare, then Grayson rushed to me, pulling my face to his, kissing me breathless.

When he pulled back, he still gripped my face. He had the look...the Grayson Crowne look that said he was about to do something terribly destructive, but when he spoke, he said, "Okay."

I gnawed on my lower lip.

"I have twenty-four hours," I said. "Will you give me what I want?"

"Anything."

I smiled. "A night with Grayson Crowne."

A ghost of a smile flitted across his lips. "Just give me one thing, Snitch."

"Of course."

"Open your fucking locket."

The inside was dark green and...wet. I touched it and my finger came away green

"Ink?"

When I looked back, Grayson was on the ground, on his knee.

"What are you doing?"

My heart beat like a drum.

Grayson's eyes were pinched, and he took a moment to speak.

"You said Mary Shelley carried her dead husband's heart...and I thought about what my heart would be. What would be inside my heart? Every single time..." He trailed off and looked away; when he looked back, he smiled. "You're the ink in my soul. You changed me. You made me different. Better. It's you."

What was in Grayson Crowne's heart?

Me.

I couldn't breathe.

"I can't sign my name next to yours on a piece of paper. Can't marry you the way I want. Can't give you the big proposal. But...I don't want to put a ring on your finger, Snitch. I want to put bruises on your body. I want to put ink in *your* soul. I want you to do the same to me. Forever."

"Forever?"

"I was never letting you go, Story. I tried and failed."

Every time he looked at it, he saw forever with me.

A future.

I thumbed the butterflied heart on my chest, feeling like it was the one inside my rib cage. "I wore this for months."

His eyes drifted to the gold, voice rough. "Yeah."

"Someday I'm going to give a proposal the whole world can see, Snitch. Some day we won't be in the shadows. We won't be in the cracks. Even if it takes us our lifetimes, I'm going to give you a proposal the world can see. You're going to wear my last name. But for now...Story Hale, will you marry me?"

SIXTY

STORY

Fate had sweetened the air for us. It was softer and quieter. The blizzard was over, and the dovecote was dappled with moonlight. Our worlds were collapsing; we'd have only this night before I'd have to leave, before we'd give in to fate.

I took a deep breath and stepped around the stone.

Into my fate.

Grayson didn't see me at first. I got to watch him. It was like years ago when I would catch glimpses of Grayson Crowne being *Grayson*. He rubbed the center of his palm with his thumb, looking up and out one of the windows.

Over and over again he rubbed his palm.

Was he nervous?

I took a step along the small makeshift aisle, and his head jolted up, eyes locking on me.

Oh, wow.

Grayson. His smile. That Grayson smile that lit up his whole face. I just stood there. Feeling warm and perfect. He was in a dark suit. Tall. The cobblestone behind him. His rose gold hair shone in the moonlight, and he was like a true prince out of a fairy tale.

In that moment, I felt like I could stand there for hours and he really would wait for me.

But I didn't want to wait.

I was so done with waiting.

I ran up the aisle.

I didn't have a white dress, but I did have the one camel dress I'd picked out. He looked me up and down.

"You are so fucking perfect."

I tucked the pocket square I'd saved into his suit pocket. His eyes reddened when he saw what it was.

"There's no use in hiding from how we got here, Grayson." I adjusted the emerald color. "This day should have been mine."

He placed a finger beneath my chin, lifting my eyes to his.

Then crushed my lips against his.

"You're supposed to wait until—" He kissed me again, and again.

"After," I said against his lips.

"We were supposed to do a lot of things, Snitch."

He gripped my face, exhaling through his nostrils. "I have so much making up to do."

I looked around the dovecote. "Don't we need some kind of priest or...*friar*?"

"Fate has been our tireless escort, so fate will be our witness now."

I know this moment between Grayson and me meant nothing in the eyes of the law. He was still married to Lottie; I was still married to West...for now.

But here, underneath the sprinkle of snowflakes falling

through the cracks in the stone roof like cold glitter, everything was perfect and right.

"You are my poetry, Story. You gave voice and power to my love, before and without you I am numb and empty. You're my soulmate. My shard matches your shard. You're my piece. My puzzle. I bleed with you."

I pressed my forehead to his. "All my life I needed someone to trust. Someone who wouldn't betray me. I found that in you. In our darkness and our secrets."

"As long as I live, Story Hale, these vows will be the only ones that matter. The only ones I honor. The only ones I cherish."

Grayson pulled my ring finger up to his mouth, sliding it between his lips, biting until my gasp steamed the cold air.

We stared into each other's eyes. "Should we seal this marriage with a secret," I joked.

He rubbed the new bruise on my finger. "I think this marriage is the secret, Snitch."

I took a breath of cold air.

It felt...monumental. Like something that should have always been just locked into place.

"In whoever's eyes count... you're mine," Grayson said. "You're Mrs. Grayson Crowne. If I were shackled to a marriage, in prison, in hell, it would always be you, Story.

"It would always be you, Grayson."

SIXTY-ONE

STORY

"Mrs. Grayson Crowne."

I smiled into my shoulder. Grayson hadn't stopped saying it, not after leaving the dovecote, not even now that we were back in his wing, in his bathroom as he insisted I take a bath to warm up.

Grayson dragged his thumb across my bottom lip. "Don't hide that from me."

He rubbed my lower lip, eyes never leaving mine. His lip quirked, like he knew exactly when his soft touch made my thighs hot, my gut ache.

I swallowed, put my elbows on the edge of his bathtub as he trailed his hand down my spine. "I always wondered what it would be like to put my elbows here and overlook the beach." Outside, the snow fell in soft flakes. "I love Christmas...The snow on the beach is so magical."

Will I still love Christmas when I'm shackled by it?

Forced to return for the Holidays like Josephine, silent as the snow.

"What happened?" Grayson asked with a soft grit. "Where did you go in your head?"

Grayson's touching was constant. Like he wanted to feel all of me. The lobe of my ear. The curve of my jaw. My shoulder.

We had this one night together. Just this one. I thought Grayson would be urgent and pressing, but his touches were slow and careful, as if we had centuries for him to explore me.

They stoked the fire in me.

"I'm thinking about the future."

He paused, then got down until his lips were at my neck.

"This room wasn't right without you," he said softly. "I felt like I was living with a ghost, but it was just you. Your memories." He kissed the hollow between my ear and neck. "Mrs. Grayson Crowne."

"I like hearing it. I like...being Mrs. Grayson Crowne."

A low sound of need vibrated in his throat, and he yanked me out of the tub, onto his lap, before I could make a sound. Water fell everywhere, soaking his clothes, as he kissed me. He grabbed a towel, covering me.

He paused. "Why the tears, little nun?"

I swiped my cheeks, feeling caught. I didn't want to ruin this moment, these few special hours.

"I'm fine."

"Story." His voice was an iron warning.

"I don't want to leave you here," I whispered. "I feel like I'm abandoning you in this dark castle. I'm worried about you."

He swiped his thumb across my cheek. "Then fucking stay. Stay with me. Don't fucking leave, Story."

"You'll lose everything."

"I don't care.

"You will." I pressed my forehead to his. "When your mom and sister are on the street. When your grandfather is trying to come for us. When West has everything and you've left a child fatherless... You will. I know you, Grayson Crowne."

I think he wanted to say something.

Argue with me.

But maybe he felt the way I did, that with only a few more hours, it wasn't worth ruining.

He kissed me more slowly, soul-deep, stealing all my sadness and giving me his passion. Getting his clothes soaked and wet as he kissed me. Yet he grabbed another towel for me, wrapping it around my shoulders as he kissed me.

My head fell back on a sigh as his lips came to the center of my throat, holding me steady. His lips slid to the side of my throat, up to my ear to whisper.

"I want to ruin you with bruises, Story. I want them down your thighs. On your neck. Inside you. When you leave me, you'll feel me. He'll know what he's taking and who's coming to get it."

He grazed his teeth across my body, under my jaw, my neck, my shoulder, above my breast, my nipple, back to my shoulder. Like he'd been holding back for months and this was what he wanted to do first, love me, hold me, touch me, like he wanted to mark me forever before I had to go.

"Would you let me, my little wife?"

"Yes," I gasped.

"I knew you'd be such a good wife, Story." He pushed

the stray curls out of my face, sliding a finger inside me, working me, devouring my reaction. "Where first?"

"Anywhere."

He gave me a deep, bone-melting grin. "That's my girl."

I waited for Grayson to wake up, fist clutching the fabric of my shirt. It was slow agony watching him open his eyes, turn his head, and search for me in the bed.

When I wasn't there, he jolted up, only to be stopped by the handcuff.

I clutched my shirt harder.

He found me standing a few feet from the bed.

"What the fuck is this, Story?"

"I knew you weren't going to let me leave, Grayson. You had that look in your eyes. You can't let me go. Not...willingly."

He rattled the handcuff. "Open it."

I can't recall a time I'd ever seen that look in his eyes, heard the timbre in his voice. Not when he'd realized he'd mistaken me for Lottie. Not even when I'd had West inside me.

It nearly made me listen.

I shook my head. "I'll be back."

"You're goddamn insane if you think I'm going to let you leave and tell the world you're having his baby."

"If you don't let me go, we'll only have ashes to live in."

He pulled again, the headboard creaking.

"You'll see. In a week or two when the dust settles, and you haven't lost everything, and we're that much closer to having it all. You'll see, Grayson. I'll be back."

"Let me the fuck out." He pulled at the handcuff. "You

call me Atlas, but you stayed for years in hell for no other reason than to care for your uncle, and now what? You're locking yourself in another hell for this bullshit? I won't let you do it. You're not thinking about what you'll have to do."

"Yes, I am." I swiped the tears blurring my eyes, then took a deep breath so my voice was steady. "I am."

He utterly froze.

Then with his stony glare locked on me, Grayson yanked at the cuff so hard, the headboard groaned. I could see the skin break.

"Stop!"

He did it again.

And again.

His jaw tight, eyes callous.

"Mr. Crowne." I tried our safe word, voice hoarse, shredded.

He yanked his arm forward, blood streaming down his wrist.

"Mr. Crowne!" I ran to him, begged him, dropping to my knees, grasping his chained hand in mine. My chest ached with the way his blue eyes cracked. I couldn't help myself...I ran my free hand down his jaw. He turned into it, biting my finger. I nearly lost myself.

Almost missed him grab me with his free hand.

I stepped back at the last minute, and he grasped air.

"Fuck!" he yelled. "Don't fucking do this, Story. Don't be his wife. Be *mine*."

I opened my mouth, but paused.

I know I should tell him I'm going to be West's mistress, that I'm doing exactly what Grayson did when he omitted *how* he planned to save me. But I need him to see we can do this first.

That this plan will save us.

He slammed his arm forward and the headboard cracked. I couldn't leave him like this, couldn't leave *us* like this, with Grayson ripping his skin open. We had to do this together. I took a tentative step closer, then dropped back to my knees.

I pressed my forehead to his.

"I *am* your wife. In all the ways that matter. Your wife. Yours. And when this is all over, when we don't have to hide, my name will be Story Crowne. If you want..." I trailed off, looking at my knees, suddenly filled with irrational insecurity, even after everything.

"Snitch," he rasped. "Look at me."

I lifted my eyes to his searing blue ones.

He kissed me. His tongue seeking mine, dueling.

"Story Crowne," he groaned, his tongue still in my mouth, lips wet on mine. "What a perfect fucking name for a perfect little wife."

The morning grew hot on my back, and I knew our time was coming to an end. The proverbial midnight had struck.

I tried to pull away, but Grayson held my neck in place.

"Grayson, you have to let go."

His thumb dug. Bruising.

"I can't let you go, Story. I've tried. I fail every time."

"Then *don't*, Grayson. Don't ever let me go. I won't if you won't. I'll hold onto you. In my heart. In my soul. In the places that matter. Will you do the same?"

I took his ring finger into my mouth, biting it like he had mine.

Begging him to see the truth in my eyes.

He watched me, lids half-mast. "I will *always* keep you inside me. Forever. I don't have a fucking say in the matter."

Still he wouldn't let me go.

"Grayson," I whispered.

"Don't leave me, little wife." His voice shredded my chest, then he slammed his lips back on mine. His kiss was calculated torture designed to make me succumb and surrender.

I broke off on a gasp, desperate to find clarity in my thoughts.

He didn't stop kissing me even as I turned my head. Kissing my cheek, the angle of my jaw—anything.

"Grayson—"

"Give in, little wife."

"Grayson, stop!"

He ripped his lips off me with a growl. "It's not just West, Story! We're going up against everyone."

"This is the *only way*. I'll get all the dirt West has on you and destroy it. You'll get the final coin, and together, we'll rewrite destiny."

"*If* it works," he said darkly. "If it doesn't? Best case: you're with *West*. Worst case: war."

I swallowed. "It'll work. I think it's fate, Grayson." I kissed him softly, keeping our lips pressed as I spoke. "It's fate you gave my uncle your coin. It's fate you never used any of yours. I don't think our fate is forbidden, I think our destiny is divided, and we just haven't found the right path."

He deepened our kiss, then shoved me off. "Go. Get the fuck away before I change my mind."

I quickly took two steps back.

"The key is in the desk...I'll write to you, Atlas."

I was at the door when his growl stopped me. "Little wife."

I looked over my shoulder. His sculpted, golden torso shone in the morning light. With his wrist shackled to the bed, he looked like a god receiving punishment.

"I'm trusting you, I'm believing in us, but I won't risk you," he said. "If I even hear the slightest whisper that he's hurting you, he's dead. I won't stop to ask your permission. I won't worry about the consequences. And if we discover the chance of failure is even one percent, it's over. We do it my way."

One percent? That was ridiculous. "Gray—"

"*And,*" he continued, cutting me off with a growl. "If I have to become *the* Grayson Crowne, if I have to become that man, I'll do it for you. Maybe I can't be my sister, maybe I can't ever leave this hell, but I can rule it."

I swallowed. "I don't want that. That's not what I want. I want us free. We'll...we'll be free. I promise. Just *trust me.*"

"I let you go, didn't I?" he snarled.

The tone clawed at my soul, but more than that...it frightened me.

I knew I had to leave. The longer I stayed, I not only risked us, but risked the urge to run to him. So I turned.

"I'll build us a world where fate bows to Grayson Crowne."

I paused at his words, then sprinted out of the room.

SIXTY-TWO

STORY

My love story started with a mistaken kiss, which led to a marriage proposal by the wrong man and ended here, bound to him. In a car to god knows where.

I hoped I'd just made enough wrong decisions to finally put Grayson and me on the right path.

"Where are we going?" I asked West.

"Scotland."

I blinked. "What? Why?"

"It's the last place he'll look for you. He'd never think to check under his own fucking nose."

I looked away. "He won't look for me."

I rubbed my palm hard.

I guess it was always my fate to leave Crowne Point. To go to Scotland.

I just thought it would be a happier occasion.

A freeing one.

West laughed. "He'll never stop. And I'm counting on

it. Once the divorce is final, we'll be back in time for Christmas."

My brow furrowed at that.

I thought West was taking me *away* from Grayson.

"Every way you look at this, I win. He touches you, I get everything. He so much as lays a finger on you, I win. If you never touch him again, then I still fucking win."

"Do you have someone in mind already?" I asked softly. West's eyes narrowed. "Someone to marry."

"She means nothing. She's well aware of the arrangement. Past the wedding, I'll barely see her."

Past the wedding...I wondered how much West stood to lose if he didn't go through with it. If it was as much as Grayson.

If he could lose more.

"What's her name?" I asked.

He dropped me and silence descended on the town car.

I looked out the window, imagining the world Josephine had described. A world where I was seen as a mistress. A world where the baby in my belly wasn't Grayson's.

I could do that. I could survive being seen as my mother, in my soul, knowing I did the right thing. The thing my mother never would have done.

I pulled out my phone. At least I had this, this shred of *me*.

I told Grayson I would write to him, and I meant it.

I opened up my Instagram—then nearly dropped my phone. I had more than ten thousand followers. In the grand scheme of people with millions, it was nothing. To me, it was everything, especially now that everything that made me *me* was about to be stolen indefinitely.

They didn't know anything about me, didn't know who I was, didn't know all the bad things I'd done.